darkness
awaits

ISBN: 978-1-952582-14-1 (print)
Darkness Awaits by Tom Leveen
Published by FTJ Creative LLC

8485 East McDonald Drive, #248
Scottsdale, AZ, 85250

Cover image generated by Midjourney

Printed in the United States of America
10 9 8 7 6 5 4 3 2 1
First Paperback Edition 2022

for Mystic

and for the Players of *TellTales* over many years

Thank you so much!

TABLE OF CONTENTS

p r e f a c e

Putting a retrospective fiction collection together is essentially like putting together a mix tape. You have to choose which story goes where in just the right order to elicit maximum emotional response.

There are pages in this book that still give me goosebumps. You're going to see a lot of spiders (*The Desert; Those We Bury Back*) and a lot of a father's greatest fears (*Those We Bury Back; Now You Don't*). You're going to peer into my own past fears (*Cooped Up*), and, with luck, even catch a laugh or two (*Dinosaurs Downstairs*).

Zombies? Ghosts? Shapeshifters? Cannibals? Check, check, check, and check! If you've ever wondered what keeps me up night, look no further than *Darkness Awaits*.

And—a word about that title:

I stole it.

I stole it from 14-year-old me, who back in 8th and 9th grades was busily assembling my own short story collection just like the two books that had and continue to have a profound effect on my writing: *Night Shift* and *Skeleton Crew*, by Stephen King.

This collection is the culmination of more than thirty years of writing horror. It cracked me up a bit when my novel *Sick* came out, because reviwers made it sound like I was trying out horror writing for the first time. Nothing could be further from the truth. My contemporary YA novels were the outliers, not the norm. The norm has always been horror, and most of it in a quick-read format like short stories or novellas.

Thank you for being a part of this journey, and I hope you find some tales in here to give you the shivers!

May you be happy
May you be well
May you be safe
And may you be peaceful and at ease.

...But also just a little scared.

~ Tom

the desert

First appeared in *Theatre Of Decay* #4

"They haven't moved since . . ." Dom started to say, then cut himself off.

I knew how the sentence ended. Since Trish and Jack had made a run for their car parked beyond the driveway, that's what he was going to say.

Since the spiders had swarmed them.

The Sonoran desert sun shone mercilessly, and the electricity was off in the new house we were trapped in; without air conditioning, we were broiling in the heat. Our cell phones collectively had no signal. Suzy's father had wanted a home "away from the damn city" and he'd gotten his wish. Despite the explosive growth of the Phoenix metro area in the past decade, Arizona was a big state with plenty of open space left for folks like Suzy's dad.

Irrationally, I hated him for this. We wouldn't be in this situation if it weren't for him.

Or, I reasoned, if we hadn't decided to spend a Friday night getting hammered before the movers brought in the new furniture.

"So whaddya think?" Dom asked. It was the fifth time he'd asked me in as many hours.

"Man, I don't know," I whispered back, as if the arachnids could hear me. "I've never heard of anything like this."

The spiders had shown up during the night while the six of us were bombed out of our skulls. At least, that's what we figured. They were already in position around the house by the time dawn broke over the mountains.

I'd seen plenty of spider-related horror movies. All of them, probably. None had depicted a swarm, if that was the right etymological term, of spiders in a perfect circle, motionless, moving only when a human dared step foot outside.

A perfect circle.

None had come indoors that we knew of. That didn't jibe with the horror movies; the hairy little bastards always found some crevice to squeeze in and drop down on their unsuspecting prey. Not so here, at least not that we had seen. These spiders just waited and watched us, a million-billon sets of eight eyes awaiting our next attempt to go outdoors.

Also contrary to my Hollywood education, these weren't some mutated super-spiders; only every species known to the desert. Black widows, strangely out of their webs, mingled with tarantulas and daddy long-legs, which stayed nearby the larger grapefruit spiders and brown recluses.

"We can't stay here," Dom said.

"I know," I replied.

We'd only brought snacks and beer. The house was otherwise empty. We'd previously discussed using duct tape around Dom's tall boots and sealing his hands in work gloves, only to discover we had neither tape nor gloves. I knew a single bite from even the most poisonous of the spiders wouldn't be enough to kill anyone apart from a child or the elderly, neither of which were in the house. Two, three, or more bites would sicken a person, but with quick attention, even several black widow bites wouldn't necessarily be fatal. How many bites, from widows and other species, Jack and Trish had sustained before they fell to the ground, I didn't know. We were all wearing shorts and t-shirts or tanks, plenty of flesh for the piercing. Dom was the only one in jeans, but his arms were exposed.

The venom—coupled with adrenalin, I guessed—had felled Jack and Trish ten yards from Trish's VW Bug. The irony was not lost on me. The creatures moved quickly, en masse, skittering over one another for a chance at sinking their fangs into naked flesh. Their numbers were so vast that our two friends had been slowed by the spiders as they swarmed up Jack and Trish's legs. After Jack and Trish had fallen to the ground, motionless, the beasts got back into position.

Into that perfect circle around the house.

If we'd stopped to think about it, it was our best chance to have escaped, while they were busy killing our friends. Dom and I were too paralyzed watching the assault. Our girlfriends hadn't watched, and I didn't blame them.

"Look!" Dom barked.

I followed his gaze, and sucked in a breath. A swarm—the correct term, I was sure—of flying insects was approaching the house. They buzzed around the house briefly before landing on Trish's car, obscuring it entirely.

"Holy shit," Dom said.

"Bees?" I asked.

Dom nodded. "Looks like. And wasps. And there's more coming."

He pointed again, and I felt my stomach lurch. Three more separate swarms were approaching. One swarm nested on my truck, another on Dom's van. The third simply flew around the house. The low hum of their sheer numbers rattled the windows.

"What's happening?" Dom's girlfriend, Suzy, asked from behind us. She didn't come close enough to see out the windows.

"Nothin' good," Dom said, and Suzy whimpered.

"So even if one of us made it to the cars," I said slowly, "the wasps would get us."

"Couldn't kill us," Dom said. "It'd take thousands of stings."

"Wasps and bees didn't kill Trish and Jack."

"Ah, hell," Dom said.

"What are we going to do?" Suzy whined.

Dom leaned back away from the window. "We wait," he said, folding his arms. "They can't stay here forever."

"Neither can we," I said.

I got a nasty look for that.

"What if they come in?" Suzy cried. "What if they—"

"Suzy, shut it," Dom said. "They haven't yet, and if they do, it'll be a good chance to run." He turned to me. "I can't back this up, but I get the feelin' if we can make it past that perimeter, we'll be okay."

I'd been thinking the same thing, though I couldn't express why. The geometry of the arachnid's circle was unsettling in its perfection, as if drawn by the hand of some eight-legged deity, delineating their boundary. For what purpose, I didn't know, but it was too well marked to be accidental.

"On the other hand," I said, "the cars are beyond the circle, and the wasps don't seem to mind."

"Think they'd attack if we got past that line?"

"I do."

"Well, shit."

"Why aren't they moving?" I wondered aloud.

"Don't matter," Dom said. "It just don't matter, bro." He sighed through his nose and began walking back toward the living room.

"We'll wait," he said, and disappeared. I heard him grab a beer from the cooler.

Night came. I stayed by the kitchen window. There was no moon to speak of, and since the electricity hadn't been turned on yet, the landscaping lights offered no clear view of the arachnids. I did think I saw something coming toward the house around midnight, but it was too dark to be certain. At dawn the following day, I saw that I'd been right.

"Dom?" I called.

Dom stumbled, bleary eyed, into the kitchen, an empty bottle in hand. "Whu?"

"Look, man."

Dom leaned over the sink and peered into the morning light.

The circle had expanded and changed color. From the front door to the outer edge of arachnids now measured about thirty yards, well past the vehicles. But it wasn't spiders that had joined the mass; it was snakes. Coiled, curled, and squiggled, thousands of the slithery bastards had extended the boundary past the spiders, a second front. Tails rattled and tongues flicked, but otherwise, the reptiles were still, just like the spiders, and like the spiders, formed a perfect circle. I recognized diamondback rattlesnakes and other vipers, and swallowed dryly. A spider bite couldn't kill you, but a rattler bite—or ten—sure as hell could.

The snakes hadn't come alone. Scorpions of varying shades of yellow and brown had joined their arachnid cousins closer to the house, looking like polka dots amid the brownbacked spiders when viewed from a distance.

The wasps hadn't left the cars.

"What the hell!" Dom screamed. He threw the bottle into the sink. It shattered, sending brown shards up and over the counter. A small piece cut his hand, and Dom didn't seem to notice.

My stomach growled. Despite my terror, I needed to eat. I wondered how Lauren, my girlfriend, was faring. I'd almost forgotten her; she'd gone into what was to be Suzy's bedroom when the swarm arrived, and we hadn't seen her since. I went in to check on her. She was sleeping. Asleep, or in shock. Either way, there didn't seem any point in waking her. I dropped to the floor beside her and hugged her close.

Night came again, our third in the house. I heard Dom and Suzy going at it in Suzy's parent's room. I couldn't blame them. The likelihood of getting out of the house alive was drastically diminished with the addition of the snakes, if they behaved the same as the spiders when someone stepped outside. I was sure they would. So would the scorpions. It made the only sense possible in these perverse circumstances. If Dom and Suzy wanted one last tumble before the end came, either from hunger or being attacked by the desert beasts outside, I wouldn't begrudge them.

I realized then that hunger was a powerful motivator. Dom and I, if not the girls, would have to try to run. The vestige of our reptilian brains wouldn't let us simply starve to death if a chance for escape were possible. We'd have to obey our basest instincts and make a run for it.

I shuddered and held Lauren, trying to command my shrinking stomach to be silent. I listened for any slithering or skittering in the air vents, and heard nothing.

Nothing *inside*.

Outside the house, I heard the ravenous cry of wolves.

legion

First appeared in *The Lost Librarian's Grave* as *Face to Face*

The exorcist arrived in a custom 1941 Cadillac Fleetwood limousine, built by American hands in Detroit, goddammit. He carried his materials on a broad leather belt of the sort feared by naughty children in certain homes. Chains clanked and sparked as he walked, threatening to catch his midnight blue robe on fire—but no spark would dare do such a thing. They whimpered out quickly, fearful of his formidable powers.

One could not see his face. His broad black hat concealed his race, his demographic, even his age. He walked with a purpose like a younger man, but an older man's beard stretched out of the shadow across his visage as if seeking light. The hairs waved and squirmed in the sunlight.

He strode up the steps of the old Victorian and let himself in without knocking. He had no time for formalities.

No one waited to greet him in the parlor or escort him up the stairs to the bedroom of the possessed. But then, the Catholic priests barreling down the narrow staircase coupled with the inhuman shrieks from above them were all the indication any sensible soul would have needed to locate his destination.

There were three priests all together, each of them older and balding, but they fled with the purpose of a mother snatching a child from traffic. The first two paid him zero attention as they thundered past, stoles trailing like pennants.

The third looked at the exorcist, eyes wide.

"Jesus *Christ!*" he cried, though not at the appearance of the exorcist; it was plainly in reaction to whatever he'd seen upstairs.

The front door slammed behind them as they evacuated.

Humming thoughtfully, the exorcist hiked the stairs and stood at the open doorway of the bedroom of the possessed man.

David Matthew White clung upside down from the ceiling, his bare and bloody feet planted flat as if nailed in place, his hair hanging down. His arms stretched wide, completing the obscene, inverted image of Christ crucified. David White, naked now with a pile of shredded plaid pajama rags lying on the bed beneath him, laughed so hard and so broad his cheeks had split at the corners.

The exorcist ignored the acidic smell of every fluid the human body could produce. The fetid mixture coated the walls; it lay in thick puddles on the floor; it stained the white sheets. The thing inside David White had been busy.

Huddled in the far corner, a man and a woman held one another and trembled. When they faced the exorcist, the man let out a little gasp.

The exorcist strode in to the room and gazed at the possessed man.

"Well, now," he said. His voice hinted at Dublin.

"*Not . . . this . . . time,*" the thing inside David White laughed. It sounded like fans at a rock concert, a thousand voices speaking in unison.

The exorcist grunted. Down to business, then.

"Were I you," he said to the couple, whom he presumed to be David's parents, who'd made the call that summoned him, "I'd head downstairs and cozy up till this is finished."

The woman licked her lips. Mothers were always stronger. "He's our son. We're staying."

"Who in God's name—" the father said.

"Suit yourself," the exorcist interrupted. "But you'll need a couple good prescriptions by the time we're done."

The exorcist hiked his robe like an old washerwoman, revealing colorless baggy leggings that further prevented any confirmation of his sex. With one booted foot, he pulled himself onto the bed and stood face-to-upside-down-face with David White.

The breath coming out of the young man reeked of the dung of cancerous cattle.

"*We will never let him go,*" the thing—the *things*—said.

"Save it for the Catholics." The exorcist turned his head over his left shoulder to get the parents in his periphery. "Whatever happens, don't come up here. Don't touch me. Don't touch your boy. Don't do a blessed goddamn thing. Understand?"

They nodded.

The exorcist turned to the possessed.

"Right," he said, and opened the heavy ebony box hanging from his belt.

The box folded out to form a tray, upon which a variety of implements and bottles were strapped tight with leather and tacks. He plucked two instruments from his tray and set to work.

The exorcist slammed an iron choke pear into David White's mouth, cutting off a round of poetic, perverted profanity from the demons within. The demons glared through shocked-wide eyelids as the exorcist turned the key of the pear. The four leaves expanded, forcing David's mouth open to its furthest extent. The exorcist adjusted the key by degrees, listening close for signs of his jaw about to give way entirely.

Satisfied he'd found the young man's physical limit—aided somewhat by the damage his possessors had already wreaked on his mouth—the exorcist chanted spells from the old times, the old ways, the era before man.

David's body convulsed. The demons within tried to curse, hiss, and spit, but the pear of anguish prevented anything more than a garbled choking.

The exorcist spoke over the noise as he gripped a pair of narrow tongs in his left hand. He struck suddenly, jamming the needle-nosed tool into an opening in the pear.

David White screamed. Flecks of larynx blood spattered across the brim of the exorcist's hat. The exorcist pulled, carefully but strongly, at the bit of stuff his pliers had gripped.

With a final pull, the thing came free.

A face.

Of what it was made, even the exorcist could not say. The face was mask-like, rubbery, and nearly human in its proportions. The face bellowed like some animal dying in a cave, its features twisting the thin skin—or whatever it might be—into unrecognizable grimaces.

The exorcist hung the writhing face on a sharp hook depending from his leather belt, and went back in with the pliers.

Face after face the exorcist pulled and yanked and tore from within the young man. Each face was distinctly male and had its own features: one with wider eyes than that, another with a broader forehead than the last. The faces groaned and wailed in an incessant choir of fury and pain. The exorcist ignored their screams, jamming the hooks through their skin-like membrane to join the others. Desiccated gray faces from previous exorcisms rattled beside them, long dead from exposure.

After a dozen such extractions, David White fell from the ceiling. The exorcist drew his cloak across the faces hanging from his belt so the darkness would quiet them like petulant birds. He knelt gracefully and expertly removed the iron pear. He replaced his tools in the box and slid off the bed.

"He will be well now. I will return in forty days for my payment. I recommend lots of water and rest. For all three of you."

The exorcist stepped from the room, cinching his robe tightly to muffle the last gasps of the faces. He moved quickly for the staircase, intuiting what was to come and wishing to avoid it.

He was right.

Most people took his work as a necessary evil and were simply relieved to have their loved one back in their right mind. Every so often, though, an outlier overreached. Wanted to know more than they really ought to know.

The exorcist heard the father's footsteps pounding behind him.

"What did you do?" the father said. He grabbed the exorcist's shoulder and yanked hard to spin the man around. "*What did you*—!"

The exorcist's hat fell as he turned, revealing what lay in the shadow beneath. It was apparent the father instantly and deeply regretted his impertinence.

The exorcist had no face. The white hairs most people took for a beard, at closer examination, were not hairs at all, but thin, independent nematodes writhing. Apart from this grotesque detail, the exorcist's head was a smooth, fleshy egg of indeterminate ethnicity.

Gagging, the father raised a fist to his mouth and stumbled backward.

The exorcist calmly bent and swept his broad hat back upon his head. Once he had it comfortably in place, he spoke.

"As I said. Forty days. Till then."

He swooped soundlessly down the stairs and left the Victorian. Climbing into the Fleetwood, he spared a look at the second floor.

David White stood at his window, his face—his real face—quite pale. The young man lifted a palm in thanks, his expression betraying simultaneous gratitude and terror.

The exorcist tugged the brim of his hat in response, climbed into the limousine, and drove across the ocean to his next appointment.

h e a r t l e s s

A full-length novel

last year

He died painfully, in white-hot agony only truly expressed in poetry.

Shock prevented the worst of it from reaching his brain, but his soul was another matter. His wife died first, and he watched. He had no choice; his attacker gripped his head in a vice, and his sheer disbelief forced and kept his eyes open while two other creatures tore her apart. Her limbs made sounds like unripe fruit being twisted between monstrous hands as her arms were sundered from her torso. Her jaw dangled open, but if she screamed, he could not hear her. His own voice gave out from shrieking by the time they cast her aside, motionless in the dirt not far from the highway. The engine of their black Jeep Liberty idled, but someone had turned off the lights.

He was still alive and conscious when they began to eat her.

His attacker held him aloft by the hair in one hand, as if he were the weight of a grocery sack. His pale Olukai shoes barely scraped the desert floor as he wriggled uselessly against the monster's strength.

The thing held up a school photo of his daughter so he could see it. It was from last year. He kept it in his wallet, which must have fallen out during his brief and futile struggle against them.

"Who's *this?*" the thing asked.

Spittle flew and dripped from his lips as he unleashed nonsensical curses and impotent threats at the creature's words.

The other two pranced toward them, each holding one of his wife's arms, which they ate like meat from a perverse picnic. He thought maybe her wedding ring winked at him under the moonlight, and he loved her so, so much in that moment. He hoped she really was dead, gone into that non-world of quiet and sleep where the pain and fear could not reach.

"I think," said the thing holding him up by the hair, turning the photo in its free hand, "we should go to the beach and say hello to her."

The implication further infuriated and terrified him, but by then his voice was completely gone.

The thing turned him in the air so they were face to face. "Don't worry," it said, with absurd sincerity in its eyes. "I will take care of her. I mean it. She'll live forever."

He writhed, simultaneously grabbing and clawing at the thing's thick forearm. It was like scratching a steel beam.

"Leave her alone!" he managed in a dry, cracked whisper.

The thing shook its head.

"No."

Then opened its mouth.

one

Baylee Ross listened to her older brother Elijah celebrating his eighteenth birthday by slaying a white dragon. He did it on one lucky roll of a natural 20 on his dragon dice. Baylee, banished to the kitchen so as not to disturb the all-important game, grinned as the nerds in Lij's bedroom all screamed "*Twenty!*" at the top of their lungs and cheered like geeky Norsemen.

Baylee tapped and swiped casually on her phone, making secret plans for later as she waited for Krista Hope to arrive. She then texted Krista to remind her to bring water. Despite the sun having gone done thirty minutes ago, outdoors the temperature still broke 100. Baylee hated Phoenix for a wide assortment of reasons; this weather ranked first among them.

Maybe second. Living with near-strangers for almost a year took top prize.

On my way! Krista messaged. **Forgot my water tho! :)**

Baylee sent her a thumbs-up. She had Krista; that was something. Lij had his gamer geeks, and that was something, too. It helped.

Krista arrived and tossed open the front door, letting herself in like a neighbor in a sitcom. "I'm here, Bails! You're saved."

Baylee clicked her phone screen blank as Krista swaggered into the kitchen, holding her Hoopla skateboard by the trucks in her right hand and a white plastic sack in her left. Her black T-shirt read, in white block letters, *Your girls play like gentlemen, and behave like ladies. ~ attrib. Jane Frances Dove.*

Baylee embraced Krista. "What's in the bag?"

"Found it at the store," Krista said, handing Baylee the sack. "He'll like it, yeah?"

Baylee withdrew a black short-sleeved button-up, em-

broidered with Harley Quinn red and black diamonds over the breast pocket.

"Jesus, yes," Baylee said. "You bought this for Lij?"

Krista leaned her board against a cabinet door and put her hands on the hips of her brown cargo shorts. "It's his birthday, so."

"Yeah, but you didn't have to do this."

"Eh. He's cool. And it was on clearance. *And* I got my discount. *And* I might have 'damaged' it a little since damaged items are discounted yet again . . ."

Baylee laughed. Krista only kept her Hot Topic gig to keep herself in ceramic wheel bearings and pro wheels for the Hoopla. With her nearly dreadlocked blonde hair and the athletic build she'd earned from years of skating, she stuck out amidst the pale vampires and tattooed sad boys who normally ran the store at Thomas Mall. They feared her.

30

Another burst of cheering came from down the hall. Krista tilted her head back to glance down its length. "The gang's all here?"

"Oh yeah." Baylee handed her the shirt. "You want to go give it to him?"

"Is Fletcher here?"

"Of course."

"Then yes."

Krista slipped an arm through Baylee's and took the lead down the white-tiled hallway. They passed framed black and white photographs of Lij and Baylee's adoptive parents, Ari and John Wagner. Krista suddenly stopped in front of one of the photos, her forehead creasing. Pictures of Baylee, Lij, or their parents hadn't been added to the display. Baylee didn't fault the Wagners for that. Lij would graduate next year; she, the year after that. Thus would end their time here with Ari and John, and that was fine by Baylee.

"What?" she asked as Krista frowned at a shot of Ari and John splashing in some fountain, quite possibly in Italy. Baylee had never asked.

"Are you guys doing something else for Lij's birthday?" Krista asked.

"What, with *them?*"

Krista's frown flipped to friendly grin. "That was subtle. You still hate 'em?"

"I don't *hate* them."

"What do you call it?"

Baylee leaned against her friend's shoulder, glaring at the photo. "I don't know."

"Sorry. Didn't mean to dull your shine, Snoop Dogg."

Baylee smiled, unable as always to resist Krista's charms. "No worries."

They continued down the hall, Baylee's clog Birks clunking and Krista's low-top Vans thwacking against the tile and echoing between the beige walls.

Lij's door was shut. Baylee opened it to an argument worthy of the Supreme Court or the late, great Gary Gygax himself. Standing side by side in the doorway, the two girls went unnoticed by the four gamers within.

"That is *totally* line of sight!" cried Chris Fletcher, jabbing a finger against a colorful map laid out on Lij's bed and covered with a thin sheet of plexiglass. Several plastic miniatures leapt from the impact. Fletcher swiped a Mountain Dew can into his hand and spit tobacco juice into it with a distinct two-syllable splat.

Baylee wrinkled her nose at the familiar sight and sound. Krista merely smirked; she didn't rattle as easily.

Ralph Silverberg, Dungeon Master extraordinaire, pushed past Fletcher with a plastic ruler in hand, which he held at an angle over the board. "Look! Right here! You're blocked by the wall, you cannot hit the troll with your Eldritch Blast."

"They're so precious," Krista said.

"Right?" Baylee agreed.

Lij caught sight of them from his desk chair. His pale eyes widened. "Sorry. Too loud?"

Baylee waved him off. "It's your birthday. Go nuts."

She thought she saw his expression cramp up when she said it. Lij turned so quickly back to the argument that she couldn't be sure.

Ralph looked up as if startled, and yipped Baylee's name. "Hey! Didn't see you."

"I try to blend into my surroundings."

Ralph laughed entirely too loudly for the joke, suddenly and irrevocably reminding the room of his year-long crush on her. Baylee made sure to not quite make eye contact with him. Ralph was okay; curly-haired and with somehow wide hips that gave him an odd shuffling gait, Baylee had never seen him wear anything besides khakis and polo shirts, like a cashier in search of a Radio Shack.

Fletcher diverted his friend's embarrassment by greeting Krista in his usual fashion: "Hey, rancid grell!"

"What's up, you unathletic little pansy?" Krista shot back with unrestrained joy.

Fletcher adjusted his jungle pattern boony hat to have a better line of sight on her. He never left home without it. "Foul she-goblin."

"Smelly-ass dork."

Fletcher spit into his can. "Weak! You jibbering scrap of kobold excrement."

"Okay, I only caught a tenth of that. Ginormous nerd." Krista tossed the shirt to Lij. "Here you go, birthday boy. Hope you like it."

Lij, expectedly, fumbled the catch badly. While tall enough for basketball, the limits of Lij's athletic ability extended only as far as rolling polyhedral dice and performing rapid-fire mental arithmetic. His T-shirt displayed drawings of the dice and read *This is how I roll* in gothic script. When he got himself untangled and held up Krista's gift, his eyebrows raised. "Seriously? Thank you!"

"If it doesn't fit, you're shit out of luck," Krista said, grinning.

"No, it's great, thanks!"

Fletcher and Ralph made jealous sounds as Lij turned the shirt left and right. Only one person in the room seemed unfazed by the gift, and she wasn't hiding it.

Baylee let her eyes drift to the group's token nerdgirl, Suze Preston. She sat in her usual place on Lij's floor, her back against one wall with her long legs, clad in frayed black jeans, stretched out before her. Everything about Suze was long: legs, arms, fingers, hair, face.

Suze's expression darkened as she stared at the Harley Quinn shirt. She coughed a bit and returned to looking at an iPad resting on her lap, open to a grainy photo of what looked to Baylee like Bigfoot. Suze's Dungeons & Dragons character sheet lay dismissed beside her hip while the boys carried on.

Baylee hunkered in the doorway, her unintentionally tanned legs jutting from short cutoffs. Krista and Fletcher resumed their insulting banter as Lij carefully folded the shirt and Ralph pretended to look at a rulebook in such a way that his gaze fell more toward Baylee than the pages.

"Is that for your book?" Baylee asked Suze, pointing to the blurry photo.

Suze glanced at her, half-hidden behind her colorless hair. She attempted a smile. "Yes."

Baylee barely heard her. Suze's default setting was a whisper. "Cool. Are you almost finished?"

"Almost," Suze said while Baylee tried to read her lips. "I need to finish chapters on the Mogollon Monster and the big birds of Texas."

"Big Bird? Like, from *Sesame Street*?"

Suze shook her head, and did not try to keep her hair off her face. "No. Literally big birds. Some people think they are Pteranodons, maybe. Living in the desert after millions of years. There's a lot of room out there. It's possible."

Baylee nodded with faux understanding; and, she knew, faux interest. Suze had been writing this book on cryptids for as long as Baylee had known her. Ralph claimed it went back years before that. Anything to do with the Loch Ness Monster, the yeti, wild men of Russia, or real-life dragons, Suze had a chapter on it. Baylee admired her work ethic; the final tome would reach upward of 300 pages. Not bad for a high school junior.

At a loss for other conversation with Suze—a typical conclusion for them—Baylee stood and turned to Krista. "Ready?"

"Yeah, let's mosey." Krista sent a flirtatious sneer toward Fletcher. "It smells like geek in here."

"You have a troubling odor yourself, sporto," Fletcher said, resuming his seat on a folding chair brought in for the occasion.

"Yeah, well you . . . ! Shut up."

"Oh, how you wound me with your rapier wit." Fletcher clutched his chest, bunching up his Slayer T-shirt in his fist.

Krista flipped him off by pantomiming a Jack-in-the-Box crank. "Next time, nerd."

Baylee grabbed Krista's T-shirt by the collar and tugged. "Let's go, lovebird."

The six of them traded various goodbyes. Everyone patiently ignored how long Ralph's eyes lingered on Baylee, and in so doing did not notice the covert scowl Suze shot up at Krista. Baylee shut the door and marched Krista toward the kitchen, noticing that Krista again kept her eyes on the framed fountain photo as they passed it.

Whatever held her sudden interest in Ari and John's romantic early life, Krista didn't bring it up, shifting instead to Elijah and his friends: "So, tell me something," she said, picking up her board. "The level of geekiness in there. Is it genetic, or is it a learned behavior?"

Baylee slung a faded red knitted satchel over one shoulder, patting it for reassurance that all her necessaries were accounted for. She pulled a stainless steel bottle from the fridge and tossed another to Krista. Krista caught it with one hand.

"It's both," Baylee said. "Where the hell is your water?"

"Bah, whatever. It's okay if you're born here, you don't need it."

"False," Baylee said as they went to the front door. "Anyone can get heatstroke and die. Even at night. I looked it up."

Krista followed her outside. As if to substantiate Baylee's point, an invisible wall of heat and dampness bashed into them. July's monsoon season was unforgiving, far from the alleged dry heat Baylee and Lij had been promised before they moved here.

"You're right." Krista winced and swigged from the bottle. "I just got heatstroke. Right this second. God, this town sucks."

Baylee agreed. San Diego beaches to Phoenix heat waves wasn't an awesome transition.

The girls followed the sidewalk north out of the neighborhood, sweating instantly beneath the punishing temperature rising up to meet them from the pavement. The city trapped heat and radiated it back throughout the night. The low temperature this evening might reach 80, with luck.

"Kyro, yeah?" Krista said, running the cold steel bottle across her forehead.

"Definitely." Kyro Café, about a mile from the Wagner's house, had become a de facto hang out spot for them, as well as for Lij and the gamers. They frequently crossed paths on accident at the funky coffee shop.

"Can I tell you something?" Krista said as they crossed an empty intersection.

"I hope so," Baylee replied casually, but a stab of adrenalin poked her belly. People who said things like *I need to tell you something* or *We regret to inform you* or *I'm afraid we have terrible news* . . . always had terrible news.

"It's not a question," Krista went on as Baylee grit her teeth, anticipating she knew not what. "It's not like something you *have* to answer. Okay?"

"Okay . . ."

"It's just that, I've known you for like a year now, and you never said how."

Baylee stopped and wrinkled her eyes. Across the street, the long-abandoned North Community Church squatted dark and unholy in a dirt and broken blacktop lot. Krista stopped walking as well, and from Baylee's perspective, the front of the church framed Krista from behind.

"How, what?" Baylee said.

"Your parents. How they died."

Baylee released a sharp sigh between pursed lips as her adrenalin calmed and began the slow process of reabsorbing into her body.

"Oh," she said, not wanting to sound relieved that Krista's inquiry wasn't something worse—like *I don't want to be friends with you anymore*, a statement she worried about hearing far more often than she had any reason to.

"I mean, I know it was bad," Krista went on, rather quickly. "Or I assumed it was bad, otherwise you would have said what happened to 'em. Yeah?"

Baylee's fear siphoned itself off, replaced now by a dull, queasy dread. Krista was right, of course; she hadn't told anyone what had happened. To the best of Baylee's knowledge, the only people in Phoenix who knew the details—or what passed for details—of how Janey and Ken Ross died, lived together in the Wagner's house.

"Yeah," Baylee said, much slower than Krista had spoken, trying to buy time. "It was bad."

That was stupid, a mere repetition of what Krista had just said. She wanted to be irritated with her friend, but couldn't muster it up. After all, good as her word, Krista wasn't asking *how*, not directly. She knew she could bow out right now and Krista would let it go; for a year, maybe, or even longer. Forever, if Baylee asked her to.

But then why shouldn't she tell the truth? Maybe it would help.

Maybe the dreams would abate. Or even stop.

Baylee took a long drink from her water bottle, aware of it being half empty now. She screwed the top back on while Krista stood quietly waiting. That was odd; Krista, standing still, quietly—three items never said in succession.

"You want to know?" Baylee looked more at the shadows around the church than at Krista. She knew from experience that the sanctuary stood alone on the lot, with a wide expanse of what had once been grass between it and an L-shaped building that appeared to have been classrooms when the church was still operational.

You could hide behind that church building. Hell, you

could park a car behind it, any time, day or night, and be utterly invisible from the streets surrounding it.

Yes, she knew that well, and it was easier to think about that than it was to look at Krista right now.

Krista snorted a gentle laugh. "I can't lie to you, Bails, yes. I do, I totally want to know. I am so goddamn curious. Yeah. But! I don't need to. You've kept it quiet and I assume there's a reason, so . . . I don't want to be all triggery. You know? If it messes you up, forget I said anything."

Baylee hesitated, waiting to see if tears would come. They didn't. Which did not surprise her, and that was sort of sad in its own way.

She banged the bottle against her thigh a few times, then blew out a breath and moved to sit on the sidewalk, knees up, the pavement quickly warming her rear end even though the sun had been down for more than an hour by then. She stared at North Community Church, and let herself wonder, briefly, how soon she might return to its secret place in the back.

Krista sat beside her, crossing her legs at first, then swearing as the trapped heat bit into her bare calves and she had to rearrange herself.

"I know I don't have to say this, but can you promise not to tell anyone?" Baylee said when they'd found moderately comfortable positions on the concrete. This wasn't something she thought she could talk about in the garish lights and bright green painted walls of Kyro Café. No, the dark was better. It concealed.

"Dude," Krista said. It was all she *needed* to say.

"I know." Baylee resisted another drink, then gave in and took one anyway. Christ, she'd need to refill the thing as soon as they got to Kyro.

"They were killed."

And there the words hung as if suspended in the hot atmosphere around them. Baylee couldn't recall if she'd ever said them out loud. Probably not. She'd never had a reason to.

Krista rested a hand, cool and damp from the water bottle, on top of Baylee's forearm.

"My dad was a video game developer. Pretty cool, right? And there was a big video game conference in Vegas, so he took my mom. They drove. And on their way back . . . it was late . . . and for some reason they stopped along the side of the road, about halfway home. And . . . something . . . got them."

Krista inhaled; either a gasp, or about to ask one or a dozen obvious questions, Baylee wasn't sure which. But Krista then audibly snapped her mouth shut and instead of speaking only squeezed her hand on Baylee's arm.

"I don't really know all the details," Baylee said. True. "But they were attacked by some kind of animal, and it . . ."

Here she paused, and a faint smile of utter helplessness crossed her young face.

"Not sure how much more you want to know."

Krista nodded. "I think I can guess from here. Jesus H, Bails. I'm so sorry. Fuck're the chances of something like that?"

"Pretty slim."

Baylee'd had the same question, and guessed the same answer thanks to the cop who'd confirmed as much in the days following her parents' deaths. Wild animal attack right off the I-15 highway between Vegas and Barstow—pretty slim chances indeed. Yet here she was, in hot-ass Phoenix, living with two family friends she'd only met in passing at the house in San Diego, and a geeky older brother who, for all his geekiness, had made three good friends the past year while she had only managed Krista. And one other.

Baylee shook her head to clear the thoughts. That wasn't fair to Krista, dismissing her friendship like that. The little skate betty had been a better friend to her than all her friends combined back in San Diego. They didn't even message her anymore.

She looked over at Krista's sincere expression and smiled again, this time with a little more authenticity. "Thank you for asking. I mean that."

Krista gave Baylee's arm a shake before dropping her hand. "Or you can call me a bitch, totally cool with that."

"No." Baylee stood and brushed tiny rocks and dust from the back of her shorts. "It was good to say it finally."

Krista joined her on her feet. "Cool. Next time I need to pry into your private life, I'll do it where there's air conditioning. *God* it's hot."

That brought a laugh from Baylee, and they marched quickly to Kyro in search of iced drinks and cold air.

○

She hadn't answered Krista's question in the hallway earlier: The answer was yes, Ari and John had held something of a celebration for Lij the night before, a small affair with a store-bought cake and array of gift cards, as if they didn't have the slightest idea what an eighteen-year-old gamer orphan might want for his birthday.

Fair enough, Baylee thought.

That was a Thursday. Tonight was "date night," and Baylee made it her business not to inquire too deeply into what went into such an occasion. Wine, she knew, or guessed; Ari was something of an aficionado, while John veered for lite beers when he bothered to drink at all, which wasn't often. She knew they went to plays and concerts; to Art Walks when the weather was nice, to movies when it wasn't—Phoenix's outdoor season spanned November to February. The two kids Ari and John had inherited from the Rosses were late teenagers, not exactly needing full-time supervision, so their date nights had continued unabated after only a month or so of Baylee and Lij moving in.

It being a date night, Ari and John were not home when Baylee returned to the house just after eleven. Krista, in her usual fashion, had kept things fun and light at Kyro after Baylee's dismal admission, which Baylee appreciated. After iced drinks at Kyro—when it had cooled to around 90—they went to the Wedge, a skatepark not far from Krista's house. Krista skated while Baylee sat and watched and daydreamed a bit about her own date coming up later that night.

Maybe "date" wasn't the right word, but she didn't care. The thought made her giggle, something she would only ever do by herself.

The Wagner's house struck her as particularly dark as she slid her key into the deadbolt on the front door. Lij hadn't turned on the porch light when the gamers left, which was odd. It wouldn't be fair to say he was afraid of the dark, but she'd noticed he'd taken to keeping some lights on around the house since their parents died.

She didn't blame him.

Baylee let herself in and felt the weight of silence on her shoulders. No one was here, or so it felt. Maybe the gamers had gone to Kyro themselves after their D&D game; the café was open 24 hours, one of its chief attractions for those denizens of the dark who chanted strange incantations like *OCV equals DCV divided by three*, and *Boxcars! CT crit!* and *Divine radiance versus kolbold chieftain*.

"Lij?" she called, closing the front door. Facing the dark hallway, she glanced into the kitchen on her left; empty and silent, lit only by the microwave and oven clocks.

No response—not exactly. But there was a sound. Soft and undefined.

She flicked on the foyer light, enjoying its yellow comfort for a moment. She walked down the tiled hallway, sandals echoing off the walls. The first door on her left opened into the guest bath, which the two of them had been sharing since arriving here. First door on her right, Lij's room; further down, her own; then last door on the left, Ari and John's bedroom. They kept the door shut all the time, like they were afraid of the teens going through their useless adult ephemera or, God in His Heaven forbid, walking in on them during sex.

It was closed now.

All the hallway doors were closed. A quiet blue light shone beneath Lij's.

Baylee knocked on his door. "Lij? You up? You okay?"

The sound again. Baylee listened carefully, then closed her eyes as she identified it.

She opened the door. Lij sat on the floor in front of his small flat screen TV. In its shadowy light, she saw Lij holding a windowed envelope in his lap, limp and flat like a dead kite. Video footage of their parents danced on the screen: they were young, not much older than Lij and Baylee, and at a beach party. Solo cups, a bonfire, and surfboards dominated the scene while barely clad young people danced and whooped and passed around smoky somethings from hand to hand.

"Lij," Baylee said softly, and came to sit as close to him as she could, shoving his wheeled office chair away. The lingering, tangled scents of the gamers jumbled into her nose, like a handful of their crazily shaped dice. "Talk to me."

Lij wept gracelessly into a jumble of black material clutched in his left hand. Most of his wardrobe consisted of graphic tees and he didn't own a suit. This button up was his only dress shirt, bought specifically for the casketless funeral service for their parents.

He didn't answer her. Tears rolled out of both eyes and dropped onto his jeans, leaving darker temporary stains.

"What happened tonight?" she said, putting one hand on Lij's knee, looking at him and not the screen. She didn't want to see the videotape, and sometimes hated that Elijah had kept them.

"I'm rich," he said.

She tilted her head.

Lij held up the envelope. Baylee took it and teased out the check inside. Her eyes popped at the number in the box, but her shock evaporated as the meaning of the check sank in: it was from the estate. Ari and John had sold off everything and, in accordance with the Ross's wills, put the proceeds into two equal accounts, one each for the both of them; half to be paid out upon reaching 18, the other half upon reaching 25. Given San Diego property values, the two teens were going to have a leg up on their financial lives after high school. It wasn't *You'll never have to work a day in your life* money, but it was certainly *Feel free to travel Europe for a year* money.

"Jesus, Lij." She put the paperwork on his bedspread.

"You'll get one too in a couple years."

"I don't care."

"Yeah," Lij choked. "Me either . . ."

He lifted his face out of the shirt and met her eyes in the dark.

"I don't wanna die, Bay."

Baylee clamped her teeth tight to withhold a sigh. It wasn't the first time he'd said it.

"They musta been so scared." Lij's eyes pinched almost shut. "You ever think about that?"

She did, but didn't have to say it. Lij knew about the dreams. Hers woke him up, too.

"Pieces," Lij said, his voice jagged like carnivore teeth.

Baylee's stomach lunged south at the word.

"That's how they found them," he went on. "Isn't it? Fucking scattered all over the place? In *pieces?*"

His voice pitched high on the last word, making Baylee wince. "Lij, don't—"

But there was nothing else to say. She hugged her brother close to her.

He cried then; awful, rib-clenching sobs that made Baylee's own nose go stuffy in empathy. A full minute passed before she realized Lij was speaking, too. Four, maybe five syllables, over and over.

"What?" Baylee whispered against his neck. "What is it?"

But Lij's voice didn't get clear up. Not at first. Another minute crept past before she realized he'd already said it a moment ago. Now it came out on repeat, a skipping, squealing audio track:

I don't wanna die. I don't want to die.

Baylee's eyes slammed shut. Tears leaked from the corners now. She understood. Not just the sensation, the vague anxiety about not being alive anymore; she understood the suddenness with which her fear of death had come on after Mom and Dad died. One minute, she was young and immortal. Then the doorbell rang, and she opened it to find a woman in a suit and a uniformed policeman asking to speak to them, and if any adults were home.

They were *afraid they had terrible news.*

Everything changed then. Some changes were immediate—the black-hole feeling in her chest as the police explained what had happened on the I-15 just the night before; the cold shock that made her sick to her stomach but unable to puke it out. Some changes were more insidious, taking their time—like when she lay in bed, unable to sleep, wondering how dark it had been when they died, how much it had hurt, what their last thoughts and words on this world were. That she would never know what they said before leaving this world.

Baylee became a vegetarian not long after. And virtually vegan not much longer after that, because she'd read vegans live longer. For a time, she read medical journals and health books obsessively, anything she could get her hands on that would promise a very long life.

Six months after they'd moved in with Ari and John,

Ari sat her down and talked about it. Ari was concerned for her. This behavior was not helpful, she said. Not wanting to have a huge, deep discussion about her fears, Baylee had quickly nodded and promised to stop reading the medical journals. And she did. She didn't need to by then, anyway; she knew everything she needed to know. She focused on what she ate and tried to get Lij to do the same without making a federal case out of it.

But all the organic kale in the world didn't make Baylee's room any less dark at night or stop her from wondering if it had been that dark in her parents' final moments on Earth.

So, yes: she knew what her brother meant. She didn't want to die, either. Ever. They hadn't talked about it at any length before, but it wasn't necessary.

Nor did she feel like trying to have that conversation right this moment.

Lij sat up and scrubbed his face with his forearms, looking angry and frustrated and more like eight than eighteen.

"Sorry," he grumbled.

"No," Baylee said. "Please."

He snorted a laugh of sorts. "Okay."

"You going to be all right?"

"You mean apart from our inexorable descent into darkness and the unknown?"

"Yeah, apart from that."

"Sure."

That was enough to get them both to smile, no matter how grimly. Baylee gave him a quick, ending hug and stood. "I'm going to bed."

Did he smirk? Just a little bit? She chose to believe not. Lij turned back to the TV screen. "Cool," he said, and turned up the volume. "And, you know. Thanks."

"No bother. What're you going to do with the check?"

"Spend it all on games."

"You're kidding, right?"

"Yeah." Being a successful video game developer had worked well for Mr. Ross, but not the kind of "well" that led to a home in San Diego; that was the result of good goddamn financial sense, and he'd passed it on to his children. Lij may very well buy a new book or two, maybe spring for pizza on the next game night, maybe even grab a few more music and game T-shirts, but not much else.

"Good," Baylee said. "Love ya."

"Love ya."

"Lij?"

He turned to her.

"It's not just you."

Elijah pressed his lips together and gave her one understanding nod of solidarity.

Baylee let herself out. She detoured to the bathroom to do her end-of-day routine before heading into her bedroom and closing the door. She also flicked the doorknob lock. Sometimes Ari came in to check on them when they got home, or even—Baylee feared but didn't know—in the middle of the night when they were asleep.

She did not turn on a light as she screwed ear buds into her ears and climbed into bed, under a comforter because by then the air conditioning had all but coated the room in frost. Another strange feature of Phoenix: locals brought wraps, scarves, and even coats with them everywhere in this damnable heat because all indoor places were kept as chilled as a meat locker in defiance of the outdoor temperatures. Sleeping with the air set somewhere in the 60s but beneath a comforter, she'd learned, was not uncommon here.

She wanted the added privacy of the comforter anyway.

Once situated on her back, she sent a text. **I'm home. You up?**

Timothy replied immediately. **Always. How are you?**

Tough night, she wrote. **Will you talk to me?**

Certainly.

Grinning at his oddly precise language—he wrote just as he spoke—Baylee nestled deeper into her three pillows and took a deep breath. The phone buzzed in her hand a moment later, and she tapped it on.

Timothy wasted no time, and Baylee deftly undid the copper button on her cutoffs and clicked her zipper down as quietly as possible, as if Lij next door could possibly have heard it. Timothy spoke, his warm voice slipping in and out of her ears as she closed her eyes and bit hard on her lip and let the rest of the goddamn world fade away for a little while.

No one knew about him, or about this time they shared almost every midnight, and Baylee was determined to keep it that way. She'd tell everyone they were together, someday.

Someday. Right now, she needed something of her very own, and that something was Timothy.

two

Baylee awoke early despite herself, and snuck out of the house without waking Lij, Ari, or John. She hadn't heard the adults come home last night, and wondered idly if Ari had tried her bedroom door and been pissed to find it locked.

Better to leave early and not find out.

The temp had dropped to 80 overnight—not so bad for an early run. Baylee lit out on a random trajectory, concerned more with time spent than distance covered. She had no special running gear; no leggings, no Sauconys, nothing but a sports bra, tank top, and some old basketball shorts she'd gotten cheap off a discount rack at Target. Thirty minutes of cardio a day would increase her life expectancy, she'd read. So she ran sixty.

Her path took her toward Kyro, and thus past the old church. It looked different in the morning light, more sad than

spooky. Baylee wondered why another religious group hadn't bought the place yet, or why some developer hadn't come along and decided to build a million condos on the property like they were doing everywhere else in town. Not that she hoped for either thing; the hidden, private back side of the sanctuary had become too useful to her the past couple of months.

It was the best place to meet Timothy.

Baylee's phone buzzed. Ari, texting her. **Hey you. Home for breakfast?**

Baylee didn't answer, choosing instead to run the entire way to Krista's house. Ari texted back an hour later: **I'll take that as a no. :)**

She didn't return that text, either.

○

The girls bummed around Krista's house all day, much of which was spent by Baylee forcing Krista to watch *Lucky 13*, a streaming series Baylee had fallen in love with just before school ended for the year. She'd seen the entire run twice through already; watching with Krista made binge number three.

"Okay, would you please explain to me your attraction to this show?" Krista demanded, darting her narrow fingers into their shared bowl of popcorn, a bowl large enough to take up the combined space of both their laps.

"What?" Baylee demanded in return. "Are you even watching it? A, Kira Thirteen is completely badass. B, Britton is totally hot. C—"

"Britton is totally gay."

"Still hot."

"Understood. Go on."

By then they were overcome with fits of giggles

and Baylee didn't go in to her feelings on the plot, characterization, screenwriting . . . or the fact that it took place in a future where some of the population had become immortal.

After sunset, they took a free local shuttle north for two miles, getting off across the street from El Dorado park. Shaded in the day by massive mesquite trees, at night they reminded Baylee of hunched old men beckoning with fairy tale fingers to maligned castle keeps, or dungeons as cold and dark as any in Lij's gamescapes.

Or, Baylee thought as they jaywalked across the dead street, I watch too much Netflix. That was more likely; when not hanging out with Krista or indulging in her best-kept secret, videos were about all the summertime in Phoenix could offer.

Best-kept secret.

She didn't like that Timothy was a secret; it wasn't in her nature to lie. But there would be questions if they knew about him. From Krista, from Ari, maybe even John, and from Elijah, and she didn't want to answer them, not yet.

Soon, she promised herself again. Just . . . soon.

Cicadas buzzed in the mesquite trees as the girls followed a sidewalk east to the skate park. The insects sounded to Baylee like alarms, warning her away from daring to be outdoors in the record warmth. But Krista didn't get this close to a sponsored position on a skateboard team by taking summers off, and Baylee respected that, even if it did mean being outside in the relentless heat.

They reached the Wedge, a concrete expanse of benches, bowls, and ramps designed for bikes and boards. Teens, mostly male and mostly on skateboards, darted and flipped and crashed, looking like scowling bees buzzing around a hive. Baylee saw Krista's eyes brighten as they approached; she loved the sport, and stood well above the majority of the guys out on the concrete. Baylee knew it, Krista knew it, and worse, the boys knew it.

Baylee flipped her foot upward to smack the rear of Krista's shorts. "Oh, go on, get out of here, you know you want to."

Krista laughed, handed Baylee her water bottle, and took the order, running hard for the Wedge. She grabbed the nose of her board at the very rim of a wide bowl, flung herself into the air, and landed perfectly on top of her Hoopla, coasting fast to the opposite rim and disappearing over its edge. Other skaters made room. They knew better than to get in the way of Krista Hope.

Baylee walked to a short wall edging one half of the skate park. Bluewhite parking lot lights lit the concrete, but cast shadows around the outskirts. It seemed to Baylee the designers had specifically wanted to create a place for illicit smokers to take their breaks between bouts of skating, as indeed several were doing at the moment. She decorously ignored them as they shot her suspicious glares, as if the sixteen-year-old girl in short denims, sports bra, and layered tank top was actually a Grown Up or Parent or Cop. Assessing her as harmless, the groups went back to their pipes and vapes.

She found a spot on the wall far from the smokers, never having cared for either drugs or alcohol up to this point. She did sometimes wonder if she was missing something by abstaining—like numbness or temporary amnesia—but since neither Lij nor Krista partook either, Baylee didn't feel any particular pressure to try it all out.

Baylee set her bag and their two water bottles beside her and leaned back on her hands, locking her elbows and kicking the heels of her sandals against the bricks. Krista zoomed and flew and skidded on the Wedge, earning both appreciative audiences and envious scowls from the other skaters. She really was something to watch, effortlessly fakie kickflipping—or whatever foreign terms Krista used—to heights and at speeds that frankly made Baylee nervous. Too often she imagined Krista failing a stunt and splitting her skull open on the merciless concrete. None of the skaters wore helmets.

Baylee sucked in a gasp as icy tentacles snaked around her midsection from behind, pinning her arms to her sides.

"Hello, beautiful," a voice said quietly into her ear.

The chill of his skin against hers did not warm, but the insides of her belly did. He kissed the back of her neck below the tip of her hastily assembled brown ponytail, and Baylee let her head drop forward and her eyes close.

Timothy.

"Hey," she whispered back.

Timothy continued placing cool, quick kisses along her neck, and Baylee reached her hands behind her to find the waistband of his jeans. She hooked fingers into the black belt loops and pulled him closer. It felt mature and unspeakably sexy.

"Don't," she said, not moving. "I'm sweaty. I'm gross."

"Not to me."

She could have fallen asleep there, sitting on top of that short wall, fully backed into her boyfriend. Eyes still closed, she asked, "What are you doing here?"

"Stalking you."

"Mmm. Okay. Krista might see you."

"No. She looks very intent out there."

Baylee cracked her eyes open. Krista was pulling off tricks Baylee couldn't begin to name, much less describe. She seemed to break the very laws of physics with each new stunt. "That's true."

Timothy gave her one last lingering kiss that lit the back of her neck on fire before setting his chin on her right shoulder. "What are your plans tonight, beautiful?"

"What are yours?" Baylee countered, pulling away just enough to meet his brown eyes with hers. He'd been vague on their messages back and forth.

"Asked you first."

"Well, I thought I might ask Krista if we can go swimming at her place maybe. This heat is killing me."

"Pools," Timothy said, pretending it was a bad word. "You don't want a pool. You want the ocean."

"I do, I really do. You want to drive me to San Diego tonight? We could be there before dawn, watch the sun rise."

Timothy laughed softly into her ear, tickling her. "That would be wonderful. But not tonight. I stopped by to see you because I've got plans most of the evening. I wanted to see you before then."

"Are you in the mob or something?"

"Serial killer, actually."

"Oh, okay, as long as it's nothing serious."

He laughed again. Then kissed her lips. His were chilly, which made sense; he'd have had the air conditioning going full blast in his car.

"What are your big plans?" Baylee asked, struggling not to sound breathless after the kiss.

"Just dinner with the family. Can't get out of it."

"Bummer."

She wanted to ask him who they were, but resisted. She understood and accepted that she knew little about Timothy's background, but it had only been a month since they'd met, and not a see-you-every-day kind of affair. They'd met here at the Wedge, while she sat watching Krista practice, exactly like tonight. Timothy had been doing the same, sitting on a low hill opposite the wall, overlooking the concrete park. Feeling a bit sorry for herself that particular night, Baylee had thrown her shoulders back and marched right up to him and introduced herself. Timothy had looked surprised, but then when he smiled, she fell apart inside. Yes, he was older, but only *some*. Not a *lot*. That's what she told herself after their first kiss, days later.

They'd been together ever since.

Baylee swung around to straddle the wall like it was horse and tilted forward on her hands. Timothy mimicked her so that they faced each other. She leaned closer, her chin now over his shoulder, their ears almost touching.

"So I might not see you till tomorrow," Baylee said in what she hoped was a seductive voice. Her lack of experience in matters like this sometimes worried her, but Timothy had thus far given her no reason to feel self-conscious.

"Probably." His voice suggested a smile.

Baylee reached up and rubbed the ends of his short black hair between her fingers. So sleek and soft and dark, she wondered if he used special conditioner or dyed it. She murmured, "But you could *call* me later."

"I could do that."

56

"I'll be home before midnight."

"I could call you a little after that," Timothy whispered. "If you want."

"Yes. I want that."

She put a hand on his leg and lowered her voice, feeling simultaneously silly, like a bad prime time TV show, and yet profoundly heady and desirable as she spoke.

"Last night was good," she whispered into his ear, and nipped his earlobe. She wanted to consume him. She wanted to be consumed.

"Excellent." Timothy kissed her cheek quickly and stood, putting his hands in the pockets of his black jeans. "I've got to be going."

"How'd you know I'd be here?" Baylee asked.

Timothy bent forward at the waist. "Because I know everything about you."

"Oh yeah?"

"*Oh*, yeah."

She felt herself smiling, relaxing into his confidence. "Can I ask you something?"

"Anything, any time."

"Do you really think I'm beautiful?"

Timothy's eyebrows pinched together. "Of course I do. Why would you ask?"

"It's just, you don't seem to want to do anything that's not over the phone."

Grinning, he said, "We do plenty that's not over the phone."

"You know what I mean. The car is great, but I mean, we haven't . . . actually . . ."

Timothy's grin slipped off as he sat back down beside

her. "Okay. When do you want to tell your family and friends about me?"

Shit, Baylee thought. Of course he's right about that.

Timothy put a hand on her knee. His fingers hadn't yet warmed in the summer night air. "I'm not asking you to. It's only been a month. We have time before I officially meet any of your people. It's okay."

"You're sure?"

"Certainly."

"And us not doing other stuff?"

"Soon. No rush. Okay?" He kissed the top of her head.

"Okay."

He stood. "Okay. Talk to you later."

"*On the phone?*"

Timothy's grin reappeared. "On the phone. Of course. Good night, Baylee."

His odd formality always confused her; *certainly* for *sure*, *good night* for *see ya*. But it never stopped her from smiling. "G'night."

Timothy ambled into the darkness of the park toward the parking lot. She watched until she couldn't see him anymore—and that's when Krista dropped beside her.

Baylee barely suppressed a startled gasp, and automatically shot a look toward the parking lot again, to make sure Timothy was out of sight; as if a guy walking around that far away would somehow be connected to her.

"It is damn hot out here!" Krista said, snatching her water bottle. "Oh my Sweet Aunt Fanny. How you doing?"

"Good," Baylee said, spinning to face the same way as Krista.

"Who was that dude?"

Baylee's lungs froze. "Huh?"

"That guy you were talking to." Krista's lips popped off the bottle.

"Oh," Baylee said, scrambling for an answer. "Yeah, I don't know. I mean, just some guy. New kid. At our school. Next year. I think."

Krista froze with the bottle halfway to her mouth again. "Ohhhh-kay. You sure about any of that, kid?"

Baylee forced a laugh and gambled. "Sorry. Just not used to getting picked up on."

"Ah-ha! That's what I thought. See, I knew you'd start attracting gentlemen callers. Way to go, Bails! Was he hot?"

"Actually, yeah." That wasn't a lie, at least. Still; she didn't want to have to keep covering, so she said, "What about all those hotties down there?"

"Psh," Krista dismissed. "Cavemen."

"Bummer. You want to go swimming later?"

"At my house? No. I mean, yes, but my dad's back again. God, just fucking get the divorce, you know?"

Baylee had no reasonable response. Comments like that invariably stabbed a blade of jealousy into her sternum. Divorce? Great—at least it meant they were alive.

The envy faded, though, and had begun fading even more rapidly the past few months. When she and Lij first came to Phoenix and started school, Baylee had made a handful of acquaintances at first, girls she still talked to on campus or exchanged meaningless social media chatter with from time to time. Krista, though, had been the only one to not shy away from Baylee's story. When the topic of irredeemably stupid, careless, or asshole parents came up in the group, the other girls would inevitably, abruptly go quiet and shoot Baylee furtive, shameful glances. Before long, they stopped talking about parents at all. After that, the only topics that arose had to do with rumors Baylee didn't care about and TV shows she didn't watch.

But not Krista. When Baylee first said her parents were dead, Krista replied, "Oh my God. What happened?" And when Baylee refused to tell her, Krista said, "Well that sucks. That's fucking awful. I'm so sorry. How do you feel now? What's it like?"

Her bluntness had been refreshing, and one of the things that made Baylee subconsciously nominate her for New Best Friend.

So Krista's reckless jabber about divorce did still leave a mark, yes; Janey and Ken Ross were only a year gone. But it also reminded Baylee why she liked and trusted this roughhouse tomboy who had never once treated her like a pariah for the great sin of having parents who'd been killed.

But not just killed. A near-silent but not-silent-enough voice buzzed at the same pitch as the cicadas in the reptilian part of Baylee's brain. Not just killed, oh no, more like *torn*—

She forced a cough to end the thought. To Krista, she said, "Sorry."

"No, never say that, that's all *Dad* ever says," Krista groaned. "Sorry I yelled at you, sorry I had another drink, sorry I missed the competition. Blah blah blah." She spat against the sidewalk with practiced ease. "Maybe he'll bring presents though. He does that sometimes. Like it helps. Last time was a CD. You know what those are? A fucking CD? Like, what *year* is this."

"What about Fletcher?" Baylee said suddenly, needing a change in subject. Her brain still buzzed with images of her parents she'd never seen but had imagined every day since getting the news.

"*Fletcher?* Oh, God, whatever." Krista rammed a shoulder into Baylee. "You wanna head out? There's too many idiots here tonight."

"Yeah, it's too hot anyway." Baylee slid off the wall and tugged the frayed cuffs of her shorts away from her thighs, which felt damp and uncomfortable, the way her legs always got on the school bus as a kid.

Krista took another slug from her water bottle as Baylee checked the time. She saw Timothy had sent her a smiley, and quickly clicked the screen blank and pulled a thrilled smile off her face.

Soon, she thought once again. Soon, I'll tell Krista. I'll tell her first. Then Lij. Then—we'll see.

They walked silently back to the shuttle stop, hopping aboard the next one that trundled by. Krista wasn't silent often, but when she was, it never seemed awkward; tonight, it did.

No, Baylee corrected herself. Not awkward. Heavy. Something either between the two of them she had missed, or something on Krista's mind; Baylee couldn't tell.

She kept her mouth closed until they got off the bus. Baylee fanned herself with the front of her tank top and finished her water. They walked toward the Wagner's house slowly, and Baylee felt again the weight of the quiet between them.

"You okay?" she asked at last.

Krista, oddly, kept her head down as if watching their steps. "No one likes me."

Baylee stopped and touched her friend's forearm. "What?"

Krista lifted her head, and she was not crying; no tears shone in her eyes beneath the orange streetlights and no tension pulled her lips taut. All the same, her normal easygoing expression had been replaced by something harder, something tilting toward anger.

"I just mean guys," Krista said, not meeting Baylee's gaze. "At the Wedge. They hate me."

"They're totally insane jealous of you, that's not the same thing."

"Feels like it." She spit again, nailing a dead leaf.

"Did someone say something?"

"No . . . I can just tell. I mean, you're all getting picked up on over there and I'm like . . ." She gave the words a singsong: "Hey, over here, surrounded by boys, someone fucking say something . . ."

Baylee almost said *Wow* out loud, but reigned it in. Krista, who she really admired, was envious over Timothy? No—not Timothy exactly, she didn't know about him as a boyfriend yet. And maybe envy wasn't the right word, but Baylee couldn't find one better. It was an odd mix of emotions in the moment. Pride, perhaps; that, yeah, she'd scored a hot boyfriend all on her own, even it was still secret; empathy, for Krista, because she was plenty cute in Baylee's opinion; then guilt, for keeping Timothy quiet this whole time. That wasn't something friends did. Now, though, Baylee thought bringing him up would make for colossally poor timing.

She cast about for something to cheer Krista up. At the end of the block, a motor revved, and the girls turned to look. Fletcher's green 1970s pickup truck grumbled down the road toward them, headed, Baylee knew, to first Ralph's then Suze's house. Game night was over.

Fletcher pulled to a stop beside them and rolled down his manual window. "Hey, ladies! How's it going?"

"Hi Baylee!" Ralph chirped from the middle seat.

"Hey," Baylee said, generally.

"Oh, hey!" Krista said, brightening instantly. "Fletcher! Quick question. Are you gonna shower this week, or . . . ?"

He gave her a tip of his boony hat. "Depends, you joining me?"

"Hmm," Krista said, feigning deep thought. "That's nauseating, soooo . . . guess not."

"You sure?" Fletcher asked. "'Cause you're pretty ripe, I can smell ya from here, you crooked-legged strumpet."

Krista raised a hand. "Oh, please. Your dork breath is making me nauseated."

"Yet you just can't seem to stop riding the Fletcher Machine, how do you account for that?"

Before he'd finished the sentence, Krista held a hand under her mouth, and Baylee thought for she sure really was going to vomit. Krista coughed, "Oh, God!" and ballooned her cheeks. Pressing her fingers against her lips, she dashed for Fletcher's open window, stuck her head in, and retched an enormous belch.

"Aw, fuck, shit!" Fletcher squealed, pushing himself back away from her.

Krista burst into laughter, hanging on the door. Baylee joined her, and after realizing she'd been faking, so did Fletcher.

"That was *awesome!*" Krista cried. "Your *face!*"

Baylee heard Ralph laughing too, and imagined she could see even the stoic Suze smiling along.

"All right, all right." Fletcher raised his hands in surrender. "You got me, well played. Fuck, man."

Krista righted herself and slapped the window frame. "Good seein' ya! Take care!"

She joined Baylee on the sidewalk as Fletcher rolled his eyes and said, "Yeah, you *hope* so. Later!"

"Bye, Baylee!" Ralph shouted as Fletcher peeled out against the blacktop.

Baylee waved. Generally. She turned to Krista. "What about Fletcher?"

Krista blinked. "*That* Fletcher?"

"Yeah. What about *him?*"

They resumed their walk. "What, like, to go out with? Are you kidding? He's a ginormous nerd."

"Yeah, but he's not scared of you."

Krista waved a hand. "Who the hell is scared of me?"

"Every single guy at the Wedge."

"What?"

"Oh, come on! They are so intimidated by you. I can see it from where I sit. But Fletcher will always be Fletcher, and, you know, honestly? I think you like that about him."

Krista laughed aloud. "*Chris Fletcher.* That gamer with the mouth full of Skoal?"

"Do you like him?" Baylee said as they neared the Wagner's ranch style home. Ari and John weren't home, and Lij had turned off all the lights again, giving the house a deserted look. She wondered how he was doing after last night.

Krista wrinkled her nose, utterly unoffended in the manner of best friends world-wide. "*What?*"

"Don't be all coy, just answer."

They paused on the Wagner's driveway. Krista stared at the house as if Chris Fletcher waited inside for her to come ask him out.

"Shit," Krista sighed. "You know, Bails . . . I do. Goddamn it."

"Well then you should hang out with him sometime." The possibility of them getting together went up like a flare in Baylee's mind. Selfishly, it would make broaching the topic of Timothy infinitely easier. "And I don't mean just like, hey, passing through, see ya around. I mean like, maybe all of us hang out sometime when they're not gaming."

"When are they not gaming?"

"Okay, fair point. But if I could make it happen? Maybe we all meet at Kyro or something?"

Krista shifted her weight from foot to foot, tapping the tail of her board against the concrete. "But like, *cool*, right? Not like, *you guys totally need to get together*."

"Right, right, not like that. Casual."

"I dunno . . ."

"Well, for what it's worth, knowing what I know about Elijah, the thing is? They're good people. They are. Loyal to the core. They watch out for each other. You can count on them. It might be a good fit, who knows."

Krista narrowed her eyes. "All right. Fuck it. Why not."

Baylee gave her friend a hug. "Cool! It'll be fun. One hopes."

"Yeah, yeah, whatever you say." A sly grin crossed Krista's face. "And that way you and Ralphie could get some good quality time together."

Baylee hammered her friend's shoulder before Krista finished the sentence. "Stop, stop, stop!" she ordered as Krista laughed. "No. Don't ever say that."

"Oh, what, I thought they were all reliable and loyal and whatever!"

Baylee gave her a theatrical sigh. "They are, but—"

She very nearly said *I'm already seeing someone*, but managed to stuff the words back in her own mouth by turning her head up to the sky as if searching for a reason to not date Ralph Silverberg. It was a long list.

She chose the simplest: "But he's not my type."

Krista dropped her board to the ground and put one foot on it. "Aw, but it's so *cute*."

Baylee made growling noises and Krista relented with another laugh.

"Okay, fine. You don't gotta marry Ralph. *Suze* though, now she's been making eyes at you."

"Oh my God, would you go home?" Baylee shoved Krista's back.

Cackling, Krista waved and set off down the sidewalk, seams popping beneath her wheels. Baylee went to the front door and squinted at her keys in the dark, whispering mild curses at her brother for turning the lights off again.

She let herself in and went right for his door, knocking loudly. "Lij? Please tell me you're okay in there."

"I'm okay in here," he called back.

"You're not leaving lights on anymore."

After a pause, his door opened. Lij leaned his tall body against the door frame and met her eyes. His TV glowed behind him. She couldn't tell what was on screen. "I gotta get better."

66

"Better how? At what? Rolling twenties?"

He took a deep breath through his nose. "I just got to thinking last night. We can't keep feeling this way, you know?"

Baylee didn't argue his use of the plural. "Yeah."

He took another breath and scanned the hallway. "I'm . . . experimenting with the darkness."

"That's good. I like that. It's a bit goth, but, okay."

She was pleased when he surrendered a smile. "Thanks."

He scrubbed his wild hair with both hands. "You, uh . . . going to bed?"

Again suspicion bloomed in her; did he know? Oh, God, had she been loud somehow and not known it? She didn't think so. *But.*

"Yeah," she answered shortly. "See you in the— oh! Um, what do you think about all of us hanging out tomorrow? Like, at Kyro maybe."

Lij sneered faintly. "With Ari and John?"

"No, sorry. The gamers. You four, me and Krista?"

Now suspicion crossed *his* face. "Why?"

Baylee tried to stay serious, but a giggle escaped anyway. The sound loosened Lij's skeptical expression. "She kind of likes Fletcher. Does he like her at all, do you know?"

Lij grinned broadly in the darkness. "Wow. *Yeah* he does."

They shared a laugh. "Okay, well, don't say anything. We'll just hang out there tomorrow night or something."

"Cool." He cocked an eyebrow. "Sleep well."

He shut his door before Baylee could interpret the expression, then decided it was probably best if she didn't.

She went to bed without calling Timothy, choosing

instead to prop her iPad up on her lap and fall asleep to *Lucky 13*.

The show followed the adventures of Kira Thirteen, a teenage girl who had survived a global apocalypse and now lived in a world inhabited by mutated humans thirsty for healthy immune systems. Lymph nodes. Tonsils. Bone marrow. Some of the living population had been treated with a serum that prevented death by any natural means, including normal aging. They were partly immortal. The only way to die in Kira's world was violently, by accident or attack.

Kira, though, was not immortal. And yet she wasn't afraid to die. She lived in a world of danger, intrigue, sex, and violence—rather like how Baylee had expected high school to be, but with more leather clothing and better writing.

The teaser of this particular episode opened with Kira staring down the barrel of an automatic rifle held by a thug working for a man called Prophet, the Big Bad of the series.

"You wanna shoot me?" Kira said fearlessly. "Roll the bones. See what comes up."

The villain laughed; Kira winked and kissed the air; the villain hesitated at her confidence; then Kira went to town on him, disassembling both the thug and the rifle in ten seconds.

By then, Baylee Ross was deeply asleep.

She woke later to the sound of her own scream.

three

Whether it was the nightmare that woke her or the scream that succeeded it, Baylee could not tell. All she knew was that the sound still lingered in the air even as Ari Wagner burst into her room. The green digital clock on her nightstand read 2:43 a.m.

"Baylee!" Ari shouted, chucking herself onto the edge of Baylee's twin bed.

Ari Wagner, mid-forties and petite enough to pass for far younger, wore a Velvet Underground T-shirt and cut-off sweat pants, her medium-length hair snarled on one side. She grabbed Baylee's shoulders, squeezing hard and chanting, "It's okay, you're okay, I'm here."

Baylee raised a weak hand, breathing hard. "Sorry. Yeah. No. It's fine. I'm fine."

A complete lie. The very last thing Baylee felt was *fine*. Her breath came out like she'd run a sprint, cold sweat clung to her skin like spilled olive oil, and her mouth felt like the batting inside a comforter.

These goddamn nightmares, she thought. Go the hell away, go the *fuck* away . . .

John Wagner appeared in the doorway, half-asleep and disheveled in his plaid pajama pants. He wore no shirt and scraped absently at his chest as he said in a voice hoarse from sleep, "Everything okay?"

"Just another dream," Ari said. "Go back to bed, hon."

John mumbled something and shuffled back down the hallway. Baylee heard their bedroom door shut.

Ari pushed one cranky curl of highlighted brown hair out of her eyes before taking one of Baylee's hands. "Bay," she said, also hoarse but awake and insistent, "you can't keep suffering like this."

"I'm not *suffering*. It was a dream, I'm okay." Baylee pulled her hand away to rub her eyes, realizing only then that she'd fallen asleep in her clothes.

"We don't have to talk about it right now," Ari said, "but I want you to reconsider getting some help."

Baylee summoned an icy glare that Ari may not have seen very well in the darkness. "I'm not depressed. I'm not suicidal, I'm not a danger to myself or others."

"Baylee—"

"My grades didn't slip all year, I have no major weight fluctuations, my appetite hasn't changed."

Those were symptoms Ari had rattled off to the teens on more than one occasion. Ari Wagner, ironically or not, for better or worse, was an adolescent therapist. She'd instructed the Ross children that if they felt any of those symptoms, they were to tell her right away. They never had, not to Baylee's knowledge.

"Sleep disturbances," Ari fired back; Baylee had skipped that one, hoping Ari wouldn't notice. "You've had nightmares two or three times a week since you got here."

"What, are you keeping track?"

When Ari didn't reply, Baylee realized, yes, she actually *was*.

Baylee also realized: Holy shit, was it really that often?

"We'd really like you see someone," Ari said. "Not me, of course, but someone at the office. Or another place if you want. Just to talk. Get things out in the open. You and Lij both. You can go together if you'd like to. Or *not*, whatever you want."

The first time she used nicknames for them, Elijah and Baylee didn't comment, although Baylee never enjoyed how it made her feel; like perhaps it hadn't been long enough since the Wagners took them in; like they didn't know the teens well enough yet. But she and Lij said nothing. Sometimes Baylee got the impression that Ari wanted them to call her "Mom."

That was not going to happen.

"We are both fine," Baylee said, awake enough now to enunciate. "I just want to go back to sleep."

Ari frowned.

"I'm sorry." Baylee squeezed her eyes shut. "I don't mean to be a bitch."

"Stop that. You're not a bitch."

"But I *feel* like one, and I'm sorry. I'll think about it, okay? I just need some more time."

Softly, Ari said, "It's been a year."

"I know, just—please. I need to think. I need to get to a place where I can talk about it, that's all. I promise."

"Well. Like I said. Don't need to decide right now." Ari sighed and brushed a single, possibly imaginary hair off Baylee's forehead. The gesture felt too intimate, too familiar, but Baylee forced herself not pull away.

Ari was okay, and John was okay—and they were not her parents.

The older woman stood and went to the hall, hesitating at the doorway as if about to add something else. Then she shrugged and said, "I hope you can get back to sleep. G'night, Bay."

Baylee watched her shadow bounce across the tile and listened to her enter their bedroom and close the door behind her.

As if he'd been waiting for a cue, Elijah peeked in through the open door. "Hey."

Baylee fell back against her comforter. "Hey."

"You all right?"

She flung an arm over her eyes. "We've really got to stop asking each other that."

"Fair enough."

"Lij?"

"Yep?"

Baylee lifted her arm and looked over at him, repeating her own earlier words emphatically: "It's *not* just you."

He drummed his fingers against the wall. "Roger that. G'night."

"Night."

Lij eased her door closed. Baylee got up and changed into pajama pants before snuggling down beneath her comforter, hoping she could go back to sleep. When it didn't come, she turned the iPad back on and got semi-lost in the adventures of Kira Thirteen.

○

"Did you get any sleep?" John asked her the next morning when Baylee came staggering into the kitchen. Lij's door remained closed, and she could hear Ari's shower going in the master bedroom. Their door was open.

"No. Did you?"

"Eh. Little bit." He smiled behind a mug of Columbian coffee. His eyes did not look nearly as sleepy and dry as hers felt.

"Sorry," Baylee said, and opened a cupboard.

John set the mug down with a bonk and slid his chair back. "Hungry? I can make you some—"

"I'm fine." She took down a box of Cheerios.

Baylee felt him watch her as she fixed the bowl with soy milk and ground-up golden flaxseed. She debated taking her breakfast into her room to get away from his eyes. John wasn't leering; it wasn't that kind of look at all. To a limited degree, Baylee thought it might have been easier if he did. No, this was sadness. At *best* it was sadness. At worst . . . pity.

She took a step out of the kitchen.

"Baylee."

She paused. Did not turn.

"Could you come sit down for a sec?"

Baylee debated ignoring him. She was sixteen, that's what sixteen year old girls did with their father figures. If that's what he was. But sixteen seemed a long time ago now. She felt much older than that, if not necessarily wiser. No—just older. Worn out. Vegan menus and daily jogs be damned, she felt like an old woman.

She turned and tried to force a smile but it failed and she knew it. "Sure."

After she'd settled in at the table—the farthest opposite chair—John said, "Ari told me she asked you again last night about some counseling."

"Mm-hmm." Baylee made sure to keep her mouth full.

"And, you don't really want to."

She shrugged, still chewing.

"You know, I've done it," he offered. "I mean, my parents are still alive, but—"

Baylee tuned out. Your parents are still alive, she thought. If you ever want to know where you lost me, pal, it was that one sunny July Sunday morning when you reminded me that your parents were still alive.

She let him ramble until she cleaned the bowl. "Thanks, I'll think about it. I got to get ready."

John's expression showed that he knew he'd misstepped, but couldn't figure out where. Then his expression changed; became matter-of-fact. "Okay, great, but one more thing. When Ari or I text you, we need you text or call back, all right? I mean, you're practically an adult and all that, and that's great, but seriously. You have to let us know where you are and if you're okay. It's not a ton to ask, we've been pretty hands off, haven't we? So, just . . . a little consideration so we don't freak out."

"Absolutely." Baylee hustled for her room, wondering if she'd said it convincingly enough.

Maybe, she thought as she got ready for the day, she really could talk Timothy into that trip to San Diego. Might be worth a try.

○

Krista went to church.

This blew Baylee's mind. She couldn't even imagine what the girl would wear. The image in her head of church-going included frilly pink dresses for the girls and severe blue suits for the boys. Janey and Ken Ross had given religion a wide berth like their parents before them, so Lij and Baylee followed naturally in their footsteps. The family hadn't been hostile to faith, not that Baylee could remember. They certainly did not, however, find much use for Easter or any other observance save for a relatively traditional American Christmas celebration that did not include a midnight mass or candlelight service of any kind.

Baylee discovered later, after having spent most of the day in the library getting lost in diet and exercise books, and one intriguing tome called *How Not To Die*, that Krista's father was the one with a religious affectation. When he was home, it was church for her.

They connected at six that night as the library was closing. Krista rode up to Baylee on her Hoopla, looking tired, furious, and relieved to see Baylee.

"Hug me. Hug me." Krista chanted this with her arms open until Baylee followed orders. "Ugh, oh my God. I like him better when he's *drunk*."

"That was a long day," Baylee agreed. She didn't mind alone time, but the hours until now had felt endless.

"You don't even know. First it was church, then it was lunch, then it was family time, and then it was chores, and then it was more family time, and, ugh, God. I could not get out of there soon enough."

"How'd you escape?"

Krista sighed. "I innocently asked what time Liquor

Barn closed. That got him out of the house. Now I just gotta figure out what to do the rest of the night because, woo boy, I think he'll be effing *tanked* shortly."

"You can stay over if you want."

"I might. I just might. Thanks, Bails." Krista gave herself one good, feline shake, as if to free herself of all thoughts of her dad. Centered again, she smiled. "All right. What's the scoop?"

When not reading, Baylee had been texting with Lij. Over the course of the day, they'd come up with their plan.

"Kyro," she announced. "All six of us."

"Oh, God, I'm not exactly dressed for this, Bails." Krista looked down at herself, appraising with obvious distaste her cargo shorts, sport bra, and tank top that looked utterly perfunctory.

"You're wearing what you always wear when you see Fletcher. It's not a date, remember. We're just hanging out."

Krista's face went taut. She placed a flat palm against her belly. "Oh, my God. I just got nervous. Holy *shit*, Bails! I just got nervous over Christopher fucking Fletcher!"

Baylee smiled. "Perfect."

They walked and shuttled to the coffee shop, with Krista keeping up such a constant stream of chatter that Baylee was able to clandestinely read a message from Timothy, **Talk to you tonight?** without being caught. She didn't dare reply though. She'd have to sneak away for a few seconds at some point to do that. If all went well at the café, no one would even notice she'd stepped outside.

Kyro was half-full when they arrived, sweaty and in good spirits. The sun cast dizzying rays of orange and pink in the west, and the girls stopped briefly to admire it. While the heat sucked fiercely, Arizona sunsets were second to none.

Baylee led the way inside, shutting her eyes against the blast of cold air that washed over her from inside the café. The coffee shop sported neon green walls and a flat-black, exposed ceiling. Local artists hung their wares on the walls in no particular order that Baylee had ever discerned. The tables, chairs, and couches inside ran the gamut from garage-sale diamonds to hotel liquidation chic. Live plants hung from every corner, studiously attended to by the staff. It was, Ari had told Baylee on their first trip here together, "a place where the rich come to feel like they're slumming it." Mornings, Kyro became dominated by undercaffeinated soccer moms and self-employed stock brokers who camped out and leeched the café's strong wi-fi. Lunch brought in the business crowd from assorted offices down the road. Afternoons saw high schoolers hanging from the rafters, while evenings tended to bring out the slam poetry and open mic crowd.

Baylee spotted Lij and the gamers immediately. Per their plan, Lij had staked out one corner of the café, securing a long couch, two stuffed chairs, and a love seat surrounding a table quite possibly built in the Civil War era. Lij and Ralph sat on the red leather couch, Fletcher in the love seat, and Suze—unsurprisingly—sat on the floor, her extraordinary limbs stretched out in front of her like in Lij's room.

"Ready?" Baylee said.

Krista jabbed her between the shoulder blades. "Bite me."

The gamers sat embroiled in a game of some kind. Each

held mismatched game cards. Baylee recognized Cards Against Humanity, Candy Land, Magic: The Gathering, Bicycle playing cards, and more, like a game store had exploded in their hands. The cards seemed to have been assembled from the dented board games Kyro kept shoved on a bookshelf along with broken-spined paperbacks and old textbooks abandoned by frustrated college students.

"What's up, nerds?" Krista said as they reached the gamers.

"Gelatinous were-pig!" Fletcher replied, not lifting his eyes.

"Hi Baylee!" Ralph said, loudly. Baylee sent him a nod with the fastest smile she could get away with.

Lij set his cards face down and stood to hug Baylee quickly. "How's it going?"

Before she could answer, Fletcher interrupted, shouting, "I call!" like they were playing bizzaro-world poker. He slapped down his cards face-up on the round wooden table. "Charging rhinoceroses, two red squares, and a suicide jack!"

"Full house," Ralph said, also laying his cards face-up. He shot Baylee a smile as if to get her approval.

"Pair of queens, the blood of the innocent, and a pair of Nightfall Predators," Lij said, showing his hand.

The gamers looked at Suze, who slid a single card face-up onto the table top.

"Hitler," she whispered.

The boys all groaned and threw down the rest of the cards. Looking pleased with herself—barely—Suze swept them into a pile and stacked them beside her leg.

"Okay," Baylee said. "At the risk of your answer giving me an aneurysm, what the hell are you guys doing?"

Ralph furrowed his brow. "Playing cards."

"You had to ask," Krista said.

"You know what's a great look for you, Kris-*duh*?" Fletcher said, dealing a new hand of mismatched cards. "Shutting the hell up. It's so hot when you do that. You incontinent kobold."

Krista took that as an invitation, and threw herself into the love seat beside Fletcher. Baylee sat down beside her brother, keeping him between her and Ralph.

"You know," Krista said to Fletcher as he dealt the cards, "I could punch you in the throat right now, and no one here would stop me."

The others all said, *It's true, yeah, she could, totally,* then laughed at Fletcher's expense. He sniffed. "You're not fast enough."

"What?" Krista cried. "Do you know how—"

"BAM!" Fletcher shouted, shooting an index finger into Krista's ribs. The attack made her squeal and double up. "Ninja attack!"

Baylee grinned. The night looked promising.

As Fletcher and Krista turned on one another—the card game was forgotten—Ralph took an obvious deep breath and held it, staring hard at the jumble of cards on the table.

"So, Baylee," he exhaled, turning to face her with his legs strangely close together in a manner that no seventeen-year-old boy ought ever do. Ralph cleared his throat, and did not make eye contact. "There's a, uh, showing next weekend of, uh, John Carpenter's *The Thing*? At Valley Art Theater? And we were, uh, thinking about going, and uh, you know. If you wanted to, you could, uh . . . you could come with us?"

He coughed once.

The entire café quieted, or so it seemed to Baylee. Certainly everyone around the table glanced her way, then Ralph's, then undertook heroic measures to be busy doing something else.

"Oh," Baylee replied in a weak voice that she hated. "Um. Thanks, Ralph. But you know, I—I think Krista has a skate competition next weekend sometime and I promised I'd be there to support her, so."

"No problem." Ralph didn't sound surprised. He hurried to take over Fletcher's dealer duties.

Ralph was a good guy, Baylee thought, it wasn't that. He just was not and never would be her type, and certainly not in competition with Timothy. She sought a way to lessen the rejection.

"But, hey," she added, and did her best to affect a British accent, something she imagined they all used during D&D games. "It is an honor to be asked, good sir."

Ralph perked up, which pleased her. She didn't want to hurt his feelings, and he seemed to understand.

"Mi'lady," he said, tipping her a courtly nod.

Lij met his sister's eyes and conveyed a silent *Thank you.* She nudged him in return.

Then everyone's lives went to hell.

four

"All right, ass-hat," Krista said to Fletcher as their insult competition ended. She raised a palm, which he promptly slapped with his own. "I need something to drink."

"Pick me up a sixer, would you, my rancid little knoll queen?" Fletcher replied.

Krista jammed his boony hat down over his face. The gamers laughed, and Krista gestured to Baylee to join her. The girls drifted over to the counter to order drinks: Krista, a large vanilla blended ice; Baylee, a green smoothie.

"So I've got a competition this weekend, huh?" Krista said under her breath as they waited for the order. "In a hundred and seventeen degree heat, no less."

"*Shhh!*"

"I'm teasing. That was a nice let-down. You're very kind, Bails."

"Thanks," Baylee muttered back. "How about you and Fletcher? When are you just going to make out with him and get it over with?"

Krista arched an eyebrow and glanced clandestinely at Fletcher. "He makes me laugh. That's the truth of it right there, my friend. That guy cracks me up."

As they watched, the gamers started an argument over whether the ace of spades was worth more than a card called a Planeswalker. "Roll off!" Fletcher declared, which sent the four of them scrambling into their various bags for their dragon dice.

"*Twenty!*" Fletcher screamed, making the Kyro patrons turn and glare. Per usual, he and the others didn't notice. Fletcher clapped his hands a couple times and cheered like he was at a football game.

"Dare I ask?" Krista said.

"Natural twenty," Baylee said. "It means he rolled a twenty without any modifiers. It's a critical hit in D&D. Which is a good thing. Best thing you can roll."

"Rolled twenty *what?*"

"On a twenty-sided die."

"There's such a thing as a twenty-sided dice?"

"Die, singular. The plural is dice. And, yes, there is. *And* I'm ashamed I know that. Geez, let's move on, I sound like my brother."

The cashier handed them their drinks and they walked back to the group. Upon getting themselves settled in the same seats as before, Krista sat up straight, reminding Baylee of a prairie dog poking out of its burrow.

"There he is," she announced.

Everyone looked. Baylee said, "Who?"

"My *husband.*"

Baylee understood instantly what she meant.

A couple had walked into Kyro: a young guy and a young girl, perhaps Baylee's age or a little older. They sauntered into the café, dressed at opposite ends of the style spectrum. He veered prep-frat, wearing a striped V-neck

Henley hugging nicely built muscles in his chest, arms, and shoulders. Baylee guessed what his abs probably looked like. He wore shorts that made her old Del Mar board shorts look sickly; she knew this because she looked down at herself to remember what she was wearing and feeling how suddenly awful it was. His hair was black, the color of shark's eyes, and he surveyed the café with a practiced, bored expression.

But something else lurked behind his gaze. Something intense Baylee could not name.

The girl, on the other hand, could have walked out of a Charles Dickens novel. Thin and narrow, she sported pure white hair poking out from beneath a brown derby hat. She wore a white button-up shirt, charcoal gray suspenders, and a pair of dark blue pants that made Baylee want to use the word "trousers." Her skin was as pale and flawless as Krista's plastic cup of crushed ice and vanilla.

Staring openly at them, Baylee scraped shamefully and unwittingly at a zit on her chin, and noticed Krista pulling her fingers through her messy hair, as if they were both suddenly the most inadequate human beings ever birthed. The gamers didn't fare much better: Suze and Ralph blinked at the couple as if they shone with sunlight. Fletcher's mouth hung open. Lij's shoulders crept up near his ears as if to protect himself from their beauty.

Somehow the pair were too good looking. And repellent, Baylee thought. She felt the most absurd compulsion to kiss them—both—and punch them hard in the face.

"Who are they looking for?" Baylee said softly to anyone listening.

"Hopefully me," Krista answered. Her eyes were wide

and focused on the guy. Her response snapped Fletcher from his reverie; he pulled back and eyed her with surprise. Hadn't things been going well?

Baylee asked her question because it's what the couple looked like they were doing: searching Kyro for someone in particular. Yet more than that, it looked to her as if they were . . . somehow . . . *shopping*.

Upon hearing some silent cue, the couple zeroed in on people at the exact same time; he, on Krista. She, on Lij.

"Oh, shit," Baylee said, for no real reason other than it felt right to say. She suddenly didn't want this girl anywhere near her brother. Yet nor could she stand; could not grab his arm, tell him it was time to go. Nothing. She could only sit and watch as if in thrall as the couple moved closer.

Krista's breath caught visibly as the guy came ambling over to her. He grinned with approximately twenty-five percent of his mouth and dropped into one of the unoccupied chairs, facing her. A completely useless and unheard-of bolt of jealousy shot through Baylee's stomach.

I have a boyfriend, she thought, who is hot and awesome and nice and sexy and . . .

And she still wanted this guy to look at her. To see her, acknowledge her existence.

"Hi," the guy said to Krista. "I'm Sean. What's your name, sweetheart?"

He had an East Coast accent Baylee could only place from watching too many movies and TV shows; Boston, she thought. He dropped the R in "sweetheart." This close to him, his age actually got *harder* to figure out, not easier. He might have been an ultra-brilliant seventh-grade prodigy en route to Harvard—or, rather, *Hahvuhd*—or else a long-tenured professor at the same school. It disconcerted her, being unable to put him into any kind of box.

"Krista," Baylee's best friend said. She was *breathless*, a state in which Baylee had never before seen her.

During this sudden courtship, the girl in the derby sashayed to the couch and threw herself into Lij's lap. Lij's expression exploded with shock—and joy. The other three gamers stared at her with a mixture of awe and anger; she was beautiful, but she was interrupting.

"Well, now," she said with a thick accent Baylee took to be Scottish. She gave Lij a pixie smirk. "Wot we got here n' tha'? Wot's your name, then?"

"Eh-Elijah."

Baylee would have laughed if the display hadn't been so grotesque. Lij was smitten.

Still on his lap, the girl drew one finger in loops around his ear. Lij's face lit up red like a stop light. He looked like a strawberry topped by dark blonde hair that needed washing.

Baylee had had enough. She stuck her head closer to her brother and said, pointedly, "Hi, how's it going, can I help you?"

Suze, Fletcher, and Ralph sent her agreeing looks that said, *Yes, thank you for coming to stop this.* Lij shot her a death glare that said, *Do not screw this up for me!*

"Easy, lass," Derby said—she hadn't introduced herself yet, so Baylee decided that was her new name. "Juss gettin' to know everyone, likesay."

She squirmed on Lij's lap. The effect it had on his teenage body, while not visible, was incontrovertible.

"I'm Fletcher," Fletcher said quickly, trying to get her attention. "Chris Fletcher. Like, Bond, James Bo—"

"Talkin' to Elijah now, love," Derby said, her eyes locked on Lij's. Baylee had heard the term "bedroom eyes" before, and now its meaning became crystal clear. Derby may as well have been naked on top of Lij the way she was looking at him.

"What are you *doing?*" Baylee said, crossing her arms with a sneer.

"Flirtin' I think," the other girl replied. "That wot it feels like to you, Elijah?"

Lij swallowed hard and nodded harder.

"Look!" Baylee said—shouted, really. "I don't know who you are, but—"

Derby's head slithered around, eyes narrowing dangerously. Baylee instinctively reared back from her ice-blue gaze.

"Easy, lass," she said again. "We'll be movin' on soon enough, likesay."

She turned her full attention back to Lij. "Want to know a secret, Elijah? Can I whisper it in your ear n' tha'?"

He nodded again. Derby had complete authority to do as she pleased, based on his expression.

Suze threw her hand of cards down and bolted to her feet, practically running to the bathrooms at the rear of Kyro. Baylee had long wondered and now could see clearly that she had a thing for Lij.

It was becoming one hell of a heart-breaking night: Ralph watched the gnarly scene between Lij and Derby with a bizarre mix of lust and distaste. Fletcher, still sharing the love seat with Krista, looked as if he could not begin to believe his shit luck.

Derby pressed herself against Lij and spoke into his

ear. His face turned brighter red.

Baylee glanced at Krista, and barely restrained a groan. Sean was tracing circles on her upturned palm, and Krista's body appeared to melt beneath the light touch.

"You wanna get outta here?" Sean said.

Krista licked her lips and nodded. Sean took her hand and guided her to her feet.

Fletcher stood, trying to puff up his slender frame. "Hey, man!"

Sean's head twisted just an inch to glare at Fletcher. The movement struck Baylee as eerily similar to Derby's a moment ago. "Fuck off, ya fuckin' cunt, I'll beat ya fuckin' senseless."

Fletcher blanched. Krista did not so much as glance at him as Sean led her straight out of Kyro, keeping eye contact with her the entire way and smiling lazily like he hadn't just threatened Fletcher with physical violence— violence, Baylee was sure, he was utterly capable of dealing out.

Then Derby was on her feet, moving like quicksilver, so fast and fluid it seemed she'd teleported like one of Lij's D&D monsters.

"Don't forget, now," she said to Lij. She tipped the brim of her hat up with one finger and slid her thumbs the length of her suspenders, up then down. "See ya la'er, lamb."

Derby stepped away from the game table, moving as if every limb was made of silk. She cast Baylee a withering glare as she left.

Baylee watched her go. The Scot turned and walked— no, skipped—after Sean and Krista.

"Well," Fletcher drawled, pulling his can of Skoal out

of one pocket and packing it. "That was nauseating."

"You gave her *your* best shot," Baylee said, but distantly, like an afterthought.

"That was before I got nauseated."

"Fair enough," Baylee said. She felt like spitting on the floor to get some phantom taste of decay out of her mouth.

She faced her brother, who, like Ralph and Fletcher too, were watching the glass door as if the couple were still there. "What the hell *was* that, Lij? Don't forget *what*, what was she talking about?"

Lij did not react. Frustrated, Baylee snapped her fingers in front of his face. He blinked and reared back.

"What."

"I said, what the hell was all that?"

Lij . . . sneered. It was a face he made when confronted with foul odors. "I can have a fucking girlfriend if I want to!"

His words and tone broke the spell the two interlopers had cast. Ralph and Fletcher spun to stare at their friend, eyes popping. Lij did not seem to notice, keeping the curl in his lip and glaring at Baylee.

". . . Wow," Fletcher said, raising his hands in a defensive gesture. "That all happened *real* fast. I am *out*."

He stooped and slung his leather backpack, something from a Ren Faire, over his shoulder.

Baylee stood. "Fletcher, wait—"

"Naw, no, I'm out, that was . . . that was crazy." He parked a wad of dip into his cheek and used his tongue to shape it, shaking his head the whole time. "I thought Krista had like a . . . I mean I thought we were . . ."

He closed his mouth, looked around, and picked up Krista's abandoned vanilla drink. He spit into it and set it back down on the table.

"I'm out," he said again, and walked quickly out of the café.

Ralph faced Baylee. They exchanged helpless looks as Lij jumped to his feet and grabbed his own bag.

"Whatever," he grumbled, and stomped outside.

Ralph took a half step toward Baylee so they stood side by side. "Do you know her? Ever seen either one of them before?"

"No. And I don't *want* to know them."

"Yeah, I'm on your team, there. I've never seen Lij act like that."

"Or Krista," Baylee said.

"Yeah, I thought she liked Fletcher or something. Isn't that why we came here tonight?"

"Yeah. I thought so too."

Suze reappeared, hair in her face and hands deep in her pockets. She stood several inches taller than both of them. "Is it over?" she asked in a grouchy whisper.

"For the moment," Baylee said, only realizing as she said it that she'd just expressed her worst fear; that this was only the beginning. Of what, she couldn't say. "But they didn't trade numbers," she added hopefully. "So maybe we'll never see her again."

"Fine by me," Suze mumbled. She perched on the couch and sorted the playing cards.

Baylee and Ralph joined in. When they'd arranged the cards in matching stacks, they gathered their things and walked out together. None of them admitted they'd sorted the cards not as a favor to café staff, but to put time and distance between them and everyone who'd just left. None of their friends or enemies were anywhere to be seen outside.

Ralph squinted up at Baylee. "You want to walk together?"

She heard no trace of flirtation in his voice. He was merely being a gentleman. A friend. Baylee knew the gamers all lived in the same general area, though Ralph lived farthest from here, beyond the Wagner's house.

"Sure," Baylee said. "Thanks."

The strange trio set off, saying nothing more. Baylee waited for the inevitable discomfort born of such silence, but it never arrived. She supposed they were each too engrossed with their own thoughts—anger, confusion, disgust—to worry about awkward silence between them.

○

Ari and John sat in the living room watching a Netflix series when she got to the house.

"Hey," she greeted them. "Lij home?"

"No," Ari said. Concern flashed in her eyes. "He said he was meeting with you."

"Oh, uh . . . we did. He left." She debated how much to tell them, and decided it really wasn't a big enough deal to loop the Wagners in. Had it been Mom and Dad, surely yes. But Ari and John didn't quite merit the whole sordid affair.

"Should we call him?" John asked.

Baylee shook her head. "He's fine. I'm sure he'll be home soon."

She hurried to her room, closed the door, and sent Timothy a message. **Weird night!**

On her bed, she tapped out a very long message detailing all the grotesqueries of the evening. When Timothy didn't reply back right away, Baylee pouted and turned the iPad to *Lucky 13*. Five episodes later, Timothy responded: **Odd.**

That was it. Baylee paused the show and wrote back, **Right? I'm not over reacting am I?**

No, wrote Timothy. **I would say you are reacting quite normally.**

Thank you. She started a new message: **What were you up to tonight?**

Dinner, Timothy wrote. **With the family. Shall I call you at midnight?**

Baylee grinned in the dim glow of the iPad and nibbled her lip and tingled inside. **Yes please.**

And breakfast tomorrow? he asked. **At our usual place?**

Yes yes yes, Baylee wrote, and checked the time. Midnight would come soon.

○

Baylee crept out of unconsciousness with languid ease the next morning. Her plantation shutters did an admirable job of keeping out the morning sunlight, but the window frame still glowed white and cast the bedroom in soft shadow. She stretched gently under the comforter and felt a feline grin cross her face as she slowly took stock of herself.

She wore nothing but her underwear; the rest of her clothing she'd shed within minutes of Timothy's call. She still clutched the phone in her left hand, though the ear buds had long since fallen out in the night. Baylee giggled and muffled the sound into one of her pillows, remembering her need to bite hard on her own arm as Timothy's voice and her hand ended her evening with excruciating joy.

It had been quite a night.

She sat up and wrapped the sheet around her body, reminding herself not to eat; Timothy would be waiting with breakfast. She noted Lij's door was closed and the house was quiet; Ari and John would have left for the day by now. Baylee considered knocking on Lij's door to see if he was home, then opted against it. He'd been such a dick last night that leaving him in time-out for the morning sounded fair.

She took a fast, relatively pointless shower—five minutes outside would render the entire purpose of showering moot—and walked to her rendezvous.

Baylee always met Timothy in a place no one would ever bother to look, and where it was unlikely anyone would accidentally stumble upon them. The walk never took more than twenty minutes, and she met him there often.

Often meaning every day. Or perhaps a little less than that, so Ari, John, and Lij wouldn't get too suspicious. Baylee sometimes wondered what kind of excuses she would have to come up with when school started up again in August. It might be tougher then. Constructing an elaborate lie about an after school program seemed impractical, and was not in her nature anyway. Well—she'd cross that bridge later.

Right now she was hungry and while already sweating under the Phoenix sun, a lingering sense of sensuality still raced through her veins.

North Community Church was peeling on the outside. The more modern, stucco classroom buildings surrounding it hadn't been cleaned or painted for much longer than a year, Baylee guessed. A mud-stained sign stuffed into the earth like a tombstone gave the church's name. The campus sat small and conservative in a large stretch of weedy land with a dusty parking lot attached on the west. The whole property struck Baylee as ghost-townish. The nearest homes were about a block away in any direction. It occurred to her for the first time that morning that maybe the church was considered historical, and that's why no one had bought it or razed it.

Or maybe, she thought, it was cursed; the site of black rites and wicked rituals since its closing.

She let herself laugh out loud. Too much Netflix?

They'd made the church their special spot because no one ever bothered them there. Its position on the block made traffic rare, which was perfect for privacy. Since the property was abandoned, at night the only light came from whatever star- and moonlight happened to get through the windows of Timothy's car. Parked in the back, behind the sanctuary, they were virtually invisible. Exactly the kind of thing a couple of teenagers would want.

Baylee never snuck out of the Wagner's house to meet him here, primarily because she never had to. Ari and John asked that the teens were home before midnight during the summer, unless they had made plans—and let the Wagners know about those plans—to sleep over somewhere else.

Baylee never betrayed that trust. If she said she was staying over at Krista's, she did. It wasn't as if she said "I'm sleeping at Krista's" and then stayed out all night with Timothy. Perhaps she could have, but then where would they go? Timothy's house? No, he had family, too, he'd said so. She just hadn't met them, or been to his house in the north part of town.

So Baylee simply never told the Wagners when she was with him, or where. Or that there was a Timothy at all. She didn't have what Ari called the "emotional resources" to let Ari and John in on the relationship. Not yet. She wanted and needed something to herself, something she could . . .

Could *cherish*. Yes, that was the right word. Baylee told herself she was not lying to anyone; that a secret was not the same thing as a lie.

She hoped.

When Baylee saw Timothy's car parked in the gravel behind the sanctuary, she put on a burst of speed. Timothy climbed out of his classic car when he saw her, and came around to the passenger side.

His car looked like something out of a black-and-white movie or TV show, like *The Untouchables* or *The Twilight Zone*. And it was gorgeous. Baylee didn't know or care to know a lot about classic cars, but she appreciated a nice ride when she saw one. This, Timothy explained to her the night they met, was a 1936 Ford five-window coupe, updated on the interior but kept classic on the outside. When she'd asked where he got it, he'd said it was a gift. His first car. Not a bad gift. Meanwhile, Baylee herself couldn't rustle up the wherewithal to ask Ari and John about getting a *license*. The idea of driving terrified her; it reminded her of her mother and father, driving along that dark road one year ago and never driving again.

She hugged Timothy tightly.

"Hello there," he said, his voice, as always, making parts of her melt that had nothing to do with the summer sun.

"Hey," she greeted him. "I love you."

Timothy tightened his hold for a moment, then pulled back to look into her eyes.

His hair was black like wet ash, with eyelashes that Baylee wanted for herself. His eyes were an impossible lion-yellow, so much so that she once asked if he wore colored contacts. Beyond that . . . in truth, he was attractive, yes, but not necessarily someone to look twice at on the street. And, yes, he had the slender, strong body of many teenage boys, the kind who can eat three burritos in one sitting and not gain an ounce.

But none of that is what hooked Baylee. And none of it was what kept her with him. She loved him because he looked into her eyes. Because he talked to her. Because he had the rare ability to know when she wanted something intimate and physical, and when she just needed quiet, or to be held, or to watch yet another episode of *Lucky 13* on her phone.

She loved him because he knew her. Baylee avoided words like "fate," not wanting to be the kind of girl who said such things about her boyfriend. Yet there had been a certain . . . inevitability.

"You're so cold," Baylee said, kissing him once before nuzzling into his slender body. "How do you stay so nice and cold in this heat?"

"Zero circulation," Timothy said. "It's a gift."

"I'm jealous."

"Well, maybe some day I can teach you how to achieve a body temperature of absolute zero."

"Please do."

"Modern air conditioning doesn't hurt, either." He pronounced it *eye*-ther.

She smiled. "Let's eat."

They split up and climbed into the '36, Baylee in the passenger seat. White leather enveloped her gently, like a hug. Timothy turned the engine and got the A/C going— one of his many interior improvements. Ella Fitzgerald sang quietly from the speakers. Timothy loved old-time music: big band, swing, and Motown.

Timothy handed her a sack full of fruit and a wheat bagel. Baylee pulled out fresh strawberries. "You're an angel."

"And you are beautiful. Have you spoken to Elijah yet?"

"No. I don't even know if he was home when I left. God, you should have seen him, he was such a jerk last night."

"Has he ever had a girlfriend?"

Baylee worked a piece of bagel out from between her teeth with her tongue, using the time to think. "No . . . not that I know of. No."

"Well, if this girl was as forward as you say, that would have left quite an impression."

Baylee scowled. "Whose side are you on?"

Timothy shook his head, his black hair catching a ray of sunlight and turning momentarily blue. He passed her a bottle of chilled water.

"No one's side. I'm just offering you the male perspective. An attractive girl comes in and pays attention to him like that? I'm surprised he didn't propose."

"Yeah, but it was so *gross*. They were both gross, her and the douchebag she came in with."

"You know," Timothy said, "frankly, I think it was a joke. They were probably older kids pulling some kind of prank. Was anyone filming? Anyone have their cameras out?"

This hadn't occurred to Baylee, though it would certainly explain a lot. "No," she said thoughtfully. "Or, I mean, maybe. It's a coffee shop, everyone was on a phone or laptop. So yeah. It's possible."

"That's probably it, then. She didn't give him a phone number, you said, so he'll probably never see her again, and neither will you. Everyone wins."

"Yeah, but *Krista*."

"Well, that I don't know, but she seems like a big girl. She can handle herself."

Baylee finished off a couple more strawberries. "I guess . . ."

Timothy ran the back of one cool finger down her cheek. "I'm sorry, Baylee. I'm being dismissive. I don't mean to do that."

Baylee tapped him on the nose with her last strawberry before popping it into her mouth. "No worries. Just a weird night is all."

She'd finished everything in the sack. Timothy crumpled up the paper bag and tossed it into the back seat. "You want me to take you somewhere? I can."

"Yeah? You don't mind?" She did enjoy being in the

Ford as he drove, especially during the day. She liked the admiring looks people gave them. It made her feel like a star.

Timothy smiled, not showing any teeth. "Of course not. We can talk more later."

She slid as close to him as the seats allowed. "You mean, *talk* to me, talk to me?"

His smile grew. "Certainly. How was last night?"

"You're the best," was all she'd allow. She could feel her face growing warm.

"Well . . . it's a team effort, hmm? Where can I take you?"

"Block from the house?" Baylee asked in a small voice, half teasing and half embarrassed. She didn't *like* that she kept her boyfriend a secret, but she wanted a little more time with him that was hers alone, not something she shared with her brother or that had previously belonged to Ari and John.

"Certainly." Timothy kissed her once—then again, longer—before putting the car into gear.

He tasted like wine.

Timothy dropped her off right where Baylee asked. After making sure no one she knew was happening by—virtually impossible on a weekday in this heat—she kissed him again and climbed out. He drove away, and Baylee walked to the house, checking her phone in case she'd not felt it buzz with a message. Her wallpaper, which showed a family photo from Thanksgiving two years ago, was empty.

No one? she thought. Not Lij, or Krista?

Panic landed hard in her belly, upending Timothy's delicious breakfast. Summertime, Monday morning—

Krista should be at the Wedge, practicing before it got too hot, but she would have texted first to see if Baylee wanted to come along.

Wouldn't she? Baylee thought. She always had before.

Her panic dimmed. Maybe, came the dismal thought, she just didn't want to talk to Baylee at all. Just like Lij last night. Maybe Sean and Derby had worked their mojo so quickly and so thoroughly that Baylee was now nothing more than a scab to be picked off and flushed away. Baylee knew such discards happened; she started her third year of high school in a matter of weeks and knew such tales of woe were not abnormal.

She decided to wait and text Krista later. Give the skate betty a chance to reach out first. But Baylee wouldn't wait all day, wouldn't risk making a thing out of it. Pride was one thing. Losing your best friend just before starting school again was simply stupid.

Baylee went inside, calling her brother's name. She'd work something out with Krista; Lij, on the other hand, still needed some straightening out as far as Baylee was concerned.

"Lij?" She walked into the hallway. "Lij, are you—"

He smashed into her.

Baylee screeched and stumbled backward as he beelined for the bathroom, smashing the door open and falling to his knees in front of the toilet.

"Jesus, Lij!" Baylee shouted, but pulled back when she saw him leaning over and retching. Nothing came out, and the fact of it seemed to make his choking all the worse. He couldn't seem to breathe, like whatever was trying to come out had a death grip on his throat from the inside out.

"Lij?"

Her brother fell backward, crumpled into a ball between the toilet and tub, shaking horribly, pale and damp. She saw he wore the same clothes as last night. Baylee took a step in, but Lij raised a trembling hand to ward her off. He was saying something—and gesturing. It sounded like "fly."

Talking to him wasn't going to do any good, he was too sick. Baylee hesitated, then turned to enter his room. She scanned it quickly, spotting his cell phone lit up and on his bed like a beacon. Baylee picked it up.

Even as she did so, text messages flew up from the bottom of the screen. Lij's browser was open to a local news page. It had today's date. It had only been "today" for a few hours now, and Baylee realized the story must have posted very early.

Then she covered her mouth and understood Lij's reaction. He hadn't been saying *fly*. He'd been stuttering Fletcher's name, trying to spit it out of his mouth as if it were a rancid thing.

Between the news story and the flurry of texts from Ralph and Suze, she realized that Lij was not sick in the viral sense of the word.

No. It must have been the headline that did him in.

Teen's Body Found In Pieces.

five

Chris Fletcher, seventeen, had last been seen at Kyro Café in Phoenix. Friends said he left there around eight p.m. They did not know where he went after that. The last messages on his phone were timestamped prior to eight. He never got home. His parents called police at four a.m. when he failed to return phone calls and text messages. At five a.m., just as dawn broke, an off-duty police officer driving west out of Phoenix on the I-10 spotted what appeared to be clothing on the side of the road, and something else. From the angle of approach, it might have looked like a dead animal, with brown hair ruffling in the mild morning breeze. But the officer was no rookie and knew from more than one experience on the force what a decapitated head looked like. He pulled over and found what was left of Chris Fletcher.

There wasn't much.

An animal attack was the current theory and no one seemed interested in trying to prove otherwise; Fletcher's limbs had been torn from his body and stripped to the bone—at least, the limbs they could find, which totaled two. Whatever had eaten him had been thorough.

Baylee read all of this in mere moments, gathering the story from the news site and from Ralph and Suze's texts. The police had talked to them both and they assumed the cops would want to talk to Lij too. Or maybe they had all the information they needed; Ralph and Suze didn't know.

The mystery was not what had killed Fletcher—the mystery was why and how he had ended up twenty miles outside of town. There was a car involved, almost certainly; he could have walked that distance in the timeframe assembled by police, but it seemed unlikely, and no one reported anyone fitting his description walking along the freeways out of town.

Baylee swooned.

Fortunately her body was positioned in such a way that she fell onto Lij's bed and not the floor. In her own short life, she'd now contended with two animal attacks and three people slain.

The odds, Baylee thought sickly. What were the odds she and Lij would know and care about three people who met their end in virtually the same fashion? Astronomical. That's what the odds were, they were astronomical, and now she wondered if something was closing in on them, hunting them, planning its next move that would end this line of Rosses forever.

Another crash brought her upright. She caught a brief glimpse of Lij bolting out of the bathroom and down the hall. Baylee lurched to her feet and stumbled into the hallway, calling for him. Lij burst through the front door, leaving it swinging open, and veered left through the small front yard.

"Lij!" Baylee screamed, and followed. By the time she

reached the sidewalk, Lij was a full block away, running harder, faster than she'd known he was capable of; fueled, no doubt, by rage and fear and sadness.

She called for him again, unsurprised when he did not stop. Baylee crouched outside, holding her arms around herself in a cramped hug as her stomach knotted and twisted beneath her skin. Lij turned a corner and disappeared from view.

Timothy, she thought. Call Timothy, have him come pick you up.

No. Ari first, then maybe John, they need to know.

No, wait . . .

Back and forth her thoughts seesawed until she became dizzy with them, unable to process a rational thought, and recognizing the sensation as how it had felt when the police came to the house in San Diego last year. It would be bad enough if Fletcher had been hit by a car or killed in some random mugging; bad, but concrete. She could have understood those things.

Another animal attack, another use of that word *pieces* . . . never would that make sense.

Baylee forced herself into the house and to her phone. She swiped and tapped and Krista answered on the second ring.

"Bails! What's up?"

"Where are you," Baylee said, sounding like a ghost in her own ears.

"Heading to the Wedge, you wanna come?"

Baylee stared absently at her feet.

"I'll meet you there."

○

She found Krista skating the Wedge, her bag tossed carelessly on top of the brick wall where Baylee normally sat to watch. She paused in the shade beneath an acacia tree. Only a few skaters were out; Krista and a handful of boys who kept a respectful distance from the obvious pro with the crazy blonde hair.

Krista was beautiful to watch. Her body moved like fluid, like liquid mercury, weightless at times. Baylee considered leaving. Krista looked so happy, so at home. She could be forgiven the way she acted last night around that Sean asshole.

Why she felt compelled to tell Krista about Fletcher before anyone else, Baylee couldn't say. It just seemed right. Karmic, maybe, or some other metaphysical urge. Up until Sean had moved in on her, Krista had liked Fletcher; as more than a friend, too, she'd admitted as much just two days ago. His sudden death was the kind of thing a person would want to know, that was all.

If it happened to drive Sean from her mind, so much the better.

Baylee walked toward the concrete bowl, taking her time, planning her words.

She'd met Krista at school back in October, after spending one month not leaving the house much, then another month at a new school where everyone wanted to look like they were from California but weren't. She and Lij kept to themselves until he met Ralph, Suze, and Fletcher. Not long after he started spending first his lunches then his after school hours with the gamers, Krista Hope sat down next to her in the cafeteria and said, "All right, your period of transition is over. Who are you, and why won't you talk to anybody? I'm Krista."

The skater became Baylee's best friend almost instantly. That's the kind of person Krista was. Thanks to her, Baylee slowly made friends with other people, too, but never quite trusted them like she did Krista.

"Krista!"

Her friend twirled in a tight cyclone, the tail of the Hoopla scratching noisily on the concrete. Krista waved and pushed over to the edge of the skating area where Baylee stood, dangling a water bottle in her hand.

"Hey, what's up?" Krista said, smiling and sweating.

"I have to tell you something," Baylee said. "It's about Fletcher."

"Oh, yeah?" Krista said. "You know, he's cool and all, but Sean, man . . . holy shit, Bails. Like, I wanna marry him, I'm not even kidding. He is just the coolest—"

"Fletcher's dead."

Krista took a step backward. "What?"

Baylee nodded. "We found out this morning. It wasn't pretty."

"What the fuck does that mean, Baylee? *What's* not pretty?"

Her rehearsed speech fled. Baylee drew a shuddering breath. "It's on the news. He got attacked by a . . . by an animal. Out in the desert, off the ten. Just like . . ."

She didn't have to finish the sentence. And she couldn't meet Krista's eyes.

"Is this a joke?" Krista said.

Baylee shook her head.

"Why are you telling me this?"

The brutality of the words made Baylee's gaze snap up to Krista's face. She'd expected terror, shock, tears— something along those lines. Instead Krista looked pissed.

105

"Wh-*what?*"

"This is about Sean, isn't it?"

Baylee couldn't get enough breath into her lungs to respond.

"Well that's just great, Bails," Krista said. "I like literally just told you I didn't feel good about myself for Christ's sake, and the instant a boy shows interest you have to shit all over it. That's just fucking great."

Baylee coughed as if punched in the stomach. "Krista . . . Fletcher . . ."

"I gotta go," Krista sneered. She marched to the wall, slung her bag, and jumped on her board. As she skated past Baylee on the way to the street she said, "Maybe if you ever had a boyfriend you'd understand."

She was gone.

Baylee stared after her, mouth open, thoughts so jumbled she nearly had to sit down. Desperate for something to cling to for stability, she called Timothy. No answer. She hung up and sent him a text.

Chris Fletcher is dead. He was killed by an animal. Just like mom and dad. Krista flipped out on me. Lij ran off. I don't know what to do. Can you come get me?

She sent it off and walked to the street where Krista had vanished. Already her friend was out of sight.

If we are friends, Baylee corrected herself. Jesus, that was fast. Was this the kind of catty shit that made girls never talk again?

She checked her phone. The text message to Timothy showed *Delivered*, but not *Read*.

"Goddammit," she said, and ran for home.

Lij was not home. Baylee had the house to herself and didn't know what to do with it. Still no response from Timothy. She tried Krista; the message showed *Read* almost instantly, but Krista did not respond. She tried calling Timothy again, hoping that since she never called during the day, the mere the fact of a phone call would be enough to get him to answer.

Nothing.

Her face tight with growing frustration, Baylee cursed and sat on the edge of her bed, hunched over tightly crossed legs. Good God, now what?

The phone buzzed.

Baylee gasped and checked the screen—Ari. Shit.

She answered.

"Baylee," Ari said, sounding breathless. "Jesus Christ, did you hear?"

"Yeah," Baylee said flatly.

"Are you all right? How are you feeling?"

She very nearly told Ari everything right then. Something in the older woman's voice flicked a switch deep in Baylee's chest and she found herself wanting to finally tell Ari about Timothy. About the weird encounter with Derby and Sean, and how Krista had utterly turned on her this morning. That Lij had run off and she didn't know where. That Ari and John were never going to be her mom and dad and that they should never try to be, that pretty soon she and Lij would just be leaving for college or maybe Europe or who-the-hell-knew . . .

"Fine," Baylee said.

Silence followed, of the sort that spoke more loudly than words. Ari didn't buy it.

But she didn't pursue. "How about Lij? I've called but he didn't answer."

"He left his phone here."

"Where'd he go?"

"I honestly don't know. He was pretty upset."

Ari made a sound of some kind, something sympathetic and worried. She swore again, and Baylee pictured her with eyebrows furrowed, lips pressed tight, trying to find the right clinical response to this distressed teenager. That's what they paid her the big bucks for, after all.

"I need to go," Baylee said abruptly.

"Baylee—"

"It's okay, we can talk later or something. Bye."

She tapped the call off. Checked her texts; nothing from anyone. She stood up and wandered the house, holding her phone tight. Staying here and doing nothing wasn't doing any good, she had to . . .

Baylee spun and raced into Lij's room. His phone lay right where she'd dropped it. She woke it up and tapped his password—0020, for "twenty," of course—and scanned his messages.

Ralph and Suze had continued texting him. The last few showed that they were wondering where he was and if he was okay, and concluded with Ralph writing **Call or text me any time ok?** and Suze sending four heart emojis. Baylee wondered, somewhat grimly, if it was one heart for each of the gamers, Fletcher included.

She weighed the phone in her hand, debating, then deciding that desperate times called for desperate measures.

She brought up Lij's contacts and tapped Ralph's number into her own. Suze, she figured, might not answer and even if she did, Baylee wasn't sure she'd be able to hear the girl.

"Baylee!" said Ralph a second later.

Baylee blinked. "Ralph? How'd you know it was me?"

Ralph made a slight groaning noise, like he'd pulled a muscle. "Yeah . . . I'm sorry. Lij gave me your number awhile back. I never had the guts to call. Sorry. For um, for having it, I mean. That's creepy."

Baylee covered her mouth. Of all the shit that had happened in the last few hours, this simple and sincere admission was the thing that came closest to making her cry. He was sweet.

"It's okay," she said. "You're not creepy."

"Good to know," Ralph said with a mirthless laugh. He cleared his throat. "I guess you know what happened."

"Yeah."

"How's Lij?"

"Well, bad. But he ran off, I don't know where he is."

"Shoot."

"That's one way to put it. How are you guys, how's Suze?"

"Shock. We don't really know what to do. But hey . . . listen, Lij told us about your parents once. How are *you* doing?"

Yes, this, Baylee thought. Someone other than Ari understanding the awful memories Fletcher's death was bringing up. Bad enough to have lost a life of the party like Chris Fletcher at all; adding the *manner* of his death to it . . .

"I feel like a bitch," she said plainly. "I hate that he's gone, and I know you guys must be crushed, and all I can think about is my mom and dad."

"That's okay," Ralph said. "It's fair. You get to feel whatever you want."

Baylee's shoulders relaxed. She'd been holding them up tight without realizing it. "Thank you, Ralph. I appreciate that."

"Sure thing. So now what, what are you going to do?"

Baylee sighed. "I guess I'll wait here. Lij didn't take his phone, so."

"Oh, that's good," Ralph breathed. "I mean, we've been trying to get to him but he wasn't responding. I'm glad he wasn't just ignoring us."

"So he didn't show up at your place or Suze's?" That had been her hope.

"No, huh-uh."

"Where else would he go?"

"I don't know . . . Kyro, maybe?"

Baylee glanced at Lij's desk. His black wallet lay where it always did during the night.

"Maybe," she said. "But I doubt it. He just ran."

"Shoot," Ralph said again.

"Well, look," Baylee said, "I'll stick around here. He has to come back sooner or later. I'll make sure he calls you guys."

"Thanks."

"Hey, Ralph?"

"Yeah?"

"You all right? I mean, I know you're not, but . . . will you be?"

Ralph said nothing for a long time. When he did speak, Baylee could hear the tears choking his throat.

"Yep," he coughed out. "Some day."

"Okay," she said gently. "Talk to you later."

Ralph said something short, but it was lost. Baylee left him to his grief.

Keeping Lij's phone with her, she went into the living room and listlessly turned on the TV. Every time she checked her phone—once a minute or so—her messages hadn't changed. Timothy hadn't read his, and Krista hadn't replied to hers.

She'd never felt more alone.

six

Ari got home first. She came in through the kitchen door leading to the garage, dropped her bag on a chair and raced for the couch as Baylee turned to see who it was; she'd been dozing.

"Baylee!"

Since her arms were already out, Baylee chose not to resist the hug that Ari gave her, sitting beside her sideways on the sofa.

"How are you?" Ari asked, holding Baylee's shoulders like she'd done after the most recent nightmare.

"I'm okay." Baylee made a show of scooting backward into the couch as if to get into a more comfortable position, concealing the fact that she didn't want Ari restraining her.

Ari sat back as well, maintaining eye contact. "How about Lij? Have you heard from him?"

"No, not yet. I'm sure he's fine, he just wanted to be alone."

She hoped that was the case. While she hadn't quite reached a state of panic yet, it was en route; Lij being out of contact this long let her imagination run wild. Wild, like an animal, like an animal who'd developed a taste for people, that lived in the deserts outside Phoenix . . .

"I'm so sorry," Ari said, bringing Baylee gratefully back from her wandering mind. "Is there anything I can do for you? Have you eaten?"

She hadn't, and hadn't realized it until Ari said so. Maybe Ari was pretty good at her job dealing with teen angst after all.

When Baylee said she hadn't, Ari bounded up. "I'll fix something. You have to eat, Bay. Salad, I assume?"

"Sure, yeah."

Ari went to the kitchen. Baylee watched her surreptitiously from the living room. Ari moved swiftly and precisely to prepare the food, and Baylee suddenly compared her to her mother. Janey Ross had been a manic pixie type, always dancing and singing some song when she made the family dinner. Ari was more straight-laced and less humorous, but more focused and attentive. Maybe that attention was what grated on Baylee; Janey was far from neglectful to the kids, but then she had the luxury of actually raising them most of their lives. Ari had been thrown into this gig, almost certainly against her will. Maybe she just thought she had a lot of catch-up to do.

"Um . . ." Baylee called, realizing only in the moment that she quite possibly had never addressed Ari directly. Not as Ari, not as Mrs. Wagner.

Ari turned, holding a carrot in one hand and paring knife in the other. She raised her eyebrows.

"Thanks," Baylee said.

Ari smiled, sadly; nodded once; and went back to work.

John arrived home not long after, and they ate together

in the kitchen, making small talk about Ari and John's work, studiously avoiding the elephants in the room: Fletcher's death, and where the hell Lij was.

He never showed.

◯

By the time the sun had gone down, the entire household was on red alert. Baylee checked in with Ralph again, who'd heard nothing. By six, Ari began talking about calling the police, and by nine, it had escalated to wanting the three of them to go on an all-out manhunt.

Baylee didn't necessarily disagree. For God's sake, he'd left without his phone or wallet, and that was more than twelve hours ago. Seeing as how no one really knew how Fletcher had gotten all the way out to the 10 when he was killed, Baylee found it impossible not to imagine the same happening to Lij.

"I'm sorry, we have to at least drive around," Ari announced at quarter after nine. She grabbed her purse and marched to the kitchen door. "John, get your stuff, take your car, we'll split up. Bay, stay home."

"Okay," Baylee said, partly taken aback by Ari's tone and partly impressed by it.

John dutifully grabbed his wallet, keys, and phone and followed Ari out to the garage. He glanced back at Baylee as the garage door rolled up.

"Obviously, let us know if he shows up," John said.

"Of course."

"Okay. Be safe."

Baylee nodded. They were gone moments later, driving

in opposite directions, with only the vaguest of ideas from Baylee on where to look for Lij.

Baylee retreated to her room, feeling too cold under the air conditioning and too hot without it. She alternately cursed her brother and begged for him to come back, wondering if this was how it felt to be a parent, and if so, there was no way in hell she'd ever want to be one.

And on that note, goddammit, where was Timothy? He'd never gone this long without—

"Oh, God," Baylee groaned, and curled up on her bed, both her and Lij's phones clutched in cramped fingers. God, what if Timothy had fallen to whatever predator had taken Fletcher? And the Rosses? Maybe—great Christ in heaven, maybe it really *was* something out there hunting down everyone she ever cared about. It got Krista, it got Timothy, that's why they weren't responding; it got Lij, that's why he wasn't home; and she'd be next.

The front door opened.

Baylee sucked in a cold breath and leaped to her feet. She turned into the hall, pulling back with a shriek as she almost collided with Lij.

"*Lij!*"

"Yes?" Lij said.

Baylee sputtered. Shit, he'd crossed the entire distance from the front door to his bedroom at something like lightspeed, and she hadn't heard a thing.

When she found her breath, Baylee said, "Where the hell were you? Jesus, I was scared to death!"

That this was a poor turn of phrase within hours of Fletcher dying did not occur to her; she was far too relieved, far too furious.

Expressionless, Lij replied, "I went out for awhile."

"Yeah, no shit!"

"No shit." Lij opened his door. "Excuse me."

He stepped into his room. Baylee followed, but did not cross the threshold. "I have to call Ari and John. They're out looking for you."

"Don't bother." He stood still in the middle of the bedroom, scanning around slowly as if searching for something.

"Don't bother? Dude, you were gone *all day*. They're worried about you, *I* was worried about you!"

"All right."

Baylee winced. "What the fuck? Are you drunk or something?"

She thought but refused to believe that he snorted a dismissive laugh at the question. "Or something."

Lij suddenly moved to his closet, pulling open the accordion doors and staring at the clothing hanging inside. At that moment, Baylee realized he hadn't turned on the light. They were standing in the dark.

"What are you doing?"

Lij didn't respond.

"Lij?"

"*Elijah,*" he said.

Now that he was safe at the house, Baylee let her anger take over.

"Oh, sorry, dickhead. *Elijah*, my bad. Are you listening to me? I was scared! Do you even care? What the hell is the matter with you?"

Lij pulled off his T-shirt and let it fall to the floor. He reached into the closet and pulled out Krista's Harley Quinn shirt and put it on. The reminder that her best friend was giving her the cold shoulder over a boy hit Baylee hard in the ribs.

Then it aided her in drawing a conclusion. She could have slapped herself for having missed it.

"Oh . . . my God," Baylee said, feeling her heart go numb. "You were with that fucking chick, weren't you. That fucking little Scottish tart."

"Nora," Lij said, absently buttoning the shirt.

"So that's it? That's where you were all day?"

"Certainly."

Baylee coughed. Unbelievable. "Lij—"

"Elijah."

"—one of your best friends died this morning and you spent the day with that Derby chick instead of your other friends?"

"Certainly."

"Oh, what'd you do, cuddle up in some . . . some . . . *haggis?*"

Of the stupid things she'd said in her lifetime, that surely ranked in the top three, but Baylee's anger was far too pointed for her to care. Furthermore, Lij didn't seem to notice.

"We read books," he said.

"Oh, *please*. You mean she's literate?"

"Quite."

Baylee rolled her eyes around as theatrically as she could. "So what did you read, rulebooks? She's gonna jump into your D&D games now?"

"Not those kinds of books." He shut the closet door and faced her.

"Lij, goddammit—"

He pointed to his TV stand, to the small cupboard beneath where he kept their parents' VHS tapes. There were twenty or so, lined up in no order that Baylee ever noticed, sealed away in plastic cases he'd gotten free from the library when they were throwing them out. All the tapes were home videos of Janey and Ken. None of them showed Baylee or Lij, because the VHS format died long before they showed up. Janey and Ken had made the tapes when they were teenagers.

High school sweethearts.

"Some of those tapes," Lij said, still pointing, "are more than twenty years old. Someday, someone is going to chuck them into a big black trash can, and they'll be buried under a million tons of other people's garbage, like they never existed. Every day, the tape in them gets older. Gets drier and more brittle. It gets more likely to break the next time someone plays them. No matter what anyone does, one day, they will simply rot."

He took a step toward his sister.

"Just. Like. Us."

Baylee's anger receded. Her voice was small. "Lij . . ."

"All of us," Lij went on, taking another step. "Sitting around, slowly rotting, no matter how many vegetables you make us eat or many times you run around the block. Do you understand that, Baylee? Do you?"

She backed into the hall to get away from him, hissing: "*Yes.*"

Lij walked into the hallway after her, his presence forcing her back until she was parallel with her bedroom door. "Then understand this. I'm going to see Nora now. I don't know when I'm coming back, or if. I'm an adult now, a big, bad eighteen-year-old, and I can do as I please." He raised his hands into air quotes: "So give 'Mom and Dad' all my love, would you? Thanks."

Lij turned and walked to the front door. Baylee stared after him, then shouted, "Is Krista with Sean?"

It made the most sense. Maybe there weren't monsters out there after all, but Lij acting like this after a day with Derby—she chose right then to never call her Nora—then perhaps Krista had met up with Sean as well.

"Don't care," Lij said without turning, and was gone a second later, with only the echo of the front door closing offering any suggestion he'd even been here. Baylee still held his phone, and even before peeking in to double-check, she knew he hadn't grabbed his wallet.

Baylee went back into her room and tapped her phone on. Her first message went to Krista: **Are you with Sean? Just tell me please.** She called John next and said that Lij had come home, but gone out again, and . . .

Here she paused. She really wanted to throw Big Brother under the bus, get him in as much trouble as possible for the way he'd treated her. He'd never done anything like that before.

But he'd never lost a best friend before. Never had to face a second killing so much like the killing of Janey and Ken. Maybe he was in shock. Hell, maybe she was too, for that matter. If spending a little time with that asshat of a girl gave him some time to process, maybe that was okay. God knew she desperately wanted Timothy to get back to her so she could hold him tight for a few hours.

"Bay?" John said over the phone.

She'd stopped talking. Baylee shook her head and said, "Sorry. Um, he's fine. He's just having a tough time with what happened this morning. He's with some friends, and he might be out all night. I don't think we should worry too much, you know?"

John sighed. "Yeah. That makes sense. At least he checked in. Okay. I'll call Ari, let her know. Thanks for getting back to me, Bay. I appreciate it."

"No problem." She wanted to add *Thanks for going to look for him*, but by the time she'd summoned the courage to do so, John had ended the call.

When the phone buzzed in her hand a mere moment later, Baylee jumped. When she saw it was Krista, she gasped, and was unable to so much as pretend to play it cool.

"Krista! Oh, God, thank you for calling back. Look, I'm so—"

"Ah, Baylee? This is Krista's mom, Charlotte?"

Something cold slithered through Baylee's stomach. "Oh! Hi. Sorry, I thought . . . I'm sorry."

"It's fine," Charlotte said quickly. "Is Krista there with you?"

"No . . . is she, um . . . *supposed* to be?" Meaning, Baylee did not clarify, is that what she told you?

Baylee already intuited the answer, though. Her very bones knew.

"No," Charlotte fretted. "I can't imagine where she is, or why she'd leave her phone behind. When did you see her last?"

Rather than speed up, Baylee's heart rate slowed, painfully, making each pump a clenched fist in her chest.

"This morning," Baylee said as her mouth dried. "We were at the Wedge till . . . I dunno, nine maybe? She was skating home from there and—"

"Who's Sean?"

"Who?" Baylee said, and could have slapped herself for sounding so stupid. She couldn't lie; after all, Timothy was a *secret* and that was *different*. Pretending not to know who Sean was, well now, that would be a straight lie.

"Sean, you just sent her a text about someone named Sean, who is that?"

Baylee sighed, quietly. No kid wants to rat out her best friend, but after the day she'd had, Baylee decided it was better to have Krista pissed at her than to keep information to herself.

"Okay," Baylee began, eyes closed as if anticipating a smack. "She met this guy, Sean. They met last night. At Kyro. My brother met his, uh . . ."

Yes, Sean's what? Sister? No. Their accents were distinct and different, and they looked nothing alike; Baylee couldn't make herself believe they were related.

"His friend, this girl Nora? So, my brother is out with her right now, so I guess there's a chance they're all together?"

Charlotte Hope's voice sharpened. She was going Full Mom now, and Baylee didn't blame her. "Well will you please call your brother and find out? And if they are together to tell Krista to get her little butt back to this house right now?"

Baylee might have smiled any other time at the tone. All moms had it.

"I would, but he didn't take his phone. Really. I'm looking at it right now."

"Are you covering for her?" Charlotte snapped. "Is she with you right now?"

"No! Ma'am, I . . . seriously, I haven't seen her since this morning. I've been worried about her too."

Charlotte pivoted: "Worried about what?"

Oh, Jesus, Baylee thought. This was exhausting.

"We had kind of an argument about Sean when we hung out this morning," she said. "You should be able to see that I've been texting her, and she wasn't getting back to me. But now that I know what my brother is doing, I'm pretty sure Krista is with them."

"But you don't know where."

"I don't, I'm sorry."

"Why did she take her bag but not her money or her phone?"

Baylee's exhaustion retreated. No money, no phone—just like Lij. Lij, being with a girl he just met. Krista, presumably with the boy *she* just met. Were they filthy rich or something? What the hell?

"I really don't know, ma'am."

Charlotte huffed a sigh. "Oh, stop calling me that, Baylee. Charlotte's fine."

Baylee nodded, uselessly, and didn't answer.

"All right," Charlotte said. "If you talk to her you give her my message, will you please?"

"Of course."

Charlotte's voice shifted once again, and Baylee marveled at how quickly a mother's tone could go from one extreme to the other. "You really think she's safe?"

I didn't say that, Baylee thought—and was unsure why she thought it.

"I'm sure she's fine. She'll probably show up later tonight."

"Okay. Okay. Thank you, Baylee. I'm sorry for snapping at you."

"It's okay. I understand. Bye."

She tapped the phone off and stared at it, blank and dead in her hand.

It stayed that way all night.

seven

When Ari and John got home, Baylee feigned sleep, even leaving her door open so it would look accidental. She heard Ari and John whispering, debating whether or not to wake her, and then giving up, promising one another they'd talk tomorrow.

After they'd gone to bed, Baylee stayed awake until midnight, hoping Timothy would call, as was their near-tradition. Her phone stayed silent. Her loneliness grew cancerous, growing like a tumor in her heart and brain. Everyone she cared about had abandoned her. It felt almost worse than when her parents died; their deaths were accidental, this abandonment was intentional. Timothy, Lij, Krista . . . they were *electing* to not talk to her. This reality cramped her entire abdomen throughout the night, and even binging on *Lucky 13* did nothing to change it.

Baylee didn't remember when she really did fall asleep, only that when she awoke, the day was well underway, and Ari and John had left for work. She immediately checked her and Lij's phones, and was rewarded with nothing except that they needed charging.

She plugged them in and forced herself to eat breakfast, although nothing sounded particularly appetizing. Halfway through a bowl of oatmeal and blueberries, Baylee said, "Fuck it," nice and loud in the kitchen and dumped out the oats, deciding that a big goddamn sugary donut was called for this fine, fine morning.

She changed quickly, not bothering to shower, dressed for the heat in blue board shorts and a white tank, with her bag over one shoulder. She locked up the house and stepped outside, hit immediately with a wall of heat that stopped her for a moment.

Steeling herself against the summer temperature and damning herself for not pushing Ari and John to let her get her driver's license—not just from her own fears but also because she didn't want to have that long of a conversation with them—Baylee marched to the sidewalk and headed for the nearest grocery store.

Her phone, fully charged, made no sound. Nothing. From anyone. The silence made her nerves twist under her skin.

Baylee got herself the biggest donut she could find in the bakery case, and scarfed it down in the store's small dining area. The sugar attacked her on a visceral level, giving her a feeling she equated to being high. Not the worst feeling after yesterday. She debated checking in with Ralph again, but didn't; after the way Lij spoke to her last night, chances were grim that he would have talked to Ralph at all.

Now what? Kyro? Just in case?

Frustrated and woozy from the sugar hit, Baylee went to the café. No one to see there, just the soccer moms and a few kids in need of a nap. Baylee ordered a green smoothie and, just for the hell of it, asked the two guys behind the counter if they'd seen Krista, or Lij, or two people looking like Sean and Derby.

Nothing.

That was the end of her resources. Krista and Lij didn't want to be found; Timothy had, very clearly she thought, broken up with her without so much as a See Ya Around; so what was left?

Clutching her cold drink that warmed rapidly in the summer heat, Baylee beelined for the Wagner's house, constantly checking her phone as if she wouldn't hear it ring or feel it buzz in her hand, even as she preached silently to herself, *Fine, so be it, I'm going to stay home and blast the air conditioning and watch* Lucky 13 *and oh by the way FUCK ALL YOU GUYS.*

She got to the house at high noon, just as a police car rolled up to the driveway.

Baylee slowed, then paused. The cop checked her out through the windshield and talked on a radio before stepping out.

"Hi there," he said.

He shut his door and walked slowly toward Baylee. Even through the trepidation building in her limbs, she felt sorry for him; he had a full uniform on: long pants, long shirt, bullet-proof vest and all. She hoped his car had great A/C.

"Are you Baylee Ross?" he asked, unsmiling but friendly.

"Yes." She clutched the strap of her bag in both hands as the heat pounded into her skull.

"You're friends with Krista Hope?"

"Yes?"

The cop squinted and gestured toward the closed garage door. The roof overhung there, and a bit of stubborn shade barely defied the summer heat. "I'm Officer Shaw. Mind if we step out of the sun for a minute?"

Baylee didn't answer, but shuffled to the small strip of shade provided by the roof overhang. Shaw came along, keeping his thumbs tucked into his Batman utility belt— she didn't know what else to call it and a lifetime of living with a gamer left her with only the one comparison.

"So you saw her yesterday, is that right?" Officer Shaw asked.

"Yeah. At the Wedge skate park." This admission made her feel absurdly guilty of some crime.

"And when did you leave there?"

"Uh . . . nine, maybe? She had her board, her skateboard, and I walked home . . ."

"Where did she say she was going?"

"Um—she didn't say, no."

"You haven't seen or talked to her since then."

"No. Is she okay?"

Shaw let the question drift past. "What can you tell me about this Sean guy she met?"

Here it is, Baylee thought. Here we go. There was something wrong with that son of a bitch, and now it's coming out, and oh God what about Lij?

Baylee answered him, giving as many details as she could, including everything about Derby, too, just to be sure, but not mentioning that Lij was probably with her right now. Shaw wrote a few things on his notepad, but not nearly enough for Baylee's liking.

"Can I ask a question?" she asked when she'd finished.

"Sure."

"Have you talked to Sean or Derb—uh, Nora?"

"No, not yet. Did Krista ever talk about running away?"

"What? No. Why would she do that?"

"Her backpack and some clothes are missing."

Charlotte's worry bloomed anew in Baylee's guts. "But she didn't take her phone, wouldn't she take her phone?"

"Maybe didn't want anyone to ping it," Shaw said. "She do any drugs?"

"No! No, look, you're asking the wrong questions, she isn't like that!"

"How long have you known her?"

"Like a *year!*" Baylee shouted—and seeing the skepticism on his face, she looked away.

It really had been only a year. And, in the interest of honesty, not even that. It wasn't as if Baylee and Lij had moved in with Ari and John and there she was, waiting for Baylee with a platinum Best Friend card. They *hadn't* met right away, and despite Krista's bold personality, it took awhile for them to really get to know each other.

Drops of sweat swirled down Baylee's arm and plopped beside her white deck shoes.

Officer Shaw observed the turmoil evident, she knew, in her face and body before saying, "Okay, well, we're looking into it. If you hear from her, you let us know, okay?"

He held out a white business card. Baylee took it with numb fingers.

"You should get inside," he offered, stepping out of the shade. "It's hot out. Drink some water. This heat makes people crazy."

Baylee nodded. Her smoothie had turned to warm liquid, and she hadn't had any water in a while; she'd been so upset and focused on getting out of the house she hadn't brought her usual bottle with her. Even as Shaw spoke, a bout of dizziness banged into her forehead. She needed water.

"Yes, sir," Baylee muttered, and walked to the front door. She went inside and watched from the front window while Shaw did something in his car for several minutes before driving off.

Baylee took a long drink in the kitchen, then shuffled to her bedroom, sticking her head into Lij's room on the way. Nothing had changed; he hadn't been home since last night.

Defeated, Baylee called Timothy. His voicemail was automatic, a mechanical voice repeating his numbers back to her.

"Where are you?" Baylee said—or whined—on the message. "Shit's getting really messed up, Timothy, please. I just . . . call me, okay?"

I just need you.

That's what she'd almost said. Baylee was glad she hadn't, but it didn't make the truth of it sting any less. She sat on her bed, her knit bag still gripped tight, and asked the empty house, "Where *is* everyone?"

◯

Lij came home at five.

Baylee was sacked out on the couch, binge-watching *Lucky 13*, right up until a season finale where Kira Thirteen went toe-to-toe with the Big Bad, a guy named Prophet who wanted to kill off all the mortals in her world, leaving only immortal humans around to serve him for an eternity on Earth.

"Hey!" she shouted, leaping to her feet as soon as he walked in. "Where the hell have you been? Huh? Goddammit, Lij! You can't do this shit to me!"

Her brother gently shut the door. His face expressed boredom and . . . something else. Baylee couldn't place it, but the word that came to mind was *distaste*.

"Sorry, your highness," Lij said, his voice slower than usual. "Had things to do."

"Oh, like your little Scottish tart?" Baylee snapped, thinking that was fairly clever.

Lij didn't reply. He raised a disinterested eyebrow and walked down the hall.

Baylee turned off the TV and ran to catch up. "Hey, I'm talking to you, Lij! Were you—"

"Elijah," he said, reaching his room. He went in and stood in the middle, arms dangling casually at his sides, surveying everything just as he had the night before.

Baylee stayed in the doorway. "Where *were* you?"

"Doing my little Scottish tart," Elijah said, not turning.

Baylee took a breath. Being angry clearly wasn't going to work. "Okay, I'm sorry, I didn't mean it. But I still need to know where you were."

"In fact, you do not." Elijah walked to his closet and again started sorting through his clothes.

"Got a hot date?" Baylee couldn't help saying.

"In a manner of speaking."

"Listen to you! Jesus, Lij!"

"Elijah."

Baylee dared to enter his room and stand beside him. "No one knows where Krista is. Fletcher is *dead*. And you're looking to dress up for your stupid bitch?"

What did not happen next was: Elijah did not glare. He did not shove her away. He did not call her any names. He did not yell.

Instead, Baylee's brother only smiled.

And said, "Where is *your* Prince Charming, by the way?"

Baylee gasped. "You *asshole*."

So there it was. The truth was out. He *did* know about Timothy.

"I didn't invite you in." Elijah picked out the black button-up shirt he'd worn at the Ross's funeral. "Goodbye now."

Baylee took a step back, relieved that at least he wasn't going to push the Timothy issue. Of course, for all she knew, there was no longer a Timothy to have issue with.

"You're not seriously going to wear that shirt, are you?"

Elijah took off the Harley Quinn shirt and tossed it carelessly to the floor.

"You're hypersensitive," he said, buttoning the black shirt over his pale skin. "Has anyone ever told you that?"

That comment—no, the way he said it—pushed Baylee backward another few steps until she was in the hallway. "Holy *shit*, Lij."

He finished buttoning the shirt and tucked it into his jeans. They were same ones he'd worn all day yesterday and the night before, but somehow, they didn't look as baggy or grungy as they should have.

And he kept smiling. No teeth showed, but the smile was unmistakable.

Elijah ran his hands through his hair, which also mysteriously looked styled now, not the usual mess he tended to shove under superhero-emblem ballcaps. Approving of himself in the mirror hanging on the closet door, he shut it and stepped toward the hall.

But he paused beside Baylee and looked down over his shoulder. The movement reminded her of a lizard.

"By the way," he said, quietly. "Have you ever stopped to ask yourself why your boyfriend won't fuck you?"

It would have hurt less, on multiple levels, if he'd kicked Baylee in the stomach; or that's what it felt like. Her abdominal muscles crunched down, making her curl forward as a sharp gasp burst out of her and her mouth fell wide open.

Elijah—her brother, her only living blood relative— smirked.

"Shame," he said.

And walked away.

Baylee didn't move, *couldn't* move. Rage flooded her veins to the point that she could not hear his footsteps on the tile, though she did hear the front door open and close gently.

Once he'd gone, she gave in to the rage.

Screaming, Baylee plunged into Elijah's room, kicking the bookshelf holding his precious gaming books. She stomped on them until the pages tore and ripped and scattered.

Not enough. She attacked his paperbacks next, throwing them mindlessly against the wall until they split apart. Only barely did she avoid sending his laptop through the window, instead choosing to tear his Harley Quinn shirt to shreds with enraged claw-like fingers.

Once her rage was spent, she knelt on the floor, surrounded by D&D pages of monsters and heroes gazing up at her, and shards of cotton shirt still hanging from her fingers like strips of flesh in a dragon's talons.

Sometimes, she thought distantly, D&D references were the only way to say a thing.

She heard the kitchen door open. Ari called out, "Hello? Anyone home?"

Baylee knew she should get up. She knew she should close Elijah's door and run to the bathroom, jump in the shower, make herself look innocent, do everything possible to cover up what she'd done in here.

But she didn't. All strength had left her limbs.

"Bay?" Ari called, getting closer. "Lij? Anybody here? Baylee—?"

She stopped in the doorway to Elijah's room. Baylee saw her red flats and black capris, showing off tan ankles and a tattoo of an ankh that looked like a regret. She could not look Ari in the face.

"Oh my God," Ari said softly. "Baylee? Are you hurt?"

Baylee's breath still came out hard and fast. She didn't answer. There *was* no answer.

Ari hunkered down beside her. "Where is Lij?"

Before Baylee could tell her anything, her phone buzzed in her back pocket. Automatically, Baylee pulled it out and checked the screen.

Timothy.

Sorry. Lost my phone. You OK? Meet at the church?

Baylee's fatigued muscles grew strong again. She jumped to her feet and bolted out of Elijah's room. Ari stood too, reaching for her, but missed.

"Baylee!" Ari called, following behind but not as fast as the teen. "Baylee, stop! What's going on?"

Baylee ran through the front door, leaving everything else behind.

○

Timothy waited for her behind the abandoned church, leaning against the '36 Ford, parked in their usual spot in the back. Baylee rushed into his arms, slamming him backward into the old car and not caring. Timothy wrapped himself around her and held tight as Baylee wept.

Crying was not something she did regularly, not since the funeral. Even thinking of that day made her remember Elijah and the black shirt, which sent another course of rage bubbling through her limbs, bypassing her tears entirely.

She pulled away from Timothy and scrubbed her wet face with her hands. "Fucking Elijah!"

"Slow down," Timothy said gently. "Here, get in the car. It's hot out. I'll turn on the air."

Baylee slipped inside and shut the door. Timothy climbed in and started the engine to get the A/C going.

"Now what's wrong with Elijah?" he asked, testing the vents with one palm.

Still snorting up snot, Baylee told him everything. About Sean and Derby, about Chris Fletcher, about Lij's sudden transformation into King Asshole. By the time she finished, the sun was low and she felt the first dryness of dehydration in her eyes.

"That is a tough couple of days," Timothy said. "I'm so sorry I wasn't here. What can I do?"

In terms of actual action, nothing came to Baylee's mind. Now that she'd found him again, and that they were still together, Elijah's barb rose to her mouth and she had to ask the question.

"Why did he say that? About us not . . . sleeping together?"

Timothy rubbed the back of his cold index finger up and down her damp cheek. "I have no idea why he would say something like that."

"But why *won't* you do it?"

Elijah had struck a tender little chord with his comment. Baylee was ready for all of Timothy; or thought she was ready anyway. She only needed Timothy to say the word. But he never did. Never tried. The truth was, for as long as they had been getting together physically, she rarely did anything for *him*. It was always his attention—his voice, his hands, his lips—on her. Never really the other way around.

Timothy's expression pinched at the question. He turned away, and Baylee worried she had upset him.

Then he turned back and looked into her eyes.

"Because I love you and respect you," he said. "Is that so wrong?"

"Of course not," Baylee said quickly. "Thank you. I . . ."

She had no idea what to add after that.

Timothy gave her one of his soothing half-smiles. "Look, I'm sure Krista will turn up at some point. And your brother . . . well, it's his first girlfriend. When that happens, boys act pretty crazy."

"Sure, but after only, like, a *day?*"

"Certainly. Happens all the time."

Baylee frowned, not liking the idea that Timothy was

absolutely right. Lij hadn't acted entirely different than Krista, really; the pair of them had been clearly smitten by Sean and Derby at Kyro.

"What about Krista?" Baylee demanded, as if Timothy knew her whereabouts and status. "She wouldn't just pack a bag and run off with some boy she just met."

Timothy smiled, more fully this time. "And you wouldn't climb into a classic car in a church parking lot with boy you barely knew."

"That's different," Baylee said, knowing it wasn't quite. "I *do* know you."

"Don't be angry," Timothy said, his voice smooth. "I am trying to help."

Baylee squeezed her eyes shut. "It's okay, you're probably right. It just bugs me. And I'm still worried about Krista."

"I would never tell you not to be. She'll hang out with this guy for awhile, he'll break her heart or vice versa, and that will be that."

"You think so?"

"Certainly. It's just how things go sometimes. Or, hey—maybe they're soul mates, and they'll get married and have eighteen kids. Either way, she's not going to just never talk to you again."

It sounded good. Or if not good, acceptable. A Band-aid to stop the worst of the emotional bleeding. Baylee nodded her agreement and acceptance of his words.

"Is there anything *else* I can do?" Timothy asked. "I want to help."

Baylee opened her eyes and met his leonine gaze, wondering if her growing dizziness was from lack of water or the golden glint she saw reflected back at her.

Maybe Krista really was okay? she asked herself.

Maybe she'd just simply *forgotten* her phone. In the heat of whatever moment Sean had introduced her to, maybe she'd just grabbed some stuff and taken off, a young girl with a crush. Was that so hard to believe? Hadn't Baylee herself considered going to San Diego with Timothy? Young hearts in love were capable of many things.

And maybe Elijah really was so taken in by a fancy accent and perky haircut that he couldn't care less about his gamer buddies anymore, even if one of them had just been slaughtered in the desert. Chris Fletcher was a good friend who just died; what had Baylee done when the stress of the last couple of days got to her? Literally run to Timothy, into his arms. That Elijah might do the same wasn't far-fetched at all.

Timothy's question lingered in the cool air between them. Just being in the car with him had a notable effect on her fears and her mood. At least *he* hadn't abandoned her after all. Elijah and Krista might be back soon, too. She just had to wait it out.

Until then, Timothy was right here, gazing into her eyes.

Absently, Baylee toyed with the laces on the waistband of her shorts.

"Talk to me," she said.

eight

She didn't want him to drop her off at the house because she didn't want Ari or John to see him. Baylee got out a block away from their house and walked from there, hoping Timothy's assurances that he didn't mind were for real. She needed water by that point; her vague dizziness had blossomed into utter lightheadedness . . .

Their house.

The fact that she'd thought of it in that term stopped her just as surely as the cop yesterday had made her pause on the sidewalk.

Not *our* house, she thought; not *my* house. *Their* house. Like she and Lij were merely visiting. But maybe that wasn't so far from the truth. Lij would be a senior next year—asshole or otherwise, she thought with a cranky sneer—and after that, college, paid for by everything Janey and Ken had left behind. Two years from now, that would be her, too. Baylee didn't envision either of them staying in touch with Ari and John after that. They'd be on their own.

Which means, Baylee thought as she followed the walkway to the front door, I need my brother more than ever. Krista, too.

She and Krista hadn't talked about their plans for after graduation, but maybe she could go wherever Krista went. Hell, maybe she could talk Krista into the University of San Diego.

Maybe Timothy, too.

Baylee went inside and veered for the kitchen to get a bottle of water.

"Baylee?" Ari called from the living room.

"Yeah," Baylee called back, rubbing her forehead. The sudden cold water gave her a headache. "Lij home?"

"No," Ari said, and the TV went mute.

Baylee sighed quietly. Ari muting the television meant it was *Time To Talk*.

She and John both came into the kitchen, barefooted and wearing shorts and T-shirts. "How are you?"

"Uh—fine. I'm going to go—"

Ari blocked Baylee's path. "Hold on. Wait a second. Tell me what happened this afternoon."

Baylee sank against the counter. John folded his arms and leaned against the doorway, though not quite in a prison-warden way. John's face showed legit concern. So did Ari's. They didn't seem pissed, which actually made things harder; she couldn't get out of this Talk by picking a fight.

Sipping more water and realizing she needed to eat, too, Baylee said, "Krista's gone. Nobody knows where she is."

"Oh, no," Ari said, raising a hand to her mouth.

"And Lij . . . Lij drank asshole Kool-Aid or something and said some vile shit today that just really pissed me off and I . . . look, I'm sorry, I lost my cool and broke some stuff in his room, but you have to understand, it was *really* not okay what he said."

"Were you friends with Chris Fletcher?" John asked.

"You mean, me, personally? I guess. I mean, he was one of Lij's best friends, like Ralph and Suze. That whole group. Yeah. I guess we were friends, too."

"So horrible, what happened," Ari added in a respectful tone. She squinted at Baylee. "That's got to . . . hit hard. The way he was killed."

Baylee nodded slowly, not meeting her eyes.

Ari took two steps closer, bare feet sliding along the tile. "Baylee . . . with so much happening right now . . . John and I talked last night about—"

Baylee raised her head and glared. "I'm *not* going to a psychiatrist."

Ari and John glanced at each other.

"It might be really helpful," John said, letting his deeper voice do the work Ari's face usually had to do.

"Okay," Baylee barked. "I'll tell you what. You get my newly minted asshole of a brother to agree, and I'll do it. You want us both to go anyway, right? That's my deal."

She crossed her arms and couldn't help pushing out one hip, the quintessential teen pose.

The adults looked at each other again. Perhaps they had telepathy, because without moving another muscle, Ari said a moment later, "That's fair. We'll ask him."

"Good luck with that." Baylee pulled a bag of carrots from the fridge and slipped between them. They didn't try to stop her.

She went to her room and fullscreened *Lucky 13* on her iPad, hoping that watching Kira kick post-apocalyptic ass would calm her down. Dammit, she'd felt so good in the car, and Ari had to go stomp on it.

Not long after the first episode ended, she was asleep.

○

Her clock read 1:26 a.m. when Baylee roused from sleep. She'd been covered with a sheet, and her iPad had slipped to the floor and shut itself off. Her door was left half-open, presumably by Ari not closing it fully behind her.

Baylee pulled herself up, hating the feel of her shoes still on; Ari hadn't bothered to take them off, maybe for fear of waking her. Baylee hated napping or sleeping in shoes, they made her feet feel clunky and numb. Groaning, Baylee leaned forward to start unlacing them.

A shadow passed by her doorway.

"Lij?" she croaked.

The shadow paused.

"Yes." His voice echoed deeply in the hall.

"Did you just get home?"

"Yes."

"Does Ari know?"

"I doubt it."

Baylee pulled off one shoe and rubbed her toes. "They want us to go to a shrink if you don't stop acting like a jerk."

Her brother said nothing, but she sensed him still there hovering in the hall.

"Lij?"

"*Elijah.*"

Baylee pulled her other shoe off. "God, really? Okay, whatever you say. Were you out with Derby?"

"Nora. Yes."

"She know where my best friend is?"

"No."

"How about that Sean freak, when's the last time he saw her?"

"I have no idea."

"I don't believe you, *Lij*."

"I don't care, Baylee."

Her socks were sweaty. She yanked them off. "What did you do tonight, then?"

"We read books."

She barked a tired laugh. "Books again, huh? Oh, okay. Whatever."

The shadow moved away. Baylee started to call his name again, but gave up. If he wasn't ready to stop being an idiot, she wouldn't chase him down.

Not yet, anyway.

She fell back to sleep and woke up to Ari and John shouting at each other about a work schedule change. Baylee stayed in bed until she heard the kitchen door slam, then waited some more to make sure they were gone.

Then she got up and immediately checked her phone.

No messages.

Goddammit.

She went to her brother's room. The door was closed, so she pushed it open, utterly unconcerned with what state she might find him in. After last night, she was game for a showdown. With Ari and John gone from the house, they could really have at it. And maybe even get past whatever the hell had happened to him.

She saw immediately his room had been cleaned and organized, and the books she'd ruined were gone. Thrown out? she wondered. He'd joked about buying more with the estate money, maybe he didn't care that she'd destroyed the old ones.

Elijah sat at his desk, feet propped on the top. Baylee got the sudden impression he had not been to sleep.

"Well well well," she said. "Look who decided to grace us with his presence."

Elijah inhaled deeply before swinging himself upright and standing. When he did, Baylee took a step back, feeling as if an invisible but tangible force had come rocketing off his body.

"I'm resting," Elijah said, moving toward the door to close it. "You can go now."

"Have you been working out on the sly or something?" Baylee asked as he slowly shut the door. He looked bigger.

Elijah paused, his face laconic. "What if I have?"

"And when did you stop *blinking*?"

He tilted his head. "Have I?"

"And answering every question with another question."

His grin widened.

"Is that so?"

"Dude, you're a nutmonkey," Baylee said, rubbing a sudden coldness on her arms. "You going to be here for lunch? Dinner?"

"I doubt it. Bye-bye now."

He closed the door in her face. Baylee stomped back to her room, changed clothes while muttering profanity at him, packed her bag without knowing why, then turned right back around and threw open his door.

"You're being a jerk!" she shouted. "Feel free to stop any time."

Lij had returned to his desk, and sat casually flipping pages in a four-inch-thick leather-bound book propped on his knees. Some D&D manual Baylee hadn't seen before, she guessed. A special collection, perhaps; something he'd bought yesterday to replace the damage she'd done to his rulebooks.

"You should really knock," Elijah said, not looking at her.

"Lij, if you're going to be a douchenozzle from now on, could you leave me a note or something? Because this new you is veering toward the asshole end of the spectrum."

Her brother turned his head to gaze at her. Still he didn't blink.

"Baylee," he said, "I am going to be a douchenozzle. I am veering toward the asshole end of the spectrum. You have been so advised. Bye now."

Feeling as though she'd been stabbed in the chest, Baylee whispered, "What's happening to you?"

"Why nothing, of course."

Furious at his tone, Baylee shouted, "You know, my best friend is fucking *missing* right now, and it makes me feel like shit. And I think your new besties are part of it! Oh, and by the way, if you recall, one of *your* best friends died. Remember that, you complete dick?"

"Gosh," Elijah said, gently turning a page. "Someone I cared about was killed. How novel."

"Oh my *God!*"

"You need to go now."

"Gladly! Prick."

She smashed out of his room, slamming his door. She stomped out of the house without breakfast, her entire body aching from the inside out.

○

She spent the day alone at the library, watching TV on her phone until the battery died. It was five before she went back to the house, surprised to find Ari and John already home.

"Baylee," Ari called from the kitchen as soon as Baylee stepped inside. "Come on in, sit down, we're about to eat."

Baylee turned into the kitchen. Her brother and John sat at the kitchen table.

Hot, tired, cranky, and sad after her long day of stewing, Baylee dropped into a chair, glaring at Elijah. "Surprised to see you here."

"Let's not start," Ari said, bringing a plate of peppered beef to the table. Lij helped himself immediately as Ari brought Baylee a big salad, filled with everything she usually liked.

"So nice to have the whole family here at one time," Baylee pushed. "Shouldn't you be out with your new buddies? Or your *girlfriend?*"

"Let's not start," Elijah said, grinning around a mouthful of meat.

Ari caught him with a short glare, but hurried to put it away. She joined them at the table, sending John a *Do something!* look.

"So!" John said brightly. "What did everyone do today?"

Silence. Just the clatter and scrape of utensils against dishes.

The adults traded another look, and John tried again. "Hey, I like what you've done with your hair, Lij. Looks good, man."

Baylee narrowed her eyes. John was right, just as she'd noticed earlier: Elijah *had* done something different with his hair. And—dammit—it did look good.

"Elijah," her brother said.

John forced a smile. "Right, sorry. Elijah."

"Elijah, there's something going on with you, and I don't like it," Ari said, setting her utensils down. "Would you please talk to me?"

"Certainly," Elijah said. "What would you like to talk about?"

"How about these new friends of yours?" Ari said.

"All right."

They both waited for the other to say something. Elijah looked like he could sit there forever, unbothered by the silence.

Ari finally threw her hands into the air and said, "Well, I don't know, exactly . . . have you met their parents—"

"I'm not going to marry them."

"—are they good students—"

"It's summer, and I place a higher value on loyalty than grades."

Baylee almost spit out her soymilk. *Loyalty?* What a bunch of shit *that* was.

"—are they on drugs?" Ari finished.

"Certainly not," Elijah said.

"But they do make you feel good," Baylee said.

Everyone looked at her.

"I just mean, when you're around them, you feel better," Baylee went on. "Stronger. Cooler."

Elijah gave her a faint nod. "Something like that."

Ari shook her head. "Well I don't understand why—"

"And you won't," Elijah stated. "But please believe me when I tell you I'm in the best place I've ever been in my life. I am not doing drugs, nor are my friends. They don't even drink alcohol. Everything is going to be just fine."

"When are you hanging out again?" Baylee said, as Ari muttered something caustic and got up from the table with her still-full plate.

"Tonight."

"Till midnight?"

"I should think at least that long."

"Mind if I tag along?" Baylee said. "Everyone else I love has ditched me."

"I do mind," Elijah said, while Ari continued grumbling and scraping her food into Tupperware. "Tonight is for . . . friends only."

Baylee's anger flared. "Aw, we're not friends anymore?"

Elijah shrugged—and smiled.

"Who the hell *are* you?" Baylee said.

"That's enough, Baylee," John said quietly, toying with his dinner.

"No!" Baylee barked at her brother. "I'm serious! What, you're her slave now because she sucks your dick, is that it?"

Ari spun from the sink. "*Baylee!*"

Elijah started laughing. John said, "Whoa," sort of under his breath; whether at what Baylee had said or Ari's response, Baylee did not know; did not care.

Elijah leaned forward, still smiling broadly. Baylee wanted to punch the asshole expression off his face.

"All right," Elijah said. "You want to talk about sex?"

He was going to say it, Baylee realized. He was going to bring it up. All of it.

"*Shut up*," she whispered.

"Let's talk about your little boy-toy Timothy," Elijah went on. "Have you told our brand-new parents about him yet? It's been over a month at least."

Baylee was so furious she didn't notice how Ari and John were reacting to the news, or to how sarcastically he'd referred to them.

"Shut up, Elijah!"

"Oh, *Timothy*," Elijah sang. "Oh, *God*, don't stop talking to me, *yes*, oh *Timothy*—"

Baylee stood, and the chair flipped backward. "You're a fucking dick!"

Her brother laughed again, in a way she'd never heard before. "I have to listen to you through the wall every night. I'm not the one doing the fu—"

"Okay, that's it," John said—not shouting, but cutting through their voices all the same. "Everyone back to your corners, this is over."

"We'll see," Elijah said. Softly. To his sister.

A car pulled up outside and honked. Baylee turned, as if she could see through the wall. "That's her, isn't it."

Elijah stood. "I have some things to attend to. Thank you for a lovely dinner."

"Hold on," Ari said sharply, and held up a hand. "Lij—*Elijah*—I'm sorry, but I'm not having this. You can't just come and go as you please with people we haven't even met, in and out at any hour you want."

"Because?" Elijah asked, innocently.

"You could start by asking permission," John said, tapping a finger on the tabletop. He didn't sound angry, but then Baylee hadn't seen either of them very angry before. Still, John's voice hit a deeper note than usual.

"Would it be all right if I attended to some things this evening?" Elijah said without missing a beat. It sounded polite, but Baylee could *taste* the condescension in his voice, the carelessness.

"What kind of things?" Ari demanded.

Elijah lifted his backpack, which Baylee hadn't noticed under the table. It looked heavy. "Reading, mostly."

"Oh, *God*," Baylee groaned with disbelief.

Elijah snapped his fingers once. "Yes. That's exactly what you sound like."

Silence slammed into the kitchen. Baylee found she had no air in her lungs, and the Wagners appeared paralyzed.

Elijah moved toward the front door, pausing by his sister's side. "He must be very good to get those sounds out of you. As if he's had . . . *lots* . . . . of *practice*."

He let the words hover. Baylee slowly turned to face him, burning something like hate into his eyes.

The car outside honked again.

Elijah smiled.

Baylee held his gaze for a moment—then leaped from the kitchen.

Ari said something behind her, but Baylee ignored it. She flew out the front door to find a nondescript brown van parked alongside the sidewalk. Derby hung out the window, wearing her hat and grinning at Baylee.

"Well now, wot we got here? Joinin' us tonight, lass?"

Baylee ran straight up to the passenger door and banged a hand on it, just below where Derby's arm hung. She could see Sean in the driver seat, smiling smugly.

"Where is she!" Baylee screeched. "Where's Krista, you son of a bitch!"

Derby gave her a surprised expression. "Chryse, you've gone tits-up, haven't ye?"

"*Where?*" Baylee cried. "Fuck you, *fuck you!* Where is she?"

"You're insane," Elijah said as he walked past her to the rear double doors.

Baylee seethed, watching him, then ran to his side. Elijah was just turning the door handle, and Baylee seized it from him, tearing the door open to look in the back.

A padded, hand-crafted bench ran along the driver's side. A rectangular chunk of carpet lay on the floor. The back went straight through, so she could easily see Derby and Sean turning in their seats to look back at her.

That was all. No Krista, no handcuffs hanging from meat hooks, no rope and gloves and masks.

Smirking, Elijah swung himself gracefully into the van, sitting on the bench. "Happy?"

Baylee stepped back, pointing a finger at Sean. "You saw her last. The cops know. If you did something to her, I swear to God I will tear your face off."

As if choreographed, Sean and Derby looked at one another; then to Elijah; then all three looked at Baylee.

"Saw who?" Sean said. Still grinning.

Baylee stared back at him as her entire stomach froze into a block of ice. "If you did anything to her, they're going to find out." She leaned down, read the license plate, and straightened back up. "And if she doesn't come home and if I don't hear from her in the next twenty-four—the next *twelve* hours, I'm taking your plate to the cops and you are fucked. Do you hear me? Both of you are fucked!"

It felt good to say, but its impact was negligible at best. Sean and Derby were laughing before she even finished, while Elijah gave her a pitying look.

"See you in the morning," he said, and pulled the door closed.

The van drove away and turned out of the neighborhood while Baylee watched, shaking. When she was able to move again, she saw Ari and John standing not quite in the front doorway, but close enough to it that they'd surely heard every word. Baylee forced herself back to the house.

John put a hand on her shoulder and gently eased her toward the kitchen. "What is it with that kid?"

Baylee shook her head and let him guide her to a chair. They'd picked up the one she knocked over.

Ari sat down beside her and put a hand on Baylee's arm. "What's this with the police?"

"I don't know," Baylee whispered. Her throat ached. "It's just, he met that girl and now he's a big jerk, and Krista met this guy who was with her, and I think they have something to do with why Krista's gone. A cop came and asked me about Krista, that's all."

Ari frowned. "Bay, I sincerely doubt Lij would know anything about that and not speak up."

She was right, and Baylee knew it—but then maybe he *didn't* know. Maybe they'd done whatever they did to her and, naturally, would not tell him about it.

But she didn't bother arguing.

Ari shook her head and sat back, leaving a cool place on Baylee's arm where her fingers had been. "Which isn't to say that I like what's going with Lij," she said. "Something's not right."

"He's just stretching his wings," John said, but not like he really believed it.

"Well I'm going to clip them if his attitude doesn't improve," Ari declared. She went to the sink and ran water.

Baylee almost smiled. It really sounded like a "mom" thing to say. Dorky and adorable and safe.

"Thanks," she said, and added, "We should've followed them. We should do that next time."

Ari blinked. "Follow—Elijah? What do you mean?"

"I mean the next time he goes anyplace with those assholes, we should get in the car and follow them!"

John chuckled, irritating Baylee all over again. "I'm not happy with his attitude this week, but I don't think it's cause to set up surveillance. Not *quite* yet, anyway."

Ari looked amused at the idea. "I know you're upset, Bay, but that's not how we do things."

"What if he really is on drugs?" Baylee said, seizing on the idea. It hadn't occurred to her before, but it would sure answer a lot of questions. Wasn't it possible that in his grief and shock over Fletcher, he'd sought some way, any way, to make the pain stop?

"I've worked with a lot of kids on a lot of different drugs," Ari said. "Lij isn't showing symptoms of anything like—"

"*Goddammit!*"

Ari froze, standing at the kitchen sink, letting water splash over her hands as she cleaned her plate. John raised an eyebrow.

"No one is listening to me!" Baylee said. "Derby and Sean are *not* good people, that's it, end sentence. And now they're doing something to Lij, and I think they did something to Krista. Why won't anyone believe me?"

Ari cleared her throat and came back to the table, sitting down and folding her hands.

"Who is Timothy?"

Baylee reared back. "What?"

"Timothy. A boy you've been seeing, apparently, without telling anyone. Who is he?"

Baylee fumbled. "Just a guy. I met. At the skate park. With Krista. Look, we're not going out or anything, we just, we've hung out a few times."

A few times per week, she thought guiltily. In secret. Behind an abandoned church.

Ari let the denial hang in the air. John leaned in, resting his weight on his forearms. "So, in other words, it's a relationship you didn't feel comfortable sharing with us right away."

"I guess . . ."

"Okay," John said, glancing between Ari and Baylee. "So, let's give old Lij a break. Not forever, he's still acting like a little punk, don't get me wrong. But let's not rush into lojacking his sneakers. Everyone okay with that?"

Baylee nodded.

But the nod was a lie. Already a plan began to form.

nine

Baylee developed the plan throughout the night as she let *Lucky 13* play in the background. Her first obvious choice was to bring Timothy on board, but she couldn't think of a reasonable way to do that. There were enough moving pieces in her plan as it was. That left the alternative, which, if she were caught, she assumed would land her in whatever big trouble Ari and John could come up with. What that might entail, realistically, she didn't know.

But it was worth the risk to find out for sure what Elijah was up to.

Plan in place, she called Krista's phone, which Charlotte Hope answered. No word on Krista. She said the police were convinced she'd run off with someone, "most likely this Sean character," but that given her history, there was every reason to expect Krista to call or show up soon.

Charlotte didn't buy it. Neither did Baylee, but she said that sounded right to her, trying to make Charlotte feel better.

If Derby and Sean were into drugs—there was no reason to believe they were, nor was there reason to believe they *weren't*—then Baylee figured there was a chance Krista was alive if not well, doped up somewhere like characters Baylee had seen on various Netflix series. Of all the possibilities, that one rang the most true. Clearly Elijah had changed suddenly, and what but a foreign substance could have that impact? The more Baylee played the possibilities out in her mind, the more this one seemed to fit best.

Now all she had to do was prove it.

Friday night would be date night. If Ari and John kept to their usual timetable, everything would go like clockwork.

○

To Baylee's surprise, it did: the first part of her plan worked beautifully.

Elijah came home to change clothes after spending most of Thursday out of the house.

That was it. It was that simple. He wandered in just after dawn and went straight to his bedroom and shut the door. Baylee and he both stayed in their rooms until John and Ari got off work; even Ari seemed to not want to risk another outburst and did not try to rouse them for breakfast.

Baylee left her room only when necessary, keeping the volume low on her iPad as she listened for any noises from Elijah's room. He stayed silent.

I'll find you, Krista, Baylee thought, over and over throughout the long, hot day. I will find you tonight and I'll fix this.

At long last, Ari and John returned home. They

shouted hellos, but neither Baylee nor Elijah responded. An hour later, Ari knocked on her door. Baylee opened it.

"So," Ari said, rather helplessly. "We're going out. You going to be okay?"

"Uh-huh!" Baylee said with as much enthusiasm as she could muster.

"You're sure?"

"Totally."

Ari clearly didn't buy it. Baylee believed she even saw Ari going through the mental process of changing her mind about her weekly date.

"You should go," Baylee said quickly. "Don't worry about us."

Ari glanced toward Elijah's door. Baylee had not heard him at all, not even to use the bathroom. "He's here?"

"Yeah, far as I know."

Ari sighed. "All right. Don't kill each other."

"Never."

"Great, thanks," Ari said—and finally relaxed. "I left some money on the table. Order something if you want."

"Cool, thank you."

"Are you, um . . . going to see him tonight? Timothy?"

Anger flared, but Baylee tamped it down. "No. Actually, I'm not sure if we're seeing each other any more."

Lie. She'd been texting with him most of the day, off and on. When she'd asked about his plans, he'd said he had a family dinner but that he could call and talk later; he'd asked about her own plans, and she'd said she was spending some quality time with Netflix and several new salad recipes. It was the most boring thing she could come up with. She did not tell him her real plot, despite how badly she wanted his help. No. It simply wouldn't work.

"I'm sorry," Ari said, at least half-sincerely.

Baylee shrugged. "Just a summer fling, I guess. No big."

Ari stepped into her room more fully. "Baylee, um . . . I've been holding back, and maybe making assumptions based on how well we knew your parents, but . . . did Ken and Janey ever talk to you guys about sex?"

Mom and Dad.

Baylee clenched her teeth, not at the question, but at the use of their names. She hadn't heard their names since the funeral.

And the answer was yes, they both had, to both kids. Pretty effectively, too, as far as Baylee knew. But then again, at the time, neither of them were exactly sleeping around.

"Yeah. They did. We're good."

"You're good, meaning . . ."

Before Baylee could answer, John walked past in the hallway. "Ready?"

Thank you, Baylee thought.

Ari frowned, but clearly was more interested in her own date right then than in Baylee's sex life. Baylee didn't know what *they* did, or when, or where, and she most decidedly did not care. All she knew was they kept their bedroom door closed at night and she never knocked on it.

"Okay," Ari said. "Well, if you ever need to ask anything, you can. All right?"

"Sure." Baylee forced a smile. Right now she just needed them *gone*. Timing the next few minutes was everything.

Ari gave her a nod, and left, leaving the door open. Baylee perched on the edge of her bed, listening to Ari knock on Elijah's door and getting no response. She could practically hear Ari shrug and shake her head.

A couple of minutes later, Ari and John left, taking John's car by the sound of it.

A very good start.

Baylee went to the living room and switched on Netflix, picking up *Lucky 13* where she'd left off. By then it was seven o'clock, and the sun still showed bright orange rays outside. Another hour, it would be full dark.

Elijah emerged at sunset. He walked past Baylee on the couch, wearing his green backpack. It clashed with his outfit, one that Baylee had not seen before. Indeed, she'd never thought of her brother as wearing an *outfit*, but tonight he looked put together.

"You need a new bag," Baylee said.

"You need a new personality."

"Wow. Nice one."

Elijah looked out the front window, between the blinds. "Thank you."

"Waiting for your girlfriend to come pick you up?"

"If you want to call her that."

"It's not the *only* thing I want to call her."

Headlights washed across the window briefly. Someone had pulled in. In that moment, Baylee felt sure he'd messaged Derby—and Sean—the moment Ari and John left.

"You might change your mind about her someday," Elijah said. "And if you don't, I truly do not care."

"Love you too," Baylee said.

Elijah snorted like she was some kind of idiot, and walked out the front door.

The instant the door latched, Baylee snapped off the TV and raced into the kitchen where Ari kept her car keys.

She'd decided to do what Kira Thirteen would do. Answer: *Whatever it took*. Even it meant a little bit of law-breaking.

Baylee rushed into the garage and got into Ari's car. Started the engine. Opened the garage door. Rolled backward to the road. So far so good. She caught the brown van turning right at the end of the street.

"Okay," Baylee said out loud, trying to use Kira's rough and scratchy voice. She borrowed Kira's catchphrase to give herself a shot of courage. "Let's roll the bones."

She had no license, of course. Her only form of I.D. was on her lanyard from school. She had driven before; a couple times, with either John or Ari, just for kicks around the neighborhood. It hadn't been hard. Plus she had plenty of time. John and Ari would be out until at least ten, probably eleven, possibly later. They always had dinner on their nights out, then went to a movie, show, or shopping . . . whatever old people did on Friday nights.

Baylee leaned forward against the wheel, the seatbelt pulling against her. The van wasn't hard to follow. Sean— she assumed it was him again—drove rather carefully, and the van stuck out readily from other traffic. Baylee counted on Ari's white car looking like a million others on the road, and that Elijah would have zero reason to expect her to be following him in the first place.

She wished Timothy was with her. It would make the adventure a lot less scary. Plus he could drive. Like, for real. That would've been the smart thing. But not knowing how the timing would work out, it hadn't seemed fair to ask him to wait in the '36 somewhere down the street, just sitting for hours until Elijah left. She was lucky enough as it was that the Wagners had left first. *Everything* thus far was luck. Trying to involve Timothy in it would have been one more thing she'd have to account for.

No. Better that he wasn't involved, not yet. Depending on where she tracked Sean and Derby to, she'd loop him in later. Tonight, even, once she had answers.

She noticed then that her heart thunked happily in her chest. An odd feeling; she was scared and nervous, quite rightly, yet enjoyed a heady rush of excitement. Already miles from the house, in a stolen car, spying on people who might have done something sinister to her best friend and were in the process of stealing her brother away from her . . .

She'd had more adventure in the last twenty minutes than in her entire life.

They drove for more than half an hour, which was right around the time Baylee realized that, in her haste, she'd left the house without a bottle of water. She made herself shrug it off; She could always stop and get one once she saw whatever it was she needed to see tonight.

They reached the outskirts of the city and turned onto a two-lane highway leading to smaller towns higher up in the mountains.

"Shit," Baylee said. It would not be easy for her to stay concealed now. Traffic on this highway was sparse.

But the darkness would offer some concealment. Thinking on this, Baylee squeaked and turned on the headlights. *That* scared her; she hadn't driven in the dark before, and good God, how close had she come to not turning on the goddamn lights?

She forced a deep breath. Okay, one minor slip-up,

nothing to panic about. She'd come this far. Outside of a car wreck, what was the worst that could happen? Baylee rationalized that she was a good kid, that she'd earned at least one Bad Kid card to play with her foster parents. Besides, if she got caught and Ari and John wanted to ground her, they could go right ahead. Without Krista, she was pretty much stuck at home anyway. And she could survive without seeing Timothy, provided she had her phone.

Two cars rolled between Baylee's and the van. She figured that was a good thing; enough distance to blend in but not so much to lose sight of the van. The highway cut a straight swath through the desert for maybe a fifty miles before sloping upward into the high country—where the hell could they be going? Meet a dealer or something?

Where they were going was off the highway.

"Shit," Baylee said again as the van rolled off the road and onto the shoulder, coasted for a several yards, then took an abrupt right onto a barely visible dirt path. By the time the van was on that path, she had passed them going fifty miles an hour.

Baylee let her foot off the gas, slowed, and pulled off the road, to much blaring of horns behind her. She stopped and turned around in the seat. The van's headlights still moved in the distance, driving deeper into the desert and fading quickly. A sliver of moon hung high in the sky, and by it, she could make out a short, flat-topped hill in the distance. The van drove that direction.

She shut off the car and kept her eyes on the van headlights. After about a minute, the van disappeared around and behind the short hill.

"How far is that?" she whispered. Depth perception and guessing distances wasn't something she needed to rely on with any regularity, much less at night. But the hill could not be *too* far, she reckoned. Three, maybe four football fields? An easy walk. The land seemed flat, the vegetation sparse.

Now: was whatever naughty stuff her brother was up to worth hiking through the desert at night to uncover? Baylee wore shorts, a tank top, and sandals. Not exactly hiking gear. And the heat . . . sun down or not, it had to be 100 degrees.

"Well, what the hell," she said, and got out.

She could afford to at least go get a closer look at what they were doing—smoking meth? shooting heroin?—and still walk back in time to get the car home before Ari and John.

She took her time picking through the scrub brush until her eyes adjusted. The going was easy enough—level ground blanketed in gravel, with ample space between cacti and bushes. Half the distance from Ari's car, it dawned on her that her phone had a flashlight, and that she'd left it in the center console. That might've been helpful, Baylee thought. On the other hand, it could've given her away. Perhaps she was more tactical than she'd thought.

That's what she told herself. Kira Thirteen would be proud.

It took Baylee twenty minutes to reach the base of the hill. It was further than she'd thought; the heat and the dark toyed with her perception. She needed water.

Baylee crept up to the base of the hill, listening and scanning all around, expecting Elijah and the others to be

162

nearby. The hill itself loomed taller than she had expected. But a path of sorts was cut into one side, winding upward and ending at the top. A second path wound around the base, circling it.

She chose the path up the hill, figuring if Elijah and the others were behind it, it would give her a good vantage point to be above them. She walked slowly, listening hard.

Nothing yet.

Then she smelled smoke. The soothing, woody notes of a campfire.

Baylee crested the hill and walked carefully east along the top. It wasn't perfectly level; little outcrops of rock stuck out of the ground at heights of two and three feet. As she climbed over them, mouth dry and hoping no rattlesnakes would jump out at her, Baylee made out a faint yellow-orange glow. The campfire.

She slowed, taking her time to slink over the rocky outcrops, choosing each place her foot fell so as to make no noise. Baylee hid behind one of the larger rocks at the edge, peeking over the top so she could see down to the desert floor below.

There they were.

They hadn't built a bonfire, exactly, but it was sizeable enough to see clearly by. Now Baylee expected to see a keg, or a cooler full of beer bottles. A pipe being passed around, or arms being tied off and injected.

Nothing along those lines, though.

What she saw was much worse.

A tree stood off to the left of the fire, its thick trunk bare until ten feet up or more—essentially a big green pole in the ground. Sean's brown van was parked several yards away from it, its double back doors facing the fire.

Across from the van sat an inimitable 1936 Ford coupe. "Timothy?"

His name whispered out of Baylee automatically. Of all the scenarios she'd imagined Elijah getting himself into, one having anything to do with her boyfriend never crossed her mind. Why would it?

Derby and Sean sat cross-legged in front of the fire, facing Baylee's direction—facing the hill—but not looking up. They might've been talking, but she was too high up to be sure. Derby dug in the dirt with something, a small shovel, perhaps. No; a knife. A huge hunting knife, glinting in the fire light and threatening to blind Baylee like a flashbulb..

Opposite them—closer to her—she saw Timothy and her brother. What the hell was Timothy *doing* here? Why had he lied about dinner with his family?

Elijah stood opposite Derby and Sean, profile to Baylee. Timothy faced him. Elijah held the big book in both hands, head tipped, reading—the same book he'd read in his room. Timothy nodded every few seconds, approving whatever it was Elijah read aloud.

D&D? Baylee thought.

Okay. Sure. This was one of those parties where everyone dresses up in character. What had Ralph called it. . . LARP? Right. Live-action role-playing. Maybe that was it. Odd, yes, but not—

Except they weren't in costume. Derby wore a similar strange outfit like she'd had on at Kyro, but the boys were dressed normally. Normally for them, at any rate, and definitely nothing like fantasy or period dress.

It didn't matter, Baylee decided. The knife in Derby's

hands unnerved her. Whatever they were doing out here, hidden away from the world, absolutely nothing good was going to happen.

Baylee flexed her knees, preparing to stand up and cry out, to tell her brother she was taking him home.

She didn't get the chance.

Elijah snapped the book shut. And when he did, the hill beneath Baylee tremored, like an earthquake, like some giant thing burrowed underneath it.

Timothy glanced at Derby, giving no indication they'd felt the quake; or else, they purely did not care. Derby flipped Timothy the knife, and he caught it deftly in his hand, with such martial skill that Baylee stifled a gasp.

Timothy handed the knife to Elijah, who traded him the knife for the book. Timothy set the book on a round rock.

Methodically, Lij unbuttoned his shirt and placed it on the rock beside the book. Bare-chested now, he faced Timothy, holding the knife in both hands.

Some kind of initiation thing? Baylee thought. So they're . . . a gang? What—

Elijah raised the knife, and drove the blade into his own chest.

ten

Elijah didn't make a sound. Didn't scream. Didn't collapse. Baylee could see the muscles in his arms—huge, rippling muscles he'd never had before—flexing from the strength he exerted.

Her brother, if that's what he was, worked the blade like his own body was a hunk of meat on a hook. Digging this way then that, staring straight at Timothy, who only nodded vaguely as if to encourage him. Baylee heard the wet crack of a rib as Elijah twisted the knife. He levered the blade up and down, forming a gap in his flesh through which he could reach one hand.

A moment later, Elijah held his own heart.

It lay in his upturned palm, drenched in viscous blood. *Beating.*

In that moment, an odd warmth flooded through Baylee, from her scalp to her toes. She was dreaming. Having one of her nightmares. Of course! Simple as that. This was a dream. All the fear left her, washed away by a dull peace. Her heart rate slowed to a normal pace. Her breathing resumed its natural rhythm. She was dreaming. Simple as that. She was dreaming. Simple as—

Elijah threw his heart on top of the fire. A jet of arctic blue flame shot from the center of the pyre, several feet in the air.

He handed the knife to Timothy, who took it with a nod, then embraced Elijah warmly. Somehow, Timothy seemed taller when he did it, pressing Elijah's ear to his chest. The embrace was utterly non-sexual. More brotherly. As if Elijah had just completed some evil rite of passage or . . .

Ritual.

How nice, Baylee thought as this odd, fluid warmth coated in her inside and out. How nice Elijah's made another friend.

Ritual.

A word that only came up around the Wagner house with any frequency because of the D&D games.

Games!

Baylee laughed.

Not loud, but laughed all the same. Relief flooded her, draining the warm peace she'd just experienced. This was no dream, and that was all right, because an even more sensical answer came to her. Any second now, some friends from school were going to pop out of the shadows with their cell phones, film her response, and post it online. Maybe this was even one of those prank TV shows. That's all this was, all it *could* be. A huge joke. Maybe even going back as far as a week, so she'd really buy into it.

Baylee shook her head, grinning. She couldn't wait to see how they did all the special effects. She even took a step from her place on the hill, ready to climb down and meet them at the fire, enjoy the laughs at her expense.

Except that's when Derby opened the van doors and pulled someone out.

Krista.

Baylee's foot froze mid-air, hovering over a large rock she'd been about to step on. Krista was bound hand and foot, gagged with silver tape. Even from the distance, Baylee could see the obvious strain on her face. Probably crying. She barely heard Krista's muffled screams through the gag.

This was some joke, all right, Baylee thought as her head swam. Yes. Some really, really detailed joke . . .

Derby grabbed Krista by the neck and jumped to the naked green tree. *Jumped.* Like a grasshopper. Thirty, even forty feet, like it was nothing. As easily as she could take a single step.

Stunned by all she was seeing, Baylee sank back behind her protective rock as Derby made short work of lashing Krista to the tree. She knew what was going to happen next. Something made it inevitable. Terror snaked through her, curling around every organ in her body and squeezing tight.

Timothy jumped next. His leap carried him even farther than Derby's. Then Sean joined them at the tree. Elijah stayed put, watching intently, bare skin reflecting the firelight.

Bare skin. Perfectly unharmed. Smooth, unmarred.

How . . .

Derby reached out to Timothy. He handed her the enormous knife.

No, Baylee thought dumbly. No, stop, it's a joke, I get it, stop.

Derby raised the knife, flat side up. Krista screamed though the tape, screamed, screamed—

Then Baylee screamed too as Derby shoved the blade against Krista's throat and sliced it open.

Somehow, by instinct maybe, Baylee had muffled her own scream into her arm, choking most of it down. It came out like a guttural hiccup. Blood gushed from Krista's wound in a flood, staining the ground black. The three of them stood before her, watching.

Savoring.

When Krista ceased moving, Derby and Sean cheered. They raised their hands and shouted to the sky, whooping and calling out nonsensically. Krista was dead, her chin hanging against her chest, awash with dark blood.

Baylee trembled. Every muscle thrummed at an impossible rate, her heart bouncing from her throat to her knees in half-second increments.

This was not a game. This was not role-playing. Krista's throat still trickled fresh blood, dotting the damp sand beneath her.

Sacrificed.

Baylee's breath came out in rapid bursts. Hyperventilating. *They killed Krista, they killed Krista . . .* it repeated over and over in her head. She tried to make her legs work, to go back down the hill, get to the car, drive hard and fast for home; no, *police*, she needed police, and oh my God, they killed Krista . . .

Derby grabbed one of Krista's arms. Sean, the other. They pulled. Krista's arms came off readily, as if yanked from her body by some macabre machinery, not the strength of two high school kids. High school kids who could jump forty feet from a standstill without any effort.

Baylee heard it.

Heard the bone and muscle give. Her mind helpfully suggested the sound was similar to poking fingers into a ripe melon and pulling it apart with bare hands. An awful, damp crunch.

She struggled to tear her eyes away from them. Instead her gaze found only Elijah, still standing by the fire, still backlit by it. He seemed to be smiling. Timothy walked back to Elijah, patted his shoulder, then took one step back.

Derby and Sean gnawed on Krista's limbs, their faces smeared opaque. Derby tossed the remnants of Krista's arm into the dark desert. It was clear now what had happened to Chris Fletcher. Fletcher and . . . Mom and Dad?

Derby whooped once before hunkering down, her knees up by her ears.

Derby began to change. Her shirt split down the back. Her spine lengthened and swelled.

Well past rational thought now, some cobwebbed corner of Baylee's mind assumed she'd turn into a wolf of some kind. But no. This thing that had been Derby was no wolf. No *anything* that ever walked the earth.

Her legs lengthened impossibly, until her knees were as tall as Derby herself had been. This made her shins on the order of five feet long, which meant her thighs, pressed against her now-elongated torso, were almost that long as well. She looked like a perverse praying mantis ready to spring at prey.

Derby's arms got longer too, dangling from broad, hairless shoulders. As she turned to show off this new,

170

morphed body, Baylee could see her eyes glowing a deep orange color, burning with their own internal, infernal light.

The thing that had been Derby tilted its head back and cackled into the night, some hellish cross between a baby's scream and a lion's roar yet which was somehow unmistakably a laugh. That sound . . . that shrieking wail became a tangible thing, shaking the rock beneath Baylee's body, something out of Hell.

After that:

Dark.

Blessed dark and silence and nothing more.

eleven

Baylee winced against sunlight beaming across her eyelids. She rolled over, wondering if she was already late for school. She must have slept in her clothes; everything was twisted around her body in uncomfortable knots. Something hard and vaguely round dug into her back. Probably her iPad, she always fell asleep watching Netflix.

She coughed. Needed water, then coffee. Or maybe vice versa.

Baylee opened her eyes. Took in the desert landscape, the rising sun. She lay surrounded by dirt and gravel, rocks and scrub brush.

Blearily, she thought, How did I get—

The memory of the previous night crashed into her brain. She hurled herself upward and dry heaved. Krista, torn apart; Elijah, impossibly eviscerating himself; Derby changing into some hellish monster . . .

Shaking and stiff, Baylee crawled to the rocky outcrop she'd been on last night and peeked over the edge, terrified of what remains she might find.

Dirt.

The tree.

Some boulders.

Nothing more.

Still quaking, Baylee shimmied along the top of the hill until she could peek over the opposite side, the side she'd climbed up the night before. Still nothing. Just an empty expanse of desert landscape. Further off, she saw the highway. Much further, Ari's white car, parked alongside the road where she'd left it, stuck out like white lint on a tan coat.

What?

Baylee stood, slowly, feeling eighty years old. Scanned three-sixty. No sign of the brown van, of the '36 Ford, of her brother, her boyfriend, or of anything else.

Panting, she rushed back to where she'd woken up, then slid-climbed down the hill to where she'd seen her best friend killed.

Nothing.

The green-trunked tree was there, but no blood saturated the ground. No sign of the campfire. No tire tracks.

"But . . ." Baylee said out loud, voice cracked and dry as she wrapped her arms around herself and rubbed them hard, trying warm up her body and get circulation back into her limbs. She'd never been so thirsty in all her life. The temperature felt close to ninety already, maybe higher.

Baylee staggered to one side, dizzy at the weight of the memory and her lack of hydration.

Here, it had been *right here*, why the hell else would I be out in the middle of nowhere in a stolen car? She dug one toe into the dirt and kicked it around, looking for blood, looking for ash, looking for one clue that a murder happened here last night.

Nothing.

"Oh my God," Baylee said, and stumbled back the way she'd come. *What is wrong with me?* She walked quickly—or tried to walk quickly—back toward Ari's car. Without its bright whiteness to guide her, she felt she might have staggered through the desert forever.

Baylee climbed inside the vehicle, relieved to find that she still had the keys in her pocket. She started the engine and the A/C before picking up her phone from the console between the seats.

Her phone was full of texts and voice mails. All of them from Ari and John. None from Elijah, none from Krista, none from anyone else.

She read the texts first. Pretty much what a teen girl who'd taken a car without permission, or license, and not come home all night gets: angry, then furious, then worried, then scared.

Not bothering to listen to the voice mails, Baylee called Ari. Ari answered immediately.

"Baylee! Is that you?"

"Yeah, hi, I'm sorry," Baylee started, but Ari's cries cut her off.

Ari wept hard, repeating *Oh thank God,* and *Are you all right?* and *What happened?* in no particular order. Baylee couldn't interrupt until she stopped to take a breath.

"I'm fine, where is Elijah?"

"Lij?" Ari said, confused. "He went out to breakfast with his friends before we got up. Where are you, Baylee? My God, John's still out looking for you, when we saw the car gone—"

"I'm safe, I'm fine, I'll be home in less than an hour. I have your car, and I'm fine. But listen—"

"Why did you take my car?" Ari shifted gears. "What on earth is the matter with you, what were you thinking? You don't even have a license—stay there. Just stay there, John and I will come and get you, where are you?"

"Stop, listen!" Baylee shouted. "You have to call the cops!"

"We *did* call the cops—"

"No, about Elijah! And Timothy and all them, Mom, I saw Krista, I found her, they *killed* her!"

Silence from Ari for a long moment.

"Where did you say you are?" she asked, very slowly.

"I'm off the Beeline Highway. I'm parked off to the side, maybe twenty minutes away from where it picks up at Shea."

"And . . . you're alone and safe?"

"Yes! But you have to listen to me—"

"Stay there," Ari interrupted. "Just stay put and we will come get you. Do not drive that car, do you understand?"

Baylee shut her eyes and rammed her head backward into the seat. "Yes."

"We'll be right there," Ari's voice was even and smooth. "Do you need anything?"

"Breakfast. Water! Water."

"We'll bring you something. Thank God you're all right."

"Ari, please, you have to bring the police," Baylee said as calmly as she could, keeping her eyes closed and trying to avoid rubbing them; doing so would only drive more invisible cactus needles into them.

"Let me call John and we'll work it out."

"But . . . !"

Baylee came up short. Fighting it was pointless. "Okay. Fine."

"Okay," Ari said. "I love you."

She hung up before Baylee could answer. Baylee guessed she had at least thirty minutes to wait, probably more. She stared at her phone, then sent a text to Elijah.

Where are you?

Then she sat back and waited.

Elijah hadn't answered back by the time John's blue Sorrento pulled up behind Ari's car. Baylee got out and met Ari halfway. She rushed over and hugged Baylee tight, then John got there and gripped them both, like a standing dogpile. They didn't say anything.

"I'm okay," Baylee said, muffled against Ari's white R.E.M. T-shirt.

John let go, and Ari stepped back, gripping Baylee's arms.

"I could smack you," she said, her expression a maternal blend of *I'm going to hug you for ten years, then for the next ten I'm going to beat you insensate with a two-by-four.*

"I'm fine. But please, you have to listen to me."

"I picked up McDonald's," John said, pointing to the Sorrento.

"*No!*" Baylee screamed. Then added, "I mean, *yes,* thank you, but just, wait, okay? I have to tell you what happened."

"You sure as hell do," Ari said.

Baylee pulled away from her. "Then listen! I followed Elijah out here last night, okay? And I saw Krista. They tied her to a tree, and then that girl Derby, her name's Nora, she . . ."

Baylee stopped and dry heaved once more. She guessed since she hadn't eaten in more than twelve hours, there was nothing inside to come up. She coughed hard and gagged, and Ari rushed to rub her back.

"Derby killed her," Baylee went on when she had her breath back. "She cut Krista's throat, I am not making this up! And Elijah, he cut out . . . he cut out . . . his . . . and-and-and Derby, she turned into this *thing*, like an insect . . ."

The words tumbled out over each other. As they did, for the first time, Baylee realized how it all sounded. The two adults watched her closely. Ari didn't seem quite so angry now; instead she wore her counselor face. John just looked concerned, his eyebrows deeply furrowed.

Yet she couldn't stop: "And Elijah, he cut out his-his-his own heart and threw it on the fire and it went up in flame . . . it was *blue*, like a gas jet or something . . . and then Derby, or I mean Nora, she turned into this monster, like a werewolf or something but not a wolf, more like a mantis . . . and Sean was there, and him and Derby, they were . . . they were *eating* Krista's arms . . ."

Wow. Insane.

That's the face Ari wore now.

"I can show you!" Baylee declared, taking a step toward the hill and pointing, but then stopping as she remembered there was nothing to show them. Not a trace.

"We should go," John said quietly to Ari.

Ari nodded back, but kept her eyes on Baylee. "Why don't you get in John's car. Eat something. We'll get you home."

"You don't believe me?"

"Not in so many words, no."

"*She killed Krista.* I saw her do it!"

"Okay," Ari said, reaching for Baylee's arm again. "We'll tell the police everything. But let's get you home first, make sure you're all right."

Baylee gave up. She let Ari lead her to John's car, and got in. The Wagners held a quick conference at the hood, then John got in and started home. In the car, Baylee ate one bite of hash brown, downed a bottle of water, drank all the coffee, and that was it. She couldn't stomach any more than that.

She assumed they'd go straight to the house.

They didn't. Clearly the Wagners had other plans. Upon arrival, Baylee thought she really should not have been surprised.

Ari's office was in the center of the city. Once they pulled into the parking lot, Baylee knew what was about to happen.

"You're kidding me," she said.

"We just need to make sure," John said gently.

"I'm not on drugs!"

"We don't want to think so either," John said, which was not at all the same as *We don't think so either*. "It won't take long."

"Are you leaving me here?"

"No, of course not." John parked in a public space while Ari parked in her covered area. "We just need some hard facts to work with, that's all."

"I'm *not* on drugs."

"Then it shouldn't matter if you do the tests. It won't take long. Bay, you have to understand what this all looks like from our point of view. Okay?"

Ari's company couldn't do drug testing itself, but the clinic right next door did. Baylee went silent and remained so as she spent the morning peeing in a cup and giving up a piece of her hair.

She had not heard back from her demonic older brother. Baylee opted not to use that phrase when Ari next escorted her to see a professional friend who ran an initial evaluation for psychiatric wellbeing on the teen.

Baylee spoke then, when the doctor started asking her questions; spoke, and told her the truth. Stealing the car, following Elijah, Krista being killed, Elijah carving out his own heart, Derby becoming a were-insect. All of it. Baylee said it all as calmly and matter-of-factly as she could manage.

Shockingly, it did not seem to help her situation.

Lydia, the woman who did the assessment, had Baylee wait in her office while she talked to Ari. Ari came in a few minutes later with Lydia and sat across from Baylee. She wore a *Please listen closely* expression.

"Baylee," Ari said, "we're going to take you home now—"

"You think I'm crazy."

"No, you're not," Ari said firmly. "I do not believe that."

The answer surprised her. "I'm not?"

"I think you saw something or experienced something unusual," Ari said. "Do I think your brother's new girlfriend turned into a monster? Not exactly. But I do believe something bad happened to you, and we'll work together to figure out what it was."

"Are you having me committed or something?"

"Sweetie, no," Ari said, smiling briefly. "You've been under a lot of stress, with Krista missing and Lij going through his . . . phase. If you say you're not taking any drugs, then I believe you, and I believe the tests will bear that out. But you've had a rough night, and *we've* had a rough night, so right now we're all going home and getting some rest. Okay?"

"What about the *cops?* You have to tell them what happened."

"We'll tell the police whatever needs to be told."

That was a non-answer of epic scale, but Baylee didn't pursue. Instead she went to her next biggest concern:

"I can't stay in the same house with Elijah."

"Okay, well, that presents a problem since you both live there."

"I am *not* staying there with him."

Ari and Lydia traded glances.

"Baylee . . . where else could you possibly stay?"

○

Ralph Silverberg had either the good sense or common decency to not look overly excited when Baylee got to his house with Ari later that afternoon. Although, she thought as a headache thudded dully behind her eyes, his being a total nerd is the least of my worries.

Total nerds didn't kill people with knives.

Or themselves.

How did Lij do it? How could he possibly have—

Baylee started shaking again. It had been happening every ten or twenty minutes. Nothing she did could warm her up. The heat of the July summer made no impact on her chills.

"You're sure this isn't a hassle?" Ari asked Mr. Silverberg as Baylee sat on the carpeted steps up to the second floor of the

Silverberg's house. Mrs. Silverberg brought her a mug of cocoa. Baylee tried to say thank you, but felt as if only dirt came out. Mrs. Silverberg gave her a momish frown-smile and touched her shoulder.

"Absolutely!" Mr. Silverberg declared to Ari. "She's welcome as long as she wants." He turned to Baylee, repeating, "You're welcome as long as you want, Baylee."

Again she tried to say thank you. Again, nothing. She hoped they could see she was trying.

Ari and John looked pensively at her. "If you're sure . . ." Ari said.

"Completely," Mr. Silverberg said, gesturing emphatically. Baylee wondered if he was a trial lawyer. He had a flair for the dramatic.

While the parents—and guardians—went on talking about Baylee right in front of her, Ralph crossed and recrossed his arms and then legs as he sat on a chair in their front room. He wasn't staring at Baylee, which she appreciated, but he wasn't *not* looking, either. His expression clearly showed he had a million questions about how the object of his affection landed in his home one warm Saturday night. It was also clear he wasn't going to ask any of them in front of the families.

Ari and John left after giving Baylee multiple hugs and insisting that she call them if she needed anything. They, too, had called and texted Elijah, but he hadn't responded.

John promised they would call the police, but by that point, Baylee hardly cared. Even if the police got involved and somehow tracked Sean, Derby, and Timothy down, she didn't believe a cop could compete against the thing Derby had turned into.

Was she the only one? Timothy and Sean had leapt like she did, they probably turned into the same awful creatures.

And what about Elijah? What was he, now?

Once Ari and John had gone, Mrs. Silverberg offered—for the third time—to fix Baylee something to eat. She managed to decline verbally. Mr. Silverberg insisted his wife leave her alone, that she'd had a hard day, just leave her be. Mrs. Silverberg gave up and went into the kitchen, where it sounded like she was going start cooking anyway. Mr. Silverberg went into the rear living room. The TV popped to life.

That left Baylee and Ralph alone in the front room. Baylee could see the weight of Fletcher's death in Ralph's slumped shoulders, as if it were a physical burden. She recognized the posture.

"So," Ralph said after a minute. His frown showed ongoing grief, but his eyes at least were lively, peering at her inquisitively. "What happened?"

Ari and John hadn't filled in the Silverbergs on the details of her story; only that she and Elijah were "having some difficulties" and that "the stress of her best friend missing" had "brought up some issues."

Baylee didn't blame them for glazing over her version of events. The Silverbergs wouldn't want a crazy person living with them, after all. And as she sat on those beige-carpeted steps in the Dungeon Master's house, crazy was the only answer that made any sense. It hadn't even been twelve hours since she woke up in the middle of nowhere; not even twenty-four since she'd seen Krista killed . . . and already it felt distant and detached.

Like, oh, I don't know, a dream? Baylee thought.

Except it wasn't. It *wasn't*.

"Have you heard from him?" she asked Ralph instead of answering.

"No. Not for awhile now. Not since Fletcher . . . not since that morning." Ralph's eyes darted between the direction of the kitchen and the direction of the living room, then back to Baylee. "You want to go upstairs?"

"What, to your room?"

"Well, yeah. They won't be able to hear us talk."

"Your parents don't care if you have a girl in your room?"

Ralph smiled at that, but not with any humor. "Baylee, I don't know if you know this, but I'm not the most popular guy around. They'll be thrilled with the idea that an actual female stepped into my room."

He stood up. "Besides, you and I both know you're perfectly safe there, right?"

Baylee surrendered. She got to her feet as the last wave of shivers subsided.

Ralph walked up the stairs and Baylee followed, leaving her backpack of clothes behind. The Silverbergs had a nice house; clean, white, and modern without being too pretentious in Baylee's opinion. Tasteful art hung on all the walls, but she didn't see a single family photo anywhere. She hoped they were displayed somewhere else. A vague scent reminding her of warm photocopier ink hovered in the hallways.

Ralph's room struck Baylee as surprisingly normal when he led her in. She'd expected posters of dragons, or *Star Wars* bed sheets. Instead, his room didn't look all that different from Elijah's. A striped comforter over a full size bed—his room was bigger than hers or Elijah's—a desk in one corner, a small flat screen TV, tablet, bookcase, closet. An antique or faux antique chest anchored the foot of his bed. Tacked to the wall beside his desk were printed photos of him and the gamers, including Elijah.

Baylee sat tentatively on Ralph's black swivel desk chair and checked out his bookcase. Two shelves were full of colorful-spined game books, the rest with fiction and textbooks.

Her gaze lingered on the rule books. She recognized several titles. "He really loves those games, you know."

"Yeah," Ralph said, sitting on the edge of his bed. "I know. They're fun. We get to be other people. Be heroes and stuff."

"But not really," Baylee said. "It's just fake."

Ralph shrugged. "I'm sixteen and I've already saved the world twice. I've died three times. I've had and lost a kid. I fought a dragon once. I brought down an international spy ring. One time, I threw a 747 jetliner over my head and into a bad guy who was about to blow up a plane full of innocent people. What do *you* do after school?"

She might have otherwise laughed. "Okay. Point taken. I guess he didn't tell you I ripped up most of his books, huh?"

"No . . . what's going on with you guys? Really."

"If I tell you, you have to promise not to laugh."

"At you? Never." Ralph leaned forward, elbows on his knees. "Shoot."

Baylee took a breath, and told him everything.

Stealing Ari's car, the desert drive, Krista, the inhuman leaps, Derby's metamorphosis . . . everything. Ralph's expression barely changed.

"That's it," Baylee finished, and peeked up at him. Thirty minutes had passed.

Ralph commented on her entire horrific experience by saying: "Huh."

Baylee stood, throwing her hands into the air. "So what *are* they? Vampires? Werewolves? Freaking homunculi?"

"You know what homunculi are and how to use the plural?" Ralph said, ignoring her rage. Then he muttered, "God, you're hot."

"Would you please focus here, Ralph? Okay? Huh? Please? Elijah *cut out his heart*, dammit!"

Ralph held up his hands. "Okay, let's take a step back for a second. Can I just make some suggestions that aren't out of the fifth edition Monster Manual?"

Baylee wrapped her arms so tight around herself she could feel her shoulder blades beneath her fingers. Then she nodded.

"Okay. Number one—what you're talking about just isn't possible."

"Oh my God, no shit, Ralph!"

"Please, hold on. I kind of need to hear myself talk this through. So. Let's look at this logically. There are only two possibilities here. You are right, or you are wrong."

Ralph stood up and paced. Baylee sat back down on his desk chair, arms still crossed.

"Let's say you're wrong for the moment. That what you saw didn't actually happen. What are some possibilities?

You were hallucinating. Maybe a drug-induced fugue of some kind—"

"I don't do drugs. Ari just took me to get tested this morning, which, can I just say, thanks so much for the trust, you know?"

Ralph blinked. "I don't think you do drugs, either, but somebody could've slipped you something."

That startled her. It hadn't occurred to her that that was a possibility. "Who? And when?"

"I don't know, that's why I'm talking out loud. So there's one option, you were drugged. Now let's say you weren't drugged. That leaves . . . you imagined it, or your eyes played tricks on you—was the moon out?"

"Yeah. Quarter, maybe. Not even that."

"So it possibly could have been a trick of the shadows."

"Except that *it wasn't!* Shadows don't do what I saw."

"Which takes us to option two. That you're right. That what you saw really happened."

Baylee kicked at his carpet. "What do *you* think?"

"I think those two kids were weird," Ralph said immediately. "And I think Lij . . . you know, looked up to them."

He grit his teeth when he said it. Baylee was struck by how much he and Suze must be hurt that Elijah would ditch them during such a terrible event as Fletcher's death.

Stop, she thought. Stop calling it that. It was murder. You saw what they did, and obviously one of them or all of them killed Fletcher, too.

And maybe Mom and Dad . . .

She couldn't begin to think of how that might be possible. Let's just say, Baylee told herself, utterly zoning out in Ralph's room, that Derby killed Mom and Dad. Why? What did it have to do with Elijah, with her? And Timothy? Dear *God*, what did he have to do with all of it?

She stared into middle space until Ralph and his entire room faded to a blur. "Ralph . . . what the hell is going on?"

Ralph pulled out his phone. "Would you mind if I called Suze over? See what she thinks?"

Baylee thought about it for a minute. It couldn't hurt; she needed all the help she could get, because so far, she still just sounded like a crazy person.

"Yes. Sure. How is she doing?"

"Okay, I guess. If you could call it that. We've been texting, anyway. I'll see how she is. The, uh . . . service is next week."

Ralph started sending texts just as Baylee's own phone rang. It was Ari. Baylee took the call in the hallway outside Ralph's room.

"Hi, Bay. We haven't been able to track down your brother yet. Have you heard from him?"

"No."

Ari sighed. "Okay. Well, we're on our way to the police station to report everything you told us, there's a Detective Mills there—"

"You are? You're really going to tell the cops?"

"Yes. We have to, hon, you know that."

"No, yeah, I get it, I just . . . I didn't think you really believed me."

"Sweetheart," Ari said softly, then paused. Baylee couldn't make out the nature of the hesitation; crying? Sad? Disappointed?

Worried?

"I still believe something terrible happened to you," Ari said. "And that 'something' might very well have involved Krista, which means it needs to be followed up on. So we'll get the ball rolling there and see what happens, okay?"

"Yeah. Okay."

"How are you feeling?"

"Not good. I mean, scared, mostly. Ari, I'm not making this up."

"I know," Ari stated, in a way that made Baylee start to believe her. "If you hear from your brother, let us know right away, all right?"

"Yeah."

"Okay. Don't go anywhere, stay there with the Silverbergs. We'll be in touch soon. Try to eat something else if you can. And get some rest."

"Okay. Thanks."

"We love you, Bay."

The words triggered a memory of that morning, one not so terrible but shocking all the same: She'd called Ari *Mom*. On the phone, after she woke up in the desert, she'd called her that without meaning to.

Baylee wondered if Ari noticed, or remembered.

"Yeah," Baylee choked. "You too."

She hung up and went back into Ralph's room. He'd fired up his tablet. "Suze's on her way."

"Thanks, Ralph." Baylee slid to the floor, her back against his bed, knees raised to her chest. He watched her there for a moment, like he wanted to say something, but changed his mind. Ralph turned back to his tablet, which he'd seated in a keyboard.

Baylee shut her eyes and leaned her head back. *We love*

you, Bay. Had Ari ever said that before? And if so, in that way? There was a difference between a casual *Love ya* and *We love you*, this factual statement. Baylee debated if she were overthinking it. Something bad had happened, so Ari just wanted to reassure her or. Okay. That was fair.

Because she is *not* Mom, Baylee told herself—although she had to force the idea just a little bit. John is not Dad. Elijah is my brother, period, the end. Whatever else he might be right now, he was that first and always, and that is the start and end of my family.

Even if he's a murderer? Her face tightened.

Even if he is, he's still Elijah. Even if he had a part in killing my best friend, and I know that he did, he's still my only blood relative left in the world.

. . . *Did* he kill my best friend?

Sitting secure in the Dork Master's house of all places, the memory of last night was still strong but . . . misshapen, somehow. Baylee could recall the entire scene, could hear the sounds of Krista's arms giving way beneath Derby and Sean's grip.

She couldn't have imagined something like that.

Other than the fact that what Ralph said was true: it just wasn't possible.

○

"Baylee?"

Her head shot up. She blinked in the afternoon sunlight coming through Ralph's window. She looked instinctively at her phone and saw thirty minutes had passed.

"Was I asleep?" she asked, voice crackling.

"Yeah, I think. You okay?"

Baylee grunted a nonsense response and nodded.

"Suze'll be here in a minute." Ralph tapped a couple of times on his tablet, then spun on his chair quickly as if reaching a decision. "Can I ask you a personal question?"

Baylee rubbed a muscle in her neck. "Why not."

"Does it ever get better?"

Baylee faced him, unsure what he meant at first. Then she saw the grief in his face; restrained, but evident. She recognized it from the mirror.

He meant Fletcher.

"Some," she said softly. "But not really. Or at least not yet. Maybe someday."

He nodded. That was the end of the deepest conversation they'd ever had.

"I'm here," Suze whispered a minute later, sliding through Ralph's doorway like a two-dimensional ghost. She met Baylee's eyes, smiled lightly, then ducked her chin and sat against Ralph's closet, long legs extended out in front of her as always.

"Hey, Suze," Ralphs said. "Okay. Baylee, can you handle telling it one more time?"

She nodded, and told them. This time, she didn't get the shivers. This time, it sounded straight-up stupid. This time, she wondered quite seriously if she was actually sane.

Suze stared at her green Converse the entire time. Ralph kept a steady gaze on Baylee. When she'd finished, Ralph explained all of his theories, darting glances between the two girls.

"So?" Ralph said when he'd explained his thoughts. "Questions, comments, anyone care for a mint?"

The comment felt like an inside joke to Baylee, except Suze didn't smile. She raised her head and said, "Can I be the voice of reason?"

Baylee blew her lips and gestured for her to go on, like it didn't matter.

"Okay," Suze said, straightening her posture against the closet door. "This guy, Timothy, you've been seeing? Any chance he had access to drugs? Prescription medication or anything else, like Ralph said?"

"No," Baylee said. "Not that I know of, I mean. I never, like, felt anything off or weird when I was with him. He's never done anything like that before."

"To *you*," Ralph said.

Baylee instinctively began to argue, but then felt his point drive hard into her guts. She closed her mouth. All she'd ever felt with Timothy was loved and secure and sexy.

Which might explain, she berated herself, why you actually don't know all that much about him, you stupid bitch.

"I think Ralph's drug theory makes the most sense," Suze said. Her delivery was gentle, nonthreatening. "I'm so sorry. Part of me very much wants to believe it all really happened, just so I would . . ."

Suze let the words hover, unspoken, but Baylee guessed the ending: Just so she would know there was a reason Elijah had suddenly turned on them. On *her*.

She cleared her throat a bit and went on: "There is a logical explanation for what you saw, and I think that's it. I also think Timothy . . . you might want to stay away from him, regardless. Even if the three of them aren't Cthulhu, I do think they have something to do with what's going on with Elijah and whatever happened to you last night."

Suze blew out a breath, like she wasn't used to talking so much. Baylee figured that was most likely true.

Ralph looked at Baylee for a long moment, like he was trying to figure something out or read her expression. Cognitively, Baylee decided Suze and Ralph were right. It did make the most sense.

But she couldn't make herself feel it was the truth.

Ralph spun decisively in his chair. "Let's try something. Just for the sake of covering all the bases, okay? Let's *pretend* for the moment that everything you saw was actually and literally true. Just for the heck of it. Cool?"

Baylee and Suze nodded.

"Okay," Ralph said, lifting his tablet. "Let's start with Timothy. What else do you know about him?"

Baylee stiffened, not liking where this might be headed—she hadn't shared the intimate details of their physical relationship, such as it was. But then after last night, there wasn't much to lose.

"Um . . . I don't know, he's got an old car . . ."

"What do you know about it?"

"It's a 1936 Ford."

Ralph started typing. "All right. Anything else?"

"He likes jazz, I guess? Or like, swing music?"

"Swing," Ralph said thoughtfully.

"Ella," Baylee added, but couldn't remember the whole name. "Ella someone."

"Ella Fitzgerald," Suze said quietly.

"That's it, yeah. He likes her. How do you guys know this stuff?"

"My grandparents," Ralph said. "They swing dance. Or they did, till Gramma broke her hip."

He wasn't looking at her when he said it, so Baylee didn't hide a smile. It was sweet. Ralph was a real person with real grandparents who did cool stuff like swing dance.

"So, here's what I'm thinking," Ralph said, scanning his search results. "In terms of brain development, we start listening to our own music around fourteen. Before that, we tend to listen to whatever our parents do. So let's say he was fourteen when Ella Fitzgerald was in her prime, say 1938 . . . that would make him . . ."

Baylee's math classes kicked in. "Ninety-seven."

Ralph spun the chair toward her. "Something like that."

"That's a jump," Suze said.

"No, I know," Ralph said. "We're just playing around. Anything else, Baylee? About him?"

She struggled, still not wanting to discuss her sexual life with them. But one thought did lead to another, taking her down a rabbit hole of memories, and another detail—not about Timothy, but Elijah—cropped up.

"There was a book," she said. "A big book, black. It might've been leather bound. I don't know. I think—sorry, I *assume* Derby or Sean gave it to Elijah, and he's been reading it at home. I thought it was just a D&D rule book."

"Black leather bound book," Ralph said, and looked at Suze. "A grimoire?"

Suze frowned at him. "Ralph, it could be filled with recipes."

"If Baylee's right about what she saw, then it wasn't recipes," Ralph snapped.

It struck Baylee as uncharacteristic of him, using a tone like that with Suze. She then understood what Ralph was trying to do. It wasn't that he had changed his mind and suddenly believed Derby had turned into some kind of monster; he just wanted Baylee to feel like he cared enough to give it consideration.

Baylee smiled again, and it hurt just a little. She paid him back the best way she knew: by playing along.

"All right, Dungeon Master," she said, kindly. "If it's all literally true, then what is she? What did she turn into?"

"Well . . . you said it was a quarter moon last night, so we can scratch traditional werewolf. You've seen them in the sun, so we scratch vampires . . ."

"Excuse me," Suze said quietly. "Since werewolves and vampires don't actually exist, we might want to take whatever make-believe rules we know about them and throw them out the window."

"What I saw was not make-believe," Baylee said.

"I'm not saying it was," Suze replied, dipping her chin. "I'm saying that traditions of vampires and werewolves must be discarded. Even if that's what they are, it's a waste of time to use movies or D&D books in an attempt to find a way to stop them."

"Stop them?" Baylee asked softly. This wasn't a plan she'd even remotely considered.

Suze looked Baylee in the eye. "We know what happened to Fletcher. What was done to his body. That's a matter of a record. Same with your parents. So either you were thinking about them when you imagined what you saw . . . or it did really happen, and if so, they're the ones who killed him and maybe your parents too. And if that's all true? Then they will kill again."

Silence.

Baylee thought such a speech ought to have been more

cinematic—a creepy musical score, perhaps, or a slow zoom up to her face. That didn't happen. Suze was just stating a fact, like she was answering a question in class.

"*If* I'm right," Baylee said, glancing them both.

Suze lowered her eyes. "Yes," she whispered. "If."

"You believe me," Baylee said to her, trying but failing to not sound surprised.

"I believe a lot more goes on in this world than we ever see," she whispered, still looking at her knees. "And I know Elijah has changed. That's all. Don't get me wrong, I still believe some kind of drugs make the most sense. But . . . who knows."

"Thank you," Baylee said, meaning it.

Suze flashed her lightning-quick smile.

Ralph's expression showed a blend of fear and possibility. "You've, um . . . got a point. Nobody imagined what happened to Fletcher."

Baylee gestured to Suze. "But I could have had him in the back of my mind and—what's it called—projected it into some kind of drug-induced craziness?"

Ralph's expression didn't change. "It's the most likely possibility, yeah. But, well, hell. Not the only one."

Baylee rubbed her eyes, exhausted. Now they were talking in circles, and it wasn't helping.

"Maybe you should lay down," Ralph said. "You look wiped out."

"Yeah." Baylee stood up, and so did Ralph. Ever the gentleman.

"Thanks for your help," Baylee said. "I appreciate it. If you hear from Elijah, would you let me know? Even if I'm asleep?"

Ralph and Suze agreed they would. Baylee carried herself out of Ralph's room and down the hall to one of two guest rooms, shutting the door behind her. The room reminded her of a hotel, everything white and sterile with no sense that actual people ever lived in it. But the bed was huge and the mattress soft, and not long after laying down on top of the comforter, she was out cold.

The nightmares started almost instantly. But they didn't wake her up. Her body and mind were far too tired for that. Baylee stayed asleep till after the sun had gone down, when Ralph woke her up. She jerked awake and blinked, startled. Ralph, who'd been standing over her, gently shaking her shoulder, took a step back.

"Uhh?" Baylee grunted, trying to force herself awake.

"Baylee," Ralph said. "It's Elijah."

"He called?"

"No." Ralph swallowed nervously. "He's here."

t w e l v e

Baylee pulled herself upright, slowly. "Okay."

"What do you want to do?"

"See him, I guess."

"You sure?"

"No."

But she walked out the door anyway. Still slowly.

"You might want to know," Ralph said quietly as they walked toward the stairs. "My mom invited him in."

"Yeah, so?"

Ralph's expression shifted suddenly, like he regretted having said anything. "I just mean . . . like, if he's a vampire? Then he's, you know . . . been invited in?"

"Um, okay," Baylee said, vaguely remembering something about vampire lore.

They reached the stop of the stairs, and Baylee descended cautiously with Ralph close behind. Elijah sat reclining in the sitting room, watching the staircase. As soon as they made eye contact, he stood up and said her name.

Baylee felt an odd sensation then; on the one hand,

he looked and sounded like her old brother. Legitimately worried, legitimately confused.

On the other hand, a part of her did not believe it. He was acting. Baylee could not specify what made her think that, and it could've just been the aftermath of whatever it was she'd experienced the night before.

Still, though.

"What the hell is going on?" Elijah said when she got to the floor. Neither Mr. nor Mrs. Silverberg were within eyesight, and Baylee didn't hear any signs of them nearby. Elijah stayed by his chair.

"You tell me," Baylee said.

He raised his palms. "Okay," he said, his eyes bugging for a moment. "How about, I got calls from Ari and John that I had to go talk to the police about something that had happened to Krista?"

"*Did* you talk to the cops?"

"Of course I did!"

"What'd you tell them?"

Elijah barked out a sound of disbelief. "That I was hanging out with Timothy all night at his house."

"So you *do* know Timothy!"

"Yeah? We met the other day. He's friends with Nora and Sean."

"Friends! Yeah, okay. More like monster friends!"

Which ranked as the number one most absurd thing she'd ever said in her entire life. Even Ralph looked like he knew it.

Elijah did not conceal one of his new smirks. "I don't know what drugs you're taking, but you've gone full-on whackadoodle."

"What about what happened in the desert, huh?"

"Sis," Elijah said slowly, "I still don't know what exactly it is you think happened, or what you think you saw. All I know is that you stole Ari's car, drove out to the desert, and passed out. And that whatever it was you dreamed about really freaked you out. So, again, what the hell is going on, and why is Ralph looking at me like I just discovered the Wand of Kolorom?"

Baylee licked her lips. She needed water. She needed a bathroom. "So you weren't out there. That's your story."

"Where? Out in the middle of the desert somewhere? No. I was watching movies with Timothy, Nora, and Sean. You can ask them."

"They were there too, behind that hill."

"What *hill*, what are you talking about?"

Baylee Ross had gone insane.

It was that simple. She was absolutely, totally freaking bonkers. That was the only realistic suggestion. Baylee ran down the list of evidence: Something had changed about Elijah, yes; she wasn't the only one who'd seen that. And truthfully, yes, she remained messed up in the head over Krista's disappearance—whether that disappearance was Krista's choice or someone else's. She was living with two people who weren't her real family. Her old friends were all out of state, her new friends only talked to her during school hours. The only guys who'd shown any interest in her were the Dork Master and . . . and what, *a ninety-seven-year-old vampire praying mantis*?

Taken all together, and accepting, at last, that real life was not a D&D game, Baylee was left with few other conclusions.

"Sorry," she mumbled.

"For what, exactly?" Elijah said.

"I don't know, I just . . . I don't know. I guess I had a really weird night, and . . . I don't know, you're *different.*"

"You called the cops because I stopped playing an RPG every single day during summer vacation? My fucking bad."

Ralph reacted to that, blinking and sucking in his stomach as if punched.

"Baylee, the next time you have something to talk to me about," Elijah said, walking toward the front door, "how about you just ask me instead."

"I've been texting you!" Baylee shouted after him.

He opened the door. "Yeah, and after this, do you really wonder why I don't feel like talking to you? Get a life, Baylee."

"Fletcher's dead!" Ralph screamed.

Baylee turned to him. All of Ralph's anger and grief was smeared across his features like crimson paint.

Elijah paused and visibly released a sigh. "Yeah. So I hear."

He walked out the door, shutting but not slamming it behind him. A moment later, Baylee heard a car start up and roll down the street.

She and Ralph stood still for a minute. He started to reach out, to touch her shoulder possibly, but then quickly dropped his hand again.

"Sorry, Baylee," he said quietly.

She stared at the closed door. "No. It's me. I'm a nut factory. I make everybody nuts."

"Is there anything I can do?"

"No. I'm going to go home."

"I can get my mom or dad to take you."

"It's okay. I think I need to walk."

"You want me to walk with you? I will."

"With all those flesh eating monsters out and about?" Baylee said, smiling painfully. "I'll be all right."

Ralph didn't see the humor. "Fletcher is still dead. Something did do that, whether it was a werewolf pack or not. Let me get you a ride. I can even take you myself, I've got my license."

"No, thanks. I really do want to walk."

Ralph didn't reply, and didn't look happy.

"It's not even twenty minutes," she reminded him. "I'm just going to go." Baylee started for the stairs, then paused and put *her* hand on *his* shoulder. "Thanks a lot, Ralph. Seriously. You really went above and beyond. I appreciate it."

Ralph took a deep breath, held it, then nodded and exhaled a thank you.

"Do you believe me?" Baylee asked, because suddenly, she really wanted to know this.

After a long hesitation, he said, "I'll tell you this. When I was about five, I thought I saw a ghost in my room. I think in hindsight it was just the way the light from the hall was hitting my door or something? I don't know. But it kept me up all night, paralyzed, just staring at this white form, you know? And I told my dad about it in the morning, and you know what he said?"

He paused, so Baylee shook her head for him.

"My dad said, 'Rollie, if there was a ghost, it probably was just saying hello. They get lonely sometimes. Or maybe it needed your help. Or maybe it was just a dream or your imagination. But don't worry about it. If you see it again, come get me.'"

Ralph smiled a little.

"And I always thought that was so cool," he went on. "He didn't say I was stupid or making things up. He just rolled with it. Like maybe it was really true, but that I didn't have to be afraid of it. I always loved that about him."

He turned his gaze toward her.

"So do I believe you? Literally? In my heart, no. I'm a geek, but I'm a skeptical geek. Most geeks are, is the thing. Maybe it was a dream or your imagination, like my ghost. But, if you see something again . . ."

Ralph shrugged a bit.

"Come get me."

The whole story and the way he used it to answer made Baylee feel more relaxed than she had in the last twenty-four hours. Or longer.

"Thanks, Ralph," she said, and went upstairs to get her bag. She stepped into Ralph's room long enough to say good-bye to Suze and thank her. She almost went to find and thank the Silverbergs, but veered off, thinking she wouldn't get her walk if she told them she was going. They'd probably insist on driving the crazy girl home. Or straight to Ari's inpatient clinic.

Ralph waited for her by the front door, and walked her to the curb.

"Thanks again," Baylee said.

"You can call or text if you need anything. I mean it, anything."

"I know."

"Good. Be safe."

Ralph stayed on the sidewalk, watching, until she'd turned the corner out of his neighborhood.

The first few minutes, Baylee expected Timothy's '36 or the brown van to come rumbling alongside and kidnap her. By the time she was halfway home, that fear had turned on her and became self-loathing.

But when she turned onto her street and saw Timothy and Elijah standing by the '36 and talking, she pulled up short. They both swiveled their heads her direction as soon as she saw them, and neither of them looked surprised. Or even angry. Their expressions said, *Well, there she is.* As if this were expected.

Baylee walked fast, taking a sharp right up the driveway, head down. If they wanted to let her go without talking, that would be fine.

Except they didn't.

"Sounds like you had rough night," Timothy said as she zoomed past.

She didn't stop.

"Sorry to hear that," he called after her.

Baylee reached the front door and opened it.

"We should hang out again soon," Timothy added in a casual shout.

He was pissed. Baylee couldn't blame him. She went inside and shut the door, walking straight back to her room and closing the door. Her heart raced as she sat on the edge of her bed, wondering vaguely if she was hungry or nauseous.

Timothy had not sounded like a werewolf, or a vampire, or even a homunculus.

Frustrated, Baylee got back up and went to the living room, peeking at her brother and Timothy through the blinds. Watching them stand there, leaning easily on the car, hands in their pockets, laughing every now and then, they looked for all the world like a couple of modern James Deans biding their time to conquer a world they didn't care about in the least.

Baylee's doubts petrified. Like being turned to stone by a medusa in a deep dungeon. Whatever happened to me, she thought, bottom line is I didn't see what I thought I did. Period. Even the idea that Timothy had drugged me makes less sense than that I . . . I've had some kind of emotional snap.

She sulked back to her room just as Ari poked her head out of their bedroom at the end of the hall.

"Bay?" she said, her eyes winced. "That you? You okay?"

Baylee went to her and hugged her close. "Yes. I'm sorry for last night."

Ari hugged her back. "No, no, it's okay, we're just glad you're safe. . . . All right, it's *not* okay, but you know what I mean, right?"

"Yeah."

"Okay. Good."

Baylee pulled back. "Listen, that drug test? It's going to come back negative."

"I don't doubt it."

"But let's just say someone slipped me something, would that show up?"

Panic creased Ari's face. "You mean a date rape drug."

"Maybe. Or something—"

204

"Are you hurt? Have you been—"

"No! Sorry, no, it's not like that. I'm just trying to figure out all the angles. I don't think that's what happened."

Ari relaxed, and toyed with her hair. "Well, me, either. Yes, it would show up. You sure you're okay here? What about the Silverbergs?"

"I'm fine."

"Have you talked to your brother?"

"Mostly. Sort of. I'll handle it. Have *you?*"

"We talked. Mostly about this new girlfriend of his. Some new clarifications are in place, let's say."

"Nice. Good."

Ari smiled. "And now, without further ado, good night. Would you both please stay in the house all night?"

"You got it."

Ari shuffled back to her bedroom and shut the door. Baylee went to her own, but left the door open, sitting at her desk, head in her hands. She whispered to herself, "Maybe you do need help."

"Help with what?"

She jumped out of her chair with a yelp. Elijah stood in the doorway, looking at least partly smug and pleased with himself.

"Nothing!" Baylee said. "Or, I mean . . . no, nothing. Hey."

"Hey."

"Listen," Baylee said, taking a step closer. "I didn't get a chance to tell you . . . or, I guess I did, but maybe I wasn't really clear . . . I just, I'm sorry about everything today."

"Duly noted."

"You really have changed, though."

"Into what?"

"Not a *what*, Lij, just . . . I don't know. You're different. And it bugs me. It *hurts*, okay? There, it hurts."

She thought she saw his eyes narrow ever so slightly. "Okay."

"Is this the new you, is this what I have to look forward to?"

"Pretty much." His voice was perfectly flat.

"Okay, well, I guess I have to deal then, huh?"

"Looks like it."

"Fine. Will you at least give me a hug?"

He looked pained. "Certainly. Any time."

She put her arms around him. He did the same. She couldn't say it was a terribly warm hug, but it was something. His skin was cool. Like Timothy's.

Baylee rested her head against his chest, and again wondered if he'd started working out, because his chest seemed a lot—

Silence.

thirteen

Baylee's breath congealed in her lungs, weighing them down. She couldn't breathe. Couldn't move. Her eyes shocked open and stayed that way as her right ear pressed harder and harder into the sinewy muscle covering her brother's chest.

Total silence.

Stillness.

Baylee pulled away from Elijah as if he were a great white shark that might strike.

"You all right, sis?"

"It's you." Baylee was unable to raise her voice above a whisper. "You—you *were* there, you *did* do it, you killed Krista."

Elijah frowned sadly and pulled out his cell phone. He began typing. "That's a hell of a thing to say."

"Why can't I hear your heart beat?"

"Eh, who knows. Maybe your ears are all plugged up with dirt. Have you even showered since yesterday?"

She hadn't. And hadn't realized it. It was the least of her concerns.

"You cut your heart out," Baylee said, slowly stepping backward. No plan, just the need to move away, to run.

"Did I?" Elijah took a step, keeping the same distance between them. That small adjustment sent adrenalin flooding her system. It was predatory.

Everything in her wanted to scream. But what about Ari and John? What would he do to them? Yet more pressing at the moment:

"What are you going to do to me?"

"Do to you?" Elijah laughed.

They matched slow steps again. "Stay away from me . . ."

"Why."

"You're some kind of monster!"

"Wow. Never thought I'd see the day my little sister became the geek of the family."

He smiled then. His teeth seemed longer.

She'd reached the kitchen doorway. A few more feet, and she'd be at the front door. Baylee reached behind her for the door knob, not wanting to take her eyes off Elijah. Except instead of the knob, she touched cloth. A shirt. Cool skin.

Timothy.

Baylee whirled around with a yelp. Timothy held up his hands. "Sorry I startled you. Everything okay?"

Now she backed into Elijah and yelped again. They were on either side of her.

"Please," she breathed.

"Please what?" Elijah said.

"Please don't hurt me!"

"Hurt you?" Elijah said. "Why would either one of us do that?"

"No, no, it's all right," Timothy said to him. "She needs to know the whole story now. Baylee? Will you come outside with me?"

"I'll scream!" she—whispered.

Timothy sighed. "I'd rather you didn't. Your foster parents seem like good people. I don't want anything to happen to them."

There.

At last, an actual threat. Any miniscule doubts she had remaining evaporated. This was for real.

Whatever "real" meant anymore.

"What do you want?" she said, her voice as dry as concrete.

"For you to come outside," Timothy said. "That's all."

"You're going to kill me."

"No, as a matter of actual fact. That is the very last thing I want to do. Come on outside, hmm?"

So she went.

By that point, terror had laid red-hot beams of steel in place of Baylee's bones, burning her from the inside. She had no spit, and her vision seemed reduced to a point the width of a quarter. But she also couldn't resist him, not if she wanted to protect Ari and John. Protect them from what had happened to Mom and Dad.

Mom and Dad. Had they known? Had they seen? Derby or Sean or Timothy or all of them, they'd killed Janey and Ken Ross. Baylee knew this with piercing clarity. Now they were here to finish the job.

Finish it, or—or what?

"I think she's freaking out," Elijah said as he put a hand on Baylee's elbow. His touch was bitterly cold.

"She'll be okay," Timothy said.

Numb, Baylee walked outside with them. A blast of summer wind cut through her clothes but did nothing to cool the panicked fire sweltering through her body.

"Put her in the car," Timothy said. It didn't sound like an order, but Elijah followed it like one. The next thing she knew, she was in the back seat of the '36 with Timothy sitting beside her, Elijah in the passenger seat.

"Now, Baylee," Timothy said. "We should really talk. Okay? That's all. Just talk."

"Y-you're a monster."

"If you want to call it that."

Stunned, she couldn't help staring at him. "You don't deny it? You're not going to lie about it?"

"You obviously saw us. That's not how I wanted this to go down, but, eh. What can you do."

Baylee turned to Elijah. He sat staring forward, not looking back.

"Derby killed Krista. You let her do it, you stood there and watched."

Elijah didn't say anything. His head tilted a bit, like he was looking out the side window, but that was all.

"I hate you," Baylee said.

"I know," Elijah said. "Just listen."

"You need to start thinking ahead, Baylee," Timothy said. "You need to start considering your future."

"You're gonna kill me."

"Why do you keep saying that?" Timothy said, and *laughed*. "No, I'm not. Nobody is. Matter of fact, if anyone tried, I'd take them out myself."

Baylee was going to throw up. No—she was going to

pass out. No—she was going to throw up then pass out. She ended up not doing either one despite the way her brain spun behind her eyes. "Why are you doing this to me?"

"Elijah? Give us a minute, will you?"

Elijah glanced at Timothy, but obediently climbed out and shut the door. He stood with his back against it like a bouncer. The '36 had only the two doors, so there was no way for her to get past Timothy or her brother. She took a deep breath, to scream, but found she couldn't. All that came out was a little squeak.

She'd watched so many movies, so many shows. Shows like *Lucky 13* where the heroine can fight for herself, and she'd simply started believing she would do that, too, if it ever came down to it. She'd watched less heroic women just scream for help in horror movies and on police procedurals. The reality was a lot different. The reality is, Baylee thought, you don't know what your body will do until it's there, till the thing is going down.

Till a werewolf is kidnapping you in a 1936 Ford.

"You're werewolves," Baylee whispered.

"What? No!" Timothy said. "Werewolves don't exist. I know this is a lot to take in, but believe me, silver bullets are not the answer here."

"You're really not going to kill me?"

"We're really not."

"How come?"

"Well," Timothy said, looking amused, "if I was broody teenager with a mysterious past on a quest for self-redemption, I'd say it's because of love. But I'm none of those things, and 'love' isn't quite the right word. It's more of a craving. You know how you're sitting in school, and suddenly you can't wait to have some specific food? Maybe it's Taco Bell, or a certain flavor of ice cream? Pretty soon it's all you can think about, and nothing will substitute for it. That's not love. But it's definitely *something*, isn't it?"

"You're . . . going to *eat* me?" Her thoughts turned swiftly to Krista. To the sounds.

"No. That would mean killing you, and for the last time, your life is in no danger whatsoever. Seriously, Baylee, that's the last time I'm going to explain that. You need to calm down and start thinking what places on Earth you'd like to visit. You're going to have lots of time."

Baylee struggled to swallow. She remembered counting the years since Ella Fitzgerald was around, or since 1936. "How old are you?"

"Three million of your Earth years."

She sucked in a breath. They were *aliens?*

Timothy burst into laughter. "Sorry! Just kidding, couldn't resist. Believe me, it doesn't matter how old I am. How long do *you* want to live?"

"I thought you said you weren't going to kill me."

"I'm asking you how long you *want* to live. Seventy years? Eighty? A hundred and ten?"

"As long as possible," she muttered.

"Two hundred?"

"Two hundred *years?*"

"How about three hundred?" Timothy went on. "How about five, or ten?"

"Vampires," Baylee whispered.

"Wow, kid. You're not paying any attention whatsoever."

She leaned forward. "Please stop this. Please. I'll do anything."

"Stop what, what are you asking?"

"I want my brother back!"

"What makes you think you lost him?"

"He's not himself. Whatever it is you did to him, it changed him."

"Or it merely revealed who he's been this entire time. Elijah will live forever. Isn't that what you want for him? Isn't that what you want for *yourself?*"

Baylee tried to block his words, but they sank in, like blades.

"Instead of worrying about how to change your brother into something he clearly didn't want to be," Timothy said, gently, "why not consider becoming what he is?"

"I don't want to be like that."

"Like what?"

"A murderer!"

"Everyone dies, Baylee. You of all people know that."

"My parents . . ."

Timothy shrugged. "Random chance. Everything is random when it comes to death. So is what happened to Krista. They happened to be at certain places at certain times, nothing more. Just like your parents."

"So you did do it. You killed them."

"They died, yes."

Arguing about it wasn't going to change anything. "And Fletcher."

"Could have been anybody. What if he was born in Michigan instead? Or Russia? It's all random."

"I don't believe you."

"Believe what you want. Considering where we are right now, you have to figure I have nothing to gain by lying about that."

215

"Just about everything else." She tried to make the words sharp, to stab him, but she could see it didn't work.

"Yes," Timothy said with a single nod. "Just about everything else. Anyone who doesn't believe in dumb luck and random chance has never been the victim in a car accident. Hasn't had to watch a kid die from some horrible disease he couldn't have prevented."

He paused.

"Well . . . all right, to be totally honest, one thing that isn't necessarily random is you."

She shrank back.

"See, when we ate your mom and dad—and we did—I smelled you. *They* smelled awful, by the way. Like casinos. But underneath that, Baylee, was you. Just as clear as a bell. And I knew you needed to be next. When I found your picture in your father's wallet, that sealed it."

Timothy shifted in the seat. Baylee jumped. He either didn't notice or pretended not to.

"See, we have to procreate every so often, just like people. It's maybe not quite as straightforward as how people do it, but it's still an urge. An imperative. We can't resist it. I knew I needed to do it soon, and I decided to find you. So I did. And as a favor for me, Nora did the same for your brother. The more I got to know you, the more I thought this would all be easier if Elijah was already one of us. We watched you for a year. Do you understand how long that is? How serious I am about giving this gift to you?"

Baylee shook her head. He was confusing her. On purpose or not, she didn't know. But she had to stay focused.

216

"I want my brother back. Whatever you did to him, whatever happened, just undo it, make it stop. Please. And then leave us alone. Okay? I'll do anything."

"Hmm. Anything?"

A cold twist of nausea unspooled in her intestines.

Timothy steepled his fingers beneath his chin. "Tell you what. Come with me, don't fight, and I'll change him back."

"What is he? What are *you?*"

"Oh, who knows," Timothy said dismissively. "We've been called so many things over the years. It doesn't really matter."

It does matter, because it'll help me figure out how to end you, Baylee thought. Followed quickly by, This cannot really be happening.

"So what do you say?" Timothy asked. "Do we have a deal?"

"I don't understand. Come with you where?"

"Out to the desert. Or wherever is convenient. We chose that spot because it was nearby, but isolated."

"So you could kill Krista!"

"Not *just* that. Outside is sort of traditional. Maybe more than that, I'm honestly not sure. We don't have to do it outside though . . . you really are hung up on this Krista thing, aren't you? We needed to eat. Now I need to procreate. Sean took care of his business awhile back, so you'll be the last to come along for awhile, if that helps. It won't be too crowded."

Unsurprisingly, Baylee had no response. She shut her mouth and wrapped her arms as tightly around herself as she could, praying to find a way out of this.

Desperately, she said, "Give me some time to think about it?"

"Okay."

Baylee wrinkled her forehead, unsure she'd heard him correctly. "Are—you're serious?"

"Sure. I'm in no rush. But then, neither is Elijah. Not any more."

"You want me to be like him?"

"Of course! I've spent all this time seeing if you were a good fit. You are."

"Why me?"

"Why not?"

"I'm serious! Why would you want to turn me into whatever the hell it is you turned Elijah into? Huh?"

"I just go where I'm told," Timothy said.

"Wh-who told you?"

"Whoever made us like this."

"Who is that?" She had some theories, but they all sounded just as insane as this conversation.

"We don't know. That's just the way he set it up."

Baylee couldn't help herself asking: "Who's 'he?'"

"If I knew that, I'd be a lot stronger than I am now. We've only ever known him as He. Or maybe he's a she, I wouldn't put it past him. Or her."

"Are you . . . talking about . . . the *devil?*"

Timothy laughed. Despite everything—it remained charming.

"The devil? Oh, sweetie." Shaking his head, Timothy went on: "There is one little flaw in the process. You have to do it yourself. We can't force you. I mean, we could tie you down, strap the knife to your hand, and force you that way, but we tried it a couple times, and it doesn't work. Also it's messy."

"That's it?" Baylee almost returned his laugh. "Well then, no! Hell no! There. Now you can leave me alone."

"Oh, I can still make you and your family rather uncomfortable," Timothy said, and Baylee's intestines twisted the other direction. "But I don't want that. I want you to choose."

"Why would I do that?"

"Like I said. I'll turn your brother back, if that's what's important to you."

"You mean you *can*?"

"Certainly," Timothy said, looking at her as if the question was insane, not the topic.

"But he doesn't h-have a . . . a har . . . a har . . ."

She couldn't say it. Couldn't even begin to consider doing it herself, whatever evil magic had let Elijah go through with his own evisceration.

"Think about it this way," Timothy said. "The kind of power it takes to keep us up and running without a heart? Not that difficult to give it back to him. You see what I'm saying? It's magic, sweetie. *Big* magic."

"Let me think about it," Baylee said again.

"Certainly."

He climbed out of the '36 like quicksilver, smooth and elegant. Baylee shoved her way out of the car and backed up the driveway. Timothy and her brother watched her.

Somehow figuring she was safe now that she was out of the car, Baylee shouted, "I'm telling the police! I'm telling them everything, you son of a bitch!"

"Feel free," Timothy said. "But you should know, I've

been at this an awfully long time. I don't think they'll be able to do much."

She didn't answer.

"Anyway," Timothy said. "Let me know what you decide. Take care, Baylee."

He and Elijah got into the Ford and drove down the street, leaving Baylee alone on the driveway in the heavy heat of a July night, wondering if maybe she'd sleepwalked out here and everything had been a dream.

But it hadn't. This whole God-awful thing was really happening, and she didn't have the first clue what to do about it. Really, unless she wanted to gouge out her own heart, there was only one choice.

She ran into the house and scrambled through her bag, pawing through books and papers until she found the business card for Officer Russell Shaw. She grabbed her cell and dialed his number. He didn't answer, of course, but Baylee left a message, measuring her words as carefully as she could.

She told him she'd seen Krista, that Derby had killed her, and the location.

She did not mention anything about monsters.

Then, holding the phone close, Baylee backed into one corner of her room and drew her legs up to her chest, shaking.

○

"Baylee. *Baylee*."

She startled awake, swinging her hands in useless fists. One of them connected with skin.

Ari grunted and fell back. "Baylee, *stop*."

She came fully awake then, blinking. Her fingers loosened and dropped the phone. She'd slept sitting up in the corner.

"There's someone here to see you," Ari said, rubbing her head where Baylee had hit her.

"What? Who?"

"A cop. Detective Mills. He said you called an officer who spoke to you about Krista."

Wincing, Baylee glared around at her room. The color and angle of sunlight bathing the walls suggested it wasn't morning.

"What time is it?"

"After noon. You've been asleep. Here, stand up."

Baylee let Ari help her up. They went out to the living room, where Detective Mills stood peering out the bay window at the street. He turned when he heard them, and gave Baylee a professional smile. He wore a grey suit that looked old.

"Baylee. How are you?"

"Been better," Baylee said, swaying from lack of food. She had to put one hand on the wall.

"Let me fix you something," Ari said. "Will you be okay in here, or?"

She nodded. Mills gestured to the couch, so Baylee sat. He took a chair nearby.

"I'm glad you called," he began.

That woke her up. "You found them?"

"Well, I wanted to come hear it from you in person. Tell me what happened."

Baylee hesitated. Tell him everything? Derby turning into a insect monster of some kind, all the rest of it?

But then, what else could she do? Glossing over the important parts wouldn't help the police find them.

"Okay," Baylee began. "I'm going to just go ahead and say everything, but it's going to sound crazy. I know that. But I, I really need you to listen. Okay? Even if it sounds nuts."

"All right," Mills said with a serious expression on his face.

So Baylee rubbed her eyes and, once more, divulged the entire story, all the way up through last night on the driveway. She noticed Mills did not take any notes. As she finished, Baylee noticed Ari standing in the doorway between the living room and kitchen, holding a mug and an English muffin on a plate. The mug wasn't steaming. Baylee wondered how long she'd been listening. Ari's expression suggested it had been long enough.

"Hmm," Mills said after Baylee had stopped talking for more than a minute. Ari blinked and came over, putting the plate down on an end table and mumbling something about reheating cocoa.

"Do you believe even a little tiny bit of any of that?" Baylee asked helplessly.

"Cops tend to be pretty skeptical folks," Mills said. "And I can tell you that I talked to the county police who went out to that hill—"

"They went?"

"Yep. It's out of my jurisdiction, but we had them check it out. Baylee, they didn't find anything out there. These are men and women who are pretty good about finding stuff."

Baylee sank deeper into the couch cushions. *I've been at this a long time*, Timothy's voice echoed in her head.

Ari returned and set the mug beside her untouched breakfast. Or lunch. Or whatever it was supposed to be. The scent of warm almond milk and organic powdered chocolate absurdly underscored the futility of any of this. Ari came around and sat near her on the couch, hands folded between her knees, and only then did it occur to Baylee that she should have been at work.

"You don't seem surprised that they didn't find anything," Mills went on.

Baylee shook her head. She wasn't. She'd seen it for herself. "What about Krista? If I didn't see her, then where is she?"

"Well, that, we don't know. She hasn't checked in, but the missing clothes and backpack strongly suggest she ran away. We see this sort of thing a lot."

"She'd take her phone."

"She could pick up a burner at any convenience store. She's probably savvy enough to know we could ping it if wanted to, that's why she left hers."

"But I have a really bad feeling about all this!" It felt stupid even as she said it.

Mills nodded in an understanding manner. "And my first response when you say that tends to be 'That's nice.' Really bad feelings often don't amount to much, I'm afraid."

"Can't you do something?"

"We're doing everything we can, believe me. But right now, she's a runaway."

"But she's not, I'm telling you, she's not the type!"

"Have you ever been mad at your parents?" Mills asked, not unkindly. "Wanted to get away from it all? Or what if a cute boy at school invites you out for a little drink, maybe smoke a little something. Anyone can be a runaway. I understand your feelings, but try to understand ours: there is absolutely no evidence to suggest that anything strange has happened. That's not to say we aren't worried, of course we are, because runaways tend to get themselves into a lot of trouble. But in terms of what we can do when a person doesn't want to be found, there's just not a lot."

Baylee sensed more than saw him trade a glance with Ari just before he stood up. "We're still keeping an eye out for her. I'm sure as soon as we find her, she or her parents will get in touch."

Baylee didn't answer. Mills and Ari exchanged thanks and goodbyes. As he walked out the front door, John walked in, looking serious. So they were both taking the day off? Except, John looked flustered, like he'd been in a hurry to get home . . .

Then Baylee understood, before they even said it.

John came into the living room and stood near the couch as Ari reached out to touch Baylee's arm.

"Baylee? We'd like you to come with us now, okay?"

"To your work."

"Just for some tests."

"I'm not on anything."

John said, "We know, Bay. Lydia called with the results. And we're not surprised by that at all. But something's going kinda kerflewy, and we need to see if we can figure out what it is."

"You think I'm crazy."

They said "No" at exactly the same time.

"But we do think you need a little help getting through whatever is going on," Ari continued. "You're definitely under a whole lot of stress, for one thing. And, in my opinion, a whole lot of backed up feelings that you've never maybe really unpacked. It's time we do that."

"What do you say?" John asked, gently. "It won't be so bad. The sooner we address this, the sooner you'll feel better."

"Where's Elijah?"

"Well, we're not a hundred percent sure," John said. "Out with his friends, as far as we know. He's probably not too hip on being communicative with us right now."

Baylee stood up. "Can I take a shower?"

"Of course," Ari said, standing also.

Baylee picked up the English muffin—she might be crazy or doomed or both, but she needed to eat. She walked toward the hallway when Ari's voice stopped her.

"And go ahead and pack a quick bag," she said, trying to sound casual. "Just, you know."

Without turning, Baylee asked, "For how long?"

"Well, we'll figure that out. Just pack, you know . . . for a few nights."

Baylee shuffled to the bathroom without a word. Shut the door, leaned on the counter, peered into her own eyes as deep as she could. Who was in there? Herself, or some shade of herself?

John, Ari, Mills—hell, even Ralph and Suze. They all had a point. She couldn't prove a single thing she'd said the past two days. She knew she was right, but her rightness was a nightmare. Unreal. Impossible. And now it was a few minutes from landing her in a psycho ward.

For a few nights.

They would come for her. The pack of them—

Timothy, Derby, Sean. They'd come for her sooner or later, and they might hurt John and Ari in the process. Or maybe Ralph would be next, or Suze. They'd already taken Elijah and Krista, and easily.

"No," she said to her reflection.

No, she would not let that happen. She had to protect all of them from what she knew.

Baylee tilted her head to look up at the narrow horizontal window inset just below the ceiling. This bathroom looked out over the backyard. The trash got picked up in an alley behind that.

"Roll the bones," Baylee whispered, only half aware she was doing so.

She went back to her room and packed the bag Ari had suggested. Enough clothes for a couple of nights, her phone, wallet, and every dollar she could scrounge up. Then she changed her clothes—black jeans, boots, fitted navy blue long-sleeve. Kira Thirteen would approve. She pulled her hair back tight and wound it up in a red hair tie. All right, so she didn't *look* anything like Kira, but Baylee definitely felt a lot more like her. It would have to do.

Carefully, she cracked open the bedroom door to make sure John and Ari wouldn't see her in these different clothes. They were in the kitchen, it sounded. She bolted across the hall and closed and locked the bathroom door. She turned on the shower, hard and loud, then climbed onto the counter and opened the window.

It wasn't an easy fit, but Baylee managed to squeeze through head-first, then wriggle her hips enough to get one leg out before falling to the ground. She landed in a pile, then scampered for the back gate, which was out of sight of the kitchen sliding door.

Heart pounding from the unusual exertion, Baylee raced through the gate, latched it quietly, and kept running on down the alley. She stopped just short of where it emptied into the street, pulled out her phone, and sent one text.

I need to roll a natural 20. Will you help?

Holding the phone, she walked briskly down the street, mentally calculating how long it would take the Wagners to break down the bathroom door and come looking for her. Ten minutes? Twenty? Did she have as much as thirty minutes?

Her phone buzzed. She checked the screen.

Absolutely, Ralph wrote back.

Ignoring the awful heat and her roaring stomach, Baylee broke into a run.

fourteen

Following Ralph's instructions, Baylee uncovered a spare key in the Silverberg's attached laundry room off their patio. She let herself into the house, grateful they had no dogs—Ralph had allergies. Both his parents were gone. Figuring she may as well commit to the role, Baylee raided their fridge for lunch. Cold cuts on French bread—because fuck it, she wanted the protein; fruit salad; and some kind of bubbly flavored water. It all tasted delicious.

Ari called thirty minutes later. Baylee didn't answer. Instead she sent one message:

I need some time. I'm safe. I'll be home soon.

Ari called again. Again Baylee let it go to voicemail. After that followed a few texts, which Baylee read but did not reply to. None of them were exactly thrilled with her behavior.

However, the last message read, **All right. If you're not home by six p.m. I'm calling the police. Don't push me on this. We love you.**

Baylee put her phone away.

Ralph and Suze showed up an hour after that, a little

breathless and eyes wide, like they'd run from the game store, where they'd decided to spend a ridiculous amount of money on pewter BattleTech figures to take their minds off Fletcher's impending service, among other things.

"What's going on, what happened?" Ralph asked immediately, sitting at the kitchen table beside her. "We both tried calling Elijah, but he didn't answer. No texts, either."

Baylee squeezed her arms close around herself again. She could *not* warm up.

"I need your help," she said, unable to make eye contact with them.

"Are you all right?" Suze whispered. She stayed standing.

"Physically, yes."

"That's good." Ralph sat back and wiped his forehead. "Because this DM does not run, and today, I ran. *Not* okay."

He offered her a crooked half-grin.

"Thanks," she said to him.

Ralph stood. "Let's go to my room."

The three of them trooped upstairs, Baylee holding her third bottle of water. Ralph sat at his desk, where several monster manuals lay open. Sheets of paper littered the desk. "You know, I'd be lying if I said this wasn't the start to a lot of interesting daydreams."

"Stop," Suze said, quietly of course, but with a big-sister grin.

"I didn't know where else to go," Baylee said.

"No worries." Ralph closed the D&D books laying open on his desk. "Research," he said, looking embarrassed. He stacked the books and moved them to one side, but

Baylee jumped up and grabbed the top book. She flipped it open.

"What did you find?" she asked, scanning the pages. Pen and ink drawings of absurd, nightmare monsters decorated every page. None looked like Derby.

"Um . . . well, nothing, really," Ralph said, scooting his chair back to give her room. "What do you . . . what happened today, Baylee? What's going on?"

"It's all true," she said. "What I saw in the desert, Krista, what Elijah did . . . it's all true, Timothy admitted it. Elijah too, essentially. You guys, please, I swear to God, you have to believe me. They're some kind of monsters."

Ralph leaned forward, his face utterly serious. "Tell us what happened."

She did, leaving nothing out.

"And now my parents—I mean, Ari and John—they want to have me committed or something. I've got till six o'clock before Ari calls the cops on me. Please, you've got to help me."

"I'm in," Suze stated.

Ralph and Baylee said, at the same time: "You are?"

Suze weighed each word carefully before speaking it. "I'm not saying I believe everything you've seen is for real. But I have been thinking about everything you said yesterday. And the fact is, something took Fletcher from this town and drove him out to the desert, and killed him, and flung pieces of him all over. It was not a mountain lion attack, or a bear. Whatever this is, I want an answer." She shifted her eyes to Ralph. "You and Fletcher and Lij . . . you are the best friends I have ever had. You're my family. Hell yes I'm in."

Ralph took a moment to absorb Suze's demeanor, then said, "Ditto."

Suze got out her iPad, set it on her lap, and swiped another page every couple seconds. "Give me a minute."

Ralph nodded.

Baylee turned back to the books. "Do have any idea what they are? I mean, look at all this stuff." She gestured to the books. "There's got to be something in here."

"Yeah, well, the irony here is that that's *pretend*," Ralph said. "Suze was right about that. We can't trust Hollywood or Wizards of the Coast for an answer."

"But what do you *think?* You still know more about this stuff than I do, help me!"

"Of course," Ralph said quickly, eyes wide. "Um . . . maybe they're not werewolves, but it's definitely some form of lycanthrope. Shapeshifters. Usually that's a werewolf, but there's legends about all kinds of were-animals. All sorts of stuff. Virtually all cultures have shapeshifter myths. Pigs, bears, tigers—"

"*Were-pigs?* Ralph . . ."

"Do you want our help or not?"

"Sorry. Yes. Timothy told me they weren't werewolves."

Ralph's lips twisted around. "What about the book? The leather-bound book you said Elijah was reading. Could you get it?"

"I don't know how. They keep it with them as far as I know. You think it's important?"

"If it *is* some kind of spell book, then yes. It could be a source of power, maybe. But I mean, you have to understand, I'm making this all up as I go."

"It's still more than I came up with. Go ahead."

"Well, Timothy told you there was 'someone else' was behind all this. He even said this was all magical. So I think the book is our best bet."

"To do what, exactly?"

"That, I don't know. Maybe if we burned it, it would kill them." Ralph shook his head. "But listen, I've looked through every book I've got, I've been to places online you don't want to know even exist, and I'm telling you, nothing adds up. Maybe you're wrong about them. Okay? I'm sorry that that's how it is, but—that's how it is."

Baylee drew a breath, ready to shout him down, when Suze leaped to her feet, eyes wide as she stared down at the iPad.

"I know what they are!"

Baylee shot a glare at Ralph.

"Of course, I could be wrong," Ralph sighed.

"What did you find?" she asked Suze.

Suze placed the tablet in the middle of Ralph's bed, and they hovered over it.

"Springheel Jack," Suze said. "Or something like it, anyway."

She pointed to the screen. An old drawing from a woodcut showed a slender figure leaping high into the night sky over a cityscape that reminded Baylee, for no particular reason, of London.

"He dates back to at least 1808," Suze said. "And there are references to him in the United States as recently as 1995."

"Who is he, I don't get it," Baylee said.

"Okay, well, understand we're not talking about something found in nature," Suze said. "This is all urban myth and hearsay and almost certainly hoaxes. There are some newspaper reports from the 1800s, in England, but just because something made it into a newspaper doesn't mean it's factual. Particularly in that time period."

Baylee touched her arm. Suze practically jumped.

"Suze," Baylee said softly. "You don't have to be logical right now. Just put everything on the table like it's gospel truth. Okay?"

Suze hesitated, then nodded. Swiping a couple of pages on the iPad, she went on.

"Springheel Jack, whatever he is, has been described as 'devil-like.' Glowing red eyes, able to leap far distances. Some people say he has a high-pitched laugh."

Baylee inhaled sharply. That fit the Derby-thing to a T.

"He's reported to have brushed off a shotgun blast like it was nothing," Suze went on. "First mention of him in the U.S. is in 1880. There are similar reports from the 1940s and 50s from Chile in South America. Whatever he is, he gets around."

Suze handed the iPad to Baylee, showing another illustration. In it, a skinny man—about as slender as Lij or Timothy, Baylee thought—was running past a woman in Victorian-era clothes. He had impossibly long fingers ending in either long claws or blades.

"In 1838, the *Times* of London wrote an article about him," Suze said. "He'd attacked a woman there. Slashed her stomach. There are dozens of other sightings reported from around the world, but all at different times."

Ralph's eyebrows furrowed as he studied the image. "Meaning what?"

"Meaning even if we're dealing with more than one

Jack, they stick together. Like, there's no report from Kentucky in 1880 and a report from Spain in 1880 at the same time, too. The Jack, or jacks I guess, bounce from place to place. Here, look."

She leaned over Baylee, swiping pages. Baylee realized as she did it that it was Suze's own book and writings she was referring to. Her monster manual.

"West Kent, England, 1837. Aberdeen, 1860. Birmingham, 1879. Edinburgh, 1880. Manchester, 1885. Newfoundland, 1928. Glasgow, 1935. He gets around. Or *they* get around, whichever."

"Edinburgh?" Baylee said. "As in, Scotland?"

They looked at each other. Derby. Nora.

"Where was the most recent sighting?" Baylee said.

"Uh . . . Boston, 1992."

"Boston," Baylee repeated. Sean. "Guys, I don't know that I need a whole lot more convincing, here."

"If this is true," Ralph said, frowning, "then how would we . . . stop them?"

Suze sighed and brushed hair off her face. "I don't know. The reports never mention anything about removing hearts, or how or why someone would become a jack. If we take what we've got at face value, then we're dealing with creatures who can shapeshift, who can leap incredible distances, have glowing eyes, and can't be killed with something as powerful as a shotgun."

"They have to be undead, though," Ralph said. "If they have no hearts, they're dead, but they're walking and talking, which makes them *un*dead."

"What's that mean?" Baylee interjected.

Ralph rubbed his forehead as if to make the wrinkles

there go away. He turned away from the iPad, turned in a tight circle, then spoke up. "Why does Dracula kill?"

Baylee wasn't sure what she'd been expecting, but it wasn't that. "I don't know. Because he's evil?"

"Is he, though? He kills *because* he's evil? What does he do with his kill?"

"Drinks their blood."

"Why?"

"God, Ralph! . . . because . . . he's hungry."

"Why?"

"Because he needs to eat . . ."

"*Why.*"

"Because otherwise he'll die?"

"Right," Ralph said, as if he only needed her input to confirm what he was already thinking. "Man is the only animal that kills because he is evil. Animals don't. Monsters don't. They kill for food, to sustain life, not take it for the sole purpose of taking it. Only humans take life for entertainment, or for vengeance. Or for—sport. Maybe we cast them as the demons without looking in the mirror. Take a look at a list of history's worst monsters. Serial killers, mass shooters, genocidal maniacs. Just going by the numbers, Timothy and them don't even compare."

Ralph had a point. A good and genuine point.

Baylee didn't care.

"They. Killed. Krista. *And* Fletcher. And my family, and now they want me to cut out my own fucking *heart*."

"I'm not defending them," Ralph said, holding up his hands. "I'm trying to figure out what they want. And maybe what they want is to stay alive."

"It sure looked like they had a fun time tearing my best friend apart."

"They need you to volunteer to do what Elijah did," Ralph said. "For whatever reason, whatever magic is at work, those are the rules. Because if you don't . . . maybe Timothy dies. Maybe they all die."

"Timothy said he needed to procreate?" Suze asked.

"Right, which is why that Derby girl changed Elijah," Ralph said. "Whatever this magic is, they must have to turn other people into jacks from time to time. Maybe it's once a week or maybe it's once a century, but they have to make more of themselves."

"But voluntarily," Baylee said, pursuing the thought. "Timothy said they couldn't turn someone against their will. They had to volunteer, just like Elijah did."

"Fascinating," Ralph said.

"So what about Elijah?" Baylee pressed. "I'm not hurting my brother. I want him back. Timothy said he can make that happen."

"It's got to be the book," Ralph said. "It has to be some source of power. Before we go decapitating people, let's try that. We could still be way, way wrong about all this, but going off and trying to kill them is a super ultra bad idea. Agreed?"

Suze nodded immediately. So did Baylee—but it took a moment.

"All right," Baylee said. "How do we get the book?"

"The way you described it, it sounds like they needed it for Elijah to do his part of the ritual, or whatever it was," Ralph said. "So we need to lure them someplace where we can have the upper hand, grab the book, and destroy it."

"Fine, how do we lure them?"

The two gamers looked at Baylee.

"Whoa, hold on," she said.

"Baylee, they want you," Ralph said. "Timothy does, anyway. You're the only bait we have."

"No way!"

"What would Kira Thirteen do?" Ralph said.

"Kira hunts bad guys for a living. I had trouble passing English."

Ralph laughed. Then said, "Sorry. That kind of sounded like something Kira would say, actually."

"Yeah? Cool. So, hey, let's revisit that calling the cops idea, huh?"

Because suddenly, this had gotten all too real. She wasn't one hundred percent sure she knew what reality was anymore, but she knew the three of them looking for trouble would sure as hell find it.

"Look," Ralph said. "Here's what I see happening if we called the police. First, they'd have to believe us. We'd have to come up with a believable lie just to get them to show up. Then, unless they saw or heard something suspicious, they couldn't even go inside a home. I think Timothy told you the truth about how long he's been dealing with police, so we'd have a hell of a time just getting the cops in the door. And let's say we did. So what? Something tells me Timothy and the others could handle a couple of beat cops."

"But then they'd call for backup, right? And like, S.W.A.T. and stuff."

"If the cops lived long enough," Ralph said. "Eventually, sure, someone would come looking for them. It might only take a minute, or it might take ten, but yes, more cops would come. And by then, all we've done is piss off the whole lot of them. Timothy, Nora, Sean. *Elijah*."

Baylee didn't reply. Didn't need to. She knew what he meant. She sat on the edge of Ralph's bed, feeling dizzy. Suze rested a thin hand on her shoulder.

"Hey, I don't like it either," Ralph went on. "I don't like any of this. So I'm totally willing to hear other suggestions."

"We need to consider the fact that none of these reports include anyone hurting a jack," Suze said. "One has never been wounded or captured that we know of. Partly that just goes to show they're urban legends, but it might also point out just how hard it would be to stop them. So the object isn't to hurt or kill them, it's to destroy the book. But we need *you* to get to *it*."

"All right," Baylee said. It at least sounded more reasonable than trying to hack someone's head off.

"How do we contact them?" Suze said.

Baylee pulled out her phone. "Easy. Call up the devil, invite him over."

"Look, that makes sense, okay?" Ralph said. "Elijah probably still has his phone, and Timothy was expecting to hear from her again at some point anyway. But we can't do this *here*. My mom and dad'll be home by dark, I don't want them in danger."

They fell silent for a long moment before Baylee sighed and rubbed her eyes.

"I know a place."

Suze and Ralph exchanged looks..

"The church. The one on the way to school."

"Yeah," Ralph said. "That works. Okay. Let's mount up."

Ralph knelt in front of the chest by the foot of his bed. He opened it, revealing a pile of medieval weaponry.

Baylee peered into it, but didn't move for a closer look. Ralph took out a fancy dagger with a wavy blade, a small axe with an ornately scrolled head, and a clumsy looking short sword, laying them on the floor beside him.

"I can't believe you just have this stuff laying around," Baylee said, unable to prevent herself.

Ralph gave her a disappointed look. "Really? You're surprised the Dork Master has broadswords and daggers in his room?"

"I'm sorry. We shouldn't have called you that."

Ralph shrugged quickly. "It's not the most clever thing I've been called. It's okay. I own it. And, hey, it's actually coming handy for once, right?"

"But why bring axes and stuff if the point is to get the book?"

"I don't know," Ralph admitted. "More cinematic, I guess."

"It might be they can only be hurt by melee weapons," Suze said, picking up the axe. She looked absurdly comfortable with it.

Ralph shut the chest. "Exactly. Better to have something than be empty handed. Believe it or not, there's not a Watcher's Guide for this."

"A what?" Baylee asked.

"Um—nothing, never mind."

"This is like some kind of role-playing wet dream, isn't it," Baylee said.

"Little bit. Not gonna lie." Ralph got to his feet. "Can you do this?"

Baylee tried to swallow, and couldn't. Her throat was too dry.

Ralph sat beside her and looked her in the eye. "Hey. I'm not letting anything happen to you."

"Nor I," Suze said, which should have sounded stupid and all *Lord of the Rings*, but somehow didn't.

"Are you both seriously this brave?"

"Huh-uh," Suze said.

"No," Ralph said. "But there's this girl watching, so." He forced a grin.

"Okay," Baylee said. "Let's roll the bones."

"Right. There's just a couple things from my parent's room I want to grab before we go." Then, faster than light, Ralph leaned in and kissed her once, on her cheek but rather near her lips.

"You're beautiful," he stated, and walked out of his room.

Baylee and Suze didn't move.

"Honestly," Suze said at last, "while sweet and heart-warming . . . cinematically speaking, that means we're going to die."

fifteen

North Community Church was just a few blocks from Ralph's home. He and Baylee walked there in growing darkness.

Baylee turned to check behind them for the eighteenth time in as many minutes. "Do you really think this will work?"

Ralph adjusted his backpack. "I don't know."

"I asked what you *thought*."

"Maybe."

"Should we stop? Go book a flight to Sweden or something?"

"We could," Ralph said. "But we're the only ones who know what's going on. What they are. We're the only ones who can help Lij."

"Yeah, I know. I was just hoping we'd both forgotten that part."

She checked behind them again—and saw him.

Baylee's breath turned solid inside her, her knees locking in place. Ralph skid to a halt beside her, starting to ask why she'd stopped, but the words shut off as if sliced from his mouth.

Timothy was not driving, the way Baylee had expected him to. No, he was walking. That same casual amble he'd had the first time she met him at the Wedge, not a care in the world. She saw him clearly as he walked under a streetlight, about a football field's length down the street.

Somehow, his pace scared her more than anything. His patience was terrifying. Like he knew it was just a matter of time.

Shivering, Baylee said, "We should—"

"Run," Ralph said.

They took off together.

They halved the distance to the church before looking back. Timothy was *closer* now, but not running. Baylee could even see the smile on his face.

"No," she heard herself gasping. "No, no, no . . ."

There.

The little church came into view. So close. No lights, no sign that anyone had been there in ages. Baylee risked another glance back, and Timothy was even closer than he'd been, somehow making up distance whenever her eyes weren't on him.

Jumping, she thought. He must be jumping. Springheel Jack.

Baylee and Ralph churned up the sidewalk, racing to the front doors beneath an ornate stone arch and throwing themselves against them. Baylee expected the doors to be locked at least, but also figured they could smash through them. Instead what happened is the doors gave way completely in a crash of wood and blinding dust.

Baylee launched herself into the church lobby, landing on her rear. Clouds of dirt blew up around them, exhaled from ancient, torn red carpet. Ralph tumbled past her, but stayed on his feet. A breath later, Timothy appeared beyond the doorway, hands in his pockets.

"Hello. How's it going?"

Ralph jumped toward him, pulling his hand out from the backpack. In it, he gripped an ornate crucifix, something he'd gotten from his parent's bedroom because Mrs. Silverberg was previously Miss Carter and a fine, upstanding Catholic. Boldly, he took another step toward Timothy with the cross stuck out in front of him in one hand.

"Begone, foul demon! The power of Christ compels you!"

Timothy winced. "Really? You got that from *The Exorcist*."

"Well! . . . yeah . . . ."

"And, Ralph *Silverberg*? Aren't you Jewish?"

". . . On my dad's side."

"Ah," Timothy said. "Well, regardless, hate to break it to you, but I'm not a vampire."

"But you drink the blood of the innocent!"

"No, I drink the blood of anyone. Although, now that you mention it, youthfulness does have a certain tang lacking in the elderly."

Ralph's arm lowered a bit. "Well then what are you?"

Timothy sighed, as if the conversation bored him. Baylee supposed it *did*.

"All I know is that we *are*." Timothy took one step closer to the doorway, and pulled his hands out of his pockets. His fingers dangled long by his legs. "Just like you. We're alive, in a manner of speaking, just like you. And just like you, we get hungry."

Baylee tightened her muscles just enough to prevent herself from wetting her pants at the carnivorous way he'd salted the last word.

Timothy pointed at them. "See, you were scared just a moment ago. Now you're verging on terrified. I can smell it. I can taste it. And it tastes good."

He slid closer. Closer. Moving on an invisible treadmill as if the soles of his sneakers weren't touching the concrete. He didn't take his eyes off Ralph.

"I don't know why," he said. Closer. "Maybe it's biology, maybe it's magic."

Closer.

"Maybe it's the cortisol racing through your bloodstream, or the adrenaline flooding your muscles."

Closer.

"All I know is that it—

"Tastes—

"*Good.*"

Timothy stopped. Stopped cold, in fact. Not so much as a hair pushed past the threshold of the church doors.

"Look!" Baylee shouted at Ralph. "He can't come in! He was bluffing!" She forced out a "Ha!" just to mock him. She was safe! Whatever he was, he was evil, and no evil could ever enter into a holy—

Timothy stepped inside.

"Without giving up my nefarious plans in the last reel," Timothy said, "or divulging my one mighty weakness that will allow you to defeat me before the credits roll, I will admit there are some places we avoid. But a church? Please. If you were looking for holy ground, you're going to have to look much further than your local Protestants. Good effort, though."

Moaning, Baylee crawled backward on her hands as Ralph skittered back beside her. Thick dirt caked her palms as she crept up the aisle, passing dusty, warped wooden pews that reminded her of giant sharks' teeth.

"Baylee, I'm kind of surprised at you," Timothy said. "Bringing this kid into the mix? That wasn't smart. I'm not sure what we're going to have to do with him now. I just know he can't live."

"S-so you do have one mighty weakness huh?" Baylee said, teeth chattering. "You want to share it with us?"

"Nah," Timothy said. "Now will you please stop running? It just makes me hungrier."

"Why," she whispered. "Why are you doing this?"

Timothy stopped. He placed his open right hand against his sternum and raised his left arm. He began to glide across the ratty carpet, taking small steps with his eyes closed. He looked like Frank Sinatra, or Bing Crosby, or some other old-timey dancer Baylee didn't know.

"Baylee, Baylee," he said, still dancing alone. "You'll be such a good partner. Isn't that enough?"

"H-hey, if you want to go to the prom or something, you can just ask."

"See, that's another thing I like. Your sense of humor."

He stopped dancing.

"Look, I don't know what it is. I don't understand the chemistry of it. But we think it has something to do with your hormones, those crazy little things going all out of control inside you. We like to make you Become when you're young. Not *too* young, but young enough to enjoy what happens after."

"Thass right," Derby added from the darkness of the sanctuary. "Young ones are swee'er."

Baylee jumped to her feet and whirled. Sean's shadowy shape sat beside Derby, carelessly reclining on the alter at the front of the room, banging their heels against it and peering at her through the gloom.

"'Allo, lassie." Even in the darkness, Baylee could see Derby's smile, wicked and white.

They were already here. The entire time, sitting here, waiting.

She'd sent Timothy the message two blocks before reaching the church, yet somehow, the jacks knew this is where they were going. They'd gotten here ahead of Baylee and Ralph. They were that fast.

Instead of them luring the jacks here, it might have been the other way around.

No one knows where we are, Baylee realized. And now we're isolated. Out of sight.

Even if they screamed, there weren't houses near enough for anyone to hear. It was part of the reason she and Timothy had chosen this place to—

The sudden memory of what they'd done together— what he'd done to her—made her ill.

"No offense, but you're all so cosmically stupid," Timothy said. "Nothing personal. I just mean young people in general. Truly! We were young once. We understand. I do appreciate your sense of immortality, though."

"I'm not immortal," Baylee said—and wondered where her brother was. She looked up at the ceiling, as if he might be crawling around up there, waiting to pounce.

"But you *think* you are," Timothy said. "You behave like you are. All humans do. But adolescents in particular have a keen sense of it. Children don't understand death, while adults very much do. But it is your youth, your particular age, wherein you straddle that line between understanding and foolishness. Death happens to other people, never to you. That makes you not the brightest animals in the pack."

"And you want me to become one of you," Baylee said, stalling. Come on, Ralph . . . come on, Ralph . . . think of something.

"Certainly. You're joining the winning team. When you do, immortality won't be just a concept anymore."

"Okay, but . . . I can't cut out my . . . my own . . ."

At last, Elijah's voice echoed throughout the abandoned sanctuary: "Sure you can."

He materialized from the darkness behind the altar and folded his arms. "I did it. It's not as hard as you think."

"Elijah," Baylee said, involuntarily.

"It's like nothing you've ever experienced," her brother said, sliding around the altar. He pulled a lighter from his pocket and lit a pillar candle sitting on top of a tall stand. The light burned blue for a moment before settling back to yellow. How had the candle gotten there in the first place? They'd brought it; that was the only answer. Good God, the only thought worse than that they'd run or jumped here before Baylee and Ralph was that they'd predicted it before the idea had even occurred to Baylee.

The shadows thrown by the candlelight deformed Elijah's face as he spoke. Except . . . no. His face really *was* deforming.

"The power," Elijah said. His voice had deepened. The muscles under his face rippled, and his mouth and nose began to stretch and lengthen. His words slurred into a terrible hiss.

"The strength. You will see things no one else can see."

Bones cracked, and his shoulders expanded under his shirt, straining the material. His legs swelled and stretched, growing him taller right before Baylee's horrified eyes. He made as if to squat down, but his bent knees grew taller as his legs got longer beneath him, turning him into some wicked mockery of man and mantis. His fingers, hanging loose by his thighs, expanded to twice their normal size. Three-inch claws slowly poked out from their tips with a sound like rotted fruit bursting. His arms grew longer.

Sean and Derby hopped nimbly off the altar and went to one of the wooden pews. They kicked at it until it became chunks of kindling, which they piled on top of the altar.

Elijah stepped into the aisle, flexing his hands. Baylee only barely recognized his face, which had stretched taut. His lips had vanished, making his mouth a terrible black hole filled with tiny razor teeth. His nose had sunk deep into his skull.

"We can have what our parents never did," he said. Baylee could barely understand him now. "Eternal life."

A squeak escaped Baylee's tightened throat as Timothy pressed up against her, seizing her shoulders from behind. His fingers felt like ice through her shirt. He smelled of fog, of stagnant ocean tide pools.

"You see?" he whispered. "Elijah knows. Now you can be with him. He's right. You can have what the rest of your family never had a chance to have. It's easy, Baylee. I'll help you. You won't feel a thing."

"Thass right," Derby called. "We can be your new best mates, likesay."

"Let her go!" Ralph said. He'd backed a few feet down a row between pews, clutching the bag in front of himself like a shield.

"Oh, all right," Timothy replied, then raised his shoulders in a dramatic shrug. "Really? 'Let her go'? Has that *ever* worked? Movies used to be so good, and now they pump out stuff like 'Let her go.' Depressing, really."

"I'll strap your ass to a nuclear weapon if I have to!" Ralph shouted. Yet he looked utterly impotent, a level one cleric outclassed by a godlike wizard.

"Like the one in Nagasaki, likesay?" Derby said. "Got a nice tan there, I did. Eh . . . it maybe stung a bit and tha'."

Baylee thought she and Ralph swallowed audibly at the exact same time.

"See, thass the thing, kiddoes," Derby said, eyeing them both. "When we're talkin' about immortality . . . that's wot we're really fookin' talkin' about."

"You said you'd turn him back," Baylee said.

"I lied." Timothy released Baylee's shoulders and moved to stand in front of her. "What is it with you people? You walk around lying to each other all day, *every* day, but when someone like me shows up and starts telling you what you want to hear, you just accept it."

The pile of wood on the altar burst into flame. Sean and Derby whooped and clapped at the light and heat. It reminded Baylee of they way they'd cheered as they tore apart her best friend.

"Plus," Timothy added, "I'm not seeing a guy who *wants* to go back to what he was."

Elijah stayed put in the center of the aisle, watching her. He seemed to be smiling, shoulders pulled back. His knees were almost level with his head, his legs impossibly long and folded into acute angles. Timothy moved away for a moment, then came back carrying Elijah's green backpack.

He reached inside and pulled out the big leather-bound book. He held it out toward Baylee.

"You don't have to understand what you're saying," Timothy said. "Just sound it out phonetically. I can help you."

The book.

Right there in his hands. She saw Ralph slide one sneakered foot an inch nearer.

Come on, Suze, Baylee thought. *Now, now, now . . .*

She needed to keep Timothy's attention. That was easy; she told the truth. "No. No, I can't do it. Please, c'mon, you *promised . . .*"

She sounded ridiculous. Derby thought so too. She said, "Ah ferd chryse," whatever that meant; possibly some shorthand for *For Christ's sake.*

"I cannae believe you insisted on this one," she said to Timothy.

"She's special," Timothy said with his toothless smile. "Can't you tell?"

Derby swung her head toward Baylee, reminding her, somehow, of a dragon. "Is she now? How would tha' be? Less go, you wee thing. Whatcha got, hey?"

She began stepping toward Baylee, chin down, eyes narrow. It was as if she'd tied Baylee to a standstill, as sure as they'd tied Krista to that tree. Derby was so thin and yet so very not fragile. She kept Baylee pinned with the gleam in her eyes and nothing more as she crept closer.

"Nora," Timothy said.

His voice carried across the sanctuary, and it took Baylee a second to realize he was addressing Derby. By that point, she couldn't think of the other girl—thing—as named anything *but* Derby.

"Well wot then?" Derby stopped two feet away from Baylee. Her tongue darted across her upper lip.

"Leave her be. She's mine."

"You're not even the eldest one here, Timmy. You should remember tha'."

"Why don't you take that up with Marquez." Timothy wasn't smiling anymore.

Something cold and dark slithered across Derby's face as she turned to him. Baylee caught something important then, something that maybe could save them, but she didn't yet know how:

They were not friends. Not lovers, not family. They worked together, they were allied, presumably out of some common need . . .

But Timothy and Nora were not at all on the same team.

"I'll kill ya for tha', Timmy," the Scot stated.

The words chilled Baylee. She'd seen guys pick fights at school. She'd even seen a girl fight at the mall once, complete with big fistfuls of hair and all. She'd watched—briefly—how Elijah and his nerd buddies play-acted their heroic characters in their games. And of course she'd seen Kira go berserk endless times on bad guys in *Lucky 13*.

What she'd never seen was the threat to "kill someone" be meant so sincerely and literally.

Derby meant it.

Timothy spread his arms open in front of him, book

hanging from one hand, inviting Derby over. A tiny grin danced on his lips. Baylee could feel raw strength in his limbs trembling the floor beneath her.

"Well," Derby said after a long pause. "Maybe not today 'n tha'."

"Maybe not today," Timothy agreed.

"*NOW!*" Ralph shouted.

Many things happened at once. Kira would have been proud.

sixteen

Suze barreled through a side door leading outside, wielding the axe from Ralph's house. She raced behind Derby and raised the weapon high.

At the same moment, Ralph pulled a pistol from the backpack. He'd slid close enough to Timothy to shove the barrel against Timothy's head.

"Drop the book!" he yelled.

A brief moment followed in which Baylee thought they were heroes. It all looked and sounded so cinematic. They were the good guys, the story was on their side.

But Suze had not seen Elijah's transformation. Baylee didn't think she'd seen *him*, period, as she'd come in. Now her brother's monstrous presence became clear: Suze sucked in a loud breath before uttering, "Oh my *God!*"

The jacks needed no further hesitation.

Derby slid to one side, then backward, then over once more to end up behind Suze, all with the ease and grace of a ballet dancer. Suze had no time to swing the axe. With her axe still raised high, Derby surrounded the taller girl with her arms and bodily flipped her in the air, with no more strain than flipping a quarter for heads or tails. Suze smashed down, her ribs cracking against one of the pews. The axe clattered away, and Suze lay still.

Things went no better for Ralph. Snakelike, Timothy dodged his head around Ralph's gun. In less than a heartbeat, the gun was useless in the center aisle where Timothy and Baylee stood, and Ralph's right forearm was twisted at a grotesque angle in Timothy's hand.

Sean jumped at Baylee, moving like a waterfall, breathtaking and deadly, to end up beside her, shoulders back, a sharp leer crossing his face.

"Gotcha," he said.

All this took one point three seconds to elapse.

"Well, that was fun," Timothy said, tossing Ralph aside with his broken limb as if Ralph were a shattered toy. "Now let's get back to business. Baylee . . . ?"

She moved on autopilot. With a scream, she shoved Sean to one side—and heard his laughter—and hunkered down to sweep the pistol into her hands. She came up holding it toward Timothy. She was farther away than Ralph had been, and hoped he couldn't move quickly enough to disarm her.

Sean didn't seem to care she had his boss at gunpoint. He faced Timothy. "You want me to break her in half?"

"No, no," Timothy said, eyeing her with the confidence of a lion. "She won't do it. She's too scared, and she'd lose her brother. That's why she came in the first place. She's going to put the gun down before someone gets hurt, and then we're going to get into my cool car and drive on out of here. Isn't that right, Baylee? San Diego sound good right about now?"

"Shoot him!" Ralph cried. His voice came out tight with pain. "Do it! Just shoot him. Maybe it'll hurt him."

"Oh, it hurts," Timothy said, keeping his eyes on Baylee. "It just won't kill me. Or, hey, you could shoot Nora. She's closer."

"You go fook yourself square in the arse, Timmy." Derby hadn't left her place beside the motionless Suze. Baylee thought maybe Suze was still breathing, but it was too dark to tell.

She pointed the gun at Derby. It shook visibly in her hands, but Derby was so close, there was no way she could miss.

At least, Baylee hoped so. They moved so *fast*.

"What do you say?" The only words coming out of her mouth were memorized from *Lucky 13*. "Want to roll the bones?"

Derby, expressionless, took two steps over to Baylee, leaned forward, and put her forehead against the barrel of the pistol.

"Aye, princess. But what abo' you?"

She killed Krista, Baylee thought.

And pulled the trigger.

Nothing. The trigger wouldn't move. Derby didn't blink, didn't suck in a breath, didn't flinch. Now, she only smiled and whispered, "Safety's on, no? Well. My turn, then."

Slowly, not moving any other muscle, Derby began to grin.

"Okay!" Baylee dropped the gun to the floor. She raised her arms. "Okay, I'm sorry, I'm done, I'll go with you. Okay? But just, please, come on, don't hurt anyone anymore. Okay? Just let everyone else go, and I'll come with you, I'll do whatever, just don't hurt anyone else. Okay? Please?"

Ralph, breathing hard, backed up to the middle of a row of pews. Elijah, or whatever had been him, hadn't moved from his place at the front of the room. His body seemed to bounce or sway lightly on his distended legs. Beyond that, no one moved.

"All right," Timothy said at last. "For you? Sure thing. Now, first, you need to—"

"Can I just have a minute? Please."

"For what?"

"For Ralph. You know he risked his life coming here with me. You know that. Right?"

Timothy shrugged a little, then nodded appreciatively. "Brave kid. The girl, too. Stupid. But brave."

"So can I just have a second to thank him?"

"Oh, I bet he'd last longer than that," Timothy said, and three monsters laughed. Elijah didn't; he only watched with glowing orange eyes.

"Sorry," Timothy said. "Couldn't resist. Speaking of which . . . do you want to know why I wouldn't have sex with you, Baylee? It's because once you have this, you never look back. Blood? Flesh? Bone? Sorry, but sex has nothing on that. You'll see." He paused, and smiled. "Isn't that right, Elijah?"

Despite herself, Baylee let her eyes glance at the thing that had once been her brother. The creature licked its thin lips as Timothy spoke. That moment, for reasons she didn't know, was the closest Baylee came to throwing up.

"Go ahead," Timothy said. "Give old Ralphie a nice going away present. You got class, Baylee. I knew I made a good choice."

"To procreate," she said, sliding cautiously toward Ralph.

"Everything's got to do it," Timothy agreed. "You'll do it someday, too. So will Elijah. Now, come on, I'm being very generous, let's get this done so we can all party."

Sean and Derby snickered as Timothy began walking past her, toward the altar. But he paused and leaned close, making Baylee stiffen and stop.

"You have no idea what you're in for," he said softly. "The power. The freedom. It's unlike anything you can imagine. It is kind of difficult to talk at first. We don't need to breathe, but you have to exhale breath in order to make your vocal cords work. So it takes a little time to get used to that. Respiration used to be involuntary. Now it's got to be on purpose. But we're never short of breath, and the *swimming* . . . Baylee, you're going to love the ocean in ways you never thought possible. When we're done here, let's go to San Diego together. I wasn't kidding about that."

Baylee met his eyes. He looked at her, talked to her, as if they were the only two people on Earth. For a moment, she believed him. For a moment, it was as if he'd had nothing to do with the deaths of her parents or her best friend or of turning her brother into a deformed demon. For a moment . . . he was Timothy again.

She wondered which one of him was the real thing.

"How are you doing this?" she whispered. "How is it possible? Am I crazy?"

"It's magic. That's all I know. What do you think keeps us up and running without a heart? Magic. We'll talk about it later."

"So that's what happened to you? You got like this because of magic?"

Something flared in his eyes that Baylee couldn't quite read.

"Sort of. Met a girl. Fell in love. Lost the girl. Searched high and low for some way for that to never happen to me." He shrugged. "Met a man named Marquez, from Spain, originally. He took care of it for me. That's all."

"So you just offered to cut out your own heart."

"He convinced me to. Every so often, we need to molt, so to speak. That's not a technical term, it's just the easiest placeholder. But we can't do it without procreating. I was his, and now you are mine."

"So you are going to—have *sex* with me?"

"No. That's not how it works. You have to volunteer, remember. You have to be willing."

"I don't buy it. People aren't going to just go around killing other people and cutting out their own hearts to turn into whatever it is you are."

"Oh, darling love . . . you have *no idea* what some people are willing to do. You've probably already met a few of us on TV. Washington D.C. Oh, yeah. We're everywhere."

He touched her forearm with his fingers, and the cold burned through her skin.

"Now go kiss your boy. Hurry up. We've got things to do and people to eat."

Timothy turned, nodding to Sean and Derby. They picked up Suze and tossed her easily onto one of the front pews in a jumble of bones. Elijah moved to stand over her, as if on guard. Still he said nothing.

Baylee sank down beside Ralph, who'd ended up sitting in one of the pews, cradling his arm to his stomach. She'd never seen a face so pale.

"It's really broken," he said. "I mean, like, *holy-crap* broken."

"What do we do?" she whispered.

"I don't know," Ralph said, looking her in the eye.

But his good hand, the left one, slid silently down toward the backpack. When Baylee tilted her head to follow, he tapped his knee against hers. She looked up quickly.

"Even if I could outrun them, Suze is hurt bad," Ralph went on. Still his left hand moved, now creeping into the backpack. Slowly, carefully, he pulled out the dagger with the wavy blade and moved it toward Baylee's hand in slow motion. The height of the pew kept it all concealed from the jacks. Elijah stared at her, but didn't seem to catch on to what Ralph was doing.

"So you're going to have to come up with something," Ralph said as Baylee gripped the dagger and concealed it under her shirt. "And you're probably going to need to roll a natural twenty. No modifiers."

He grinned, sickly.

"Sorry I couldn't be your hero, Baylee. I really wanted to."

"You've done plenty," Baylee said. "Thank you."

As she said it, she managed to slide the weapon into her waistband and pull the hem of her shirt over the top.

"Time's a-wasting," Timothy called from the altar. "Let's get this party started!"

Baylee squeezed Ralph's good hand and stood. The dagger was concealed perfectly—as far as she could tell. She came out to the aisle, fighting an urge to spin and run out the main doors. But she couldn't do that, not after what the gamers had done to help.

And there was Lij. If she could still get a hold of the book somehow . . .

Which, it turned out, was the easy part.

When Baylee got to within a few feet of the altar, feeling the heat from the fire tightening her skin, Timothy handed the book to her.

Baylee took the book in both hands. It felt warm in her fingers, like the leather was alive. It must have weighed at least five pounds, and she thought she caught an odor of singed hair.

"What is it?" she asked. "What is it *really?*"

"Well, we pretty much call it . . . 'The Book.' Not very original, I know. But books like this don't usually have titles. It's one of those—*no!*"

Baylee ran.

She sprinted toward the pyre on top of the altar and threw the book on top of it.

"No!" Timothy shrieked again.

The book went up in flame instantly, like tissue paper. A wicked squeal rose from the fire, like the burning of an animal, and the flames turned blue. Baylee literally raised her hands and cheered, feeling pure white victory pulse through her limbs.

She turned to face Timothy, waiting for him to burst apart in flames, or melt where he stood like the Wicked Witch, or . . .

Or . . .

Stand there with a snarl on his face.

"Baylee? Why did you do that?"

". . . You're still alive?"

Derby scowled and marched up to her. "Tha' pishes me right off, tosser."

"Oh, shit," Baylee said, her eyes closing helplessly.

"I get it," Timothy said, ambling toward her. "You thought if you burned the book, we'd all die in some sulfurous explosion of energy, right? Points for trying, but you have no idea what it is you're up against."

"Well now, she's sure set us back a bit n' tha'," Derby said.

"There are other books," Timothy said, his eyes not leaving Baylee. "We have time."

Baylee sank into the front pew beside Suze's motionless body. She wanted to cry and somehow couldn't. The dagger pinpricked her leg as she collapsed. So that was it— her only remaining defense was a Dork Master's play knife. Except she felt a warm drop of blood where the tip had nicked her skin. The tip was sharp.

Timothy stood beside her.

"The problem," he said, "is that now, you're stuck being just plain old human Baylee. Which means you can't hang out with us. Which pretty much reduces you to a midnight snack. Sorry, kid. You had your shot."

"'Bout fookin' time," Derby said, and removed her hat.

Baylee pulled out the dagger and screamed as she shoved it as hard as she could into Timothy's stomach.

The blade went in, resisting at first, then sliding in as if through some gelatinous thing.

Timothy looked down at the knife, then at her. He shook his head, laid his hand over hers, and pulled the dagger out.

"Got that out of your system?"

seventeen

Keeping his hand on hers, Timothy hauled Baylee up to her feet. The wavy dagger stayed locked in her grip. Timothy's blood coated the blade, sticking and dripping like congealed oil.

"You had such spirit," Timothy said. "I could smell it on your parents. That's one of the reasons I wanted it to be you. What a waste."

He marched toward the altar, but paused as Elijah put a clawed hand on his shoulder. Huge muscles still filled out his entire torso and arms.

"This wasn't the deal," he said to Timothy in his slurred monstrous speech.

Timothy glanced down at Elijah's sharp fingers. "You're new. So I'll let you remove your hand of your own volition this time. Next time, you'll lose it. All right, friend?"

"I mean it," Elijah said. "Let her go. This was not the—"

In a blur, and without loosening his grip on Baylee, Timothy grabbed Elijah's wrist and flipped him up over his shoulder. Elijah crashed into a series of pews several yards away, smashing them to splinters. Sean and Derby clapped and cheered again, having a grand old time.

"Lij!" Baylee screamed. Her brother did not get up.

"Now let's everyone calm down," Timothy said. "Clearly we all need a bite to eat. So let's handle that, and then we'll head out. All right? How about Brazil? We could—"

He let Baylee go, lurching backward into the altar where the fire still burned. Only after Baylee realized this did she hear two gunshots.

Ralph stood in the center of the aisle, the pistol clasped in his good hand. He looked like a cop, the gun black and deadly in his hand, and trained perfectly in his grip.

"Baylee, go!"

Two shadows blurred along the opposite walls before she could make her feet move. Ralph tried to track them with the barrel, but by the time he'd sighted in on one of them, the shadows had dropped behind him, blocking the front doors. Sean and Derby now stood between the two teens and the safety of outdoors. They snarled in tandem, and lowered themselves, ready to pounce.

"All right," Timothy said.

Baylee and Ralph whirled. Timothy was on his feet, rolling one shoulder around in the socket. Two red spots punctured his chest.

"Now I'm pissed," he said casually. "Would one of you please kill that kid while I eat this bitch? I'm sure someone heard those shots, so we need to go."

Sean and Derby leapt. Ralph twisted toward them, firing wild.

But the monsters didn't reach him.

Elijah burst up from the wreckage of the pews and intercepted the two of them in his absurdly long arms. Tangled, the three of them crashed into more pews, smashing them to pieces.

Ralph pivoted toward Timothy. Baylee screeched and ducked to one side as Ralph unloaded shot after shot. Each report rang with two syllables of explosive power.

Timothy chanted along with each one as the bullets drilled into his body.

"Yeah!" he shouted. "Yeah, yeah, yeah! Good one! Good one!"

Ralph stopped firing as the pistol locked open. He stood with his mouth open, staring in shock at the multiple wounds staining Timothy's torso. That appeared to be all they were: mere stains to be washed away.

"Whoa!" Timothy said as his fingers elongated. "Damn good shooting, son, damn good. You are gonna taste *great*."

A roar dragged Baylee's gaze toward the mass of hairy limbs in the center of the pews. Sean and Derby had twisted free of Elijah, and now each held him by an arm. An image of Krista came to Baylee's mind, and she all too readily saw them about to tear her brother apart—monster or not.

With the bloody dagger still in her hands, Baylee screamed and raced toward them. Derby spun and lowered her head, grinning ferociously as she neared. Baylee couldn't stop herself, even knowing there was no way she could reach the girl, or even hurt her.

But they had her brother and she had to try . . .

Roaring, Elijah brought his arms together in front of him. With superhuman strength, he clapped Derby and

Sean together. The jolt disoriented them. They growled and stepped back to get their bearings.

In that moment, Baylee jumped. Raising the dagger overhead in both hands, she brought it down hard into Derby's shoulder.

Derby screeched and batted Baylee away. She landed in the aisle at Ralph's feet, realizing how stupid she'd been, how pointless it all was. Timothy had been stabbed in the gut, and just shot with a magazine full of bullets. Her little poke with the knife wouldn't even faze Derby.

And then . . . Derby staggered.

Sean released Elijah and stepped away. Elijah, too, backed off in the opposite direction. To Baylee's shock, Derby stumbled over her own feet and fell to the floor amidst the wooden rubble of the old seats. She reached for the dagger, but once she had her pale fingers around the handle, she didn't pull on it. A mewling, pathetic whine came from deep in her throat.

"Oh . . . bleedin' chryse . . ."

Derby fell flat on her face, sprawled on the floor with her limbs spread wide. Motionless.

"You bitch," Timothy said from where he stood by the altar.

Still cowering on the floor, Baylee watched him start down the aisle. She felt Ralph's hands under her arms, trying to hoist her up, but he couldn't do it, not with his broken arm. He ended up kneeling behind her instead. Baylee backed up into him.

"I was going to do this quickly," Timothy said, taking slow, deliberate steps toward them as Elijah and Sean lingered nearby, watching. Timothy changed with each step.

It seemed he could control the metamorphosis, choosing which parts of his body morphed first.

"I was going to cut your throat, let you bleed out nice and quick," he said as his legs swelled with muscle that split his jeans down the side. His shoes were destroyed almost instantly, shredded beneath his widening feet. Curved claws sprouted from each toe and tapped dully on the ancient carpet.

"Now," he went on, "I'm going to play with you a bit instead. Sean?"

Baylee looked back at Sean. He curled his back, preparing to pounce toward Elijah. She saw, though, that he concealed one hand behind him, like a mugger with a knife.

Then she noticed he was slowly penetrating his own rear flank with claws extending out of his right hand. Why would Sean be drawing his own—?

The dagger.

Timothy's blood on it. The wound she'd given Derby hadn't been mortal even to a human.

Something else had killed her.

Elijah matched Sean's steps, circling, preparing for the strike. Thick fluid dribbled onto Sean's right-hand claws as he snarled at Elijah.

And then she knew.

"Elijah it's the blood!"

Elijah turned his attention to Baylee for a split second. It gave Sean the opening he needed. Sean sprang and tackled her brother, taking them both against the far wall in a flurry of claws. Sounds like a hellacious cat fight screamed from their mass of slashing limbs.

Timothy struck almost instantaneously, loping toward her and Ralph. He swatted Ralph away as effortlessly as a beach ball. Ralph flipped once in the air before landing near the front doors. He did not move.

Timothy dropped to a hunker beside Baylee, his flattened snout inches from her. She heard the feral growls and tearing flesh of Elijah and Sean fighting behind her, but couldn't turn away from Timothy.

"You could have had everything," Timothy said carefully around his misshapen mouth. "You were chosen. I would have given you the world. Now you're nothing."

He grabbed Baylee's throat and lifted her to her feet—then raised her even higher, her toes dangling above the carpet. She grasped his thick wrist with both hands, wheezing, her heart a jackrabbit behind her ribs.

"And you killed Nora," Timothy went on, walking toward the altar. The fire still burned, though not as brightly as before. "I wasn't particularly fond of her, but she was one of us. That's going to add an hour to our special time together."

He backed Baylee up into the altar. Flames singed her hair as she kicked uselessly at him.

"So let's start," Timothy snarled in her face, "with fire."

With his free hand, he reached past Baylee for a chunk of burning wood.

She realized, just a moment before he was going to plunge the coal-hot lumber against her face, that Timothy's weakness wasn't necessarily physical.

It was his arrogance. His assumption that Sean would kill Elijah.

Behind Timothy, she saw Elijah flying through the air,

at least eight feet off the ground, legs fully extended, his arms high overhead. He roared in mid-flight, and landed precisely behind Timothy, dragging all ten of his claws—with Sean's fresh blood infusing them—down Timothy's muscular back.

Timothy howled, releasing Baylee and the chunk of wood simultaneously. He lurched forward, spraying the flames all along the rear of the church. Baylee sank down, momentarily by his knees, before scrambling to the side and aiming for the cover of one of the few remaining benches still in one piece; the place where Suze still lay and just then began to stir.

Timothy recovered and spun to face Elijah. Elijah stepped back with his hands raised before him. Crimson-black fluid dripped from his claws. Baylee risked a glance at the area where he'd struggled with Sean. Sean was crumpled in a heap against the wall.

As Suze flickered her eyes, Baylee moved toward Derby. On her hands and knees, Baylee scooted on the floor until reaching Derby's lifeless form. She grabbed the dagger and pulled hard. It came out and into her hands after a struggle. Then she skittered backward until she rammed into an upright bench.

Timothy and Elijah hadn't moved. Though still in his monstrous form, Timothy's face seemed relaxed somehow. Loosened. Then slowly, he shifted into his human shape. Enormous holes still punctured his chest and abdomen where Ralph had shot him.

Once fully human—or human-esque—Timothy stared at Elijah, who had not yet changed.

"This isn't what I had in mind," Timothy said. "Oh, my."

He fell to his knees . . . *crying.*

"Come on," Timothy said, hanging his head. "Please. Please . . . I don't want to . . . come on, why do you think I did it? Come *on . . .*"

For one fleeting moment, Baylee felt pity for him. Timothy's whole body shook, shoulders lurching up and down, braying great sobs like she herself did for a week after losing her mom and dad.

Ralph had been right. He was scared to die.

"I just . . ." Timothy moaned, and raised his head to the ceiling. Behind him, flames licked the back side of the altar, spreading along the far wall. The whole place would go up before too long. Even in the shadows, Baylee could see tears washing his face.

"*Please—!*"

Then Timothy's body seized tightly, as if pulled taut by some internal rope. He froze that way for a moment, then fell face-first to the carpet, dead.

Elijah watched him for a moment. Then, slowly, he pivoted to face his sister.

Baylee stood on quaking legs.

And pointed the dagger at him.

Elijah started taking on his human form, piece by piece. The change was not as elegant as Timothy's transformation had been. Finally he stood as the brother Baylee knew and loved, although much larger and much more frightening even without his monstrous attributes. They stood twenty feet apart.

"Don't come any closer."

Elijah spread his arms. "So what now?"

"I don't know."

"You're going to kill me? I'm a superhero, sis. I could change the world."

He was so big now. So imposing. "Superheroes don't kill people."

"Maybe I don't have to do that."

"It's the only way for you to stay alive."

"There's time. Before it has to happen again. Maybe there's another way."

"I don't think so, Lij. Elijah."

"You know I could take that knife away from you in a heartbeat."

"*Heartbeat?*" Baylee coughed. "What is that, a joke? Some kind of irony?"

"It wasn't meant to be. Now that you mention it, it is sort of funny."

Neither of them laughed.

Baylee did not lower her hands. Elijah came no closer. Behind him, the flames spread. Now the entire back wall of the crumbling church was on fire. Smoke clogged her eyes and burned them. They were standing in a tinder box.

Someone stumbled into her and Baylee gasped. But it was Ralph. He stood beside her, hunched over, cradling again his broken arm. Suze crept off her bench, and backed away from Elijah. He made no move to stop them.

"We need to get out of here," Suze grunted, limping toward the front doors. Baylee couldn't believe it when she swooped down to pick up Nora's derby. "I think I'm pretty hurt . . ."

"We're coming," Ralph said weakly, but didn't leave Baylee's side. "You go, Suze. Go."

He and Baylee stood staring down her brother until Suze got out of the church.

270

"I'm going to go now," Elijah said at last.

"Where."

"I don't know. Away."

"I can't let you do that."

"But you can't stop me, either."

Something splattered against Baylee's arm. She didn't risk looking away from her brother, but saw peripherally that a single clear drop had hit her skin. She was crying.

"I love you," Baylee said.

"I love you, too," Elijah said. "Believe it or not."

"I do . . ."

He tilted his head. For just a moment, he didn't look like a monster anymore. "You do?"

"Yes."

Elijah licked his lips. "I won't let anything happen to you. Ever."

"Or Ari and John. Or Ralph. Suze . . ."

"Or any of them, of course. I promise."

"Okay."

"I'm walking away now, Baylee."

Elijah took a step backward. Then another. He kept his hands raised to the side, fingers spread. His footsteps made no sound, not even against the wreckage on the floor.

She kept the point of the dagger aimed at him until he reached the side door where Suze had entered. At last he turned away and pushed it open.

"I'll hunt you down."

The words came on their own. Baylee hadn't meant to say them. But she didn't try to take them back.

Elijah froze, still facing the door. Baylee could see the muscles in his back flexing, and wondered how many leaps it would take for him to get to her. To tear out her throat. One leap, she figured. Maybe two at most. He could be here and on top of her before she could scream.

Elijah didn't move.

"I know," he said.

He pushed the door open and slid out into the night.

Baylee stood rooted to the spot, dagger still raised. Eventually her arms dropped, then her entire body fell to the floor. She didn't let go of the weapon. Baylee studied its edge, watching Derby's blood drying on the metallic surface.

As far as she knew, it was now the only weapon in existence that could kill her brother.

"Baylee?" Ralph crouched beside her with a groan. "We have to move. This place is coming down."

Baylee slid the dagger into her waistband behind her before reaching for the scraps of Timothy's black jeans. She shook them until his keys dropped into her hand. Only then did she let Ralph help her off the floor. They slouched outside as the flames behind the altar ate away the rear wall of the sanctuary.

Outside, they found Suze across the street, leaning against a fence. Baylee immediately scanned for signs of Elijah, to make sure he wasn't waiting for them. She saw nothing.

Ralph held a hand to his head, then winced against a sudden burst of flame from the roof of the church. "We'd better move."

Suze's eyes were winced tight. She held both hands to her side and wore Derby's hat on her head at a cockeyed angle. "How many experience points you think this was worth?"

No one laughed. Still; they needed the joke.

Baylee searched the street and saw what they needed a little ways down. "Follow me."

She led them to Timothy's Ford, parked further up from the church, in shadows where she and Ralph hadn't looked earlier; they'd been too busy running. The first wails of sirens met her ears as she turned the engine and drove away from the smoking church, headed for Suze's house. They were gone in the darkness before the trucks reached them.

"We'll call 911 when we get to your place," Baylee said, driving slowly. "If you're sure you guys can make it."

"We'll make it," Suze said.

"We're gonna need a good story to explain what they find back there," Baylee said.

"I'm DM," Ralph said. "I'll come up with something."

"Where's the gun? The cops will—"

"In my bag," Ralph said. "I don't think there'll be any sign of us."

"What about the bodies?"

"Let's roll those dice when we need to."

"Where'd you learn to shoot like that?" Baylee asked as the sirens grew more faint.

"I'm not a *total* dork," Ralph said. "I shoot with my dad all the time."

They reached Suze's house in safety; battered, bruised, and smelling of smoke, but safe. Her parents were not home and to Baylee's shock, their entire adventure that night had barely taken an hour.

"I'll get us some water," Suze said. She shuffled into the kitchen as Baylee and Ralph dropped onto the couch in the living room.

"What's your plan for the car?" Ralph asked, grimacing and holding his arm.

"I got a few places to park it. I think I earned it." She rested a cramped hand on Ralph's knee. "Thanks, Ralph. I'm alive because of you."

"Yeah?" Ralph said. "Cool. Does that mean you might eat lunch with us sometimes when school starts?"

She took his good hand in hers. "Stranger things have happened, huh?"

eighteen

The Wagners brought her to an adolescent psychiatric hospital the next day. Baylee didn't fight it. When the police showed up later that afternoon, she knew from television not to say anything without a lawyer, which Ari and John quickly summoned, using funds from the estate. Her story was far from watertight: She'd broken into the old church with her boyfriend and two of his friends. They'd lit a fire on the altar. Sean—she didn't know his last name—and Timothy got into an argument. Nora tried to intervene. There was a fight, and after that things got blurry, she said. She thought Sean shot Timothy and that he stabbed Nora. But by that point, Baylee claimed, she was just looking for a way out of the church without attracting attention, and couldn't swear to anything that happened thereafter.

Best way out of a jam, Kira Thirteen had taught her: admit to something stupid or illegal. Give them something to nail you for and distract them from the real thing.

Breaking and entering and arson seemed to do the trick, though that process took several weeks, during which she dutifully went to her counselling sessions, both private and group, and quickly learned from other patients how to hide taking her pills.

She did not want her reflexes dampened in any way.

After two weeks her doctor released her. It was just before school started. More cops came with more questions, and the more they asked, the more she said she didn't know.

Where is your brother? I don't know. Where is Krista Hope? I don't know. Did you ever meet Timothy's parents? No. We can't identify two of the bodies. Oh really? You said those kids killed Krista Hope. Yes. So then what really happened, Baylee, tell us the truth!

I don't know.

And in many ways, that answer was the most truthful. After all, she had tried to be honest weeks ago and no one believed her. Why bother trying to tell the whole story now?

With Ari's blessing, she walked to Ralph's house on the last afternoon before school began. Ralph met her at the door with a smile. Baylee hugged him close.

"Suze's here," he said, taking Baylee upstairs.

"Do you still have it?" Baylee asked. She didn't need to say what it was.

"Yes," Ralph said. "It's safe, don't worry."

"Any sign of him?"

"Nothing."

In his room, Suze stood and also gave Baylee a warm hug. "It's good to see you," she whispered.

Baylee flicked the brim of the derby hat Suze wore and grinned. "You too."

They took seats. Baylee filled them in on everything that had happened with the cops so far.

"Will you have to go to jail?" Ralph asked nervously.

"Probably not. My lawyer doesn't think so. We'll make a deal."

"Do they believe you?" Suze asked softly.

"I don't think so, but they can't prove anything. I think you're safe."

Suze shook her head, but replaced the long hair behind her ears. "That's not why I was asking."

"What about at home?" Ralph asked.

Baylee shrugged. "I'm keeping my head down and my mouth shut. I think they blame themselves for Lij being gone. Ari and John, I mean. I feel kind of bad about that, but I don't know how I could talk them out of it."

Ralph and Suze voiced their understanding of that conflict, and then the room fell into silence.

"So," Baylee said, sitting up straight, "there is one other thing."

She watched the two gamers trade glances.

"It's something Timothy said. I don't know if you heard him. He said they were everywhere. On TV, in Washington D.C. It wasn't just them."

Ralph nodded. "I remember."

"I'm getting my license next week," Baylee said. "And we still have the car, right?"

"I've been moving it around," Suze said. "It's safe."

"And I've got a lot of money coming before too long," Baylee said. "So I've been doing some research."

She pulled a folded print out from her pocket and handed it to Ralph.

"Martial arts schools. Real ones, like krav maga and jiu jitsu, bulletman, stuff like that. Not the sport kind. I think

I should check those out. As many as I can."

"I think we all should," Ralph said, handing the list to Suze. "That's a good idea. It's smart. I don't know if it's enough, but."

"Right," Baylee said. "I know. But we have to start somewhere."

She paused, and looked back and forth between them.

"I mean," she added, "I do. I have to start. Just knowing that there are more of them out there—"

Ralph spun in his chair and grabbed something green and roughly spherical from his desk. He passed it to Baylee.

"Roll the bones," he said.

"You guys don't have to," Baylee said. "It won't be any safer than the church was."

"Elijah," Suze stated. "One day, some day, he'll be back. Can't you feel it?"

Baylee nodded slowly. She could.

"We're in this with you," Ralph said.

Baylee took a deep breath, held it—then sighed. She almost said Thank You, but realized by the expressions in their faces that there was no need.

She juggled the die in her hand before tossing it onto Ralph's desk. The three of them huddled over the result.

"Twenty."

the end

heartless

This short story, written many years earlier,
became the basis for the novel of the same name.

A burnt moon glared down at the southwestern desert, it was a quarter to midnight, and the weather was right for a killing.

But Matthew didn't know that.

His gaze scampered back and forth across the backs of the skulls of his three friends: Michael, the driver; Joel, in shotgun; and Timothy, on the bench seat beside him.

Even in the darkness of the station wagon that bore the four boys, Matt could see the smirk on Timothy's face curving like a tusk. He knew Timothy was watching him, scrutinizing his every movement and subtle shift in mood without so much as blinking an eye.

Matt narrowed his eyes at Timothy; did he blink at all?

As if in response, Timothy's eyelids drooped and fell, then rose sharply again. Matt jerked in his seat, startled.

"Enjoying the ride, Matthew?" Timothy asked, turning his crystal eyes toward Matt.

Matt swallowed heavily and prayed Timothy hadn't noted the reaction. "Sure," he burst out, his voice loud in the vehicle, "it's real pretty out here."

The other three erupted into laughter. Matt blinked for a moment, then joined them, confused but not wanting to be left out.

"He's scared to death!" Michael exclaimed, twisting the steering wheel in his hand. The car veered left, off the blacktop highway. No cars had passed them for half an hour. "Remember when Joel became?" Michael went on, giggling. "He was so freaked out that he . . ."

"Now, now, Michael," Timothy said, his voice carrying a warning note. "We don't want to make Matthew jumpy, do we?"

Michael's hilarity shrieked to a halt. "Of course not," he replied, and focused on the drive.

The station wagon bumped and shook over sandy potholes as grim cacti marched past the car. Matt guessed they were a mile from the highway now. Alone. He wished for one of those big brick portable phones the rich chicks at school toted around in their purses. If something happened out here—the car blew a tire or broke down, or some desert animal got a hold of one of them, or hell, even a rattlesnake bite—help would be a long time arriving.

Matt swallowed and longed for a glass of water. "There's that word again," he said. "Became. Became what?"

They said nothing. Joel drummed a nonsense beat absently on the dashboard.

Matt rolled his eyes and sunk down in his seat, bracing his knees on the back of the driver's seat in front of him. Moonlight shone through the windshield, illuminating the two boys from the front, and Matt stared at the rhythmic heartbeats pulsing steadily in Joel and Mike's necks.

Matt had known the group for a month now, and it had

been the best month of Matt's young life. Wait; no—not quite best. It had shown him the enormous potential of being acquainted with these three. His grades, always poor, had begun crawling up slowly but steadily, though he didn't remember doing any more work than usual. It was as if his teachers had simply chosen to increase his grades. His parents, formerly stern and forbidding, had begun to let him do as he wished, sometimes even funding his evenings out with the three guys. Matt's standard-issue blemishes had grown smaller and more infrequent, revealing strong, taut skin shining with vitality. Girls he'd only fantasized about talking to were—almost alarmingly—now talking to him first. Some had even hinted at romance. Not a few had hinted at sex.

Matt was a newborn star in the high school heavens, and he knew it was thanks to these three.

He simply didn't know why.

Timothy had approached him at the start of the year, and Matt's mouth had dried under Timothy's searing gaze. Popular kids blanched when the three guys approached; lifelong bullies took wide paths to avoid them; girls batted eyelashes and prettily swung their hips toward them as they passed in the halls; teachers only called on them when they had correct answers. They were gods. So when Timothy came up to him and asked—or was it instructed?—Matt that they should have lunch the next day, Matt agreed quickly. It was a strange friendship, Matt knew, and didn't care. He was now in, he belonged, and he didn't care why Timothy had chosen him.

But as the station wagon tore through the serene, opaque Sonora desert, Matt felt the first ticklings of fear on the back of his neck, of things not being quite right. It wasn't the first time, he admitted to himself. Timothy and Michael and Joel were usually silent, stalking through hallways at school, as if in slow motion to wicked theme music only they could hear. They rarely smiled, yet commanded authority over all they surveyed. Matt had always respected them, like everyone did, but now he wondered where the line was drawn between respect and fear. Michael and Joel were less impressive than Timothy, Matt had noticed. They were subservient to him, as though whatever power they shared was more readily controlled by Timothy.

"So where are we going again?" Matt asked. He still wanted a drink of water.

"A favorite place of ours," Timothy said, gazing out his window at the curtain of night shrouding the desert scrub brush. "I think you'll like it."

"Yeah," Michael said. "You'd better."

Matt shuddered under his clothing. But there was no going back now. His dreams were being fulfilled. He'd do whatever they asked.

"That's good," Timothy said, and Matt jerked.

"Huh?"

Timothy turned toward him and grinned. "We're close enough," he said, and Matt realized Timothy had been speaking to Michael.

Michael brought the car to a halt. The three boys climbed gracefully out of the vehicle; Matt stumbled over his own feet and almost crashed to the dirt, bringing chuckles from Michael and Joel. Matt cursed and righted himself.

They closed their doors and began treading toward a nearby hill. Matt could barely make out a slim trail snaking upward, with a bent and unidentifiable tree crowning the summit. He perpetually kicked up rocks and tripped over bushes, and noticed uneasily the other three trod the ground without any missteps. They probably have the place memorized, Matt reasoned. They've been here before. Probably hang out here and drink or smoke out or . . . something.

At the base of the hill, the trio stopped and looked at Matt. Timothy nodded to Joel, who reached into one oversized pocket of his cargo shorts and pulled out a thick black book. He held it out toward Matt.

"Put your left hand on the book, Matthew," Timothy instructed.

Matt did, and felt something akin to relief. This was an initiation, that's all. Whatever it was these guys knew, they were going to share it with him. While Matt's dreams were becoming reality lately, he still felt distant and disconnected, living vicariously through the other three. Using borrowed power. Maybe after tonight, he'd have what they had in his own right.

"Now, repeat after me," Timothy said, and slowly recited a string of words foreign to Matt. Matt followed orders, repeating the sounds.

Matt gasped at the last syllable, and heard Michael and Joel chuckle again. A strange strength surged through him. His slight frame filled with some other thing, some force making his muscles contract and ready to spring. He sensed he could leap to the top of the hill in one jump if he had a mind to.

"What . . . ?" Matt asked breathlessly.

"You are becoming," Timothy said, and motioned for Joel to put the book away. "Come."

Timothy led the way up the trail, followed by Joel, then Michael, with Matt at the end of the procession. Despite the rhythmic pound of his heart and strength pulsing through his limbs, Matt still stumbled upon the trail. He lifted his eyes, and was struck by the lithe pace of his friends. They looked as if they were floating up the trail, but when Matt looked down at their legs, their feet were in fact still touching the earth.

Matt rubbed his eyes—the moon must have been behind a cloud earlier, surely it must've, because the world was brighter now. Almost as bright as day. Matt paused and glanced down at the car. He could read the license plate from fifty yards away.

"Whoa," Matt breathed.

"Matthew," Timothy said ahead of him. "We are on a schedule. We mustn't keep her waiting."

They continued up the hill. Matt was amazed at the ease of which his lungs were operating, his breath slow and steady and deep with no trace of strain. Until ten minutes ago, he would have had to sit down and rest by now.

And his teeth were beginning to ache.

"Hey," Matt said, "my mouth hurts."

"Yep," Joel said in an offhand sort of way, and added nothing more.

The other two gave him no response.

Moments later they reached the top of the hill, a small plateau thirty yards across. Matt could see the tree easily now, a tired old joshua, with a squirming girl roped to its trunk.

Matt stopped in his tracks. He recognized the girl from school; from having had lunch with her the day before, in fact, but didn't remember her name. Thick nylon ropes secured her to the tree, her mouth bound by grey tape wound around her entire head.

Only her throat lay exposed.

"Guys," Matt said, and gagged.

The others had reached the tree. Timothy pulled a gleaming knife from behind him. Matt didn't remember seeing it as they walked, but there it was, one smooth edge, one jagged, reflecting rays of moonlight into Matt's eyes.

"It's time, Matthew," Timothy said. Matt realized distantly that Tim was speaking softly, but he could hear the words as if Timothy were beside him instead of thirty yards away.

"I—I can't do this," Matt said, but took a step toward them.

"You can," Timothy said, "and you will. The alternative is . . . bleak."

Matt looked to Michael and Joel for guidance, and recoiled as they smiled at him, carnivorous teeth glowing beneath the moon, their lips utterly too wide and broad, their mouths gaping holes of impossible dimensions.

"Become, Matthew," Timothy said, his voice still soft.

Matt walked to him.

Timothy held the blade in his hand, offering the hilt to Matt. Matt took it and pulled, but Timothy would not relinquish his hold.

"Go on," Timothy urged softly, "take it."

Matt stared at him, fell deeply into the black opaqueness of Timothy's eyes; all trace of his crystaline irises were gone.

Matt yanked on the weapon, hard. The dagger tore from Timothy's grasp, and Matt was certain he had sliced Timothy's palm; yet Timothy merely smiled wisely and nodded.

"Now go," he said. "You know what to do."

Matt turned slowly and took a step toward the fettered girl. He paused and glanced at his feet, uncertain, and noticed Timothy casting a sharp shadow against the sandy ground. In shadowplay, he watched Timothy curl his right hand into a fist and appear to squeeze down, catching drops of liquid in his upturned left palm. The cupped left hand disappeared into the shadow of Timothy's head, and Matt's ears detected a quick sipping.

Matt acted quickly. The blade slid easily across the girl's throat, spilling her blood in great gushes on the desert plateau floor. She died moments later, and Matt fell to the ground, exhausted. His nose twitched at the overwhelming stench of life, of blood, pooled at the young girl's feet, and he was struck quite suddenly by a monumental craving to bury his face in the damp earth, to savor the aroma of her, to drink.

Michael and Joel whooped and cheered. They slapped Matthew on the back while he was yet on his hands and knees. Timothy squatted down beside him.

"That's it," he said.

Matt tilted his head up toward Timothy, both repelled by what he had done, and relishing the power seeping into his whole body.

"What are you?" Matt asked, his voice a hoarse whisper.

"The question is, Matthew," Timothy soothed, steepling his fingers beneath his chin, "what are we."

Michael had picked up the knife and sliced cleanly through the ropes holding the girl. Matt watched, repulsed and somehow pleased as he and Joel each grabbed one of the girl's arms and yanked. The arms detached readily, as if pulled apart not by adolescent boys but by heavy machinery built for just such a macabre purpose. The two began fencing crazily with the pale limbs, spattering gore upon one another as they laughed aloud.

"There is one more step," Timothy said, watching his friends play. "If you wish. But you don't have to, Matthew."

Matt climbed slowly back to his feet as Michael and Joel stopped their horseplay and watched. Matt turned to Timothy.

"What must I do?" he asked, and was thrilled at the deep timbre his voice had assumed. His fear was a vague memory.

Timothy smiled and rescued the knife from Michael. He handed it to Matt, then took Matt's head in his hands. Matt did not struggle as Timothy pulled Matt to his chest, paternal.

"What do you hear?" Timothy asked.

"I hear nothing," Matt said.

"Yes," Timothy hissed, and released his grasp. He fixed Matt with steel in his eyes. "The choice is yours."

Matt understood. Joel and Michael looked curiously reverent as Matt took the knife from Timothy. He recalled observing the pulse in Joel and Michael's necks, outlined in moonlight, and understood they had not taken this step, hadn't the courage to follow Timothy wholly, and were shamed by it.

Timothy smiled marvelously, his mouth growing

wide and deep as Joel and Michael's had, his sinewy frame beginning to bulge and ripple, threatening to tear his clothes from his body.

Matt pressed the knife against his chest and drove it in between his ribs. The others gazed on, immune to Matt's agonizing screams.

Several minutes later, only partly aware he should be dead, Matt held his silent organ in one hand, the bloodied knife in the other. Without direction from Timothy, Matt walked to the edge of the hill and tossed the heart over the edge. He glanced down at his chest, and saw nothing but the bloody shreds of his t-shirt, and smooth, unmarred skin over his torso, now thick with muscle Matt did not remember.

And as his lips parted and stretched, as his teeth elongated and filled his maw, as some unseen force rebuilt his skeleton and muscles, filling them with otherworldly strength; as Joel and Michael knelt at his and Timothy's feet and muttered strange archaic sounds, Matthew knew he had Become.

those we bury back

A novella

If charnel-houses and our graves must send
Those that we bury back, our monuments
Shall be the maws of kites.

~ *Macbeth*, Act III, Scene iv

one

The house remembered him.

Pulling up alongside the splintered red wooden fence surrounding the front yard, Braden Clark felt it. Even before he'd entered the neighborhood, he could feel the house awakening. Knowing. Smelling him in the vicinity.

Braden sensed its memory waking, shaking off the dust of a two-decade slumber, probing for him, seeking him out. And it found him. Its incorporeal tentacles reached for and enveloped him whole. They penetrated the interior of the truck, sniffing for him. The mechanical muscle of the new-model-year Toyota Tundra provided him and his son no more protection than a hospital gown. It was as if in the twenty years since he'd been here, his childhood home had accumulated more filth and rot and smell and rancidity, enough to make it live. Enough to make it breathe. Enough to make its fetid vapors tangible.

Three-year-old Josiah Clark didn't seem to notice anything unsettling. Braden nearly offered a silent prayer of gratitude for that small mercy.

"Whose house this?" the toddler wanted to know from his car seat in the back.

294

"It's my old house." Braden sat still in the cab, clutching the wheel, his knuckles tight knobs pressing the tendons into white strips. Scar tissue across them flexed as if threatening to snap open and bleed anew.

"You live there?" Josiah asked, frowning.

Braden wasn't sure if Joze meant to use the present-tense or not. Preschoolers hadn't quite mastered tense.

Doesn't matter, Braden thought. *The truth is what matters, and the truth is I do not live here.*

This excursion didn't make any sense to Josiah, Braden guessed. They lived together with Mommy in a new house, so this one clearly could not be where Daddy lived.

"I don't live here anymore, I just used to," Braden answered his son.

Shouldn't have brought him, Braden thought. *Should have found someone to stay with him at home, or taken him to Grandma's, even if it was just for ten or twenty minutes so I could get this stupid thing over and done with.*

Except sitting there, staring at the house with its tan, peeling face and frowning blank window eyes, he knew he'd brought his son on purpose. Not as a sacrifice, though once the word flashed in his head he had trouble dismissing it; no, not for that. More as a talisman. As a relic, an emotional splinter of the True Cross from his abandoned faith. Josiah would unwittingly protect him. His sheer simple love would ward off any panic, Braden believed. That the presence of a toddler would calm his nerves made for a bitter pill to swallow, but Braden didn't mind. At the moment, he didn't give one tiny shit that he was using Josiah as an emotional crutch.

Of course, the decision to bring him had been made

earlier, when not parked in front of the old house. In the clean light of the Phoenix day, under the glimmering cabinets of their home—their real home as a family—it had just made logistical sense. His wife, Ashley, worked late on Fridays, and he usually picked Joze up from preschool and after-care at six.

Bring the kid along, no big deal. In and out in five minutes, no sweat. Then take him out for ice cream! Get a treat, you'll both deserve it.

Then you never have to think about that goddamned house ever again.

Yes, it had been easy to think that way yesterday. This morning, even.

Now, parked here, he found it harder to justify having brought Josiah along.

Now what he wanted to do was throw the stick into reverse and say the hell with this.

"What doing, Daddy?"

His son's voice startled him. Braden released the wheel and sat back, realizing his hands had cramped.

"Hmm? Oh. Nothing, Joze. Nothing. Just thinking."

"You o-tay, Daddy?"

"Yeah," Braden lied.

Now the choice loomed before him like a tangible pendulum. No middle ground, only the two extremes:

Leave his boy in the car, which you were never supposed to do; or bring him inside? Into the lair of demon memories?

He'd let fate choose. Fate seemed to have chosen his path this far, anyway, so what the hell.

"Josiah? Do you want to come inside or wait in the car?"

It would, after all, only be for a second. A minute, a full minute at most. Josiah wouldn't roast in the car. Even if he somehow got locked inside, which he wouldn't, kids and pets didn't die in cars in November. June, yes. July, August, absolutely. Not fall, not November, not a week past Halloween, they didn't.

"Come inside," Josiah proclaimed.

And Braden had known it. Of course he wanted to go inside, Josiah always wanted to go inside. *Inside* was not here, the car, the old, the familiar. *Inside* was always new, exciting. Of course he'd want to go in.

"Okay," Braden said. "But just in and out. Real fast. All right?"

"O-tay, Daddy."

But Braden didn't move.

The woman who bought the house hadn't changed anything. Not one thing. *Who does that?* he wondered. The ranch-style house featured a deep front yard covered in tan gravel. From east to west: two kitchen windows looked out over an unadorned concrete porch. On the opposite side of the front door, one small window in the master bathroom and one larger window in the master bedroom glared like transparent eyes, shaded with off-white aluminum awnings. The awnings reminded Braden of a smoker's teeth.

When he and Ashley bought their place, it had already been close to a dream home, "close" being the operative word. The home had needed some interior paint changes—one particular mustard-yellow accent wall drove them both crazy—and the back yard resembled a blank, brown slate. Over time, though, they'd painted inside, built a red brick patio in the back, and installed new double-pane windows throughout. Braden still wanted to turn the back yard into a sort of park for himself and Josiah, with plenty of trees and lush grass.

This woman had done *nothing* to the Clark's former house. The same dust-colored exterior paint Braden had put on himself, some twenty-two years ago, still clung stubbornly to the wood slats. The rotted red wooden split rail fence stood in place, useless for anything other than a perfunctory property demarcation. The trees and bushes had either continued growing, overwhelming the roof and long front yard, or else died in place, shedding tinder-brown needles and leaves. The monster acacia rooted beside the driveway had grown immense, nearly obscuring the concrete front porch running from the carport to the front door.

Braden blew breath out between his teeth with a hiss.

"What doing, Daddy?" Josiah asked again. He frequently asked many things again.

"Sorry, Joze. Nothing. Just thinking. You ready to go?"

Josiah cheered, "Yaaaay!"

And Braden thought, *He has no idea what happened here. And that's a good thing. Dear God, I love you, kid.*

He checked his phone; 6:30 on the nose. Dumping the phone into the center console, Braden opened his door. Cold wind blew in, whipping the cuffs of his jeans with a sound like startled birds.

And clouds slid overhead, heading west to obscure the sun.

two

Braden Clark's first novel had not been a success, not by any conventional measure. Conventional measures didn't interest him, though. One doesn't set out to write a Shakespearean mystery thriller with hopes of international acclaim. Or if one does, one doesn't admit it publicly. He'd been thrilled to have been offered a ten thousand dollar advance. Likewise, he'd been thrilled—and a little terrified—to take the small stage at his local independent bookshop the day the book released and talk about it, and answer questions from the few dozen friends and family who'd shown up to celebrate with him.

More importantly, his editor wanted another book. After a year of struggling with titanic writer's block and the birth of Josiah Andrew Clark, he'd finally hastily scribbled a bank heist story. In it, two teenagers planned what they thought would be the perfect holdup and getaway, a sort of Bonnie and Clyde for digital natives. That one caught the attention of librarians and educators, and quite unexpectedly, his years of teaching Shakespeare at the junior college level came in handy. Schools wanted him to come talk to their kids, conferences wanted him to speak or teach classes.

Braden gladly did it all. Even after three years, the moderate success made him dizzy, and Ashley's pride in him thrilled him endlessly. She happily continued her work with disabled veterans at the Department of Economic Security, because they learned quickly that book-writing and conference-going didn't pay many bills. Josiah ran and giggled and tantrumed his way through life as usual, proud of his dad for nothing more than being his dad, which helped keep Braden's ego in check—Stephen King might be a millionaire, but Braden guessed he'd still had screaming toddlers to deal with.

Local papers wrote stories and reviews about Braden and the new book, and the bookstore invited him back again to launch the second novel. Braden accepted, and the crowd had been bigger that time. There were even a handful of people whose faces he did not recognize, which to Braden indicted his greatest success of all—more people than friends and family knew of him and cared enough about the books to come to the book event.

And the old woman had shown up.

She loomed at the back of the crowd, wearing a gray overcoat against the unusual storm that had broken that Tuesday night of the launch party. She'd stood there, unsmiling, hands dangling straight down, arms motionless, watching him speak. Ten years of teaching had given Braden that teacherly ability to quickly pick out who was paying attention and who wasn't; or who, as in this case, simply didn't fit in.

She bothered him as soon as he noticed her. The woman

didn't seem to blink, and made no discernable expression throughout his talk. By the time he finished and sat down to sign books, he'd been perspiring from the strain of not openly staring back at her.

The line for books lasted perhaps thirty minutes, and she'd waited for all of it, scuffling along at the back of the queue. Braden's heart had pounded just a little more with each step she took nearer the table.

She had no book in her hand when she got to him. Braden forced the best smile he could, looked up at her, and said, "Hello."

"I read about you," the woman said, each syllable colored the same as her overcoat. "There's a box for you at the house."

Braden said, as most people would, "Uh . . . ?"

"I bought your old house," she said. "Mildred Malkin."

"Oh!" The sound came out of him before he could have even attempted to stop it. "That's . . . I . . . okay. And, I'm sorry, you said . . . ?"

"A box came for you. Think it's books. The return address says Donelly & Sisters Publishing."

"Oh," Braden repeated, but softer. Donelly & Sisters, a small imprint in New York, had published his first novel. Part of his contract stipulated twenty free hardcover editions to him, which he'd received two years ago. The novel had gone into paperback, which meant he'd receive an additional twenty copies in that format. They'd never arrived, and he'd never really thought to ask for them.

"How did they get there?" Braden asked.

But of course Mildred Malkin couldn't answer that and did not try. "Heavy box," she said. "Couldn't lift it. It's been in the kitchen for months. You'll have to come get it."

"I see," Braden said, aware that, and unsure why, he was stalling.

"Any time's good," Mildred went on. "I'm always home."

The word *always* came out with a bit of emotional seasoning Braden couldn't quite identify. Bitter, maybe? Sad? Lonely? So far, it was the only word that hadn't sounded identical to the others.

Braden ran mentally through his schedule quickly and said, "Friday, maybe? Six-ish?"

"Friday's fine," Mildred Malkin said, and with a curt nod, went on her way.

By the time the launch party wrapped up—the store manager, Eddie, said they'd sold fifty copies of the book—Braden felt anger boiling a pot of acid in his belly. Ashley noticed it immediately and, per her usual manner, addressed it just as immediately.

"What's wrong?" she asked as he slammed the door of the Tundra. Braden winced at himself; the truck wasn't more than a couple of weeks old, he needed to be more careful with it.

"How did she get it?" Braden said, nearly shouting. "How the hell did a box from Donelly end up *there?* Jesus!"

"You think Jesus put it there?" Ashley said with an innocent lilt.

His anger decreased from a boil to a simmer. Ashley had that effect on him. Braden snorted a surrender and started the truck.

"I moved out, lived on campus, then got the apartment, and then we got the house," he said as he drove out of the parking lot. Ashley, of course, knew all of this, but let him speak—and he knew *that*, too. "They had the apartment address, and they have the house address. How the hell did the box end up at my old place?"

"Well, it must have something to do with the move," Ashley said, tucking a piece of blonde hair behind her left ear. The gesture never failed to tickle him inside. She'd done it several times the first time they met, six years ago, and still it worked magic on him.

The magic dimmed slightly that night, though, as he wrestled with the mystery of the box of books. "That's just it, there's no way. They would never, ever have had that address for me. Never."

"It *is* weird."

"Yeah."

Braden began gnawing on his lip, and Ashley rested a hand on his leg, assuring him of her presence. She also said nothing; another one of her insightful gifts. He knew she was tuned in to his ugly thought: *I can't believe I have to go back to that goddamn house.*

"You could just leave the box," Ashley said when they were halfway home. "You don't *have* to pick it up."

"Yeah, but what if there's something else in there? Maybe there's a royalty check, or even just a statement, or—I don't know."

"I can go on Saturday afternoon if you want. Just me. I'm happy to."

Braden considered it for a while before saying, "You know what, no. No. My parents aren't there, right? I'll just go in and grab the box real quick, no big deal. I already told her I'd be there Friday anyway."

"You're sure?"

"Yeah. It's just a house. Who cares."

Except it wasn't just a house. Ashley knew it as well as he did. Later, after they'd relieved Ashley's mom and dad from babysitting duties and put Josiah to bed, sex helped diminish his apprehension, but not well and not for long. Ashley, attuned to him as always, noticed and said nothing.

He hadn't slept well.

three

Braden got Josiah out of his car seat and hoisted the hefty three-year-old to the ground; Josiah ranked above the fiftieth percentile for his age and size. Joze reached up for his dad's hand, and Braden took it gladly.

Joze will be a big kid, Braden thought as they took slow, deliberate steps up the carport cement. It seemed like the boy's hand had grown larger overnight somehow. Physiologically, of course, that must be true in some barely measurable way; but today Josiah's hand felt particularly mature even if his gait did not.

Braden stopped them when they passed the front bumper of the Tundra, realizing he'd been automatically heading toward the door beneath the carport, which opened into the kitchen. Where they'd stopped, a pale flagstone path led from the uncovered portion of the driveway to the front door, and Braden realized they ought to go that direction. *Owners* used a kitchen door, *guests* used the front. The distinction actually made him feel better momentarily. He was merely and gratefully a guest now.

"Let's go this way, buddy," Braden said, urging the toddler to the right.

Josiah didn't protest. He merely asked, "What we doing?"

"We're picking up a box of Daddy's books."

"Why?"

Here we go, Braden thought, but smiled. Joze entered the "Why" phase several months prior and showed no sign of relenting. Usually Braden didn't mind. And he didn't mind now; it kept him distracted from the window-eyes of the house that followed his movement up the path.

"Well, some books got sent here by accident," he told Josiah.

"Why?"

"That's a question I'm asking, too, m'man. But you know what?"

"What!"

"I'm super glad you're here with me."

Braden thought he detected a lift to Josiah's step after saying it.

They reached the front door, and Braden's eyes immediately shot to the roof overhang. Here is where the spiders loved to wait.

It seemed every summer of his entire life, these enormous brown, wolven arachnids would arrive and park themselves on the ceiling here, ostensibly to feed on the tiny fliers gathering around the porch light. Then why, Braden always wondered, were there always so many bugs? Their population never decreased when the spiders showed up. The sight of their hairy, splayed bodies never failed to give him chills. Whether they were venomous or not didn't matter, the buggers scared him. A few times, in his youth, he'd tried to kill them as they hung upside down in that unnatural way of theirs; they'd hang and wait to either hunt bugs or, as Braden believed only half-jokingly, to race inside and terrorize him in his own bedroom. Never once had he killed one. He'd learned the hard way that spraying insecticide was a bad idea. Upon contact, the nebulous poison often caused the spiders to drop and swing acrobatically from draglines, suspended in midair, and somehow always at the exact height of his eyes, where their angry legs would tremble and reach for him. Trying to squash them with sticks from afar never worked; they'd sensed the attack and run full speed along the ceiling to some previously unknown hiding hole. Their hideous speed always caused him to shriek and hurriedly pull the front door closed, breathing hard and swearing never to try *that* stunt again.

Being a chilly November day, though, and still technically daytime—although gray clouds floated thicker and thicker overhead—he saw no spiders. Grim relief caused Braden to exhale audibly.

He reached out for the doorbell buzzer, but stopped and asked Josiah instead, "You want to press the button?"

The doorbell sat much higher than the boy could reach. Joze loved pushing buttons. Sometimes Braden found it cute, occasionally even helpful; other times it created disaster. Braden hadn't realized how many household buttons were within reach of a toddler until recently.

This time, though, Josiah seemed hesitant. Joze gazed at the once-red front door, now a dismal rust color covered in fine dust, as if uncertain the portal could in fact be opened.

It's a door, Braden thought as he watched his son. *It's just a door, dude.*

Yet even as Braden finished the thought, Josiah scooted back a couple of inches—not quite seeking refuge and safety from behind Braden's leg, but definitely edging closer to his father.

"You okay, Joze?"

Josiah nodded.

"You want to push the button?"

Josiah shook his head.

So Braden hit the doorbell. He saw no point in trying to convince Joze to do it, and no point standing around wasting time. He heard the old chime clang dismally in the front hallway, a tired *dang-dang* curse rather than the crisp, lively *ding-dong!* of happy houses.

Happy houses? Braden thought. *So this one's sad, is that it?*

Yes, he replied to himself. *Yes, this one is sad. Among other things.*

With a stunning crack, the front door pried open. Braden jumped, and he felt Joze tensing beside him. Braden realized suddenly, and for no useful reason, that perhaps the door had not been opened since he'd lived here. An image of archaeologists using a crowbar to pry the stone lid off an ancient sarcophagus came to mind.

Mildred Malkin peered out from the darkness of the house, and Braden found his breath sucked up and out of his lungs.

The two kitchen windows offered weak sunlight to spill into the short foyer; weak not only because of the storm clouds shifting into position overhead, but from the gargantuan acacia tree as well, which darkened the front yard even on the sunniest days. Once past the threshold of the front door, the kitchen lay to the left, and a long hallway to the right—also dark, Braden remembered clearly. Straight ahead from the foyer, they'd enter a nearly circular room with a fireplace, but no windows; further beyond the fireplace room sat the living room, where the TV and couch used to be. That room took a left turn, where—at last—additional windows faced east into the back patio and yard.

No natural light in the fireplace room, Braden thought. Not when the front door was shut, which had been most of the time when he'd lived here. Just darkness, even on the brightest day. The bend in the living room floorplan prevented sunlight from creeping into the fireplace room. And besides, trees branched out over the patio, shading it year-round, so little sunlight got into the living room anyway. The left-hand hallway also lacked natural light, which meant the heart of the house lay in darkness.

How did the sun ever get into this place? Braden wondered. *Or maybe it didn't, and I just didn't notice.*

"You came," Mildred Malkin said.

"Yeah, hi," Braden said, trying for a smile and not sure he succeeded.

"You brought the boy."

Go. Now.

This first, immediate internal response shocked him. It wasn't so much a red flag or an alarm bell as a gentle, almost maternal tug at the back of his conscious mind.

Go, now. Please.

The most recent newspaper article about Braden and the books had mentioned Josiah, in terms of his answering the questions "Do you have children, and does having them change what you write about?" The answers had been yes, then no. Or not really, not that he could tell. Joze couldn't read his father's novels for many more years, so it never occurred to Braden to write any differently, or to change his style for the sake of his son.

So Mildred—Braden wasn't sure if she had a Mrs. in front of her name or not—must have simply realized that the little boy at Braden's leg was that child he'd mentioned in the article. That's all.

Still—her phrasing tugged again at him. *The boy.* Who talked like that in the real world? For one terrible moment, Braden thought he saw his parents shadowed in the darkness behind Mildred; wicked beast versions of them, with horns and tails, as he'd imagined them and dreamed of them when still a boy himself.

Stop it, he told himself.

"Yes, this is Josiah," Braden said, rather gamely, he though. "Joze, can you say hi?"

"Hi . . ." Joze said cautiously.

Here is where the tension will break, Braden thought. *She's an old lady, all old ladies love kids, it's in the Constitution or something.*

But Mildred said nothing. If her eyes darted toward Josiah at all, Braden didn't see it. Then again, her withered face sank deep into the gloom of the old house, and he couldn't deduce much about her reactions.

"You'll want to take a look around, I suppose," Mildred said. "Old times and all."

"Actually—" Braden began, but Josiah took over. Joze could not resist an invitation.

"Yaaaaay!" he shouted, and hopped up and down in place, tugging Braden's hand.

"Well, I guess that answers that," Braden said, and tried to give a courtesy laugh. It dropped dead on arrival.

Mildred opened the door further and stepped away. "Feel free. I'll be in front of the fire."

Fire? Braden thought. *I didn't smell the fireplace going.*

At least, not until right that very moment, when the old familiar odor of wood smoke tickled into his nose and he could see the dim orange light cast by the fireplace; a fiery pupil in the sclera of darkness.

The front door sat a couple of inches off the concrete porch floor. For the first time in twenty years, Braden Clark stepped up inside the house.

He still held his son's hand. Tightly.

f o u r

Braden marveled briefly at the colossal effort it took him to shut the door behind them, and when he did, it sounded like a vault door being whisked shut with a deep boom.

"You live here?" Josiah asked his dad, tilting his head at all angles to take in the short entryway.

Braden matched his son's examination. The cream-colored tile floor must not have been cleaned since the house went on the market; the grout had turned brown. To the left, the kitchen retained its old blue and tan wallpaper, its cabinetry still pale oak. The hallway to the right, leading to bedrooms and bathrooms, lay as dark and long as ever, a great maw awaiting tribute.

"I used to," Braden said. "A long, long time ago."

"What's there?" Josiah pointed down the dark hallway.

"My old room. We're not going that way, bud. Come on, come this way."

Josiah followed his prompting forward, past the kitchen and the hallway, into the fireplace room. Josiah went only haltingly, his free fingers edging into his mouth as he kept a watchful eye on the hallway as they passed it.

He's like a cat, Braden thought. *When they wake up suddenly and just stare at something no human can see.*

It seemed to Braden at that point he could detect the faint smell of ammonia, that cat-piss smell unlike any other on Earth. His family had kept a few cats over the years, here at the old place, but no more. One of his first goals upon getting into his bachelor's apartment had been to get a rescue dog. Jake. Jake had been a medium dog, good for walking, but already sporting a white-haired muzzle. Dogs could be stupid, and a pack could be dangerous, but most wanted nothing more than to utterly and completely love a human being, and Jake fit that bill. Braden had sworn to never own another cat so long as he lived; they were capable of too much disdain, too much hate. At least, until you had something they wanted, then the suckers would play all their nice cards. You couldn't trust a cat. A dog—whether stupid or dangerous or loving—let you know immediately what he was all about. No secrets.

The acrid scent of cat piss wafted past Braden again, and he wrinkled his nose involuntarily. Another difference between the cats and the dogs: dogs might get messy, yes, but if a cat decided to spray something—say, your brand-new favorite fifth-grade backpack—no force under Heaven could remove that smell. A fifth-grader might get called a lot of interesting names that year because of that faint odor that never, ever went away no matter how many times he washed it.

Just for example, Braden thought.

"Daddy?"

"Huh?"

Braden jerked. He'd come to a stop, not quite past the dark hallway, looking down its length, remembering.

"You squeeze my hand," Josiah said, pulling gently away.

"Oh. Sorry, buddy. I didn't notice. Sorry."

"This way," Josiah announced, forgiving the indiscretion immediately. He stepped into the fireplace room.

Mildred Malkin sat in a stuffed chair upholstered with a dismal flower print cloth. Her knotted hands expertly worked two knitting needles, though Braden couldn't say yet what the old woman was building.

He noticed immediately that, like the front yard and kitchen, Mildred had changed nothing in this room. His parents had painted all the interior walls flat white before putting the house up for sale, covering 70s era chic wood paneling. But Mildred had let the walls stay white and empty, with no art or decoration. A dining nook contained a table and four chairs, smaller than the enormous table his parents had kept in the same place. Mildred's furniture looked out of place in there, like doll toys. The hardwood floor, original to the construction and resealed in the weeks leading up to the house going on the market, still appeared serviceable but unswept.

Braden assumed then that the entire property inside and out had been preserved. No; not preserved, but neglected. Clearly Mildred had found the house she wanted, tossed her things inside, and left it at that. Such a careless act carried with it an air of depression, but Braden shrugged it off. He wasn't here to offer decorating advice.

"The place looks good," Braden said, unable to help himself. He meant it sarcastically, and it came out that way, but it lacked the sharpness to penetrate the way he'd wanted it to.

Mildred didn't bother to reply, choosing instead to continue working on her knitting. Her fingers reminded him of the spiders' legs he'd dreaded as a kid.

Braden glanced toward the living room, which lay to the left of the fireplace. It had been an addition built by his father for the sole purpose of containing a regulation pool table, one of the few joys the house had brought Braden. A tiled step up led into the living room, forming a sort of theatrical proscenium arch of the threshold. The pool table stood intact there in the dark, reminding Braden of a sports car in a forgotten garage, waiting only to be dusted and started up and allowed to cruise to its full potential. He still wanted a pool table of his own, but his and Ashley's home didn't have the space.

Josiah must have intuited his gaze. He pointed at the big table and shouted, "What that!"

"That's a pool table," Braden said, taking steps toward the tile step. "You want to see?"

"Poo table?" Josiah asked, perplexed.

Giggling a little despite himself, Braden said, "Pool table. Like a swimming pool."

He caught the error as soon as he'd said it; Josiah seized on the image and asked, "For swimming?"

Oh, boy. "Just come take a look," Braden said, and guided Josiah into the living room.

But stopped on the tile step after he heard the creak.

The hardwood floor conducted a quiet symphony of its own from place to place, tiny tweets and stringlike twangs that followed walkers around. But in front of the tile step to the living room lay a baritone brass, a wooden creak that could not be stepped around, one that had foretold the arrival his father all those years ago while Braden watched cartoons in the living room after school.

"What that?" Josiah proclaimed, looking at his feet.

"Just the wood," Braden said. "It creaks a little."

It creaks a lot is more like it, he thought. *My God, it sounds exactly the same. Exactly.*

Josiah lost interest immediately and rushed for the pool table. His little head barely poked above it. Braden joined him, and frowned with a flash of anger—Mildred Malkin had not covered the table at all, not protectively. On top lay only balls of tangled yarn and . . . yes, a cat. A goddamn cat on the pool table; a fat, cantankerous alley with tiger stripes and a yellow belly. The animal bore multiples of toes it did not need, and when it spoke to him, its voice came out like a witch's shriek.

Josiah made a face. "What that?"

"That is a cat, on my pool table." Braden used the possessive without thinking about it. The cat's presence on the dusty green felt irritated him. Anxious now to get away from the insulting creature, and since they'd come this far anyway, Braden decided he wanted to say hello to the best friend he'd had here as a kid. He asked Josiah, "You want to see the yard?"

"Yaaaaay!"

Braden turned to ask Mildred if she minded them checking out the backyard, but Mildred had silently disappeared, leaving the tangle of blue yarn behind on her chair. The fire had lost its roar.

Shrugging, Braden led his son behind an ancient couch—upholstered the same as Mildred's knitting chair—and to the back door leading to the porch. Curtains were drawn across the single-pane picture windows, leaving them to navigate only by shreds of gray light.

What is it with people living in this house and hating sunlight? Braden thought. *Like both sets of owners were goddamn vampires.*

He ushered Josiah through the back door, closing it behind them. This door, too, had its own distinctive swish-whoosh sound as it opened and closed. Each little noise felt like the needleprick of a syringe, injecting him with memories.

Josiah toddled out across the red brick patio and out from underneath the porch roof. He held his hands palm up. "It's raining, Daddy!"

Braden joined him, and felt the tiny drops. Overgrown trees formed a low-hanging, thick canopy shielding them from most of the drops, but a fine mist crept through the leaves.

"Yeah, it's raining. Not bad though."

Josiah marched out to the yard, which formed a half-acre U around the back side of the house. Braden followed.

Quickly it became clear the backyard fared no better than the front under Mildred Malkin's care, or lack thereof. An old tin shed sat still on its concrete slab, as pointless now as it had been in Braden's youth. The trees had grown taller and thicker or else died and withered; the former never pruned, the latter never removed. The ground lay barren, only hard-packed dirt and occasional patches of gravel. The brown cinderblock wall encircling the back yard seemed miscast, belonging more to a prison than a suburban home.

Josiah wandered through the yard, heading west, toward the next bend in the yard.

"Wait!" Braden cried.

His son paused, looking back, concerned—why was his will being thwarted?

Braden licked his lips, not wanting Josiah out of his sight, not in that part of the yard. Not without him. He hurried to catch up, not realizing he'd stopped to survey the whole property. It seemed that the treetops bent now and formed a thicker ceiling than they had just moments ago, but Braden chalked the sensation up to the growing cloud cover and weight of rain as it fell on their branches.

Josiah dismissed him and continued walking, slowly following the bend in the yard. Braden skipped to catch him, but slowed again as he neared the pine tree.

This immense pine must have been older than the house itself, stretching high toward the sky. He wanted to call it majestic, but it wasn't; it was old and tired, still green but shot through with brown, much like Braden's own occasional beard now betrayed stray white hairs.

He approached the trunk with a sort of reverence, reaching out and letting his hand rest on the crumbly bark. The tree seemed to pulse to life beneath him, though obviously it was only the beat of his own heart through his fingers. For an absurd moment, tears stung his eyes, and Braden thought, *It remembers, too.*

It remembered the countless times he'd scaled the branches to the top, to the dangerous top, to the fatal top if he ever lost his grip. Yet not once in a decade or more of climbing it had he ever fallen from this tree. Never once had it bit him or drawn blood, never once had any creature slid down his shirt or dangled before him like the spiders on the front porch. This tree was a sanctuary. He wasn't sure if his parents knew he climbed as high as he did. The pine must have been forty or fifty feet tall, and from its summit, he commanded a view encompassing most of Phoenix. Or least it had seemed so. Braden fought the urge to scale up it again, one more time, see the sights from on high.

"I think I missed you," he whispered.

Wind murmured through its branches, and a soft, wooden groan like an ache issued from some branch high above. Standing at the trunk and looking straight up its length, Braden thought briefly that two of the lowest branches dipped low toward him. A trick of the stormlight gathering overhead, he figured.

"What these?" Josiah's voice broke his reverie.

Braden turned, and the warmth left his body.

The wire mesh chicken coop. Still there.

And Josiah too close.

"Red light!" he called instinctively, and Josiah froze in place. Braden quick-stepped toward his son and grabbed his hand again, then hunkered down beside him.

"Sorry, bud," he said. "I didn't mean to scare you. It's just, it's dangerous over here, okay?"

Josiah nodded as if he understood, though Braden knew he didn't. Couldn't.

The coop took up the north-western corner of the yard, stretching about thirty feet across and fifteen feet deep. The rear consisted of the same brown cinderblock that surrounded the rest of the yard, while the front and one side of the coop were made up of hexagonal chicken wire stretched tight over cedar posts cemented into the ground.

No chickens, though. There hadn't been chickens

back there since before the house sold. That made sense; Mildred Malkin clearly didn't venture into this yard much, if ever. Raising anything other than the asshole alley cat in the living room didn't seem fitting in Mildred's lifestyle.

"What that?" Josiah's never-ending question.

"It's a chicken coop," Braden said. "You raise chickens in there for their eggs. It's like a little farm."

"Mommy eats eggs!"

"Yep, she sure does. C'mon, let's go back in." Braden stood.

"Why you in there?"

Electricity raced through his spine. "What? What, Joze?"

"Nothing," Josiah said. He hadn't moved, just stood planted on the dirt staring at the structure.

"C'mon, let's go," Braden urged. "Look, it's starting to rain more."

Josiah looked upward. Here by the coop, the foliage thinned overhead. Some days—*most* days in this part of the country—sunlight would trickle down. Today, it was rain. The storm clouds thickened and grew darker, puffing up like dragon bellows, preparing to roar.

Then they did. In one enormous peal of thunder that rattled Braden's ribcage and made Josiah cry out, the torrent came. Great heaving drops poured down on them as the sun set completely.

Pulling Josiah close, Braden ran instinctively for the big pine tree, huddling by its two-foot-diameter trunk. The tree protected them instantly from the worst of the downpour.

"It's raining," Josiah announced.

Braden smiled, overcome by affection. He never

wanted Josiah to grow up. There were times, as there are always are, where he couldn't wait for the kid to get out of the house, go to college, find work he loved, the whole nine. But those times were fleeting. Most days with his son, most *moments*, he never wanted to end. Soon enough he'd stop snuggling on the couch. Not long from now, they'd probably lock horns over school or girls or cars or all of the above. Right now, though—right now, he loved Josiah as much as the big pine tree seemed to love him throughout the years. And like the old tree had done, he would get to watch Josiah grow up.

"Yeah," he said. "It sure is raining. We should get inside."

But they didn't, not right away. In moments the brown dirt became a gray sludge, the trees no longer enough to keep the water out. Under the pine, the ground stayed relatively dry, giving for all the world the appearance that they'd found a desert island in the ocean.

"I'm told," Josiah said.

"Cold," Braden corrected. "We need to work on those *kuh* sounds, Joze."

All the same, he picked the kid up.

"Ready to run for it?"

"Yeah!"

"All right, here we go."

Braden gave the pine one last look, tilting his head back to scan up its entire length. Again he thought he heard the soft creak of branches moving, and again believed it to be the wind. He lowered his chin, and darted through the sudden bog of the backyard.

The going wasn't as fast as he'd thought it would be.

Mud sucked hard at his shoes, crummy Sauconys from his running days, as if working against him, trying to prevent him from reaching the red brick patio. The journey took twice as long as he'd figured and he felt breathless and old by the time he and Josiah made it to solid ground. He tried to set Josiah down, but thunder erupted and the toddler squealed, clinging tighter and strangling his dad.

"Joze, relax, you're choking me. Let go a little. Okay? Okay?"

Josiah obeyed, but falteringly. When Braden could breathe again, he said, "That was a big one, huh?"

Josiah nodded.

The thunderclap presaged another deluge. Braden sank to the bricks on one knee, keeping his hold on Josiah but turning to watch the rain smash into the yard. It sounded like a chorus of demons out there; the wind that had murmured beneath the pine now bawled with rage.

Lightning struck.

Shouting in shock as the bolt crackled from the sky, Braden twisted away from the yard and toward the house, protecting his son. An explosion went off—close, but not beside them. The lightning had definitely hit the ground, and close, but not in their immediate vicinity; when he turned to check, the backyard and patio seemed unscathed; drenched, and already flooding, but not blackened.

"Enough of *that* shit," Braden muttered, and scurried for the back door. He pulled it open, dumped Josiah inside, and shut it behind them. A moment later, he locked it, too, though for no good reason he could come up with.

"All right," Braden said. "So this has been all kinds of fun, but it's time to get out of here. Okay, Joze?"

Josiah nodded. Then yawned.

Too much excitement for one evening, Braden thought. *Let's get the hell on out of this place.*

Together they walked past the couch again, which faced an ancient tube television on the counter at the front of the room. The yellow tiger tabby howled at them again as they passed the pool table, and Braden flipped it a finger as they walked by.

Stepping down into the dark fireplace room, Braden paused, scanning for Mildred. She'd either disappeared, or else blended into the shadows thrown by the dying fire.

"Hello?" he called. Josiah echoed him.

No response. A single loud *pop!* from the fireplace startled him, but nothing more.

"All right," Braden sighed. "That's it. Let's go."

He guided Josiah to the intersection of the entrance hall, long hallway, and kitchen doorway. Hadn't she said the box was in the kitchen? Leaving Josiah there at the intersection, Braden eased into the kitchen, surprised at its mysterious lack of smell. No ghosts from his past, and no hints from its present. The kitchen felt lived in, and decades-old stains on the countertops remained; the tile here, too, needed a thorough cleaning; and Mildred hadn't put up any art or other decorations. If she'd cooked recently, he couldn't smell it. The stove was new—or rather, not original to when he lived here, anyway. It must have been installed not long after Mildred Malkin moved in, because it definitely showed twenty years of use on its flat four-burner range.

Braden walked the length of the kitchen, but saw no box. He paused at the kitchen door, which led into the covered carport. Mildred's car was as nondescript as the rest of the house—a beige sedan of indeterminate model.

Thunder shook the foundations, and Josiah called for him. Braden went to him, frowning. Where was the goddamn box? Standing in the intersection with Josiah again, he glared down the hall.

"Hello? Mrs., uh . . . Malkin? Hello?"

"Where she go?"

"Man, I don't know, Joze. Here, let's go ahead and check down this way."

Josiah snaked his fingers into Braden's hand and gripped tightly. Braden led them down the hallway, slowly, as if expecting a trap. They passed a guest quarter-bathroom on the right, small and painted tan. At the end of the hall, before the left turn, the door to what had been his parents' bedroom stood closed. He glanced to the left; two additional bedroom doors were also closed. One had been his, the other his mother's sewing room.

Impulsively, Braden stepped into the short end of the L, and flicked on a light switch. The architects had apparently realized just how damn dark it could get back here, and installed a hallway light. It popped on, sickly yellow, but at least chased the worst of the shadows away.

"Hello?" he tried again, but already knew somehow what would happen.

Nothing.

Braden stepped back to the master bedroom door and knocked. "Mrs. Malkin, I can't seem to find the box. Hello? It's really storming out there—"

A punch of thunder drove into the house.

"—and we need to get going. Hello? Are you all right?"

It occurred to him then that maybe something horrible had happened to the old woman. What if she lay in the bedroom, choking to death or having some kind of heart failure? Yes, it was possible . . .

Or maybe she's in the master bathroom taking an enormous dump, that too is possible, Braden thought with grim humor. *God* he wanted out of here.

"Know what?" he said, half to himself and half to Josiah. "Forget the books, not even worth it. Let's just go home."

Josiah, to his surprise, didn't seize on the idea right away. Instead the boy glanced down the shorter hall, toward the two bedroom doors.

"What down there?"

Oh, boy, here we go, Braden thought. "That's uh, where Daddy used to sleep. C'mon."

He tried pulling Josiah down the hall. Not happening. Josiah's curiosity was piqued.

"Can I *see* it?"

"No, we gotta go, Joze."

"But *why?*"

Ah, shit, not now, Braden thought. "Because it's raining really hard and we need to get home. Okay? Let's go."

Josiah let himself be coaxed down the hall and into the kitchen. Braden paused for one more look around; the fire had nearly extinguished itself, and still no sign of the old woman.

He pried open the front door as another boom of thunder went off above them. Josiah sucked air between his teeth and huddled closer to Braden.

"All right, off we go," Braden said, and they stepped onto the front porch.

And stopped.

"No *way*," Braden said.

They'd found where the lightning hit.

f i v e

The acacia tree had fallen squarely over the Tundra, its forked main branches forming an embrace on either end of the vehicle. It seemed as if the tree were gripping the black truck with enormous claws. Where the lightning hit, the trunk of the tree still smoldered beneath the punishing rain.

"Dammit," Braden said. "Wait here."

He ran to the tree as Josiah screamed for him from the front porch, the sound all but lost in the wind. Before even reaching the tree, Braden knew: There would be no moving it, not with brute force. It would take a chainsaw and an hour or more to free the truck. They were going nowhere.

Yet he tried anyway, forced by his own sense of parental responsibility to at least make an honest attempt. For God's sake, they couldn't stay *here*, not this house, not one moment longer . . .

The tree didn't move as he first pulled, then switched sides and tried pushing on the trunk. The branches may as well have been steel I-beams.

Trapped, he thought. *The fucking thing has trapped us here. It wants us here.*

Braden blinked rain from his eyelashes. What the hell kind of thinking was that? It's a storm, a tree, and a problem. His creative mind had started tiptoeing to the fore, pushing reason aside.

We'll stay on the porch, he thought grimly, still shoving hard against the trunk. *We will just stay on the goddamned porch until the rain lets up if that's what we have to do, goddammit, why won't this thing move?*

Except he knew that staying on the porch was no more feasible than freeing the truck. Thanks to the wind and sheer volume of rain, water soaked the concrete almost as far as the short step up into the house at the front door. It would be miserable staying outside, even with the roof offering a modicum of protection.

Braden yanked at branches, wondering if there were at least some way to get into the car, stay holed up in there until help arrived, but the tree had done its job admirably. Not only was there no moving the car, there was no climbing into the damned thing at all.

He abandoned the tree. Squinting through the rain, he rushed back to the porch. He knelt down and hugged Josiah tightly with drenched arms, again considering just staying right here on the porch. But no; it was too cold now, far too cold. At the very best, Josiah would be forced to endure a piercing chill, not to mention the furious wind and rain. The porch offered nothing more than dampness compared to the rest of the neighborhood's cascades.

The neighbors, Braden thought wildly. *I can go to a neighbor's house.*

The front door opened behind them with its bank-vault whoosh. Mildred Malkin peered out at them. Something had changed about the old woman, though Braden couldn't identify what. More pale, perhaps. Her face loomed somehow, a vacant white space in the darkness behind her.

"Looks like you're stuck," Mildred said.

"Yeah, I think I'll need a chainsaw or something. You don't happen to have—"

"No."

Braden wasn't surprised, and it didn't matter, not yet. The storm had unleashed with pernicious force, and even if Mildred had a chainsaw lying around, using it in that gale wouldn't be safe.

So, on to step two.

"Well, I'll probably call my wife," Braden told her, not liking the idea but seeing no alternative. "She can come pick us up, and then tomorrow, maybe, we can get someone to come cut up the tree. I got a guy who—"

"Streets are blocked," Mildred said. "You'll have to stay here."

No, a voice whined in his head. *No, no, no, I want to go HOME.*

"Really?" Braden said. It hit him that he and Josiah were still on the porch, and that his son shivered in his arms. "Did you see that on TV?"

"Radio. TV's out."

"Daddy, I'm *told,*" Josiah said.

"All right, Joze. We'll go inside."

He stood up and ushered his son toward the front door, unable to stop himself from glancing up as he did, searching for those hairy spiders. He saw nothing. Mildred

Malkin stepped back, keeping a hand on the door knob as they re-entered his old house.

"Thanks," Braden said as Mildred shut the door. "Do you have a towel or two we could borrow?"

Mildred moved off down the hall without a word. Braden guessed where she was going; a built-in linen closet faced his old bedroom door in the short end of the L-shaped hall. And indeed, Mildred disappeared around that left turn, as quiet as a ghost.

"Here, let's, uh . . . here," Braden babbled, and took Josiah into the fireplace room. The hearth had a protruding rock ledge, most of which was taken up by a freestanding three-pane screen, but enough space at the edge of the hearth remained to form a sort of bench; a perfect perch for warming up one's back, so he sat there with Josiah beside him. The fire, having already died, left only coals to emanate heat, and even those coals did little. It felt to Braden as if the house was cold, and the red-hot remnants were only *less-cold*, not warm. It would have to do until Mildred came back with the towels.

He considered taking the initiative and going for more wood himself, rekindling the blaze. Clearly the old woman kept wood on hand. His father used to keep a cord or so in a fenced off area of the front yard, at the far southeastern corner. His mother used to hang clothes to dry back there. Mentally, he could distinctly recall the clicking-clacks of the gate latch opening and closing; an oddly precise auditory memory.

"You good?" Braden asked Josiah.

The toddler nodded, still shivering. Braden hugged him close for a moment, then went into the kitchen. He'd seen the same old tan corded phone on the wall by the kitchen door; he could call Ashley at work, have her come get them.

The phone gave him only a faint buzz. No dial tone. He smacked the cradle a few times—never having understood what effect this was supposed to have, but driven to try it anyway. No response. The line was dead.

"Radio says there's a flood."

Braden spun. Mildred stood in the doorway, forearms out like a forklift. She carried on them a stack of towels that may or may not have once been white.

"Hundred year flood," Mildred went on. "Don't get those much."

"Right, probably every—I don't know, hundred years or so," Braden said with a moment of bitter joy at being able to lash out.

Mildred neither saw the humor nor took offense. She turned on her heel and headed into the fireplace room. Braden hurried after her, not wanting her to be alone with his son.

She dumped the towels on her chair. "You might have to stay the night."

"Oh, no," Braden said, picking up the top bath towel. It practically snapped in half as he unfolded it. An odor like mildew and mice greeted him, making him wince. "We won't be here that long. When you say flood—"

"Intersection's gone."

He knew instantly what she meant. The closest stop light was near the main artery out of the neighborhood. Only one way in or out. The neighborhood resembled a gated community without the gate.

"Prob'ly it will drain fast, but the rain's got to let up first," Mildred went on.

Thunder boomed. Braden rolled his eyes. Yes, this day was getting more perfect by the moment.

No—this night. The sun had disappeared while they were in the back yard.

"Even if you did get that tree moved," Mildred went on, oblivious to both the wrath of the storm and Braden's growing frustration, "your car will stall out trying to get through the water. Might carry you away to the wash. You and your boy."

If for any godforsaken reason the woman wanted them to stay here—perhaps out of miserable loneliness, perhaps out of boredom, who knew—then she knew right where to hit him. Braden instantly conjured an image of the wash about a mile east of the house. For about 363 days out of the year, the wash was merely a nice park with a concrete bike path. But the park had been constructed primarily to act as a drain for these occasional storms. If Mildred was right about the intersection's level of water, and it wouldn't be the first time it had happened in Braden's memory, then the wash was certainly flooded. People occasionally tried to cross the wash when it flooded like that, folks from out of town or who thought their bad-ass jacked-up truck could conquer the water. Few ever did. Every year, a handful of idiots had to be hauled out of the muddy torrent. Every other year or so, a couple of people would die trying to cross the wash in a tiny sedan.

Kids died when their parents let their stupidity take over. Braden had seen such tragedies on the news before. Tundra or not, he wouldn't risk crossing that wash tonight.

Of course, to entertain the possibility, the truck would need to be cut out of the damn acacia tree.

Mildred wasn't exaggerating about the intersection being impassable. Braden knew it happened from time to time. Once he'd ridden his bike out to see it, and ended up walking the bike back home because the water had been too deep for him to ride in. He needed no other reminder that, on his own, sure—he might have the temerity to forge the wash and take his chances in the truck if it were free. With Josiah in the car, no way.

"That's a good point," Braden said as he considered all of that. "Maybe we are here for a little bit. If it's not too much trouble. Certainly not overnight though, the storm can't last that long."

Mildred dismissed him. Putting her hands on her knees, she leaned in toward Josiah. Another inch and Braden would have interposed himself between them. People always thought they could get in kids' faces or touch them without permission. He hated that.

"Would you like to hear a story, little boy?"

Braden handed the towel over to Josiah, expecting the boy to decline her invitation. Plus he must be getting hungry for dinner by now.

"O-tay," Josiah said to the old woman.

Mildred smiled, if it could rightly be called that; a thin black line slithered across her lips.

"That's okay," Braden snapped, snatching up the second towel from her chair. "You don't have to do that. We can just wait in the—"

Mildred turned and picked up the knitting materials she'd left earlier. She sank into the chair, keeping her eyes tight on Josiah, who sat directly in front of her with his back to the still-cooling fireplace.

"This is a story about a little boy just your age," Mildred said.

Braden thought but couldn't have proved that her sharp tongue darted between her lips just once as she spoke. She hesitated and peered up at Braden. "How about you get our fire going again? You know where the logs are kept."

"It's wet," Braden said. Shouted, practically. Anger began settling into his stomach. The old anger, the bad anger. The anger that got things broken. Or . . . maybe he needed dinner, too.

Mildred said, "There's some under the tree in the drying yard."

That's what his family had called the fenced-off area out front; apparently she'd inherited the phrase.

"That'll be dry enough," she went on. "Bring some in. Warm us up a bit."

Braden looked at Josiah, who'd wrapped himself in the towel. He himself looked a little like an old woman clutching a brittle shawl. He still shivered, though.

Dammit, Braden thought. He didn't want to leave the boy sitting here alone with Mildred Malkin; but the kid was cold. They both were. He knew without asking that Mildred wasn't about to turn on the heat. His father never did, either. Nor could he make Josiah come with him out in the pouring rain to rescue a handful of logs. His son needed just this small act of valor, and Braden needed something he could control. Wrestling a few damp logs into the fireplace and getting it going again might release just enough testosterone to see him through the storm and get them both back home.

"All right," he said, not liking the taste it left in his mouth. "I'll go get some wood. Do you have some newspaper or something we can use to get her going again?"

"In the laundry room."

A tiny room at the back of the carport had been partitioned off to hold a washer and dryer. Braden knew it well. As well as the rest of the house, he supposed, and fought a sudden surge of nausea. The laundry room was yet another spot in the house he hated going into.

"Great," he said, feeling anything other than that. "I'll be right back." He knelt in front of his son. "Joze? I'm going to get some wood, get the fire going again, and we'll warm right up okay?"

"O-tay, Daddy."

Josiah didn't look frightened or even sad; just wet and chilly. Braden wiped a damp lock of Josiah's blond hair off his forehead, and smiled. Looking into Josiah's trusting face always had that effect.

He kissed Josiah hard on the forehead. "Be *right* back."

Leaving the two of them behind, Braden took the kitchen door to get to the carport, struck by the sensation he would never see Joze again. He fought the feeling, and went on into the carport.

First he checked the laundry room. Like the other noises of the house, the sound of the laundry room door opening had not changed. The hinges offered the same cranky squeal they always had, like out of tune violin strings.

Braden found that like the stove, the washer and dryer had been replaced, but most likely right after she'd moved in. Both units were different than the ones he'd grown up with—and grown to hate—but looked barely serviceable. In the tiny room, no larger than a walk-in closet, the washer and dryer sat against the back wall. To Braden's right, an industrial laundry sink sat bolted in its same old position. Seeing it twisted something in his intestines, and he reflexively grabbed at his abdomen.

Don't pretend, he told himself. *Remember what Dr. Bennett said. Don't pretend like it didn't really happen because it really did and you need to accept that.*

He thought he'd buried them. Buried all of this. Not all at once, and not easily; not quickly, and not cheaply. Insurance companies were possessed of the ability to remotely determine that a client no longer suffered and could be roundly dismissed from coverage, and this had happened once already with Dr. Bennett.

"Not cured," cautioned Dr. Bennett, Braden's most effective therapist to date. "There's no cure for what you went through. There's healing. But no cure."

Forcing himself to breathe through his nose, Braden scanned the laundry room. Above the washer and dryer, warped and sagging shelves held old magazines and newspapers in yellowing stacks. On another shelf, a variety of household cleaning supplies and detergents, their bottles looking like they could stand a good cleaning themselves. Among them, he recognized a yellow bottle of Ronsonal lighter fluid, most likely used for its label-removing abilities. Braden considered and dismissed using it to get the fire going quickly.

He stepped backward out of the room and shut the door, ignoring as best he could the returning violin screech of the hinges. His intestines shrank again at the sound.

Those things did happen, he thought. *They did. Stop fighting.*

"Not now," he said out loud through gritted teeth. Being at the very place where everything went so very wrong might bring up the memories, but this was not the time to go diving into them.

Quickly, Braden rushed out from the safety of the carport and into the storm. Thunder roared as if welcoming him, daring him. He cast a frustrated glance at the Tundra, which sadly had not managed to extricate itself from the fallen acacia under its own power.

By the time he reached the spruce dog-ear fence surrounding the drying yard, his shirt had soaked through. Braden unlatched the wide gate and slipped into the fenced-off area, wondering what fresh memories the place might bring.

He didn't wait long.

Grunting, he gripped his stomach and fell to one knee. His jeans splashed in a brown puddle, drenching the denim. Braden shuffled to his feet and took refuge under the small maple in the corner of the area, where he found—and dismissed—Mildred's slightly drier firewood.

Here it came. Eighteen years compressed into one single, vivid home movie of rot and pain.

Braden slowed his breathing, and used every technique his therapist had taught him so far. *Maybe one day,* he thought crazily, *I'll be a black belt at it.*

Bracing his back against the tree, he rode it out.

six

Why his parents did what they did, Braden didn't know. Not then, and not now looking back. The confusion that plagued him through his childhood had only grown sharper as an adult; less vague and nebulous, more refined and concrete. The questions ultimately always boiled down to the one key item, the one inquiry that if answerable might have accelerated his own recovery and well-being as a grown-up:

What the *fuck* was the matter with them?

It began with the beatings, irregular but terrifying in their irregularity. He never knew what might set his father off with the belt, or his mother with one of her arsenal of kitchen implements; wooden spoons, spatulas, and other tools he could not to this day identify. Were any of the attacks earned, he wondered? He didn't recall being a bad kid, and raising Josiah now with Ashley's clear-headed guidance and assistance, he understood the difference between a kid simply being three versus being maliciously disobedient. He felt sure he'd never been the latter.

But then, perhaps his parents had never given him

the opportunity; maybe that's where the beatings had stemmed from. No "spoiling the child," maybe. They were not Bible thumpers, though. Sometimes, Braden wished they were. Then he could hate God, hate the Good Book, hate the Baby Jesus, and come away with some semblance of an answer to his life-long question of Why? Instead, his parents seemed merely intent on enforcing their will, whatever it happened to be in the moment.

Besides the random attacks, there were the clothes dryer incidents. Braden told Dr. Bennett he thought they started around age two, but couldn't be sure; the only real clue was that he must have been small enough to fit inside the gas-heated tumbler. Because that's where his mother put him.

He knew the first time came after a short bout of playing in the rain in the back yard. He'd come back inside, she'd gone ballistic, and dragged him into the laundry room. There, she'd shoved him bodily into the appliance and turned it on.

Physically, he hadn't been terribly hurt. Maybe she'd come to her senses and shut it off quickly, or maybe she'd only intended to terrorize him—in which case, the ploy worked. Braden screamed himself hoarse. Apparently, this pleased Mrs. Clark, because she used the tactic several more times, for reasons Braden could not fathom then or now.

But he'd grown out of the dryer. He physically became too big. Something else was needed.

Around age three, his father began locking him in the chicken coop with the animals. Naked. Braden could hear his own screams echoing down the years; still remember the way he'd jumped up and down, begging to be let out, to not be left alone in here with them, and yet that is exactly what his father did. Due to either his age or the trauma itself, Braden didn't know for sure how long he would be left in each time. Maybe only a few minutes, maybe hours. Never overnight that he could remember. When he'd first described these incarcerations to Dr. Bennett, Braden had actually sounded *generous*: "See, it could have been worse, they didn't leave me out there all night, Doc."

While Dr. Bennett stared quietly, Braden had gone on at great length about the delicious cooking his mother did, that his father had bought him his first bike and first car, how both parents were active in fundraising for a variety of civic and nonprofit groups.

Dr. Bennett had gently explained that even the most abusive people couldn't be abusive twenty-four hours a day. It didn't make what they'd done any less harmful or wrong.

And Braden—*My God!* he thought as he recalled it—hadn't fully understood the therapist. *They were good people,* he'd argued at first. *They made some bad calls, they were probably stressed out, it's not that big a deal.*

Ashley's pregnancy had occasioned the first appointment with Dr. Bennett. For years Braden struggled with a wild, unpredictable anger that he never understood nor tried to. *Everyone gets angry!* he'd argue, with himself if no one else.

But not everyone destroyed their own property, Ashley had said, gently. She was right, too. He'd done thousands of dollars in damage over the years: doors kicked down, walls punched through, dishes shattered, electronics beaten to early deaths with his bare hands.

There's power there, though, he's tried to say. *There's strength when I get like that, so no one can ever hurt me, or hurt you, I can protect us both!*

Yes, Ashley had agreed. But what is its source, and what does it cost?

As she always did, she left Braden to draw his own conclusions, and a week later, he'd made the appointment. A tiny life was due to come out of her in seven more months, and he wouldn't let the child see him enraged and destructive. He'd never once in his life hurt another human being in these blind rages; always he'd focused on some inanimate thing. But with a little one around, who knew what could go wrong? It wasn't worth the risk.

He'd been with Dr. Bennett for all three years of Josiah's life. Three good years. The therapy had been slow, and expensive of course, but now . . .

Braden stood up and ran both hands through his hair, then shook them free of water. He glared out at the drying yard with a grim snarl.

He hadn't broken anything in more than a year. He still got upset, but never like he used to. It seemed those days had finally passed, to his surprise and gratitude.

But whenever he imagined Josiah, his beautiful son, enduring what his parents had put him through, Braden's fears came back; the terror that somehow, he'd end up like his own parents and would do to Joze what they'd done to him. It hadn't happened, and most days, Braden didn't really believe it would. He had Ashley. He had new roots. He'd gotten rid of every reminder of his childhood, and hadn't spoken to his mother or father in two years, by choice. They had never met Josiah. Braden would not allow it. For that matter, Ashley would never let it happen, not after learning about their various abuses.

Braden forced a deep breath through his nose. The worst of the flashbacks had passed for the moment. The memories had been bound to happen from the moment Mildred Malkin introduced herself at the bookstore on Tuesday; just a matter of time before those memories reared up and struck at him. So now they'd come, and he'd survived, and eventually, the rain would stop and he and Josiah could go home. Maybe make an appointment with Dr. Bennett for a little sooner than his usual once-a-month.

He picked up an armful of logs. They weren't drenched, not quite. He wasn't convinced they'd burn. Still, worth the try. Braden trudged through the storm back to the carport.

Five steps from the kitchen door, he saw it. About twelve inches directly parallel to the door, spread across the ceiling: one of the hated wolf spiders of his childhood.

Waiting.

"Shit," Braden said, freezing in place. He suddenly became hyper-aware of the logs in his arms, and wondered what kinds of critters might be hiding in them, how upset they may be that he'd jostled them from their dry home.

One of the many things that irked him about the wolf spiders showing up like this: where in the world had they come from? The carport was painted white. There were no holes in the ceiling. One moment it looked like a vast, plain expanse, awaiting some Michelangelo's brush; but turn your back for a second, and there it is, an enormous hairy spider waiting to drop on you.

Nervous now, Braden considered going to the front door instead. Both it and the kitchen door were closed, of course; he hadn't thought ahead to how he might open either one with his arms full of firewood.

He backed away from the kitchen door, keeping a sniper's eye on the arachnid. It didn't move. Braden eased away from it, then took a sharp turn to go to the front door.

Another spider waited for him there. It clung to the ceiling, directly over the door.

"God*dammit!*" Braden shouted as chills crept up his arms and legs like invisible spider legs. How did they know, how did the little bastards *know?*

Huffing furiously, he backed away as far as he could without leaving the concrete porch. Maybe the acacia tree coming down had something to do with the sudden appearance of the wolf spiders; maybe they'd been living peacefully there, and the lightning bolt had chucked them clean out of it, or otherwise fried their little hairy sensors and they'd evacuated themselves.

Braden knelt down, wincing as runoff from the roof coated his back. Well, no bother there; he hadn't exactly dried since coming in from the drying yard—*No irony intended*, he thought. He let the logs fall to the concrete, then stepped back from them, waiting for a cadre of wolf spiders to come charging at him. But no, the logs stayed still.

Cursing again, Braden steeled himself and made a quick lunge at the front door, keeping his head tilted back and an eye on the spider. He managed only to crash his knuckled into the doorknob, making him screech and pull back, shaking his fingers out.

What a stupid fucking day this is turning out to be, he thought, and cursed again, loudly, because that always made things feel better for just the slightest of moments.

On the next grab, he looked before he leapt, and got the knob to twist satisfactorily. He gave the door a shove, then grit his teeth as he imagined the spider scrambling inside. That would be the end of refuge in the dry house for him; he'd have to spend the rest of the night out here on the porch.

The rest of the night.

Braden risked a look back at the flooding street. Were they really stuck here? Here, of all places, overnight? That didn't seem possible, and certainly not reasonable. He couldn't manage a short jaunt into the drying yard for firewood without a major flashback attack, what the hell would sleeping—or trying to sleep—in the old house do to him?

One thing at a time, he told himself. He picked up a log in each hand, made sure the wolf spider hadn't darted closer or into the house, and rushed inside, booting the door shut behind him.

Real Medal of Honor stuff there, soldier. You can't handle a bug? What's the matter with you?

Braden shook his head rapidly in an effort to change what Dr. Bennett called "intrusive thoughts." That Medal of Honor crack was his father's voice, not his own. It was the kind of thing that if Ashley had heard it—and Braden swore she could actually read his mind sometimes—she would have said, "There's no forward motion there."

"No forward motion" was code for, "Get over the dumb shit your parents did to you because you deserve to be happy."

The headshake seemed to help. Stomping into the fireplace room, where Josiah sat enraptured by Mildred Malkin's story, he nudged Josiah to the side, and Joze followed the direction without taking his eyes off the old woman.

"And the little boy was never heard from again," she whispered.

"Wow!" Josiah said appreciatively.

Braden's stomach curdled at the words. What was this, a ghost story? Well, certainly the atmosphere had conjured enough disturbed spirits. He threw the two logs onto the andirons, then slumped down onto the hearth where Josiah had been sitting. He'd have to get the newspapers from the laundry room, and no matter what direction he took, that meant two encounters with the wolf spiders—one on the way out, another in.

"How you doing, Joze?"

"Good," Josiah said, and yawned.

Braden's chest shrunk under his shirt. The kid was tired. The kid needed to lie down. It was only by the grace of any gods in the universe that he hadn't started melting down yet.

"You want to take a rest?" Braden asked, for the first time in Josiah's life hoping his son would say no, which he usually did. He couldn't bear the idea of putting Josiah down anywhere in this house to sleep.

"O-tay," Josiah said.

Shit, Braden thought.

He turned to the old woman. "I don't suppose there's anyplace?"

"Your old room," Mildred grunted, heaving herself out of the chair.

"How do you know which one was mine?"

"It's pretty obvious," Mildred said, and offered no clarification.

Well, it was only a matter of elimination, Braden figured. A three-bedroom house, with the master at the end of the hall, she had a fifty-fifty shot at guessing.

Still. Her guess disconcerted him.

Braden picked Josiah up in one arm, mostly to prove to himself he could still do it. Josiah weighed in at around thirty-five pounds, and Braden had the upper body strength of a novelist not engaged in regular exercise beyond that of caring for a toddler. But he liked how Josiah fit into the crook of his arm, the way Joze's hand fell lightly on his shoulder. It made him feel strong. Competent. The opposite of everything his parents had ever made him feel.

Mildred Malkin led them down the L-shaped hallway. All of the doors were closed, even to the small guest bathroom. Mildred didn't bother turning on the hall light back on, and Braden experienced the discomfiting sensation that Mildred disappeared in the darkness before him. It took all his effort to not reach out and flick the light on again himself.

Josiah, oddly, didn't seem bothered by the darkness in the least. All the same, Braden held him closer.

"Here," Mildred gruffed, and opened a door. She shuffled out of the way so Braden could walk in.

He expected a fresh wave of nostalgia when he entered his old bedroom. Instead, the wave resembled nothing more than apathy. Maybe his journeys through the rest of the house and property had already drained him of his nostalgia and—*Let's be honest,* he thought—fear.

"It looks good," he told her, somewhat magnanimously.

The old woman grunted something unintelligible. A noise of gratitude, or maybe a mere acknowledgement.

Perhaps because his posters, action figures, books, and furniture were no longer there, the bedroom held no real sting for him The walls gleamed clean white, and stood unadorned like the rest of the house. What did this woman have against pictures?

His bedroom had two windows. One faced west, looking out at the far side of the front yard; a dead plot of land, home to nothing but gravel. The other window faced south. Overlooking the chicken coop. He'd always hated that this view stood as a reminder of his parents' tortures, but on the other hand, he could see his old pine tree, too. That seemed to split the difference. Somewhat.

Instead of his twin bed, the room came equipped now with a crib, placed beneath the western window. The crib seemed rather high quality, he thought; dark wood that looked hand carved, though he couldn't have said for sure. The crib didn't match the rest of the house; Braden thought the wood might be oak. A matching rocking chair, carved with deep scrolls like the headstocks of violas, stood near the head of the crib. The bed had what appeared to be fresh white sheets and a baby blue blanket, as if waiting for just such a little boy to occupy it. A two-foot tall vintage baby doll of vaguely male features, wearing a blue cotton work-style shirt sat propped in one corner of the crib, staring dumbly at the far wall.

The sliding closet doors Braden had removed in high school to make extra room for his desk hadn't been replaced, but nothing hung on the bar nor graced the shelf space above. Under the southern window, a counter ran the length of the wall, where he'd spent hours upon hours warring G.I. Joe versus Transformers, or plastic army men; or racing and crashing Matchbox and Hot Wheels cars. The wooden top had been a scarred and carved thing when he left, testament to his entire youth. Since then it had been sanded and painted white. Dull, boring, white. Built-in bookcases stood atop the counter anchoring either corner, with additional cabinets beneath. They weren't packed like in Braden's heyday—if in fact he'd had a heyday—but a few board books suitable for littler kids stood upright and ready. He resisted an urge to peek into the cabinets; surely there must be something stored in this room. The old woman hadn't actually said she had grandchildren; but with the crib and rocker, shouldn't there be diapers and other baby ephemera in the cabinets, close at hand?

But he knew instinctively that if he opened those cabinets, they'd be empty. They'd be stripped of the polka-dotted shelf paper that had been inside since as far back as he could remember, probably since the house was built.

"What do you think, Joze?"

Josiah gave no indication of whether he approved or not. Braden stepped past the threshold, aware only then that he'd been hesitating at the doorway, taking it all in before daring to put his child inside.

"Linens in the closet," the old woman grunted, and shuffled down the hall.

Braden thought to say thanks, but didn't. It didn't seem to matter. He kissed Joze close on the head and set him gently onto the mattress, on top of the blue blanket. He expected Josiah to protest, to have a grand mal meltdown.

Instead, the boy seemed to cozy up to the setting just fine, and arranged himself on his belly just like his father usually slept.

Unsurprisingly, Mildred had not changed the curtains. They were the same old rough brown that Braden had grown up with. They reminded him of burlap. Unable to resist the urge, Braden went to the southern window and yanked on the cords that opened them. The familiar whisking-snick sound of the pulley jolted his spine like so many other sounds had done that day.

The coop had blown down.

Shocked for a moment, Braden tried to understand the physics of it. Most of the coop consisted only of chicken wire fence, so how had the wind uprooted the cedar poles? A moment later, he didn't care; the damned thing had fallen, and that was good. Now maybe Mildred would have it removed, or maybe she'd leave it there to rust, and either way it didn't matter. Braden would never have to step foot on this property again once the storm had passed.

He savored the peculiar sense of exultation for another few seconds before turning back to Josiah.

Josiah stood up on the mattress and pointed. "Tan I have a book?"

"Sure thing," Braden said. He pulled a handful off the shelves, feeling an odd sense of relief that they weren't his own. That would have been impossible, of course, but the day had taken so many odd turns already. It wouldn't have come as a shock to see his old copies of *The Monster at the End of This Book*, or *The Very Hungry Caterpillar*.

He handed the books over to Josiah. "Here you go, bud."

Josiah sat down cross-legged and began poring over the books. He chose one—it had a dump truck on the cover, a sure-fire winner—and started pretending to read the words aloud to himself. Braden hunkered down, balancing on his toes and lightly gripping the bars of the crib. He recognized the words Josiah spoke as being from one of his books at home. The kid had memorized it by virtue of he and Ashley having read it so many times.

Josiah had been out of a crib for months now. Seeing him back in one brought on a sudden nostalgia that made Braden smile and want to cry at the same time. He recalled watching Josiah sleep as a baby, usually only when Ashley was at work; long stretches of silent time where he would watch and listen, paranoid the infant would suddenly smother himself to death unless Braden kept a careful eye on him. Later, as Joze got older, Braden stayed to listen to him sleep because he liked the sound of his son's breathing.

"Joze, you want me to sing to you?"

"Noooo," Josiah said, and rammed two fingers into his mouth, still carefully turning the thick cardboard pages of the truck book.

"Okay. I love you, buddy. I'll check on you, okay?"

"O-tay."

"Sure you don't want a song?"

Josiah shook his head. Such a bundle of contradictions, these little guys. One night he could ask for ten dozen songs until Braden's head felt ready to explode, or it could be a night like this where he wanted nothing, and there came with the boy's refusal a needleprick of regret, or even vague resentment. Parents couldn't win. Feast or famine. And Braden knew, watching his only son nodding his head, fighting a dead-tired sleep, that he wouldn't trade it or change a thing.

Thunder cracked just then, a high-pitched, teeth-jarring crash that rolled over the entire city. Josiah whined loudly, "Daddy!"

"Hey, hey. It's just thunder." His voice shook, though, and he hoped his son didn't notice. That had been a loud one, all right.

"Thunder hurts!"

"No, no. Thunder can't you. I promise. Thunder can't hurt you."

"Yes it *tan*."

Stuck for a moment, Braden reached in past the doll and pulled two pillows out of the crib. "Hey, Joze . . . can clouds hurt you?"

"No . . ."

"Can pillows hurt you?"

A small, shy smile from Josiah. They did pillow fights all the time at home. "No . . ."

"Right. Now listen." Braden smacked the pillows together. They issued a soft thud. "You hear that?"

"Yes?"

"That's just like thunder. When you smack the pillows together they make a sound." He illustrated again, and Joze's smile widened. "And when *clouds* crash together, they make a sound too, and that's thunder. But clouds can't hurt you, and pillows can't hurt you. They just make noise. Okay?"

It took Josiah a moment to process all that, but soon enough he said. "Yeah, o-tay," and grabbed the pillows away from his father.

Braden gave them up. He touched Josiah's head. "See you in the morning, and we'll go right home."

"O . . . tay," Josiah said through a yawn. He turned the last page of the truck book, and slowly toppled over, asleep.

"Love you," Braden whispered, and patted his own chest, an odd silent gesture he'd developed over the past three years; *You're in my heart, Josiah*. He never did it when Joze could see him, never did it in front of others. Maybe it was for the benefit of God, letting the deity know he would stop at nothing to protect his own son. That was more than God could say, wasn't it?

As usual, Braden stayed for a moment and watched his son sleep. The doll watched too, as if trying to read the board book over the sleeping toddler's shoulder.

The doll turned its head and looked at Braden.

At first Braden assumed the toy had fallen, that his son had bumped it and caused it twist around. But no. The doll's body stayed still. Only its head, impossibly, turned to gaze at Braden with glassy brown eyes. The linen material around its neck stretched, but popped no seams.

They stared at each other.

Though virtually expressionless, the doll conveyed a dark malevolence in its idiot, dead gaze.

See what I can do?

Braden's face fell slack, as in the moment before vomiting.

I can move whenever I want.

Josiah sighed in his sleep, oblivious to the terror transpiring inches behind him.

So when you leave, the doll seemed to say, *I can do whatever I want to him.*

352

. . . And I will.

Warm chills spilled from the base of Braden's neck and spread over his arms, then cascaded down his thighs.

The toy seemed to grin, although its rosy lips didn't part. It turned its head back toward Josiah. Braden reached for the thing with parental instinct—

The toy spun its head around again toward Braden, fast, fast like a snake striking, and the unimaginable horror of it drove a groan up from Braden's guts and out his mouth.

"Daddy . . . ?" Josiah said, turning over and blinking sleepily.

The doll twisted itself back to normal—or whatever passed for normal in that possessed thing, so Josiah wouldn't see it had moved.

Imagined it, Braden chanted in his head. *Just pretend, just imagined it, the house is getting to me, that's all.*

And yet it wasn't; or that wasn't all, at any rate. He felt it at the base of every hair on his arms, his legs, as they stood rigid and at attention. Each goosebump testified to the awful reality that this stuffed toy had truly moved of its own mind, and it would hurt his son.

"I'll fucking kill you," Braden whispered savagely to the creature, whose back was now to him, just as it had been while Josiah had read his book.

Josiah . . .

"Huh?" Joze said to him. "Huh?"

Thinking now only of his son, Braden stood up, reached into the crib, and yanked the doll out, using both hands to wring its puffy neck. He shuddered even as he did so, waiting for the thing to writhe in his hand, to come alive and bite at him.

And it did. The doll shifted noiselessly in his hands. Braden bit back a scream as he stepped away from Josiah's crib.

"It's okay, Joze," Braden said, his voice sounding as if he were being strangled. "Go to sleep."

I'm going to kill whatever is stitched inside this thing, Braden thought as he whirled toward the door. That's what made actual, reasonable sense: something alive had become trapped in the doll through a loose seam or hole. That was all. Maybe it was even wolf spiders. Not a cheery thought, but a damn sight better and more sane than thinking the toy had moved on its own.

He shut off his—

He shut off the bedroom light and pulled the door closed. The doll squirmed again. Braden felt its blue cotton shirt sliding across his palms.

Enough of this *shit,* he declared to himself, and quick-stepped to the fireplace room. By that point in the day—evening, now—he didn't much care if the old woman got angry about it. This doll was going to burn.

He found Mildred sitting in her chair in the fireplace room, in the dark. He marched directly to the fireplace, only to realize, of course, that he hadn't re-lit the fire yet.

Goddamn, he thought. So much for burning the doll.

He held the doll out to Mildred. "Here. This was in the crib. It, uh—scared Josiah."

Mildred Malkin tilted her chin up and smiled no earthly smile. The woman looked insane. And of course, she must be; buy this big house and do absolutely nothing with it? Not so much as a chintzy art print on a wall? And if she had grandchildren, as the crib seemed to attest, why no photos anywhere?

"You keep it," Mildred said, and in the dark, Braden swore her teeth never came apart. "I'm going to eat."

Something about the phrase turned his stomach. The old woman got up from the chair, her joints creaking.

And Braden realized . . . she hadn't looked this old at the bookstore.

Looked strange, yes. And that hadn't changed. She'd been an odd duck from the moment he saw her. Watching her now as she shuffled across the hardwood floor and turned down the hallway, Braden compared the yardstick-straight middle-aged broad who'd startled him Tuesday night to the hunched, malicious shape of the woman who now inhabited his old house.

Compulsively, he asked, "Are you all right?"

Mildred Malkin laughed, and disappeared around the hallway corner.

The doll squirmed in his hands.

Braden dropped the wicked thing to the ground and stomped on it. Once, twice, again. Even as his foot squashed down on the toy, he could feel that nothing living lay inside it, no breathing thing; not a snake or spiders or a goddamn capuchin monkey for all it mattered. Just batting and . . . and whatever made it fucking move.

Shivering now, and doubting his own sanity, never mind Mildred Malkin's, he picked the thing up and dove for the front door. He glanced up automatically, looking for the spider; gone.

Good. Fine. He chucked the doll into the driving rain and slammed the door shut again. Breathing hard, he stood there at the intersection between the front entry, hallway, kitchen, and fireplace room. And, after a moment or two of getting his breath back, he shut his eyes and squeezed his hands into fists.

Okay, man. You just threw a toy into the front yard. You're imagining that inanimate objects are coming to life, that a crazy lady has aged decades since you got here, and that the whole damn world is out to get you.

It wasn't true. Couldn't be, obviously. The house, the stupid house, after all these years, it had its hooks in him. And even that image he forced himself to think away; houses were neutral, they had no feeling. This was fully and completely the work of his parents, their ghosts lingering in his neurons. That's it.

"Daddy!"

Despite his attempt to reassure himself, the sound of Josiah's voice propelled him down the hall at a run. Back home—his real home—if he heard the cry, he'd haul himself up off the couch or out of his office chair and meander toward Josiah's bedroom. Here, with all that had happened or all that he'd imagined happened, he couldn't let Josiah's cry go unanswered.

Skidding a little on the tile, Braden lurched for the turn in the hallway, just as some shrieking banshee attacked his face.

Braden shouted and instinctively swung both fists, connecting solidly with a great hairy beast attached to his face. As the bedlam eased momentarily, he realized it was the asshole cat from the living room. Having dropped away from him, it stood militant in the short end of the hallway, blocking his way to the bedroom.

Frustrated more than scared, Braden moved to go around the creature. The cat hissed like a vampire and slid in his path.

"Really?" Braden said to the cat as he began to seethe. "You're not gonna win this one."

He tried again to go around the cat. And again, the cat slid over with a growl that sounded like a bandsaw.

"Daddy!"

That was it. Braden screamed and kicked the cat squarely, hating himself and hating the cat, hating the house and hating that he'd ever bothered to come here.

The tiger-striped tabby crashed against the far bedroom door with a thunk and a screech. Braden didn't stop to assess if it was hurt, only lunged for his bedroom door and opened it. The cat yowled and scrambled on its multi-toed feet behind Braden, escaping down the hall, claws scraping against the tile.

"Joze?" Braden breathed.

He flicked the light back on in his old bedroom, and his chest cinched tight.

Josiah was gone.

Truly, plainly gone. Missing. And the reason was immediately clear:

Braden was looking into his own old bedroom, exact in every detail, as he'd last lived in it.

seven

The panic of not finding Josiah would normally have overridden anything, any surprise, any shock. But this . . .

Braden rubbed his eyes and blinked rapidly to make sure he was seeing what he thought he was seeing.

The image didn't change. The room now sat bereft of the crib or the rocking chair. Even the white paint was gone, returned now to Braden's poster-covered hideous wood paneling. Yet these details are not what convinced him that this peculiar place in the universe had suddenly traveled backward in time.

The smell did.

"God," he gasped, and raised a hand to his nose.

It wasn't a pungent miasma; not an assault. For the most part, the scent of the room was perhaps only a few parts per million. But it existed, sure enough. The underlying odor consisted of cat piss, that pinching, sour odor that could be mistaken for nothing else. On top of that, a grim staleness that he could not specifically identify wafted into his nose.

And something else. Rancidity. Not of milk, not food gone bad and rotted, but something deeper.

His loft bed, built with a friend during high school, stood guard above the western window, bare wood topped by a thin twin mattress. Instead of the hardwood floor, his old carpet had come back—narrow, colored stripes, and likely the source of the various odors that came creeping into his nose.

Braden thought he might puke. He squeezed his eyes shut. This visit to the old house had certainly been doing a number on him, clearly. But this—this was vivid on an entirely new scale.

"It's okay, Joze," he said, keeping his eyes shut. "I'm right here, buddy. Just give me a second."

His son did not respond.

Braden began hyperventilating. Like obscene echolocation, he knew when he opened his eyes, he wouldn't see Josiah and the crib. It would still be his old room. His voice had carried differently when it had been the converted nursery; the way it bounced back as he tried to console Josiah just now, the quality of the sound had been different. Muted. Not the echo associated with hardwood floors and less furniture.

Slowly, Braden let his eyes slide open.

Yes. Still there. Still the old room. This was no flashback.

Braden squatted down in the doorway, trying to sort out the inexplicable sensation of wanting to go in—*needing* to go in—and see and touch everything just as it had been before he finally moved out. The only problem, the only *slight drawback*, was that he had clearly gone insane, because old bedrooms didn't just pop back into existence.

Impulsively, he shut the door again. Still balancing on his toes, like he had beside the crib when the doll had looked at him, Braden counted under his breath to twenty. The longest twenty seconds of his life.

No, he thought, *there were some times that felt longer. Being locked in a fucking chicken coop or shoved into a dryer comes to mind . . .*

His eyes snapped open.

Braden stood and threw open the bedroom door again. And again, it remained his old room. Old bed, old desk, old books. Everything.

"Okay," he said out loud. "Okay. I get it."

Chills blew gingerly on the back of his neck as he took a step into the bedroom.

"You want me out, right?" he went on, trying not to marvel at how familiar the old raggedy carpet felt beneath his sneakers. "That's fine. I'll go. I'll walk, I'll *swim.*"

Thunder roared above, as if punctuating his acknowledgement that the neighborhood still roiled in the throes of a hundred-year storm.

"I just want my son back." Braden resisted an urge to touch the unpainted two-by-four posts that held up his bed. What might happen if he did? If it felt real, if it was a tangible thing that could give him a splinter, what would that mean? Would that underscore the fact that he'd gone backflip batshit looney tunes?

Or it might it confirm something darker.

And which was worse? Which was more dangerous for Josiah?

His path took him toward the southern window. Again Braden spoke aloud. "Whatever this is, I just want Joze back. And we'll go. Okay?"

He reached the window. The curtain was still drawn

back, and he leaned over the counter to peer outside. Lightning flashed at that instant, giving him a snapshot of the back yard and—

The wire fence had spread.

Like some kind of living malignancy, somehow the chicken wire from the coop had grown. It had become thicker and longer, making a wire floor halfway to the pine tree.

It would take a couple of rolls of the stuff to achieve that, Braden thought. *At least. Maybe more.*

No—surely his math was wrong. There must have been a lot of the wire used to surround the entire coop, and now that it lay on the ground, it just looked like more.

Except . . .

Except he'd already seen it on the ground once before, only a few minutes ago really, when putting Josiah down in the crib. One layer, barely visible in the muddy earth, laying no more than six or seven feet from the posts that had once secured it. Now it stretched out twice that far, and with what looked like three or more layers on top of it.

Which is not possible, Braden thought.

Then again, neither was anything else happening right then.

Braden turned to face the room. With the one set of curtains open behind him, the other still closed, the windows gave the unsettling impression of a giant looking in at him, squinting one eye closed to peer more closely.

Panic climbed up his throat with insect legs. *Stop, stop,* he told himself. *Just wait a second. Think it through.*

. . . Find the old woman.

That made the most sense in these obscene

circumstances. It was her house now, not his, not his parents'. If there were answers, Mildred Malkin had them.

Chin tucked down, Braden strode through the bedroom and stopped outside the threshold, calling Josiah's name. He opened the opposite bedroom door, frighteningly unsurprised to find his mother's old sewing room. It, too, smelled vividly authentic—of machine lubricant and disintegrating brown paper patterns. He went in, looked in every possible hidey hole, then went back to the hall, shouting again for Josiah. He tried not to sound terrified, and wasn't sure he succeeded.

Braden strode down the short length of the hallway to the master bedroom. Not bothering to knock, he gripped the handle—cold and greasy, exactly like his parents' bedroom twenty years ago. It did not move.

He tried again. The door was locked.

Part of him relished this fact. Now he had a tangible thing to fight against. Many doors had fallen to his fists and feet before he'd gotten therapy; this one would pose no difficulty.

He pounded with one fist. "Mrs. Malkin?" he shouted, well beyond knowing or caring if she'd ever been married. "Mrs. Malkin, my son is gone. Where is he? What the hell is going on? Hello?"

The door rattled beneath him. Mildred Malkin did not respond.

"Fuck it!" Braden shouted.

He stepped back, cocked his right leg at the knee, and slammed it against the door, just left of the doorknob. Brief satisfaction flooded him as the flimsy door burst apart and flung open.

But the room assaulted him right back.

It had become his parents' bedroom.

Braden forced himself in. He had not been in this room in twenty years; and in fact, probably thirty-five or more. He never came in here as a kid, not for anything, not if he didn't need to. Though the biggest bedroom in the house, it felt oppressive as kid. Prison-like. Even his own bedroom had borne a sort of pall. Except for being off the property entirely, at the library or a friend's house, only while climbing the tall pine tree did he feel secure here.

Those trapped sensations returned as he scanned his parents' artifacts for Josiah. He even dropped to the ground and peered under the queen-sized bed, half expecting some wicked clown from a *Poltergeist* movie to drag him beneath it forever. But no, beneath the bed lay only stored sweaters in plastic bins. He recognized them immediately—they belonged to his father.

Braden hopped up and moved to the master bathroom. He sneered at what passed for the "modern" art on the walls; it always reminded him of intestines smeared on the canvas. Among their other sins, his parents lacked taste.

"Mrs. Malkin? I don't know why everything looks like my old house or if this is some kind of TV prank—" That theory made the most sense so far. "—But I want my kid back, right the fuck now!"

He threw open the bathroom door.

And knew the night would be a long one. Mildred Malkin was dead.

eight

Mildred Malkin had lain dead for more than a day, Braden felt sure of that. She lay on the floor of the master bathroom, dress hiked up past her sallow calves, an orange prescription pill bottle clutched in one hand. Her clothes did not match any he'd seen her in; not at the bookstore, and not here inside the house.

Here inside the house.

Four words which, with this grisly discovery, took on an entirely new grim meaning.

With a sudden insight he could not prove, Braden knew she had died before whatever thing pretending to be her had come to the store.

The house had . . . baited him here.

He took no further steps closer to her body, but did note—not so much with terror now as morose acceptance—that the master bathroom had reverted back to how his parents had left it.

It didn't matter. It seemed clear to him that Mildred Malkin had taken her own life, and Braden felt sure the house had played a role.

"Daddy!"

Josiah's voice came from somewhere in the hall.

"Joze!" Braden screamed, and darted out of the bathroom to go get his son—

But Mildred Malkin stood waiting for him.

The bedroom door had closed silently while he'd been in the bathroom, and now the hunched, wicked form of Mildred Malkin that had let him into the house earlier stood in his way. She rocked easily side to side on spindly legs, her lips pulled back from black, misshapen teeth like shards of obsidian. From somewhere deep inside her gut, a hoarse whisper like the sound of TV static came forth in one long, unending stream unbroken by breathing.

Braden froze stiff, his lungs twisting inside-out beneath his ribs. Slowly, he forced himself to look to the left—and there lay the real Mildred Malkin still, younger and less sinister than the apparition by the bedroom door, but very, very dead.

He turned back to the specter. The Malkin-thing's fingers wriggled and snapped.

"I just want my son," Braden said brokenly, each word a hunk of rock that fell hard to the floor.

"*You can't,*" the creature said, grinning through its filthy teeth. The strange hiss continued without hitch or interruption.

Josiah, Braden thought. *He's out there.*

"I'm going to get him." Braden was pleased to hear some strength returning to his voice—though *pleased* was not quite the right word under the circumstances.

"*You can't.*"

He clenched his teeth and cast one last look at the body on the bathroom floor. Still there. The real Mildred had passed on. This one in front of him . . .

Braden marched toward the thing. She shifted to put her body in front of the doorknob. Barely holding back a revulsed moan, Braden pushed her shoulder.

The creature felt solid enough, but also soft. Yielding. He fought nausea as a scrap of the Malkin-thing's skin fell from her face.

"You can't!" she squealed triumphantly.

Braden screamed and pushed her with both hands. The creature barely moved, her body still in front of the doorknob. She began to laugh over the odd static hiss still coming out of her mouth.

"You can't, you can't!"

"FUCK! YOU!" Braden screeched and swung a fist.

His knuckles crashed into her cheek. More skin came off her face, revealing dry muscle and the first hint of ivory bone. The Malkin-thing took the blow, and continued laughing, cackling, now clapping its withered hands together like a child.

"You can't!"

Screaming incoherently now, Braden let his red rage take over. Like he'd told Ashley years ago, there was indeed strength in anger that black, that deep. Adrenalin coursed through him, overriding his terror, seeking only to destroy this grisly thing and find his son.

He charged at her again, now wrapping both hands around her neck. He squeezed, hard, yelling in her face.

But the Malkin-thing only cackled at him as if being tickled.

"I will fucking end you!" Braden cried, shoving his own face even closer to her own.

The specter slowed its laugh as he continued to choke it. But he could tell even in his rage it had no effect. This drove the rage higher, sharpened it. He would expend every last breath on destroying her if that's what it took.

The Malkin-thing stopped laughing at last. The smile dropped away.

"You can't," she whispered.

And a moment later, her entire form burst into dust beneath him.

Braden backed away, choking on whatever substance had animated the creature. He spit on the floor, and rubbed his face furiously with both arms. Then he lunged for the door. No time to consider anything that had just transpired—Joze was still out there.

But he was not in the hallway. Braden took methodical steps toward the intersection of the hall and kitchen.

"Josiah?" he said, still breathing hard and trying to slow his enraged heartbeat. "I heard you buddy, where are you?"

No response. Josiah's voice had sounded different somehow; not muffled, but deeper. As if using one of his many pretend voices. Maybe he'd run outside to evade whatever horrific thing was after them.

Impulsively, Braden opened the front door.

And there it stood. The doll. Standing on its two stuffed legs. Braden's mind, or perhaps what was left it, quickly calculated the physics of the doll's weak joints, knitted together with nothing but thread and batting, and decided in a nanosecond the likelihood of such a toy being able to balance so perfectly without crumpling to the ground were next to zero. It wasn't possible, and yet—

The toy took a step toward him.

As a kid, he'd seen all the classic horror movies featuring possessed toys—*Child's Play*, *Tourist Trap*, *Puppet Master*. Hell, there'd even been a *Goosebumps* episode on TV with a talking ventriloquist dummy. Braden had watched them all, and been delightfully frightened; delightful, because any fool could see all you had to do was stomp on the little suckers and end the movie. They were only six inch dolls, some of them; even the life-sized mannequins in *Tourist Trap* were only made of plastic and wood—take an axe to 'em!

But now, staring at the doll on its two legs, Braden understood where the terror in those films came from. It wasn't that the toy posed a threat, at least not that he could see; it was more like the helpless horror of watching a car crash. Some feral, animal part of you wanted to reach out and just *stop* the cars from hitting. But you knew that couldn't happen. *Could not.* So instead you'd be gripped by paralyzing fear, unable to act, unable to turn away. The unreality of the whole thing is what made it so frightening. This was something so utterly otherworldly, something having no business on this plane of existence, that it shrank his freezing feet inside his wet shoes and made every open hole in his body shrivel up tight.

It did not *belong.* That was the short version. The specter of Mildred Malkin had at least been semi-human. Maybe the dead Mrs. Malkin had had a crazy twin, and that's who attacked him . . . not likely, but at least possible.

This doll, this stuffed toy, that had twisted its own head to look at him in the bedroom and which now took halting, jittery steps toward him . . . this thing had no reason to it.

Like the wolf spiders, which were really only vaguely venomous to humans, the toy couldn't possibly hurt him. Knowing this didn't make the scenario any less unsettling. The toy took another uneven step. Braden groaned as gooseflesh erupted down his neck and across his arms, a sickening fear that nearly drove him to his knees. He managed to shut the door and throw the lock, though whether a locked doorknob would be of any use in this damned place, he tried not to consider too deeply.

Houses can't be bad, Braden told himself, backing into the fireplace room. *Not in and of themselves.*

. . . But what if they could become *infected?*

He yelped as he backed into the floral-print loveseat that used to sit in this room twenty years previous. Of course it had returned along with all the other emotional detritus of his past. Braden reached down and grabbed it for stability, urging himself not to collapse. The fabric felt exactly as it had in his youth—crisp, somehow, and antique.

Slow down, he told himself. *No forward motion like this. Slow down, man.*

This house had probably been built with a certain sense of love, with old-school labor and materials that were built to last, utterly unlike the look-alike houses found in the outskirts of town these days. No, the house had only ever had two owners: his parents, and Mildred Malkin. The first had given it a cancer.

Then what about the old woman? *Who's dead in the bathroom,* Braden's subconscious reminded him, and he told it to shut up.

Mildred Malkin was real, or at least had been; whatever unholy thing he'd fought with at the bedroom door, that was no ghost lying dead in the bathroom. Her involvement in the night's events had likely been unwitting. Most likely, she had just been a lonely old woman needing some space to spread out.

Or maybe she was broken, too. Broken like his parents. Just as poisonous and wounded people tended to attract one another, perhaps the house had attracted her, as well. Maybe she didn't even know it, or couldn't put a finger to it. Maybe the house had sought out someone as cancerous as itself, someone it could easily infect.

Or possess.

Braden shook his head. There wasn't time to ghost-bust. He had to find Josiah, and by God *walk* to freedom if that's what it took. He might be nearing forty, but in a life or death . . .

He raced to the guest bathroom and switched on the light, his hands next reaching for his face. He turned his chin this way, then that, checking every angle.

He hadn't changed. The little guest bath, with its sink and toilet only, had turned its own clock back like the rest of the house, but Braden himself had not regressed. He didn't know how to feel about it, although relief fought its way to the top.

Braden lurched out of the bathroom and stopped in the hall. *Think,* he ordered himself. *Think this through, dammit.*

And his immediate thought after that: *Stop fighting this.*

He rested his back against the wall, focused on his breathing. He was a lifelong student of horror movies; among the many atrocities committed by his parents, one of the slightest was allowing him to watch the bloodiest, goriest films around at the time—or, perhaps more accurately, not bothering to care that he was watching them. Who would allow a seven or eight year old to watch John Carpenter's *The Thing?* Or *The Exorcist?* Back when there were such things as video rental stores, he'd grab these films by the armload, moderns and classics alike, and watch them in the living room. His parents saw the VHS cases lying on the pool table, they knew he was watching them, and they didn't say a word. Neither he nor Ashley would ever let Josiah watch those things. Not *ever*, hopefully, but definitely not until well into his teenage years.

As a student of these films, Braden decided to accept his situation for what it appeared to be: a goddamn haunting.

The protagonists in these stories always made the dumb call. Their scripts required a certain level of stupidity in order to move the story forward. Many modern films, though not as many as he might have thought, had taken the tropes of seventies and eighties horror and turned them in on themselves. The stupid protagonist was sometimes replaced now with a stubborn protagonist, or even a cautious one—not the type to say, "What's that noise? We should go check it out. I'll go by myself into the dark woods where our three friends have disappeared one by one."

So accept this, Braden thought. *Just accept it. Maybe you're insane, maybe you've snapped. Okay. Or maybe this is really happening. Don't hurt yourself or your kid, and everything will be fine.*

That would be rule number one. No matter what he saw or heard, he would not hurt Josiah or anything resembling him.

Of course, he had to be found first.

Next: Go with the haunting. Braden didn't particularly feel insane, though of course he doubted any insane people did. But Ashley had seen the old woman at the bookstore, she knew where he and Josiah would be.

She . . . *had* seen Malkin, hadn't she? Suddenly Braden wasn't sure.

Doesn't matter, he thought. *She knows where we were going and what we were doing, so she'll come looking if we don't come home. That much is for sure. In fact, she'll call the police eventually. I just have to find Josiah before then.*

"Josiah?" he said. "I know . . . I think you're in here somewhere, buddy. And I'm going to find you. All right? Daddy's gonna find you."

He pushed himself away from the wall and pulled his shoulders back.

"And anybody or anything else in here who's got a problem with that? I will burn you to the fucking ground if my boy's hurt. You got that? Huh? You hear me, motherfucker?"

The house shook. Not with thunder, though the storm still raged outside and thunder had almost constantly been roaring above. This was different. This felt like an earthquake. A big but localized event. Local to just this property.

Braden smiled. Maybe he'd gone insane, and maybe not. But if not . . .

The house had just shown its cards. It could hear him. It could respond.

It lived.

"So it *is* you," Braden whispered. "All right. Now we're getting somewhere. Let's do this."

He moved swiftly through the kitchen toward the carport door, ready for war.

nine

He knew now that the house had his son. Where, he couldn't say and couldn't guess. Maybe some otherworld, some hell of ectoplasm and anguish. Braden didn't dwell on the possibility. It would cloud his judgment.

Braden stalked to the kitchen door. He peered up through its solitary window at the ceiling, and spotted the spider immediately. It seemed bigger, but whether that was true in some phantasmagoric sense or just his brain assuming the worst, he didn't know and it didn't matter.

Steeling himself against the prickly fear from his childhood, Braden swiftly opened the door and slammed it shut behind him, all but running for the safety of the laundry room.

The spider followed.

Fast.

"Shit," Braden wheezed and lunged into the laundry room, yanking the door closed. Through the window in the door, he watched the arachnid sprinting along the ceiling in its spindly, inhuman way, and shudders wracked his body. The spider stopped about two feet from the door, and Braden swore he felt waves of hate emanating from the hairy beast.

Then it dropped on a wire-thin strand of web, making Braden yelp and leap away from the window. The enormous arachnid lowered itself, legs extended, and hung there at Braden's eye level, slowly spinning on the other side of the door.

Waiting.

"Son of a bitch," Braden said. The spider hung close enough to the door that running past it or under it would be all but impossible. The hairy bastard knew it. Never mind being outweighed by a factor of ten thousand; the spider sensed his fear and waited for him.

Okay, Braden thought, not daring to take his eyes off the spider. *Waiting for what? What can it really do? Scare me, okay. But those things aren't poisonous to people. Even if it bit me, it might hurt, but it can't kill me.*

Not normally, no. Except normal no longer applied.

Braden backed up into the dryer and leaned against it. The washer and dryer too became the old gas models he'd grown up with. He realized for the first time how badly he needed a drink of water. He considered but rejected drinking from the industrial sink faucet. The idea repulsed him. The entire house repulsed him. Ingesting anything from its rancid pipes could only end badly.

And why? Because the goddamn place was haunted. That had to include the water. That had to include the spiders. No spider he'd ever seen behaved like this one— like it had an agenda. He'd never seen a toy doll walk around under its own power, for that matter. No, everything in and about the house was bad; rotten. Water would have to wait.

He had extra bottles in the Tundra, but he couldn't get inside it without power saws, dry weather, and plenty of time. Out beyond Mildred's car, he could see his new truck sodden and trapped under the acacia, begging to be let out, wanting to attempt to forge the undoubtedly raging wash separating him from home.

Home . . .

"No," Braden said, out loud to assure himself of his own voice. "No."

He'd come to the laundry room specifically to grab a weapon to destroy the stuffed doll outside the front door, if in fact that's where it still stood. That one of the spiders had been waiting on the ceiling outside the kitchen door wasn't surprising. That it attacked, that it showed agency and planning . . . Braden hadn't anticipated that.

And then, because that's how the evening was shaping up, a second wolf spider, presumably from the front door, marched around the corner on the ceiling and took up position by the kitchen door.

Braden swore they were laughing their fuzzy little asses off.

"Son of a *bitch*," he said again.

Suddenly from the house: Josiah's voice. It called for him, as if from the kitchen—"Daddy!"—and the plaintive sound drove Braden to action.

He looked for the slender bottle of Ronsonal lighter fluid, but of course now that the house had somehow regressed into the past, the bottle was gone. Fortunately, a substitute sat in almost the same place: charcoal lighter fluid. Braden grabbed it, found it more than half full, and booted the laundry door open. The spider hanging from the web began wriggling, trying to swing toward him. The sight of it tickled wicked chills down Braden's back, and he couldn't help a shriek of disgust as he dodged around it, never letting the bastard out of his sight. But he'd have to, and fast, because the other spider was now behind him, waiting . . .

Braden spun to his right, facing the kitchen door. The second spider anticipated him and dropped in front of his face on a dragline. He spun again, aiming for the front porch, and ran, skidding on puddles of rainwater pooling on the concrete.

The doll waited for him there.

Braden slid to a halt, almost landing on his rear; and he knew that if he had fallen, the toy would have swarmed him, maybe showing razor teeth or extending bladed claws from its fabric arms.

But he kept his feet and glared at the evil thing even as his limbs began to quake at the sight of it taking those uneven, silent steps toward him.

Gonna getcha, the doll seemed to say, or maybe it was telepathic. *Gonna getcha, Braden.*

Braden sucked in a breath and could not move. The doll may as well have issued a command to freeze. It came tottering at him, as if in wicked stop-motion animation, its glass eyes locked on his own. What could it do, what could a toy possibly do to him?

Scare him to death, maybe.

Again the logic of the scene played itself out as a self-defense mechanism: whatever wicked force manifested itself here, and unless it actually did extend teeth or claws, the doll could not hurt him. Its only weapon was fear.

Yes, Braden thought. *Fear. That's it. That's what this is about. It knows I'm afraid. And it's using Josiah against me.*

The doll reached him. No matter how much logic or reason he mustered, it still took all of Braden's will to reach down and snatch the thing by the neck and race for the front door.

The toy shrieked. Whether aloud or only in his mind, Braden didn't know, but it shrieked at an impossible pitch and writhed in his hand like a snake, squirming and pawing at him. The sound of it pierced his mind, making his eyes water.

Struggling to maintain a grip on the thing, Braden pushed the front door open as thunder crashed. He ran for the fireplace, praying his plan would work.

Braden knocked aside the freestanding fire screen and chucked the stuffed doll into the fireplace. It screeched louder, if such a thing were possible, as its fabric skin touched the still-hot andirons. Braden saw red coals beneath them. As the toy tried to scramble out of the fireplace, Braden opened the lighter fluid, pointed it at the coals, and squeezed the bottle.

Yellowish fluid leaped from the tip and hit the coals. They burst upward in flame, engulfing the toy in a blaze of green fire. The doll squealed, and danced onto the hearth in what Braden sincerely hoped was exquisite agony. When the toy fell off the hearth and onto the hardwood, he curbed an impulse to stomp on it, crush it; that attack might put out the flames, and it had shown itself impervious to being crushed anyway. So Braden stepped back and watched the toy go up in flame, its body releasing fumes of burnt cotton batting and plastic.

A minute later, the doll fell motionless. Braden nudged it with his foot, fully expecting the thing to leap back to life, mewing for his blood. It didn't happen. The doll seemed finished.

Braden used a poker from a set of fireplace tools to get the toy back into the fireplace, where he doused it again with the lighter fluid. Little remained of the toy by the time he finished.

"Daddy?"

Braden whirled. "Joze!"

Nowhere. Nothing.

Braden jumped into the living room, keeping the poker in one hand and lighter fluid in the other, like some bizarre version of a knight errant. He scanned the living room as he went, sliding one foot in front of the other along the tile floor.

"Josiah? Answer me, buddy. I'm here. Where are you?"

Then Braden found him.

"*Josiah!*"

His son stood on the back porch, plainly visible beyond the picture windows. Braden lurched for the back porch door, threw it open, and ran outside.

Only to discover Josiah back *inside* the house.

Forcing himself to slow down—which meant fighting every instinct he had—Braden approached the window. Two things struck him immediately, two things he'd missed just a few heartbeats ago.

First, it *was* Josiah . . . but Josiah *older*. Not by much. A year, maybe two. At this age, though, a year brought immense physical changes. This morning Josiah had been as tall as Braden's hip; now he'd probably be up to Braden's ribs. And while he hadn't lost the adorable baby fat all toddlers hung on to, he'd definitely gotten leaner in the face.

Secondly . . .

Josiah wasn't in the house, either, as Braden had first thought.

He was *in* the glass. He somehow existed only as a two-dimensional reflection.

Braden approached, still gripping the poker and charcoal fluid bottle. He let the poker drop and dangle between his thumb and forefinger as he reached out to the glass and touched it.

"Daddy!" Josiah cried. And disappeared.

Braden took one step back, gripped the poker, and cursed, swinging as hard as he could. The window shattered, spraying shards inside and out. Terror glared bright in his eyes for a moment as he considered the possibility that he'd somehow killed his own son with the sudden maneuver; but Josiah's broken body didn't appear, either in the shattered glass or in real life.

Plus his voice sounded again, this time from the backyard.

Braden cried out and ran off the porch into the yard, dropping the poker and bottle of charcoal fluid, repeating Josiah's name. Rain cascaded into his mouth, nose, and eyes, trying to drive him back. He ran instead for the relative safety of the pine tree.

He saw then that the wire fence on the ground had grown thicker. Braden wiped water from his eyes to confirm what he thought he saw, but there was no mistaking it. The chicken wire now lay several inches thick, and had stretched to within just a few feet of the base of the pine tree.

Also, it moved. Undulated, like a bucket of fishing worms. Braden thought maybe the rain and darkness were playing tricks on him; but then again, the wire moving was no more out of place than seeing his aging son trapped in glass . . .

Wait, Braden thought. The one word punctured through his tired brain. *Just wait a second.*

From the laundry room, he'd heard Josiah inside the house. From the fireplace room, he'd heard him in the family room. Then outside.

"Shit," Braden whispered, shivering in the cold.

The house had used Josiah as bait. Luring Braden out here.

No sooner had the thought occurred to him than the wire fence came alive and lunged for him.

t e n

It came as a tidal wave, slithering toward him, rising from the ground, curling backward on itself, then slapping forward. Braden released a guttural yelp and forced himself back against the tree trunk. The wire spread toward him, inching along, as if using a million tiny fingers to creep nearer.

That's what this was, Braden thought, nearly subconsciously; he couldn't make himself move, and panic drove all rationality away. *The house lured me out here with Josiah so it could get me.*

He screeched and batted at his face when something soft brushed past it. After his encounters with the wolf spiders he felt sure they'd returned and were moments from burrowing into his ears.

Instead, it was the delicate scratch of a pine needle. One of the pine's branches, about as thick as Braden's arm, bent down toward him. Not stopping to consider the ramifications, he grasped the branch and used it to haul himself up, thankful he'd maintained his life-long slenderness. Kicking off the trunk with his feet, he yanked himself higher and managed to settle on the branch in a standing position.

The branch moved beneath him, lifting away from the hexagonal wire fence. The fence, like a thinking creature, stopped advancing no more than a foot from the tree trunk. Braden could have sworn he felt rage emanating from the twisted strands of metal.

"Thank you," Braden gasped, not considering who or what he might be thanking.

The tree waved gently. Too gently, really, considering the gale-force winds of the storm. He didn't bother to think deeply about it.

Braden slid down carefully, nestling himself into the pine branch. It was the safest, most secure he'd felt since driving into the carport. The pine had never betrayed him, had witnessed many of the depravations foisted upon him by his parents. The pine knew about the coop. And it had protected him, in a certain sense; it had provided a psychological escape. Three stories high, young Braden had been safer at the top than anywhere inside the house.

Rain continued to batter the yard, flooding it. For sure the wash a few miles east would be overrun. The dirt yard beneath him—except where the wire fence now covered it—had become a bog. Even if or when he dropped down and tried to run from the fencing, Braden didn't think the mud would allow for fast travel. It might even work in coordination with the wire fence, sucking his feet down, paralyzing him.

Yet here, in the lowest branches of the pine, the worst of the rain ran elsewhere. The tree simply had too much foliage above, too many branches and cones and needles to siphon the worst of the storm away from him. This place, this exact place was the driest part of the yard right now.

Licking his lips, fearing again for his fragile sanity, Braden said, "Can you hear me?"

No voice came back. But the branch beneath him swayed and creaked softly. Braden shivered, as if put off by what he was going to attempt next.

He tilted his head back and estimated the height of the tree. It had, of course, grown taller since he'd lived here. Then he peered across the yard at the roof of the house. He ran something resembling calculations in his head, then breathed deeply, hoping. Perhaps praying.

"I need to get to the roof," he said aloud, while thinking, *You've gone absolutely nucking futs, buddy.* "Can you help me? They have . . . the house, I mean . . . I guess . . . it has my son."

Immediately he began berating himself. Talking to trees? Won't Dr. Bennett be impressed with *that.* Braden readily imagined cartoon dollar signs popping up in the therapist's eyes, and the image almost made him laugh, except the laugh would have sounded a lot like a scream, so he didn't let it out.

Above him, the old pine swayed in the storm.

And then began to bend.

Old wood straining against its grain first alerted him to it. Braden looked up, and saw that the pine no longer merely swayed, but leaned, tip first, toward the house. It sounded for all the world like a door hinge in need of oil, but immeasurably louder.

Braden swore under his breath, then grabbed hold of the branch beneath him. He nearly wept as the pine continued to force itself down, closer and closer to the roof.

At the same time, the wire fence beneath him started crawling again. It seemed to multiply on itself like a cancer, spreading across the muddy ground and encircling the tree. Even before it began, Braden knew what would happen next.

It's angry, he thought, nearing delirium. *Son of a bitch, the house is pissed at the tree because it's helping me.*

The top of the pine didn't quite touch the roof, but it did extend several feet past its edge. Braden scrambled to follow the main trunk, skirting through branches almost as easily as he had in his childhood. The branches were still in the same place, after all, and he found his hands and feet finding holds as effortlessly as when he'd been ten.

He could hear the wire fence scraping up the trunk after him. It sounded to him like a box of his mother's sewing needles dropped over and over again on a tile floor. Breathing hard, Braden ploughed through the branches of the pine until he was safely over the roof, then dropped down. The tree righted itself immediately, and the wire fence continued its march upward. Braden started to turn and run for the far side of the roof, but found he couldn't, not yet; he stayed and watched as the chicken wire engulfed the entire pine tree, crushing its branches beneath some unholy strength, until the whole thing looked like a dull gray sculpture three stories high.

"I'm sorry," Braden said. "Thank you."

Then he turned and raced for the far side of the roof.

He jumped off of the roof on the front side of the house, near the dirt—now mud—where the acacia had stood. Quickly, he spun around to check for the wolf spiders, but did not see them. He ran past the property line into the street, then turned to face the house. He laced his fingers and formed a visor over his eyes to protect them from the worst of the storm. Flood water lapped at the tongues of his shoes, far higher than he'd ever experienced on this street. Had the house brought the storm? Or was the deluge coincidental?

Maybe—probably—it didn't matter.

He screamed Josiah's name, hoping against hope something would give, some clue would arise, or maybe his sheer rage and love would make the house surrender. Only the sky roared in response. From here on the street, he could see the top of the pine tree out back, ensconced in the wire fencing. Somehow, that made him feel better—or rather, feel less insane. If it could be seen from the street, it seemed reasonable he wasn't imagining it. That's what he told himself.

Braden glanced at the other houses. He could try going to them; ask for help. But of what kind? What possible story could he tell people to make them come to his aid? And even if someone deigned to go into the house with him, what could they do?

Whether an instinct or something more insidious, Braden felt sure at that moment that anyone else stepping foot inside would find Mildred Malkin's colorless house and belongings, the old woman dead in the bathroom, and Braden needing to answer a hell of a lot of questions.

No. He couldn't ask for help, not yet.

So then what?

"Joze," he said to himself. Nothing else mattered.

The curtains in his parents' old bedroom window fluttered. Braden didn't move, choosing instead to pretend like he hadn't seen the movement, draw whatever entity had made the motion into a sense of confidence—with any luck. He kept his face pointed away, but his periphery fixated on the spot.

The curtains fluttered again, and when the blond boy appeared, looking out, searching for Braden, he fought hard not to scream and rush back inside.

The boy was Josiah. He knew it like he knew Joze's eye color and sound of his breathing as he slept. The boy was Josiah, but older. A teenager.

Just a ghost, Braden thought, but didn't believe it. Another piece of the nightmare puzzle popped into place as he realized the house's plan.

It was stealing Josiah's time. His life, his youth. Just as Braden's parents had stolen his.

Braden thought then, with no particular logic, that Josiah's physical life was not in mortal danger—the child wasn't going to be killed, per se, but rather aged. Drained. The house would take from Braden the childhood he'd so enjoyed for three years with Joze, day by day taking steps to ensure his son wouldn't suffer the same abuses he had. And it was working, too. Braden knew it. He'd studied enough to know that Joze was on a good path, better than most, if for no other reason than he was being raised by two adults who loved him and would always be together for him. If nothing else.

If nothing else, Joze will never be locked in a fucking chicken coop, for instance, Braden thought as these theories pinwheeled in his head. *How does it help you get him back?*

Braden took a step toward the house through the floodwater that had now reached his ankles. *The house made Mom and Dad do that heinous shit,* he thought, and giggled brokenly; he stopped walking and bit down on his lip, hard. He could hear how crazy that little laugh had sounded, but his turn of phrase unearthed more memories. Things they'd done. Things they'd scrubbed into his face, that he'd *swallowed—*

No! he thought. *Not now, not yet. Get through this. Get your son. Then you can melt down all you want. Focus.*

It wasn't easy, but he forced himself to take another step. He could still see Josiah—older Josiah—behind the bedroom window, hands pressed against the glass, not *in* it, searching through the storm. Braden even believed, whether he'd heard it or not, that Josiah was calling his name.

Braden smiled.

Not a lot. Not large. But a smile. Because for one moment, like the sun poking through storm clouds, the house had made a mistake. Small, tiny really, but a mistake.

He knew what his son would grow up like. The house had given him a glimpse of Joze's future. He was tall, and strong, and healthy. Now that might be phantasmagoric or imaginary or worse, but it was a glimpse all the same, and for that, Braden smiled.

And broke into a run as soon as his feet touched the gravel yard.

He ran for the front door. Magically, or perhaps it only made sense at this point, one of the spiders lay in wait on the ceiling. It dropped in front of him on a dragline, wriggling. Braden smacked it with one open palm, shouting with both revulsion and courage. The spider flew several yards down the porch, righted itself, and came racing toward him. Braden faced the arachnid, raised a foot, and brought it crashing down on the hairy beast. The spider splayed flat, guts painting a spray pattern on the concrete. It was the first spider he'd ever killed.

Braden took no time to celebrate, though an exultant rush did flood his veins. He opened the front door, threw himself inside, and rushed for the master bedroom. The bedroom door had closed, so he booted it open, leaving a smear of wolf spider innards on the wood near the knob.

Josiah turned from the window.

Braden stopped in the center of the room, breathing hard. He hadn't fully expected Joze to actually be there; he'd assumed the vision would vanish, as surely as it had in the living room window. Natural parental instinct had brought him here, no matter what he figured would happen when he arrived. But no; there Josiah stood, aged maybe seventeen or eighteen, taller than his dad, and scared.

"Daddy?"

Braden nearly choked. Josiah's voice had become deeper, mature; but the tone and the look on his face showed Joze to still be three years old inside.

What must it feel like, Braden wondered vaguely, *to be so small and stuck in a body so big?*

"Joze?" he said. "Is that you, buddy?"

Josiah came to him, and Braden recognized the clumsy step as belonging indeed to a toddler, and his chest ached.

His son embraced him and Braden hugged him back. Josiah certainly felt real; his breathing sounded deep and regular, his eyes were the right color, and body heat radiated from under his shirt.

His shirt . . .

Hating to do it, Braden pulled away from Josiah, and looked at his son's chest. It took a moment, but he recognized the shirt. It wasn't the one Joze had worn that morning. It was one from Braden's own high school days. AC/DC, Back In Black.

That's right, Braden imagined the house saying to him. *Just like you, Braden old chum. Older every moment, one day closer to death, and nothing to show for it. He'll grow old and die here before you'll ever see the sun again.*

"Josiah?" Braden said.

"What happening, Daddy?"

The words tore through Braden like a chain saw. Yes, this was his son—and wasn't. The real, three-year-old Josiah was in there, somewhere.

"I don't know," Braden said, fighting to keep his voice level. "But we're going to work it out, okay?"

"O-tay . . ."

Braden cringed. The voice mismatched the body so badly it cramped his stomach.

"Where did you go, buddy? Do you remember?"

"Um . . . nooo . . ."

"That's okay, that's all right. Here, sit on the bed for a second."

The enormous boy obeyed, perching gingerly on the edge of the queen-size mattress. Braden shifted to the side and peeked into the bathroom; Mildred Malkin still lay motionless on the floor, unmoved from where he'd left her. He took that as something of a good sign, though couldn't justify why exactly.

Braden turned back and sat beside Josiah. "We're going to figure out a way home, okay?"

"O-tay."

"You don't remember anything after I left you in the crib?"

"Noooo."

"Did you see anybody? Do you remember seeing any people?"

"There was a monsters."

Braden's guts tightened. "What kind of monsters? More than one?"

"Yeah . . ."

"Did one of them have horns?"

"Yeah . . ."

Braden knew immediately what the rest would be, but he plunged on anyway, just to be sure.

"Horns that came out of his head?"

"Yeah . . ."

"Was there another monster?"

"Uh-huh!"

"And she had a long tail and long fingers?"

"Yeah!"

Yeah, Braden agreed silently. *I know.* These were the images he'd conjured as a little kid, not much if any older than Josiah. He recognized the two monsters immediately.

"Did they do anything to you, Joze?"

And if they did, so help me sweet baby Jesus, when I get that truck free, I'm driving across the state to find them and end them.

"No," Josiah said thoughtfully. "They chased me."

"They did?" Braden said, instinctively resorting to that sing-song voice parents use when they need the real story and don't want to frighten the child into silence. "What did you do?"

"I ran away!"

"Good!" Braden said. "That was a good choice. Did they hurt you?"

"No. I ran fast."

"Good job, buddy." Braden wrapped an arm around the broad shoulders of this grown boy. "That was very good. Do you know where they went?"

"Noooo."

"Okay, that's all right, that's fine."

With sudden clarity, Braden thought, *It wasn't the house that made them be the way they were. It might be haunted now, but it wasn't then. It was them. It's always been them.*

He didn't know if the revelation would amount to anything, but he felt this discovery to be true in his bones. His mother and father still lived, up in Utah now. When this house was built, it had probably been just a regular old place, made with 1960s sensibilities. But there hadn't been anything wrong with it, no fundamental eldritch flaw.

No, that had come after. The house had, perhaps, absorbed too much of the poison inflicted by his mother and father. It had become corrupt. Then they'd left, and the house sat and festered, a rancid growth that someday would burst. Today had been that day. Only the pine tree, the one place untouched by their sickness, remained immune and had come to his aid.

That's insane, Braden thought, then quickly followed up with, *And your point is?*

"But they were here," he heard himself whispering. "Maybe you couldn't touch them, but they were here someplace."

"What, Daddy?"

"Hmm? Oh. Nothing, Joze. Just talking to myself."

So that's what this is? Braden thought. *A monster movie?*

Well . . . in a sense, maybe, his subconscious went on without him, poking up from the depths of his mind. *Just maybe it is a movie.*

There was, after all, no earthly way his three-year-old son had suddenly added fifteen years. No physics in the universe would allow for that—or at least, no physics that would allow his brain to still be toddling while his body outgrew it. Light-speed travel could wreak havoc with time; he knew that much from nights spent watching the Discovery Channel. But this sudden growth with no attendant mental aging? No.

And houses didn't suddenly re-acquire all the trappings of their former selves; all the furniture, the carpeting, the *odors*.

A movie, on the other hand . . . like aiming a video projector at a wall but not setting up a screen, the light and images would bounce around on any surface because nothing interrupted its waves and particles. Maybe everything, even the very bed he sat on with Josiah, was a projection. A pretty goddamn real and tangible projection, but still just that—imaginary.

If he was anywhere near correct in these hypotheses, then Josiah could still be physically, tangibly saved. This whole day could be undone. All he had to do was end the projection.

How? An exorcism? Braden figured his sessions with Dr. Bennett were about as close to spiritual exorcisms as he could come. No, today's events might well be supernatural, but that didn't make them demonic. Not in any Biblical way, at any rate. Human beings did just fine when it came to torturing and hurting one another. They didn't need a devil's help. Therapy, likewise, served as the modern equivalent of an exorcism. It got rid of the ghost demons haunting him, or at least let him move past them. Maybe the sheer act of coming back here had been enough to trigger all this.

Braden glanced around the room, as if seeing it for the first time.

"Hey, Joze?"

"Yeah?"

"Come on out here with me."

His son's hand crept into Braden's own, and while the sensation of Josiah's huge adolescent hand made Braden's skin crawl, it also comforted him—Josiah was in there. Josiah was *here*. Somewhere.

He led them into the hall and past the intersection, pausing only long enough to see if the burnt doll would make an appearance from the fireplace room. It didn't, so Braden went on into the kitchen.

His mother had kept an array of high quality knives in a butcher's block on one counter, and the house did not disappoint; there it sat, as it always had during Braden's childhood. The block included a cleaver, a broad axe he'd seen her use on certain cuts of meat. Braden pulled the cleaver out and hefted it.

Okay, he thought. *Let's see what happens.*

And he swung the blade as hard as he could.

eleven

The blade bit deep into the frame edging the doorway from the kitchen to the hallway intersection. He felt Josiah jump, but Joze didn't scream. The cleaver stuck there, and only with some effort could Braden pull it back out. A chunk of wood fell to the floor.

The house rumbled.

Braden grinned, a ferocious expression that momentarily disfigured him.

"That's what I thought, you grouchy old bitch," Braden said.

It could feel.

"Mommy says you not supposed to say that bad words," Josiah reminded him.

"You're right, buddy. I won't do it again. Come on."

He walked them through the dark house to the back porch. Cold wind blew through the picture window he'd shattered, and Braden took hope from it—the house hadn't repaired itself, an act of haunting his Hollywood education had led to him to expect. He peered out the window, searching for signs the wire fence had encroached, but saw only the red brick porch, and beyond, mud.

The can of barbeque lighter fluid and the fireplace poker remained where he'd dropped them. Braden turned to Josiah.

"Put your fingers through my belt loop. Here, in back." Josiah did it, looking perplexed. "I need my hands free. You hang on there, stay close, don't let go. Okay? Can you do that?"

Josiah nodded dutifully.

His eyes, Braden thought. *They're still three. It's just his body that's aged.*

He took them back into the house, to the guest bathroom. The house had kept every detail, and sure enough, twenty year old copies of *Time* and *National Geographic* still lay in a wire basket by the toilet. Almost—but not really—amused at the predictability, Braden grabbed the entire basket and brought it to the fireplace. He threw the entire contents into it.

"Help me in the kitchen," he told Josiah. "We need to bring all those chairs in here."

The round, wooden kitchen table stood surrounded by tall-backed wood chairs with woven straw seats. He and Josiah pulled all four chairs into the fireplace room. The remains of the doll still smoked on one andiron.

"Stand here," Braden instructed. "Where I can see you. But stay clear, okay?"

He began bashing the chairs to kindling with the poker. With the first hit, he could feel the house shifting, and he imagined it watching him, trying to second-guess his plot. Even when he'd finished destroying the chairs and tossed the chunks of wood into the fireplace on top of the magazines, the house only creaked and groaned a little.

Braden shot a stream of the lighter fuel onto the coals. The fireplace burst to life, and the ancient chairs lit up.

"Wow," Josiah whispered.

"We're almost done," Braden told him. "Let's go."

They went back into the kitchen. Braden went to the stove and fired up a burner. The stove clicked five times, a subtle timpani. Braden shifted the knob past Lite before the flames could catch, and sniffed the air. The gas came through strong, its rotten-egg odor bursting in his nose.

"That's it," he said. "Let's go, Joze."

"What doing?"

"Going home. Come on."

He peeked through the window in the kitchen door. He did not see the spider, so he assumed it clung to the wall above the door, waiting to drop down on him. "When I open the door, we're going to run to the street, all right? As fast as we can."

"O-tay."

"Ready? When I count to three. One, two—"

The phone rang.

Braden's parents rarely saw need to upgrade anything. They had a corded, rotary phone attached to the wall, which had been there for as long as Braden could remember.

He stared at it, a pale tan hunk of antiquated plastic. Kids like Josiah, or even older than he, didn't know what a dial tone was. Braden had even read that kids below a certain age, when faced with a doorbell, used their thumbs to press the button, while people Braden's age and older tended to use their index fingers; unintended and harmless consequences of being born into the touch-screen generation. Even now, Josiah looked at the phone like an alien entity. Braden saw he was having trouble with the sound.

"Lines are down," Braden said to himself. Then again, maybe they weren't. Maybe they'd been repaired.

In this storm? he thought. *No. No way.*

Answer it.

He picked up the receiver, but said nothing.

"Turn it off, Braden."

Braden's eyes slammed shut. Every muscle locked, including his heart.

"Dad?"

"Turn off the gas, Braden."

It was his dad, but not. Like Josiah, it was some older thing, older than any human had a right to be. But the tone was him, through and through.

"No," Braden said. It wasn't his real dad. Couldn't be. And even if somehow it was, so what?

"Turn it off."

"No."

"I'll take you outside."

Braden remembered what that meant; could never forget what it meant. It meant locked up. It meant the belt. It meant his mother picking up a handful of warm chicken shit from the coop and scrubbing it into his face until he choked. That's what happened when you were bad at the Clark house.

Braden slid to the floor, holding the phone with both hands, pressing it hard against his ear.

"Because you're a big strong man," Braden seethed. "Isn't that right? Isn't that what she looked for?"

This was a quote. Braden had kept his childhood quiet,

never told anyone, not until Ashley. When he finally caved and sought out Dr. Bennett, the psychologist had, at first, recommended confronting the Clarks. It could be by phone, or letter, or email, or in person, but he was not allowed to be alone if and when it happened.

Braden had opted for email. He listed their atrocities using calm, dispassionate facts. No accusations or heated language. Ashley had proofread it before he sent it, and confirmed it was factually stated rather than inflammatory; perhaps even kind, considering the right he had to show them his anger. The email had instead just been a recitation of the truth, concluding with one question: Why?

His mother had replied: *I like a strong male figure. Your dad is a strong man.*

His father had replied: *Get over it.*

That day, after a surprisingly short conversation with Ashley, Braden cut off all contact. He deleted their number from his cell and blocked their email addresses from his account. It so happened he and Ashley were about ready to purchase the new house, so he left them no forwarding address.

They'd offered no denial, nor any apology. It took Braden months to accept those things, if indeed he ever had. Even complete strangers who accidentally bump into one another—while in line at a grocery checkout, for example—accept as an American cultural norm to, at minimum, mumble a quick "Sorry." People did it every day automatically, even if it wasn't heartfelt.

So to not even put up a show of apologizing . . . to not even use the old passive-aggressive twist, "Well I'm sorry if *you* think something happened . . ." That perplexed him as much as anything else.

On the phone, whatever creature was speaking to Braden, it didn't rise to the bait. "Turn off the stove, Braden. Or you'll go outside."

Braden reached out and grabbed Josiah's hand.

"Make me." He felt seven years old when he said it, and yet it tasted wonderful. "You blocked my car. You threw in some spiders. A baby doll. Ooooo! That all you got? Is it? Because I'm going to *blow this fucking place sky high*."

Braden got up and slammed the phone down hard enough to break the cradle. That, too, felt wonderful. Holding tightly to Josiah's hand, he threw open the kitchen door.

No spider dropped as they ran out into the carport. Braden shut the door behind them, then rushed to the street. Again he wondered about neighbors, if they'd seen him, but disregarded the concern. Someone would know he was here soon enough.

Then the wire came for them.

twelve

The hexagonal chicken wire fence rolled up and over the walls separating the back yard from the front, like wicked kudzu in fast-forward. Braden watched it slithering toward them with helpless awe, his face slackening as if being melted by the pelting rain. He and Josiah, not really dry for quite some time now, were utterly soaked through, and shivering from the cold.

"It coming," Josiah said softly from where they stood at the end of the carport, beyond the acacia tree and Braden's pickup.

Braden didn't answer. Still holding Joze's hand, he pulled them backward through the flood. His feet were underwater now, an event never known in this neighborhood. The street dipped to allow drainage, but before much longer, floodwater might be lapping at Mildred Malkin's front door.

Mildred, Braden thought. *I'm sorry for whatever happened to you.*

Had the house attracted her there, a poisonous soul to occupy it? Had she somehow sought out a place of despair? Or had she merely been an unwitting victim to the house's vengeful whims?

It didn't matter much now. Braden slogged through the water and rain, barely able to keep his eyes open, as the wire fence grew and thickened and tumbled toward them. It moved too fast, far too fast for him to outrun it on foot and dragging a six-foot tall toddler along.

Then—the hit.

Braden and Josiah fell forward into the water on the street with joint splashes. To Braden, it seemed as if a body-sized hammer had knocked them both down. Every bone in his body seemed jolted one inch upward from its normal position. Only a moment later did the sound bang into his ears: a deep, sharp boom that seemed to liquefy his eardrums.

Braden searched for Josiah. He hadn't disappeared, fortunately, and instead was already climbing to his hands and knees, crying—and that sight twisted Braden's heart further than he thought possible at that point. The kid still looked like a teenager, yet everything in his expression and voice showed his real age. Braden forced himself to his knees, unable to hear the worst of Josiah's screaming because of the deafness wrought by the explosion behind them. He hugged Josiah close. Over his son's shoulder, he surveyed the damage.

His childhood house was gone. Not utterly; many walls still remained, but smoldered or burned outright. The kitchen lay demolished, and from his angle on the street, Braden could see to the living room, where the pool table now supported several beams from the roof.

The chicken wire fence had vanished.

Braden got to his feet, pulling Josiah up with him. Together, they slogged back onto the property, aiming for a gate separating the front and back yards. It had been blown off its hinges, and Braden went through carefully. Small fires peppered the entire area, most of them already dwindling under the punishing rain.

"Where going?" Josiah asked.

"Someplace safe," Braden said, hoping he was right.

He took Josiah through the yard. Mud and wind-blown detritus from the storm sucked at their feet and tapped into their shins. The pine tree looked haggard now, drenched with rain and broken from the assault by the wire fence. Braden looked in the direction of the old chicken coop as soon as he came within view it, and saw the entire structure had been destroyed. He saw no evidence of the fence having grown or surrounding the tree. In fact, other than the teenager in his arms as they pushed through to the relative serenity beneath the pine tree, Braden saw no evidence of much of anything except that a house had exploded.

They reached the pine. The ground was damp, but still not soaked. Braden sat down with his back against the trunk, and Josiah joined him, curling up beside his dad.

"You o-tay, Daddy?"

"I'm fine, bud. Are you okay?"

"Yeah."

Braden made sure he had a tight arm around Josiah's shoulders. "I'm just gonna close my eyes, okay? Just for a minute. You don't go anywhere."

"O-tay."

"Okay. I love you so much, Joze."

"I love you."

Braden shut his eyes.

When two policemen in rain gear woke him up, the first thing he did was look down at his arms. Josiah, age three, lay nestled against him, fully on Braden's lap and sucking sleepily on two fingers.

Braden wept, and they led him away. The rain had stopped.

thirteen

"I've got your statement from the night of the accident," said Detective Hennessey. He wasn't the type, on first impression, to cast fear into anyone, Braden thought. Or maybe Braden just didn't fear much of anything anymore.

"It's just, there's a few things I'm a little confused about," the detective went on. "Hoping you can clear it up."

Braden nodded. Three days had passed since he and Josiah were escorted off the property. An ambulance had taken them to the nearest hospital, where they were both released after a night of observation. Ashley had, in usual form, been nurturing to them both. Braden didn't tell her the entire story until they were all safe at home. When he did finally tell her, he'd left out nothing. Not one small bit of information or even so much as an impression. Ashley took it all in with her usual grace and calm. She asked serious questions, or questions designed to make him think she was serious. Either way, Braden didn't care. She listened, and didn't judge.

"It's this thing about the stove in the kitchen,"

Hennessey said. "You said you smelled gas when you came inside the house?"

That was the best lie Braden had been able to concoct. He chose to stick with it. "That's right. I tried to get Mrs. Malkin to get out of the house, but she wouldn't. I would've carried her out myself except I had my son."

The detective nodded absently. "Well, that's kind of the problem. See, Mr. Clark, according to records and the investigators, that house hasn't been fitted with natural gas for about two decades."

Braden didn't think his face betrayed anything, but inside, his organs grew cold.

"Wow," he said.

"Yeah, that's what I thought. 'Wow.' Can you explain that?"

"No. Not really. I can't. Um . . . but if the house wasn't fitted for gas, how the hell did it blow up?"

"Tell you the truth, I was hoping you could come up with a great story about that, too."

Braden allowed a smirk. The detective had meant his phrasing to needle him. Clearly, he'd done his homework on author Braden Clark.

"Sir," he said, "I'm telling you exactly what happened. We got out as soon as I smelled gas."

Hennessey nodded again. "Yeah, that's a funny thing. The investigators smelled it, too. Damndest thing. You know, the gas companies, they put in that smelly stuff so people know when there's a leak. Otherwise natural gas has no odor, did you know that?"

"I think I've heard that somewhere, yeah."

"When a house goes up like that, the smell lingers. You

can't miss it. The investigators reported on it. All intents and purposes, it was a gas leak that led to the explosion. Except for that part where there wasn't any natural gas hooked up."

Braden nodded slowly.

"That is a mystery," he said.

"Maybe you'll write a book about it, eh?"

"Maybe I will."

They stared at each other. Braden's face was as impassive as the doll's had been.

The detective let him go after another thirty minutes of questions. He didn't expect any charges to be filed; Mildred Malkin's body had been relatively untouched due to her position and location in the master bathroom. No one could come up with a good motive for Braden to have bombed the place, and they found no evidence of other foul play. Mrs. Mildred Malkin's death was ruled a suicide—an autopsy revealed fatal amounts of an anti-anxiety medication in her system—and Braden Clark was free to go and live his life.

Those words meant more to him now than ever.

In the days that followed, every so often, Ashley would give him a look like she wanted to ask more about that night, but she never did, not until a month later when her parents came by to baby-sit Josiah. Little Joze himself seemed none the worse for wear. Braden had feared nightmares or anxiety, but the toddler went on speeding through life like nothing strange had ever happened. Braden accepted it as a gift.

For their first date night out since Braden had been cleared of any wrongdoing, he and Ashley went to their favorite seafood place where crab and lobster were served in plastic bags on tables shrouded in butcher paper for easy disposal between customers.

"What do you think really happened?" Ashley asked before their course was delivered.

Braden sipped water. "You think I snapped."

"No. I wouldn't be living with you if I thought that. I wouldn't let Josiah anywhere near you if I thought that."

"You don't think I killed her?"

"Not once have I thought that."

He believed her. God, what a woman.

"What do I think really happened?" Braden said. "I think the house wanted to die. It's taken me a bit to come to that conclusion. But I think it did. It wasn't out for us. Out for *me*. It wanted to be destroyed. When the phone rang in the kitchen, my dad—whatever was acting like my dad—tried to get me to stop. But then something *else* led me around, gave me the idea to blow the whole thing up. And I think it was the house itself. Maybe it tried other ways to demolish itself over the years, and none of them worked. Maybe whatever made Mildred kill herself gave it the power to do something, or maybe it killed her first . . . I don't know. I mean, I *really* don't know, I don't know *anything*. It's just a guess. It's all I'll ever have is guesses. But that's the one that makes the most sense. To me, I mean."

He paused and sipped more water.

"It wanted to die," he said again.

Ashley laid a hand over his. "I'll buy that. It makes sense. It's twisted, and very, very sad. But it makes sense."

Braden squeezed her hand. They talked next about which TV series to binge on, and that was that. Ashley never brought it up again.

Later that night, they made love, and when he was sure Ashley was asleep, Braden let himself into Josiah's room and knelt by the edge of his new twin bed, watching his son's relaxed face and listening to his gentle breathing. Josiah had two pillows with Superman pillowcases clutched in his hands, but no stuffed animals. Braden had asked Ashley to take all the stuffed toys out of Josiah's room and burn them. He didn't know if Ashley had actually burned them or not, but when he and Josiah got home from the hospital together, the toys were gone. Josiah never asked for them.

"I love you," Braden whispered to the sleeping toddler. "I love you so much, Joze. And I'd do it all again if I had to. I'd go through hell for you. I'd stare down God and all his armies to keep you safe."

He brushed a lock of blond hair off Josiah's forehead, then quietly got up and climbed into bed beside his wife. He slept almost immediately.

The following weekend, he and Josiah planted a young pine tree in the back yard.

t h e e n d

tree fort

originally published in *Aoife's Kiss*

Clown walks into a bar. Bartender says, what'll you have? Clown says, bartender, gimme a treefort! Bartender looks at him, says, well what's in a treefort? Clown says . . .

Porno books and cigars, hee-hee!

I smiled but did not laugh. Tommy's voice rang clear and cold in my ears, telling and re-telling his stale old jokes. I heard him as clearly as if he were still standing there beside me. Our fort never had porno books or cigars; those would come as we aged, but our fort was free from such degradation.

I stopped smiling.

The fort looked like it was still in decent shape. I craned my neck back as far as it would go, studying the warped plywood that served as the fort's floor. I saw cracks, but no splits. I gazed down the length of the trunk. The wooden crossbeams we'd nailed to the trunk all those years ago had been swallowed partially by the growing tree. Where once the rungs were weak and prone to popping off, they were now embedded in the bark. I grabbed the lowest rung and pulled on it. It was like trying to pull off a branch. The rungs were safer now than they'd been when Tommy and I first nailed them down.

I grasped the lowest rung and began pulling myself up the ladder, careful not to disturb the lower branches as I ascended. We'd built the tree fort when we were ten, and no grown-ups had helped. We'd nailed the old wood together with nails pilfered from Tommy's father's workshop, and he'd never missed them. We'd surrounded two sides of the plywood with a short wall, constructed out of two-by-four scrap. One side of the fort was camouflaged with green netting I'd asked my mom to buy us. From the ground, you had to look closely to see it. It was like a sniper's nest, exactly what Tommy and I had intended. We even had an emergency exit, a thick nylon rope tied to a branch above the fort that we could drop out and slide down in case the fort was ever overtaken—or if we just wanted the thrill of sliding down the rope, which was often. It was a straight drop of twenty feet or so, a stupid height to be jumping from, but we had faith in our rope and our immortality. The rope still held firm even now.

I reached the trapdoor opening and shoved it up. The hinges complained bitterly, but didn't resist. The trapdoor fell to the floor and startled a flock of birds, which took flight with a cacophony of whistles and caws. I glanced down, making sure their flight didn't disturb the lower branches.

I pulled myself cautiously up through the hole. I weighed a good deal more than I had when I was ten. Back then, Tommy and I could scramble up the ladder and be hidden behind our netting in about five seconds. Imaginary foreign invaders were always chasing us, but our cap guns held them at bay once we were secure in our fort.

The floor held my weight, but it wasn't big enough for an adult to crawl onto. I knew this already; I visited the tree fort once a year since Tommy died. Sort of a commemoration. It was ironic and somehow appropriate that Tommy had died here. As if the invaders had finally taken one of our own. Tommy hadn't gone without a fight. He'd fired his cap gun empty before the end came, and I admired him for that. Even to this day, I admired him.

I heard myself sigh. Tommy never gave up on anything, I remembered. Even when our imaginary enemies invaded the fort and took us hostage—Tommy and I had tied the rope on ourselves—he was always full of ideas on how to escape, and of course, they always worked. When we were ten, eleven, and twelve, we were able to switch roles on a dime, better than any actor. Make-believe required it. I had to switch from fearless defender of American freedom to cold-blooded mercenary at the drop of a hat. Tommy took his turns too, though his mercenaries were always better—that is, more evil and more sadistic—than mine. I envied his playacting as much as I did his stubbornness.

We were best friends, I almost said aloud as I began working my way back down the ladder and shutting the trap door above me. Even when Tommy got loud and obnoxious, which was frequently, I still loved him. I didn't have the maturity to call it that when I was twelve, but looking back, I knew that's what it was. It seemed only logical that the two of us would get our first crushes on the same girl upon entering junior high school. We were that much alike. Like brothers. The object of our crush, Lindsey McNaughton, had been swayed by Tommy at first, but in the end, had come to enjoy my company more.

Maybe it was because she felt bad for me when Tommy died. It didn't matter to me at the time. Of course, by senior high, Lindsey and me weren't an item anymore, and Tommy was still dead. Lindsey had only gone out with me as a sort of comfort, and I didn't mind. Tommy wouldn't have either, I figured.

I dropped the last couple of feet to the ground, careful not to disturb the lower branches. I glanced up at the nylon rope that hung taut from above, making sure everything was still in place. Tommy hadn't questioned me when I suggested we play War one more time, even though at that point video games and girls had become much more important to us both. He'd joined me in one last daring escapade, this one involving more mercenaries than we'd ever faced before. Our cap guns almost glowed red with the amount of imaginary hot lead we rained down upon our enemies. We were outgunned, in the end, but determined as ever to go down fighting, even as the mercenaries climbed into our fort. I'd prepared for them, setting a neat trap with a slipknot in the rope that served as our escape route. When the mercs burst into the fort, guns blazing, I'd dropped the noose over Tommy's head and shoved him out the escape hatch. Tommy stayed in character till the end, firing his gun at me all the way down.

I've never heard a sound like the one I heard that afternoon, the wet-stick snap of Tommy's neck when the rope had played out. With that sound, the assault had stopped, and I never played make-believe again. There was no need. Lindsey didn't play make-believe, and certainly never played War. She wouldn't understand that I was a hero, that I had saved us both from Tommy's incessant, know-it-all attitude.

I sighed again and shoved my hands in my pockets as I watched Tommy's bones sway gently from the end of the rope. The police had never made it this far out of town when they searched for him, and I didn't feel like helping them out. So here Tommy stayed, where he belonged, his weathered bones and leering skull protecting our fort from all invaders, foreign and domestic.

I wondered how long his skeleton could remain intact. Tommy's blue jeans were crusted solid on the ground beneath his fleshless feet where they'd fallen several years ago, his green t-shirt tattered and almost gone completely. But Tommy's old stubbornness must have run as deep as his bones, for the skeleton was a model of perfection. It looked like a fake, something you'd find in a biology classroom, except for small tufts of brown hair clinging to his dry, ivory scalp. I watched the lower branches sway again in a light breeze, fearful they would disintegrate whatever remained of the sinews and cartilage holding Tommy's bones together, but the lower branches veered away from the specter, as if in respect.

"What's in a tree fort?" I asked.

Tommy's skull was still and silent, smiling.

He loved that joke.

crimson candles

Tony and Michelle drove to the mountain again. They held hands, but it was perfunctory, not even tradition so much as muscle memory.

"You don't think he'll really show, do you?" Tony asked.

Michelle's hand stayed limp in his own. "It doesn't matter. We still have to go. We still have to try."

Tony figured she was right about that. If they did have any traditions, it was going to the mountain to see if Owen would show or not. It was an annual thing now. They'd been doing it for five years. By this point, neither of them really believed anything different would happen.

But isn't that where all good stories begin? Tony thought.

He tapped the brakes lightly as something darted in front of the headlights. "Did you see that?"

Michelle was already leaning forward in the seat, squinting. "Something. Was it a squirrel?"

Tony didn't answer. He didn't need to. Squirrels weren't that big.

Earlier in their relationship, he might have pointed

that out. To do so now would lead only to misery on both their parts, so he kept his mouth shut. He leaned back in his seat, not realizing until he did it that he, too, had been leaning forward.

Michelle mirrored his movement, settling back into her bucket seat. Whatever the thing had been, it was gone now.

"It looked white," Michelle said quietly. "Did it look white to you?"

"Little bit," Tony said. "It was kind of fast. Hard to say."

He glanced at her. Michelle looked uncomfortable.

"It was just some animal," he couldn't stop himself from saying. "Don't worry about it."

That was the bit he should not have added. He could feel her scowling in the darkness of the truck. But Michelle didn't say anything. She did remove her hand from his, and folded her arms.

Tony returned his right hand to the steering wheel. "Have you ever told anyone we do this?" he asked after a long silence.

"Not specifically. Some friends from school know that we go out on this night, but I haven't told them where, or what we do."

"That's good," Tony said, as if it mattered.

"What about you?"

"No," Tony said quickly. "Nobody."

"Maybe this should be our last time," Michelle said softly. "I mean, five years. That's a long time."

Tony did not answer, though he had the same thought. Five years. That was a nice round number. A nice even anniversary. The world loved patterns; the world appreciated anniversaries, special dates and times, even as the broader universe could not care less. There was something about the calendar that kept the world going.

Five years. Surely, that would be enough for Owen. If he was watching.

They reached the base of the mountain twenty minutes later. It loomed tall before them, a dark mass, darker than the purple-black sky behind it. Tony found a dirt place to park the truck and turned off the engine.

"Are you sure you want to still do this?"

Michelle nodded in the darkness. "Let's just go."

"You sure you have everything?" He'd asked several times already, including at her house when she got into the car.

"I'm sure."

They got out of the truck and walked almost by instinct to something resembling a path winding up the mountain. Tony had a flashlight, and he knew Michelle had two more in the backpack she carried over her shoulders, but she didn't pull one out and he didn't turn his on. It was part of the tradition. The anniversary. There was a certain way to do things, and finding their way in the dark to the top of the mountain was among them.

They did not speak. They did not hold hands. They moved slowly at first, letting their eyes adjust to the darkness. Midway along the path, they could see almost as well as if it were sunset. It happened every time this way. They never spoke of it to one another, yet somehow knew all the same.

They also seemed to know, without sharing it, that if they came up one day before or one day after, this is strange ability to see better in the dark would not happen. It was unique to this date and time.

They reached the summit thirty minutes later. Wordlessly, Michelle hunkered to open the backpack. She set up the crimson candles in their particular places while Tony scanned the area for wildlife, park rangers, or anything to indicate that this was anything but just another spring night.

Michelle finished quickly, and sat cross-legged at one end of the pattern of candles. She gestured to Tony, who sat across from her in the same manner.

"Right," she said. "Let's start."

They each took a deep breath, held it a moment . . . then began the chant.

Although they never practiced or rehearsed, all the words—older than the stars above them—came fluently. The strange syllables and archaic consonants sounded like animal gibberish even in their own ears, yet their mouths worked automatically.

Halfway into the ritual, Tony knew it would be another bust. Five years running, they had come here and tried to bring Owen forth, to beg his forgiveness for the accident, with no success. And tonight would be no different.

He'd just completed thinking the thought when the candle flames burned blue.

That was new.

He glanced at Michelle, who frowned at this new thing. He wanted to ask her what was going on; could see she wanted to ask him the same; yet they did not stop the ritual.

The temperature at the top of the mountain dropped precipitously. The warm spring air turned cold, bitter— like a snow storm. It pinched the hairs on Tony's arms and legs. He saw Michelle shiver.

The candle flame turned a deep and secret violet Tony had never before seen. Not in a candle flame for sure, but anywhere else for that matter. Purple was not even the right word, but there was no earthly word for it.

Twin tears fell down Michelle's face as she stared at the unearthly color. Only then did Tony realize he, too, was crying.

Though not from joy. And they weren't tears after all. As the crimson candles flared their eldritch color, something else dripped down their faces, hot and fatal.

The world loved calendars. It loved anniversaries.

Owen did, too.

now you don't

Author's Note: Of all my novels, this is a "hard-R" for graphic violence. If that is not something you wish to read, please continue reading on page 517.

one

Travis awoke believing he was having a heart attack but instead it was a monster. It perched on his chest, weighing him down, pressing him into his memory foam mattress until it took the shape of an inverted Egyptian sarcophagus. The thing must have weighed more than a hundred pounds; two hundred, maybe. It had knees, for they were pressed into the hollows of Travis's shoulders, preventing him from moving his arms. He thought its feet were positioned in such a way as to keep his thighs immobile as well. The thing apparently knew Brazilian jiu-jitsu because holy shit he could not move.

He had only enough time upon waking to see that it had a tiny hole of a mouth, a small black disc in the darkness of his bedroom that reminded him absurdly of a blow-up doll, though he'd never actually seen one of those in person. The skin of its cheeks was pulled taut, giving the thing a gaunt, ghoulish appearance. Its skin was something on the Caucasian spectrum, not quite pale and not quite tan. The forehead rose high and sloped backward with sparse baby hair sprouting along the crown. The fineness of the hair reminded Travis of his daughter's scalp when she'd been born twelve years ago.

Darla, he thought as the terror of his situation lit his nerves on fire. Darla, where is she?

The monster was naked. In the half-second Travis's brain had to assess all these facts, it also registered that some small, limp, cold limb lay across his belly. A penis, chilled and damp, as if having emerged from a swimming pool.

"Whut—" A sound less than a word belched from Travis's mouth as the thing atop him tilted its head, staring down with blue eyes lit by the beam of a streetlight shooting from between the dark wood blinds.

The monster raised its right hand. It looked spider-like in the dark, shadowy and segmented. Its nails were overgrown, inches long, jagged and sharp.

It tilted its head again before plunging a finger into the soft skin where Travis's eyelid met his eye socket.

Travis had enough air to scream as the finger pierced deep. The monster drove its finger down, then to the right. Travis felt the rough skin and sharp claw sliding behind his eyeball and heard the chilling squish of the eye popping neatly, though not cleanly, from out of his skull.

The monster laid its other hand across Travis's mouth as he bellowed. The skin of its palm was calloused, warm, and dry. Every muscle in his body cramped as Travis fought against the monster's weight, against the fear for Darla's little life, against the rich, bright pain in the cavern where his eye used to be.

He felt a tug deep in his skull, like tightening a shoelace. Then a brisk snap and the eye let go from its mooring.

Travis's other eye, his right, was wide open. Even in the dark and despite the rampage of cascading hormones released by pain and terror, Travis's one remaining eye beheld the monster hold up its hand. The eye swung from the monster's finger tip by the stalk, wide by default since it had no lids, gazing blindly back at its owner, accusing. Travis wanted to vomit, wanted to pass out, wanted the horror to end.

Darla! he screamed, but the sound was incoherent and muffled under the creature's palm. Travis tried to close his eye but couldn't—a warm disbelief flooded his system, convincing him this was a dream, what else could it be, surely this was a nightmare from which he would awake any second now, *any second now . . .*

The monster tilted its head back and raised its hand, dangling the eyeball above its face. It issued a short sucking sound. Travis heard it, or imagined he heard it, over his ongoing muffled screams. The eye slipped neatly into the beast's circular mouth.

It lowered its chin to stare at Travis as its jaw worked. It studied him as a bird might study a worm. Travis stopped screaming, overcome with wretched disgust and nausea as he watched the monster eat. The thing itself didn't seem to blink, or if it did, it was too quick for Travis to notice.

Of course, what he really noticed was that he had just had his left eye pulled out and eaten by a naked humanoid monster.

Perhaps, Travis considered mildly in that cobwebbed corner where such space is reserved for insane thought, that is what I should be focused on right now.

His cries for Darla shifted to a cry for help. The monster gave him what was, for all intents and purposes, a pitying look. It then curled its right hand over his left eye and began working at it as he had the other.

Right-handed, Travis's brain pointed out. Look at that, it's right-handed and having a little trouble. That must be why this one hurts more. Oh, wait—*Look* at that? Haha, I get it. Very punny.

His voice went coarse as he lost all vision. The dark world in front of him did not fade to black or red or white; it simply ceased to see in one quick pop. The eye came out less gracefully than the left had. Explosive pressure burst somewhere just above his face, and Travis felt the viscous goo of the eyeball drip onto his cheek. Then came a slurping noise and his brain advised he not think about what that sound meant.

Please, he begged silently through his raw screams. Please don't let me die please not like this sweet Jesus God please don't let this be how I go out please . . .

The weight vanished. Travis bolted upright, hands flying to his face, covering his cavernous eye sockets. The space left behind sickened him and his pizza dinner burst forth from his mouth, coating his boxers and naked thighs, still warm from where the creature had perched.

Senselessly he swung his hands down for a pillow, which he found and stuffed against his face. His brain, operating on brute instinct, questioned whether or not bleeding to death were a real possibility.

Someone would come now, he thought, or semi-thought; conscious words were well beyond his abilities now. Someone would hear what passed for screams and come running, call the cops, call the paramedics, they'd get here, save his life . . .

But because of the depth and breadth of his screams, his voice was utterly destroyed. All that came out were slick tendrils of puke and a hoarse grunting that no one could hear past his own bedroom door.

Instinctively he got to his knees on the mattress, swiping his bookshelf headboard for his cell phone. He found it readily in its usual place beside his framed photo of Jenny and Darla and got it into his hands where it rested with its knobby, familiar comfort.

He groaned, then wailed as the futility of it hit him— if it was a landline and he could calm down enough to rationalize, he could have called 911 by feeling for the buttons. But a touch screen? The chances of guessing what numbers he was hitting, if any at all, were remote at best. He remembered there was some push-button way to automatically dial the emergency number, but could *not* remember what the hell it was.

"Fuck!" Travis screeched noiselessly, the first actual word he'd managed to form since the monster had climbed onto him.

The monster—where?

Panicked, Travis slid from the bed and huddled against the wall, drawing his knees up to his chest and scrambling for the pillow again to staunch the blood and gore he felt trailing warmly down his face. Where had it gone? Still in the room? He bit the pillow to force himself into silence and listened.

No sound but his own pumping heart and the short snorts of breath from his nose against the pillowcase. The floor was carpeted, it could be standing right in front of him for all he knew.

Travis kicked out. His feet scraped carpet, but nothing else.

Darla—

He heard no screams from her room. Maybe the thing didn't know about her or didn't care. Or maybe it had already silently killed her in her sleep before coming for him.

Or, or, or . . .

Groaning again Travis tossed the pillow aside and crawled forward. He'd be lined up with his bedroom door from here. Whether or not the thing that had blinded him was still here or not, he couldn't help that. He could think of no practical way to defend himself against it if it attacked again. That left Darla, making sure she was safe somehow.

But if he couldn't defend himself, how could he possibly—

Travis let the thought fly away. No helping that now. He had to know if his daughter was safe.

He found his bedroom door open. Maybe that meant it had left; he slept with the door closed, he and Jenny always had back when they actually shared a house. He crept past the threshold and turned right, knees abrading from carpet burns.

"Darla!" he croaked, reaching out with his left hand, sweeping broadly, seeking the dip in the wall that would indicate her doorframe. His fingers found the lip and he pulled himself toward it, calling her name again.

Darla's door was shut. He shoved stupidly, blindly into

it for a moment before reaching up for the door knob and twisting with one slick hand.

Travis fell into the door which flew open and banged against the wall.

"Darla!"

He heard her mumble something nonsensical, then say, "Dad?" A catch in her voice gave it two syllables.

Travis rose to his knees and said her name, reaching out for her.

A moment of silence followed, broken next by his daughter's piercing, endless scream.

○

Jim didn't know whether to knock or just what, so he let himself into the hospital room without announcing himself. He later berated himself for the truth: he wanted to see what he'd be getting into first. He wanted to get half a look at Travis before committing to going into the room, because Jesus Christ, what if he was all gored up and shit? Unlikely, given their location, but still. The image and idea stuck in his head.

He peeked around the wall and saw Travis in a room by himself, his head and eyes bandaged thickly with bright white gauze. No blood stained the wraps. He lay quiet and still, mouth slightly ajar, breathing on his own with a slow, regular rhythm. Some invisible man was talking to Travis, and it took Jim another second to realize it was an audiobook whispering from Travis's phone, which lay on a nearby tray beside a yellow plastic pitcher.

"Am I awake? Who's there?"

Travis's voice was dry and ragged, but his face—the half Jim could see of it—didn't tense.

"Hey, man," Jim said, sliding closer. "I'm gonna go ahead and say 'How's it going' because that's what we always say. I understand it's a bit fucking stupid to ask."

Travis grunted. Jim saw the corners of his mouth twitch as if trying to smile but giving up before the expression could be realized.

"I been better." Travis's mouth barely moved. "But I'm here, man. I'm alive. You know?"

Jim moved closer. He didn't like hospitals much, and he sure didn't like good friends getting . . . what, de-eyed? He didn't like that much, either. Maybe whatever curse had fallen on Travis would fall on him if he got too close.

"That's cool." Jim shook his head, wanting to slap himself. "I mean, that's a good way to, uh . . . to look at it."

To *look* at it? Jesus Christ, he thought. You should maybe not try to help, Jimbo, huh?

Travis's next grunt came close to taking the form of a laugh, and the corners of his mouth stayed just a little bit turned up now. "Dude. It's okay. I wouldn't know what to say either. Don't worry about it."

Relief settled in Jim's stomach. He went to the side of the bed, unsure if he should take his buddy's hand or just what. So he didn't, but he did lean on the raised side of the bed so Travis could at least sense his proximity.

"Man, I'm sorry. Just—*sorry*. I don't know what else to say. This is some fucked-up shit. What happened?"

Jim got the oddest and most disconcerting feeling that Travis's gaze slid over toward him beneath the bandages. Except Travis would never *gaze* again.

"You really want to know? Or you want the cop version?"

Jim straightened a bit. "Did you tell them something different than what happened?"

Travis moved his head about an inch to one side then the other. It finally dawned on Jim that he must have a dozen different painkillers and other meds coursing through his body.

"No. I told them everything. I told them the truth. But I know they don't believe the details."

"I don't get it."

"I told them exactly what happened. Everything I saw before I couldn't see anymore. They're not gonna argue that someone did this to me. But I know they think I was delirious or something as it happened. Dreaming, even. They think it was just some guy."

Jim leaned closer, drawn to his friend's phrasing. "You mean it wasn't?"

"Naw, man." Travis's hand lifted a bit off the sheet as if in the beginnings of wave, then dropped again. "It wasn't just some guy. It was a dude, yeah. I mean, male. I felt his dick laying on me, I think—"

Jim's lip curled.

"—but it wasn't a normal person. You know how in horror movies no one ever believes the kids when they say there's a monster out there?"

Jim nodded. Cursed himself for trying to use body language to communicate with a blind guy. Said aloud, "Yeah."

"Well that's what this is like."

Travis lifted his right hand again, this time with dim

430

urgency. Jim regarded it for a moment, then clasped it in his own.

Travis squeezed, not tightly, but emphatically all the same. "I'm telling you. It wasn't human. It was something else. Some monster. And it's still out there. You gotta watch Darla for me, okay? Okay, man?"

"Yeah, yeah, okay."

"No!"

Sudden strength flared in Travis's grip and Jim winced at the shock of it.

"It has claws. Or something like it. It weighs a ton, it moves quietly. It fucking *ate my eyes in front of me*. You gotta watch out for Darla and Jenny, make sure they're safe."

"Hey, hey," Jim said, putting his free hand on Travis's shoulder. "They're fine, bro. I texted with Jenny just a while ago, they're okay."

"That's not what I mean." Travis let him go. "The cops kept asking me about enemies, and drugs, gambling, debts . . . stuff like that. You know I'm not into any shady shit."

"Yeah." To Jim's knowledge, Travis was nothing but a straight-shooter who played hard ball on the basketball court and nothing more. His party days were long past, and he didn't seem to live a millionaire life on his run-of-the-mill investment banker's salary. He did okay, better than Jim, but that was all.

"So then maybe it was something else, something I forgot. I don't know. But it came for me. *Me*. It might come for the rest of my family too."

"Trav, if whoever did this wanted to hurt Darla or Jenny, why didn't he do it when he was in the apartment?

Darla was right there. She's fine."

"Dunno." Travis's voice carried a stubborn edge. "Maybe it'd eaten its fill."

Jim's lip curled again. He thought of the dinner scene in *Indiana Jones and the Temple of Doom*, of Shorty and Willie stirring a soup full of eyeballs. He decided he'd skip lunch today.

"Just promise me, man."

"Dude, what the hell am I supposed to do?"

"You got a gun?"

Jim coughed. "Got one? No, I rent every so often. Trav, that's for shits and giggles, I'm not trained."

"More than me, you are."

"Trav—"

"I don't trust anyone else."

Jim blew out a sigh. "I thought you said you weren't into anything shady."

"I've known you longest. C'mon, man, we got twenty years behind us. I don't have that with anyone else. Business guys, Jenny's friends. That's it. I'm talking about my daughter's *life*."

Jim clutched the railing and took a step back, stretching out one calf and then the other. "All right. What is it you saw?"

Travis told him. Jim decided he'd skip dinner, too, when Travis finished up.

He also reckoned the cops were most likely right. Obviously someone had attacked Trav and done some serious damage. After the trauma he'd survived, it could and almost certainly would wreak havoc with his mind, his memories. It had to have been some psycho with a penknife or, Christ, even a utensil; some nutbag with a fetish for his grandmother's collection of tea spoons from Great Britain, who the fuck knew?

But a monster? No. Not the kind Trav described anyway.

"You don't believe me."

Jim blinked. Travis had been blind for less than forty-eight hours, had he already developed some of those Marvel mutant powers to compensate?

No, Jim told himself; no, he's just being perceptive.

"I'm having trouble with it, yeah."

"That's fine," Travis said, surprising Jim. "Honestly it doesn't matter to me if you do or not. What matters to me is you keep an eye on my kid."

An eye on her? Jesus, was that a joke? No, Jim realized. Just an idiom. Travis hadn't caught it. He asked, "What about Jenny? What do you want me to do?"

Travis grunted again, not so much a laugh as a dismissal. "Sure, yeah, Jen too, whatever. Bitch."

He'd tacked it on, perfunctory. Jim smiled mildly, and for the first time since arriving; for the first time since yesterday when Jenny had called to tell him what had happened. She'd already been to see her ex yesterday and to take care of Darla.

Jim started to say something else, but Travis had grown quite still, head a bit to one side, mouth again slack. He stood straight and touched Trav's shoulder.

"Trav?"

No response at first. Then Travis made some kind of noise that may or may not have been a word or two.

"I'll go," Jim whispered. "You need to take it easy."

"Jim . . ."

"Yeah, bud."

"If I'm makin' this up . . ."

"Yeah?"

"Then what did he do."

Jim tilted his head. "Do?"

"With my eyes."

Jim's mouth dried.

"Because the cops didn't find 'em. So if I'm lying or I made it up or I was delirious, that's fine. That motherfucker still took my fucking eyes with him. Who does that?"

Jim tried to get saliva back into his mouth. He wasn't successful. He patted Travis's shoulder again. "I gotta go. I'll come back later, okay?"

When Travis didn't answer, he took that to mean his friend was asleep. Jim let himself out of the room—quickly—and into the hospital hallway. He kept his pace brisk as went to the elevator and rode it down, happy to at last feel the warm Phoenix sunlight on his face.

He lifted his head and shut his eyes against the Arizona sun. For the first time in his life, he really felt the eyelids, the muscles around them, the different shades of red that played against the inside of them as he squeezed his eyes shut.

His eyes were where they were supposed to be. It was a beautiful thing.

"Fuck," Jim uttered, dropping his chin and opening his eyes again.

He got into his Jeep Liberty and took off fast.

○

"He doesn't know," Jim said while Jenny spun a mug of coffee between her fingers, scraping it against the kitchen tabletop.

"You're sure?"

"Pretty, yeah. This has nothing to do with us, whatever it is."

Jenny looked up sharply, trying to parse his words: what was the "whatever" he was referring to?

Jim sighed. "I mean, whatever attacked him, it has nothing to do with us. How is Darla?"

"Freaked the fuck out, what do you think?"

Jim bit back a response by washing his hands at the kitchen sink, turning the water on as hard and hot as he could. He loved her, but goddamn if she didn't get bitchy sometimes. Travis was right about that, and of course he'd know best.

Jim turned the water off just short of scalding himself and wiped his hands on a dishtowel hanging from the oven. "It was a stupid question, it's not what I meant."

Jenny let the spoon clang inside the mug. She rubbed her eyebrows with her fingers. "No, I know, I'm sorry. I'm the one who's freaked out. She's okay, more or less. Probably want to get her into some therapy just to be on the safe side. Jesus, can you even imagine what she saw?"

Jim nodded. He'd thought about it a lot since leaving the hospital. Seeing Travis with all those bandages, that was unsettling. Being there, in the moment, with the blood coating Travis's face and those eyeless black sockets staring but not staring right into him . . .

He kept drying his dry hands. "Yeah."

Jenny let her shoulders slump as she looked up at him

with puppy dog eyes. "Can I give you a hug?"

He tossed the dishtowel and opened his arms. Jenny went to him, holding him close. Jim held the back of her head, her dark brown hair tangling in his fingers while he pressed her into him. Yeah, that was better. Such a good fit.

"We were already separated," Jenny said, resting her cheek on his shoulder.

Jim grunted an agreement, but that was all. He'd grown tired of the refrain. He knew it himself, she didn't need to keep bringing it up. Jenny and Trav had been on the outs since . . . well, hell, since about a week after their wedding, and everyone knew it. That they'd lasted long enough to have and raise Darla into a functional pre-teen was either a miracle or an act of sheer willpower.

How *much* willpower, Jim tried not to think about. As a matter of course, fearing he'd give himself away, he never asked Trav if he'd strayed during the marriage, and he didn't ask Jenny, either. Mostly he'd forced himself to assume they had, and that it didn't matter. That was then— whenever it was—and this was now. He didn't believe in "once a cheater, always a cheater," because, goddammit, he and Jenny *weren't* cheating. The divorce had been final for months. This keeping it a secret from Trav was just . . . just friendship, really, Jim told himself. They'd tell him when—

When you're sure, Jim thought. When you know Jenny is in this for the long haul and not just a rebound. Right, Jimbo? Right?

"You sound guilty when you say that," Jim told her.

"I know. I have to stop that."

He pulled her back just far enough to allow a kiss.

"You really do."

The single kiss grew to multiple, which grew to one long mouth-to-mouth.

"I sent Darla to school," Jenny breathed, coming up for air. "I wasn't sure if I should, but she wanted to go. She said she couldn't stand just sitting around."

She kissed him again. Jim glanced at the kitchen clock over her shoulder. Two p.m. Darla wouldn't get off the bus till three.

"Is this weird though?" he asked, unbuttoning his shirt even as they continued kissing.

"I don't care." Jenny turned and leaned over the kitchen table, forearms flat across the surface, presenting her ass to him. She wore denim shorts and a yellow T-shirt, and knew he enjoyed disrobing her himself like this. "Let's not think about it. Just fuck me."

Sounded good. So he did.

Jim tried very hard not to picture Travis's bandaged eyes, watching without sight, as he banged Trav's ex-wife in their former house.

It wasn't easy.

t w o

Frank Montrose only slept a few hours a night anymore. Maybe four. Six if he was exhausted, but that was rare. An eighty-year-old man could only do so much gardening anyway. Frank kept good tabs—just shy of a diary, in fact—of how his old-guy buddies were doing. They talked cholesterol and prostates and cancer and angina, like every aging man in the history of the United States when they gathered for pool or bocce at the senior center. Some of the guys had been in wars, but not Frank. Hell to the no, his granddaughter might say, and he'd laugh when she did. She had a mouth on her, and he approved. It drove her grandmother mad.

But Grandma Grace didn't live with Frank anymore. Their divorce had been back in the eighties, when such things were uncouth and scandalous. Frank didn't care, and knew Grace didn't either. They hated each other and hated that their parents had talked them into the marriage when she got pregnant. Good Christ, a one-week stand and then get saddled with kids and a life together when they hardly knew each other? Who thought that was a smart idea?

He didn't miss his parents much.

Frank heard the first noise just as the bad guys on *Sons of Anarchy* were starting a gunfight. Of course, in that show, who were the good guys and who were the bad wasn't easily distinguished. It was one of the reasons Frank liked it. The whole world was one big gray area, as far as he was concerned, so the anti-hero approach to storytelling made perfect sense to him. He'd been watching it well into the wee hours on The Netflix on most nights just like this.

There it was again. The sound. Muffled and cautious. Something trying to be stealthy.

He muted the TV and turned his head toward the bedroom of the little bungalow he rented. Small but neat, the tiny home lay in a renovated part of town where it once would have cost an eighth what he was paying. One bedroom, one bath, little kitchen and a tiny living room big enough for his chair and the TV. Vegetable garden in the back, grass in the front that he paid some punk kid a couple bucks to trim now and then. The place suited him fine.

But the noises . . . these were new. Not part of the usual settling that happened this late at night in a house as old as he. They'd come from the bedroom, but what were they?

Another sound.

The window, Frank thought. By God, that was the window closing. Which meant the other sounds were the window opening.

Opening then closing—to let someone in?

Frank almost called *Hello?* but realized that would be stupid if someone was actually breaking in. And—goddammit—his revolver was in the bedroom, naturally. Fuckballs.

He reached for his cell phone, laying in its usual place on the side table by his recliner, but his hand merely hovered over it. Do it, he told himself. Don't be a stupid old man, swallow your pride and call the damn police.

Except what would the boys say tomorrow when they shot pool? Ol' Frank's crossed the line, they'd josh. Ol' Frank gave up bein' a man, took his own nuts off, heh heh heh . . .

Nope. Not doing that. Hell to the no.

He carefully pushed the footrest down so the recliner was upright. He tapped the remote so the sound came back on.

Don't let them know *you* know they're here, he thought. Pretend like you decided it was nothing.

Frank stood, taking his time, just to be on the safe side. His legs were still in pretty good shape; the gardening and bocce kept him just limber enough to prevent falls, or so he hoped. He knew broken hips were all but a death sentence at his age.

Since the gun was in the bedroom, he had to find a weapon. He glanced around the room and into the kitchenette, debating using a knife. Nah . . . that seemed stupid, too easily turned on himself. Something more like a bat would be better.

His umbrella stood at a cockeyed angle in one corner near the front door. That would work. Frank shuffled to it and picked it up. It felt good and right in his hand.

Turning, Frank lowered his chin and strode purposefully toward the bedroom, heart pounding, reminding him he was still alive and still a man, by God. This sucker in the bedroom would regret choosing this old man's house to burgle.

The door was open a crack, no more. He left no lights on, so nothing spilled out. Steeling himself, Frank kicked the door open wide and poked the metal tip of the umbrella in before him.

"Get outta here, you sonofabitch!" he shouted.

The man on the bed didn't move.

Frank gasped. Real fear cascaded over his skin now—he hadn't quite believed there'd be an actual thief in the room, Jesus, this had just been a little show for himself. There wasn't supposed to be a real fucking *guy* in here.

The man on the bed wore nothing. He sat perched in the middle of the twin-sized spring mattress, looking for all the world like a hawk or maybe a gargoyle; knees bent, arms stretching down so his palms rested between his feet.

"The fuck!" Frank roared—or so he thought. The words were much more like a fart of useless sulphuric gas than an authoritative demand for answers.

The man cocked his head, reminding Frank of the chickens his parents raised. For some reason, the guy was pursing his lips halfway, making his thin lips into a small black orifice about the size of an "OK" hand signal. Apart from the backward sloping head and bald crown—and his buck-ass-nakedness—the guy had no other distinguishing features that Frank could discern in the half-light that spilled into the bedroom from the hallway.

"I—" Frank whispered.

The man sprang.

He tackled Frank into the hallway. Frank lost the umbrella along the way as the full weight of the intruder smashed into him. He heard his old ribs snapping as the attacker landed on top of him, pinning him to the tile floor.

Frank issued an involuntary groan as his head cracked against the tile. He struggled to draw breath into his bruised lungs while his assailant perched atop his prone body.

A long slow vowel sound rattled in Frank's throat as he rocked his head side to side, trying to figure out what to do first to extricate himself from this position. Goddamn the guy was heavy . . .

A hand slapped against Frank's mouth. He tried to scream in response, but his busted ribs and the guy's firm hand prevented much more than a muted moan. Frank opened his eyes just in time to see his attacker lifting his right hand as if showing Frank his fingers.

Claws, Frank saw. The guy had fucking claws. No, that couldn't be right—but yes, that's exactly what it looked like. Christ Jesus, *claws.*

And his mouth—it wasn't that he was purposefully pursing his lips. It was that this was the actual shape of the man's face. He looked as if some monstrous god had gripped his face and pulled forward, drawing all the skin down into a point within his mouth. Frank saw no teeth, just the endless black circular hole.

Frank resisted as best he could, but it was useless. Whatever this thing was, it had snapped too many ribs for him to breathe properly. Even if he could've breathed, Frank lacked the strength to shove the heavy creature off him.

Creature. Yes. No man, but a thing. An animal, maybe—some escaped bald-ass chimpanzee or great ape, maybe.

The thing pointed at Frank. Frank widened his eyes in response, trying desperately to communicate. *Yes, yes, I'll do anything you want . . .*

Sharp pain pierced Frank's left eye just at the edge of the bony socket. The creature slowly, craftily—like a demented surgeon—hooked its index finger claw into the skin and flesh there. Frank squealed under its hand, feeling the rough texture of the claw slip behind his eyeball.

The squeal became a shriek. He lost sight in his left eye. Fluid poured out of the eye socket and down his face as Frank screamed and screamed.

The thing pulled on the cords that kept his eye attached, like it was pulling a knitting stitch tight. Then it gave one more tug that lifted Frank's head off the tile an inch or so. With his remaining eye, Frank saw the thing above him holding his left eyeball from the stalk, twirled once around its finger like a strand of spaghetti.

Frank shit himself and did not know. Piss flooded out of his penis and warmed his crotch and he did not know. All he knew was terror on a level he would not have dreamed possible before this moment.

The creature raised its hand, studying the bloody white sphere as some kind of specimen. It tilted its head back.

Don't do it, Frank thought incoherently, feeling madness beginning to edge into his consciousness. Don't you do it, don't you do it, aw Jesus, no . . .

The creature fed itself the eyeball. Frank saw no tongue pop out as it neatly stuffed the organ into its black hole of a mouth. The mangled cord dangling behind it got sucked up like a noodle a moment later. The creature chewed on it all, working its mouth like a baby on its thumb, its mouth never quite closing all the way. Something green and gelatinous dripped from its mouth and landed on the tip of Frank's nose, warm and slick.

Frank stopped screaming. Stopped breathing. There was nothing more to do but hope to die. He'd never had that thought before, this concrete desire to be simply dead because dead would be a Christ of a lot better than this hell.

The creature shook its head as if to get the last bits of food down its throat before peering down at Frank again.

It lifted its gore-encrusted finger.

No, Frank thought. No, no, no, Christ no—

New pain shot through his right eye. This time the orb was pierced directly, and the creature uttered a low, mewing sound as if disappointed. It dug around with the claw, scooping for all the viscera it could find while Frank found the wind to scream anew.

He was blind. Then the weight was gone. Frank's hoarse cries echoed uselessly in the tiny home, loud enough only to conceal the creature's departure. Frank climbed shakily to his hands and knees, puked on the tile, and tried to crawl for the living room. His hand slipped in the vomit, and he went down, chin splitting open against the tile.

He forced himself up, groaning nonsensically like a sick bovine lowing. He shuffled forward, dimly wondering if he was even going the right direction, but the sound of the TV oriented him. He was missing *Sons of Anarchy*, and now he'd miss it forever.

Frank kept going, feeling unknown fluids dripping onto the tops of his hands as he crawled. He threw up one more time and felt slick feces trailing down his backs of his thighs before crashing headlong into the side table where his phone lay.

The table crashed to the ground, taking the phone with it.

"God, God, God!" the old man chanted in a thin, reedy voice as his broken ribs threatened to puncture his lungs.

He scraped a hand across the floor, searching for the phone. At last he found it, and pulled it into his shaking hand. Frank sat up, back on his heels, feeling shit squish beneath him, and gazed sightlessly, stupidly down at the phone in his hand.

No buttons.

Just a smooth layer of plastic screen.

Frank screamed.

○

Adobe Creative Cloud crashed for the third time that morning, and Jim was about ready to take a sledgehammer to the goddamn CPU. Normally he wouldn't have put off working on the EnerJuice account—the owner was a nice guy, laid back, and trusting in Jim's skills for a great print ad—but the shit with Travis had rattled him more than he thought. He couldn't shake the feeling that it was his fault somehow; or, more correctly, his *and* Jenny's.

Guilt was a bitch, Jim decided, thumping his thumb on his desk while the computer rebooted again. He knew, functionally, that's all it was. No connection could exist between Travis's attack and Jim's relationship with Jenny. Why would *his* sin hurt Travis? That made no sense.

So maybe it wasn't that, Jim reasoned. No, not that; it's that something shitty happened to Travis on top of how shitty things had already been going.

But, Christ, they were divorced now! Sure, the

motives and machinery behind the affair—*if* that's what it is, Jim corrected himself—were as trite as any made for TV. While Jenny and Travis had never been on the best footing, divorce and the ending of a long relationship, not to mention its effect on Darla, were still sharp and painful. Jenny was smart woman, but she wasn't excessively handy, so when the bathroom sink backed up, she'd begged Jim to come fix it if possible; she didn't have the money for a plumber, and since he and Trav had cleared a similar block two years ago in the kitchen, couldn't he just come over real quick and take a look?

Old porno music, the type that had become a staple in comedy acts, played loud in Jim's head. Bwow-chicka-bwow-bwow. The plumber is going to . . . *come* right over all right, bwow-chika-bwow-bwow . . .

Jim half laughed, half sneered. Yeah—pretty fucking trite.

He'd never married, and the ladies weren't bashing in his door lately. Maybe it was a being-forty thing. Maybe it was time to make some changes? Have a mid-life crisis? Maybe that would help. Go to the gym, buy a new car.

Sandy, his editor, knocked on the frame of his open door of his small office. She didn't look happy. Her bulk, flattered by well-tailored suit, took up most of the doorway, pageboy haircut glimmering beneath the florescent lights.

God, now what? Jim thought.

"Jimbo. Uh . . . look, there's someone here to see you."

Shit. Jenny. Had to be. Who else was there?

Happy, though, to walk away from his CPU for a bit, he stood up. "All right. Who is it?"

"Cops."

Jimmy hesitated. "Cops?"

"A detective. Didn't get his name, the receptionist told me."

"Why didn't she buzz *me?*"

"Because she's a nosy little trouble-making cunt, you know that." Sandy offered a grin.

He couldn't argue. "All right. Thanks. He's in the lobby?"

"Yeah, I didn't see any reason to let him back here. Jimbo, you good? What's up? Seriously. If you tell me now I can run interference or damage control."

He came around the side of his cheap desk. "I have no idea. I haven't done anything."

Except fuck my buddy's ex-wife. Not yet a crime in this state.

She blocked his way out and made sure he met her eyes. "No shit, Jim."

"No shit, Sandy. I have no fucking clue. I'm not embezzling, I'm not a mule, I'm not any watchlists. That I know of."

She stepped aside. "All right. But you let me know. I love ya, Jimmy."

"Love you too."

One of the many reasons he liked working here. The company was small, didn't pay what he was worth, and insisted on Windows of all goddamn things for the creative team, but Sandy ran things free but with boundaries, and kept things nice and family-like. He appreciated that.

Now on to the fucking cop, Jim thought, and walked out to the lobby.

The lobby was isolated from the cube farm in back by

a single door. The lobby itself was a tiny, tiled room painted almost-white, with broad windows letting in morning sunshine. Dori, the receptionist, look appropriately flustered as Jim walked out.

"Oh, Mr. Luxe, there's a—"

"Got the message, Dori, thanks."

By this time, the enormous black man in the gray suit had turned away from the windows where he stood and appraised Jim. Jim tried not to look too intimidated; the guy had to have played professional football in a former life. As he lumbered forward with his hand extended, though, Jim noticed a jerk in his hip that spoke of an injury of some kind. The detective could win any stand-up fight, but no way was he going to be chasing any crooks down any alleys.

"Detective Beard," the cop said. He showed credentials.

Jim shook his hand. "Jim Luxe. How can I help you?"

Beard hitched his pants. "You friends with a guy named Montrose?"

"Yeah, Travis. What's going on?"

Beard glanced at Dori. "How about we step outside for a minute?"

Jim raised his empty hands. "Just a sec, no offense, but am I under arrest here?" He didn't see any uniformed officers outside or cars in the lot.

Beard laugh gently. "No, no, nothing like that. It's just, the details might get a little gory."

Ah, shit, Jim thought. Something about the attack, of course. Though what light he could shed on it, Jim couldn't guess.

"Sure," he said, and led the way outside. He glanced back once to note Dori's fake expression of concern, which lay like a mask atop her real emotion which was frustration at being kept out of a doubtless juicy story to tell the rest of the company in the break room.

The men walked a bit down the sidewalk and stopped beneath an acacia tree that offered shade. "Is this about the attack?" Jim asked, crossing his arms.

Beard somehow nodded and shook his head at the same time. "How long have you been friends with Mr. Montrose?"

"Oh . . . almost twenty years now? Something like that."

"Mm-hmm. You ever meet the rest of his family?"

Jim tried not to hesitate too long as he considered his options. "Sure. His wife—ex-wife, Jenny. His daughter Darla. Why?"

"His mom? Dad?"

"Oh! Well. They've been broken up a long time now, if I remember correctly. I never met them. Trav didn't talk about them much, not to me."

"Past tense, huh?"

". . . I'm sorry?"

"You just used the past-tense to describe Travis Montrose."

Cocksucker, Jim thought. Bullshit TV cop show games. "Well, if I did, I didn't mean it that way. What's going on, may I ask?"

"You don't know where his folks live?" the detective asked instead of answering.

"No. In town, it sounded like, but that's it. Look, I'm sorry, I'm in the middle of designing some things right now and I'm running behind, what is this?"

Beard sighed heavily, like his job was the weight of the

450

world. Then again, compared to being a mid-level graphic designer at a family-owned firm, maybe it was. "Mr. Montrose—senior, that is—Frank Montrose was attacked in a similar manner as his son late last night."

Jim's upper lip wrinkled up. "God. You mean the . . . like, his eyes?"

"Yeah," Beard said ponderously. "You've been to see Travis Montrose, is that correct?"

"Yes. Day before yesterday."

"So you saw the kind of condition he was in."

"Yeah." Jim unconsciously placed his palm on his abdomen.

If Beard noticed him doing it, the cop didn't comment. "Can you think of any reason someone would tear into your buddy like that?"

Jim had already spent hours thinking about that very thing, and had nothing to offer the detective. "No. Travis was—"

Fuck. Past-tense. Here he was, an innocent man, and the detective had him on the ropes.

"Travis *is* a pretty good guy. I mean, you know, he throws an elbow here and there on the basketball court, but that's about it. Plays hard. But he's a good dad, he's a good friend."

Then why are you fucking his—? *Shut up.*

Beard nodded. "Pretty athletic guy."

"I guess so. He worked out hard."

"I'm trying to imagine what kind of person could keep him pinned down long enough to inflict those wounds."

Jim glanced down meaningfully at his own body. Travis had fifty pounds on him, handily. "You're not thinking *I* do?"

Beard gave another friendly laugh. "No sir, I do not. I also think he would've mentioned it if his assailant happened to look like a friend of his. Just checking all my bases. The fact that father and son were both assaulted the same way . . . that raises some flags. Means I need to dig around some. Might even mean Feds getting involved. Could be a cult thing, maybe. Family grudge. Dunno."

Pieces snapped into place. Jim stood up straight. "Jesus, Darla."

Beard met his eyes. "That's right. Maybe the ex-wife, too. We're a little concerned about that. One attack on one guy, well, that's an incident. Two attacks on two guys, now, that's a pattern. The same attack on two men directly related by blood . . . that's a problem."

Jim held then wiped his mouth. Goddamn. No. No, he couldn't let anything happen to that girl, and not to Jenny either. While he hadn't exactly envisioned marrying Jenny, he also hoped to still be a part of Darla's life regardless. She was a gem. Good God, he'd met her the day after she was born, when it looked like Jenny and Travis had found something to unite them. That feeling hadn't lasted, but that day, holding that baby girl for the first time—

"Is she in danger?" Jim demanded.

Beard frowned. "Impossible to say. Nothing imminent. Not that we know of. Do you have any reason to think she is?"

"No . . . no, Christ, I can't even imagine what is going on. Is someone keeping an eye on her? *Fuck* . . ." A distant piece of his brain tittered, hee hee! Keeping an *eye* on her, get it?

"She's at school," Beard said, holding up a calming hand. "And her mother's aware of the situation."

Jim blew out a breath. That wasn't enough. He'd stay the night, he'd stay every night if that's what it took. Never mind what Travis might think of it. Hell, he'd probably suggest it the next time they talked. The animosity he had toward his ex was one thing; keeping his baby girl safe was entirely another. And for fuck's sake, it's not like he wanted bad things to happen to Jenny, either; he just didn't want to deal with her anymore.

Beard scratched his head. "How, uh . . . well acquainted are you with *Mrs.* Montrose?"

Jim's nervous expression dropped, his eyes narrowing. "Why don't you ask her."

"I have. Now I'm asking you."

"What's it got to do with some psycho tearing out people's eyes?"

"Maybe nothing."

"You just get off on it, or?"

A slim smile creased the detective's face. "Getting awfully defensive, Mr. Luxe."

Jim clenched his teeth and looked away. "Fine. I'm sleeping with her. Happy?"

"Nope. I got a little girl related by blood to two men who were mutilated and blinded within the last forty-eight hours. This is what we call due diligence, making sure I've looked at every possible angle so the same doesn't happen to her."

Jim deflated. That was fair, and he knew it. "Does Travis have to know?"

"I have no reason to tell him that. Like I said—"

"Due diligence."

"Correct."

They stood in silence. Jim stared at the pebbled sidewalk, debating his next move. Beard let the silence grow before saying, "Well, I think that covers things for the moment. You should keep a close watch on the girl, call 911 immediately if anything looks out of place. Even if it feels stupid, do it anyway, that's what the cops are there for. Don't mess around with this psychopath."

"Count on it." Jim looked up. "Wait, does she know? Darla. Does she know what happened to her grandfather?"

"I couldn't say. I don't think so. That would be between her and her folks."

Jim nodded. Of course it would be.

"Thanks for your time, Mr. Luxe, I appreciate it." Beard didn't offer his hand. "I'll be in touch."

Jim waved weakly, already consumed with how to best protect Darla. He walked in the direction of the office but went past the door and on down the sidewalk, taking a right turn around the building as he pulled out his cell and called Jenny.

"Jim?"

"Jenny. How's Darla?"

Jenny sighed like she'd just sat down. "Okay. She's at school. I talked to a cop today—"

"Beard."

"Yeah, that's his . . . how'd you know?"

"He just left my office. He knows about us, FYI."

Jenny said nothing for a moment, then said, "Fine, whatever. That's irrelevant."

"That's what I said." He did not know, suddenly, if he had in fact said that to the cop, but Jenny got the message.

"Jimmy, would you come with me to get her after

school? I don't want her on the bus by herself. I mean I know there'll be kids and a driver but—"

He was answering before she'd finished. "Of course, of course I will. Jenny—do you have a gun?"

"No! Of course not." The offense in her voice waned as she asked, more quietly, "Do you?"

Jim wiped the first glistening of sweat from his forehead. "No, but I'm thinking about it."

"How long would it take?"

He barked dismissively. "In this state? Hour. Two tops, I'd guess."

"But like, legal, right? You wouldn't go messing with the wrong people."

"Jesus, of course not, Jen. I'm not that stupid."

"Okay. Okay, good. Thanks."

"Have you talked to Travis? What the hell happened to his father?"

"Oh, God, Jimmy, it was the same sick thing. Whoever it was took his eyes out. And then . . . Ugh, *God*."

"And then?"

"Well," Jenny said, her voice green, "the cops couldn't find them. Just like with Travis. And he says the guy . . . you know . . ."

Jim hurried to cut her off. "But no idea who or why?"

"No."

"Did you tell Darla?"

"No, God, no. I'm not sure how. You think I should?"

Asking him a parenting question. Was that a good thing or a bad thing? Better not to think about it. There were bigger issues to worry about right now.

Still. It was nice to hear.

"Maybe not just yet. Let's you and me talk about it some more first. But I mean, whatever the hell's going on, she's going to have to stay vigilant. She can't or won't do that without knowing why. But yeah, let's talk some more later about it."

Let's. Let us. Let us both. Let us both talk and determine the best choice for your child who is not mine. Cripes.

Jim squeezed his eyes shut, then rubbed them for good measure, trying to erase the images that screened in his head, most of them having to do with Darla and the sick fuck who had an eyeball fetish. "What time does Darla get out?"

"Three fifteen."

"How far away?"

"Couple miles. A few minutes."

"I'll be there by three at the latest."

"Jimmy . . . thank you. I know you don't have to do this."

"There's nothing I wouldn't do for Darla. Period. Okay?"

"Okay. Thanks."

"You got it. See you in a bit."

They hung up. Jim stood still, letting the sun bake his scalp through his hair. He checked the time: just shy of lunch.

He wasn't hungry.

three

"Hey, Champ," Jim said to Darla as she climbed into the back seat of his red Jeep. He instantly felt like a douchebag for having said it.

If it bothered her, Darla didn't show it. "Hey."

Jenny turned in the passenger seat. "Hey, baby. How you doing?"

Darla let out a dramatic sigh. "*Fine.*"

The adults glanced at each other. That was a pretty promising answer from a twelve-year-old. An attitude like that could only mean that things were, in fact, fine, despite the myriad crushing blows of junior high.

Jim drove them out of the parking lot.

Turning again, Jenny asked her, "You want to go visit your dad tonight?"

Jim's grip tightened on the wheel.

Darla rested her head against the window, staring longingly out at—basically anything that wasn't in this car at this moment with these people, near as Jim could discern. He didn't have kids, but he remembered being one.

Darla shrugged inside her bulky rugby jersey, a

style which she'd been favoring of late. And, being fundamentally a dude in all ways, Jim had needed Jenny to explain why. He was glad he hadn't accidentally teased Darla about it. She'd never have spoken to him again. Or at least not till her early twenties.

"I'm sure he'd love to see you," Jenny pressed on.

Darla's voice was just as caustic and sarcastic as any bona-fide junior high girl. "I'm sure he'd love to *see* anything."

Jim laughed.

He did manage to catch it before it burst out of his lips, coming out instead as a rather painful snort that choked his soft palate. He coughed quickly to cover it.

Jenny spun around in her seat to face forward. When Jim looked out of the corner of his eye, he saw her pressing a fist into her mouth, her lips curling inevitably upward.

Jim let go. He let the laugh out and it was awful and wonderful. Jenny clearly took it as permission and laughed loudly with him. As he checked the rearview, he saw Darla heroically pulling her own giggle inward.

"That's *awful!*" Jenny cried through her laughter, tears toppling down her cheeks now.

When he had control of himself again, Jim shook his head. "It was necessary. Tragedy plus time and all that." He looked in the mirror again. "Thanks, Darla."

The pre-teen didn't answer, but her shoulders lurched forward a few times as she continued to suppress her laughs. Jim took that as a minor victory.

At the Montrose home—three bedroom, two bath, two car garage, nice neighborhood, mature trees—Darla beelined for her room, but did not shut the door; another good sign, Jim decided. He and Jenny stuck to the kitchen, where Jenny started a pot of coffee and pulled a DiGiorno out of the freezer. Supreme style. She held it up.

"Sure," Jim said. "You want me to stay?"

Before she could answer, he waved her off.

"Never mind that, I'm staying, I don't much care if you invite me to or not."

Jenny set the pizza down. "I was going to say yes. I was going to *ask*."

She moved to him and hugged him warmly. Jim tensed, worried that Darla would come in and catch them, but the nature of the hug was purely nonsensual. He returned it, tightly.

"What do you think?" she whispered. "No bullshit."

He pulled away to look into her eyes. "What do you mean, about what?"

"About these attacks. Do you think someone's coming for her? Someone with a grudge against Travis and his family?"

Jim opened and closed his mouth silently a few times before settling on the imminently unsatisfactory, "I don't know."

"I know you don't, I'm asking what you think. Tell me she'll be okay."

He lowered his head to meet her gaze squarely. "I'll tell you that I'll stay here as long as it takes to find the asshole who did it. I'll tell you I'll stop at nothing to keep her safe. Okay?"

She nodded, even though her expression betrayed doubt. Doubt, or just a mother's fear—Jim wasn't sure.

He also saw an unrivaled fierceness there, burning

brightly behind her gaze. One thing Travis and his father hadn't had in their favor was a mama bear's rage. No matter what hadn't gone right between she and Travis, there was no questioning either of their love for Darla.

Jim pulled her close again, squeezing her. "Come on out to the car."

"What for?"

"So I can show you something."

They parted, and Jenny sent him a questioning glance; was this a prelude to sex? Because if so, he needed to rethink that idea post-haste, her expression said. He smiled at the idea.

They exited through the kitchen door and into the garage. He guided her to the Jeep tailgate and opened it up, revealing a white plastic bag. From this he pulled a small black plastic case.

"I got this during my lunch break. It wasn't even forty-five minutes."

Jenny stepped backward. "Is that a gun?"

"Yeah. It's a, uh . . . Glock 17? I think that's what he said. Maybe 19, I forget now. With hollow point bullets."

Jenny's lip curled. "What's that mean?"

"Guy at the shop said they're designed to stop in the body. Reduces the chances of the bullet going through the target and into something or someone else." He shrugged. When he went shooting at the range—and that had been a few years ago now—he'd used what the rangemasters sold him. Full-metal jacket. Good for target practice, less good for home defense.

"You know how to use it?"

"Well, I mean, point and shoot. Like a camera."

460

She clearly didn't see the humor in that. Jim put the case back into the bag and shut the tailgate.

"I've shot before, it's just been awhile. There's a range up north I'd go to sometimes. We even did it in Scouts, believe it or not. Part of a safety course. Better to know how to use it than not, keeps people safer. That was the rationale, anyway."

Jenny winced up at him. "You think you could actually 'point and shoot' a person?"

Jim met her gaze. "If that person was threatening you or Darla, you're goddamn right."

He hoped he looked as confident—no, competent—as he sounded. He wanted to be a man, goddammit, but he knew that ultimately he was still just a guy who drew pretty pictures for a living and hadn't so much as run a lap in ten or more years. Naturally slender, he didn't have a weight issue to contend with, and he ate mostly okay; he avoided most fast foods these days and didn't really drink too much.

But Jenny's point wasn't beyond him. There was a world of difference between owning a firearm and being the type of guy who was good and goddamned trained to use it. Cops and soldiers, people who routinely carried, they trained for this shit over and over and over again. Blowing a few hundred bucks at the gun shop on your lunch hour wasn't the same thing.

That didn't make his promise any less valid, he told himself.

Jenny waved at the case. "Just, keep it in here for now, okay? It still makes me nervous. Bring it in tonight."

Jim dutifully put the case back. He hadn't even opened it.

He closed the gate and they went back inside. Jenny immediately called, "Darla?"

"What?" came the irritated reply.

"Just checking," Jenny said to Jim. She sighed. "This is going to be a long night."

Jim held up the DiGiorno. "Yeah, but there's pizza."

When she smiled, he felt some of his tension ease. Maybe everything would be all right.

○

The old woman had a room to herself, which was how she liked it. Laying in her bed, a knit afghan covering her frail body, Lorene knew many things: She knew the nurses didn't like her too much, she knew she didn't give a shit, and she knew it wouldn't matter for much longer.

It was an odd feeling, this dying business. What had Peter Pan said? To die will be a great adventure? Yeah, easy to say when you're eternally eleven years old. Try seventy-nine on for size, you little shit.

Lorene's skin had grown thin, and sagged even more than it had the last few years. She rarely ate anymore, and when she did, it wasn't much. Some tender fruit once in awhile, or some toast when the nurses could coax her into it. Everything and nothing hurt all at once. Each muscle complained when she moved, including her heart, which seemed to sigh with each contraction and release. It wanted a break. Fair enough, it had been going nonstop for almost eighty years. That's a long time to do one thing over and over.

Interesting, Lorene thought this night, and heard

herself giggle; you'd think that would make a muscle stronger.

She wanted to roll over but couldn't quite make the shift. It took too much energy. She'd always been a tummy-sleeper but the hiatal hernia prevented that now. It could wake her up gagging, choking, feeling like she couldn't breathe. Not fun. So instead she slept on her back, propped up by a few pillows, so all the bile and acid would stay down where it belonged.

Lorene reached for her plastic water bottle and gave herself a sip. Good Lord, wasn't this just the worst? She had a TV in her private room but didn't feel like turning it on. Nothing good on this late anyway. She could read, but that would mean wearing those heavy glasses, and the paperback brought by the late-night nurse—Shannon or Sharon or something—was a regular pocket book, not the large print Lorene generally needed.

So she lay there and thought and bitched quietly to herself, and sometimes, just sometimes, wished her son would come to see her.

Lorene gasped at the sound of something metallic near her window.

She turned her head against the cool cotton pillowcase, narrowing her eyes. What had that been? The plastic blinds were half-closed, letting in only the vaguest light from the lit walkway outside. Palm Court Community was roughly horseshoe shaped, the two-story buildings surrounding an immaculate series of paths around a stone fountain. Many of the residents took their walks there, or were wheeled around it by nurses or family members. Lorene hadn't been wheeled around it in a week now. The nurses knew how to punish bitchy old ladies.

"Hello?" she croaked. That seemed silly. Who would be at the window?

A short grinding sound pierced her ears, making Lorene take in a breath of air. It sounded like metal on concrete, like . . .

Like the bars on the windows being yanked out of their moorings.

But why would someone be doing that right now? It was past eleven at night. All the old, dying folk like her were abed, their keepers staffed down to the minimum.

A burglar.

Oh, sweet Aunt Jesus, someone was breaking in! Some rat-fuck son of a bitch was breaking into her room!

Only that made no sense either. Perhaps, if the criminal had time and patience to search every single room in Palm Court, he might make off with a few valuable trinkets, but not much more. By the time a person lived long enough to make it to the last stand that was Palm Court Community, most of their possessions had been stripped away, sometimes already sold off by greedy grown children just waiting for Mom and Pop to kick the bucket.

So then what?

A sex criminal!

Of course. That was the only answer.

Lorene turned herself over to the right, searching half-blindly for the nurse button on the cord, just like in the hospital she'd recently been released from. Dammit, it was here somewhere. She'd never used it. Refused to use it, in fact. So of course now that she needed a hand—

The window slid open readily and silently, as if recently lubricated. Lorene turned her head and kept scrabbling for the buzzer.

"Who is it? Who are you?" she demanded in a high, wheezy voice. She wished suddenly for the cantankerous presence of Frank, who at least kept a revolver in his bed stand all his life. Now that would be something, popping this sex fiend one in the chest with a .38!

The lacy curtains split apart.

Lorene froze as a figure angled itself over the sill and slipped into her room. A man, she felt sure. Once inside he hunkered down, like a monkey, and reached up to close the curtains behind him.

Her old heart woke up now, quickly beating an emergency rhythm that she could do nothing with. Ancient adrenalin spilled into her crusty veins, motivating her to at least try to scream.

Too late.

The man leaped from the floor in one great heave, like a frog. He landed on the bed somewhat rather gracefully, from what Lorene could tell through her terrible vision and growing panic.

The old woman froze as he placed a hand over her mouth, just enough to keep any screams from being too loud. Even this close, she couldn't make out his features; her bad eyes and the dark conspired against her.

The man reached out with his right hand toward her bedside table and picked up the remote for the TV. He thumbed buttons and the screen came to life. Something British on PBS.

He turned back to her. His head moved with an odd precision that reminded Lorene of pantomimes . . . or chickens.

She moaned through his fingers, and he pressed them

tighter against her. A warning. Don't scream, he was saying. Don't scream.

Lorene didn't. She didn't have the strength now. He was straddling her, knees on either side of the sheet and afghan. The bedding drew right across her body by the weight of his shins, making her blanket an effective straightjacket.

The man on top of her kept his hand pressed against her mouth, but she could breathe. Through the haze in her vision, she detected him reaching for the bedside table again.

She gasped as she felt the weight of her glasses sliding over her head.

Lorene blinked rapidly, trying to hydrate her eyes. By the blue glow of the flat screen in the corner, she could make out the man's features now.

Her old muscles locked in place, then relaxed utterly. Her heart beat slowed suddenly into hard, heavy beats beneath her fragile ribcage.

The thing on top of her stared down, its small, circular mouth a black hole against its pale skin. It removed its hand from her mouth and peered into her eyes.

Lorene's mouth went slack. A slick of saliva dripped down her chin.

"Oh, no," she whispered plaintively as her eyebrows cinched together. "No, no, no, no. Oh, please. Oh, not you. Not you. Oh . . ."

The thing leaned close. She smelled something acidic on its breath.

It did not possess full articulation of its jaw. When it spoke, the little hole of a mouth pulsed only mildly, like a sphincter.

Its voice was soft and breathy, forcing words rather than forming them. "Ow . . . ew . . . hee . . . mee."

Wild tremors shot through Lorene's body. "Yes . . . yes I see you."

The thing nodded. It took her glasses off, gently, folded them, and placed them beside the remote. It slipped its hands beneath her head, lifting it gently off the pillows.

Still shaking, Lorene felt the creature's thin lips on her forehead, pressing down. A kiss. Its lips were dry and cracked, like her own skin.

Its thumbs rested lightly against her temples as it cradled Lorene's skull like a lover.

She wept then. "Please . . . oh, please . . . I never—"

Lorene screamed as the creature's thumbs pushed slowly into her eyes. The pressure was intense, filling her head with crushing weight. The thing took its time with her, pushing, pressing, until first her left then right eyeballs ruptured.

Lorene sucked in a scorching breath, which then parked uselessly in her lungs. She stopped breathing entirely. Her near-blindness was now complete. Half-mad with pain and fear, she still felt the thing's claws now digging into her eye sockets. The tips scraped around the edges of bone, like a kid scooping every last bit of ice cream from a bowl.

A slender expulsion of air came from Lorene, a tire losing pressure. The weight of the thing above her shifted. She felt its almost bald head beside hers as it let go of her. She sank slowly back into the pillows as her lungs expelled their last in one long near-silent gasp.

But she heard. She heard it all. As the creature hovered over her, its smooth, dry cheek beside her own, its mouth by her ear, she heard.

It chewed slowly. The mouth was clearly open, the inner workings of its maw seeming to savor each squelch as it consumed her eyes.

It wanted her to hear. It wanted her to know.

Lorene heard it swallow. One damp, cat-vomit pulse.

Then it breathed on her, gave her another kiss on the temple, and then the weight was gone.

Lorene Montrose did not take another breath.

○

The sex was perfunctory, Jim thought. Good, as always, but not . . . *there*. First of all, Darla was asleep down the hall, that was one thing. Not enough to stop Jenny's advances or make him turn her away, but still. The knowledge creeped him out a bit. Christ, what if she walked in? But the door was closed and locked, and Darla had crashed by about eleven, and it seemed clear she wasn't apt to rise any time soon. Jenny had closed her door quietly, then turned to Jim in the hall and taken his hand.

They'd said nothing, just walked into her bedroom, shut the door, and immediately fell into each other's bodies, kissing, groping, sighing roughly in one another's ears. When the last piece of clothing hit the floor, Jenny reached out and flipped the doorknob lock, and that was it. They'd fallen into the king-size bed, right on top of the comforter.

Jim had pressed his lips together hard as he came, feeling like all the stress and worry of the last couple of days was exploding out of him in several exquisite pulsations. By the time he was done and collapsing on top of her, he already knew Jenny hadn't come, despite the fact that she'd gripped the wrought iron headrest behind her as if bracing, but she didn't comment on it and didn't seem to care. She just pulled herself closer to him as he rolled onto his side, and held him close.

Then the doorbell rang.

Jim tightened and sat up fast. Jenny followed suit.

"What the hell?" he barked, and looked at the clock. Nearing one.

Jenny clutched his arm. "What if it's *him!*"

Jim got the implication instantly. They parted, sliding off the bed, stumbling into their clothing. The gun, goddammit, the gun was still in the fucking Jeep!

The doorbell rang again.

Jim held up a hand as Jenny flicked on the bedside light. "Wait, wait, wait. He wouldn't ring the bell."

"We don't know!" Jenny snapped, and raced from the room into the hallway.

Barefoot, Jim followed as she opened Darla's door. The girl lay sprawled at an angle across the bed, her oversized nightshirt twisted around her torso.

Jenny breathed out and shut the door again. "Let's go see."

Jim nodded. They crept to the front door. Jim peered into the spyhole—and dropped his shoulders.

"Shit," he said, and opened the door.

Detective Beard stood beneath the porch light. His face was grim.

"Mr. Luxe," the cop said, and raised his eyebrows a bit as if peering over Jim's shoulder. "And Mrs. Montrose?"

Jenny came around Jim's side, arms around her middle.

"I haven't changed it yet," she muttered, then to the cop said, "What's going on?"

"Everything all right here?" Beard asked.

The two traded worried frowns. "Yes," Jim answered. "We just checked on Darla, she's safe and sound. What is it? It's one o'clock in the goddamn morning."

Beard nodded as if that's what he either was expecting to hear—or just hoping. "There's been another attack. Travis Montrose's mother."

Jenny bit her lower lip and pressed herself into Jim's shoulder. Jim gripped a handful of his own hair in one hand. "Are you serious?"

A stupid question at one in the morning while talking to a police detective, but the cop clearly didn't mind.

"Yes, I'm afraid so. Felt like coming by here might not be the worst idea, you know."

Jenny peeked up. "Was she killed in the . . . *same* . . .?"

"The same manner, yes, it appears that way. If there was any doubt about this being all connected to the Montrose family, that doubt has passed. The FBI is getting involved now."

"Oh, God," Jenny groaned before Beard finished, and turned to Jim again.

"Have you told Travis or his dad?" Jim asked, choking a bit on how dry his throat had become.

"Not yet, they're both still recovering in the hospital. We'll tell them in the morning. That's another little part of what brings me out here right now. I'm a dad myself, so . . . it might be better, Mrs. Montrose—"

"Jenny," she said, pulling herself up. She stood tall now, but kept Jim's hand clasped in her own.

"It might be better, Jenny, if you were there with Travis

when we told him," Beard said. "A thing like this, he's going to need someone familiar around. Plus there's his daughter, he'll want to know she's all right, I assume."

"Yeah," Jim said before Jenny could. "He'll *need* to know that."

"How about we meet at the hospital around ten," Beard said, and it wasn't a question.

Jim turned to Jenny, who nodded tightly. "That would be fine."

"All right. I'll see you there." The detective turned.

"Uh, sir? Are you leaving anyone here overnight? A police officer?"

Beard shook his head. "No, we can't really leave a uniform here, but I will make sure there's a cruiser coming by as often as possible. Keep your phones on and ready to dial if there's an emergency, we'll be here right quick."

"Okay. Thank you."

Beard turned once more, but hesitated. "You two folks have been home all night, I assume?"

"Aw, *Jesus!*" Jim spat. "You know what—?"

Jenny squeezed his hand. "Jimmy, don't. It's all right. Yes, detective. We've been here at the house since a little after three with my daughter. Would you like me to go and get her?"

Beard waved. "No, that won't be necessary. Sorry for the bad news and disturbance. I'll see you at ten."

"Good night," Jenny said, closing the front door as Jim stewed in the entryway.

"The nerve of that fucker!" he said in a harsh whisper once the latch was closed. "Can you even—"

"*Shut up,*" Jenny barked.

Jim froze.

"You shut up and listen to me," Jenny went on, pointing a finger at him. "Someone is out there killing or trying to kill every member of my daughter's family. And until this is over, I will cooperate fully and completely with anything the police want to investigate, do you hear me?"

Jim nodded quickly. It was all he could do.

"Good," Jenny said. "I'm going to go lie down and try to sleep, knowing that I goddamn won't, so that I can get up in the morning and tell my ex-husband his mother is dead. I'd appreciate it if you'd stay up and make sure nothing happens to my child."

She turned and marched down the hallway and into the bedroom, opening Darla's door on the way and leaving hers open as well.

Jim gazed down the length of the dark hall for a long moment, then went into the garage and got the Glock.

four

Jim stayed up the entire night. He loaded and unloaded the Glock a dozen times, and checked the locks on the doors twice that. He alternated between standing at the living room windows and the kitchen windows, his eyes drying out over the course of the night, until the sun finally rose and Jenny came out.

"Anything?" she asked.

"No. Did you sleep?"

"A little. Not much. You?"

"No."

Jenny shoulders drooped. "You really didn't."

"That's what I said." And he was pissy enough to prove it.

"Go lay down," Jenny urged. "I'll get breakfast for Darla."

He wanted to fight, something petty and immature, but in the end he was too damn tired to do it. He walked past her to the bedroom just as Darla poked her head out of her room.

"Oh! Hey, Jim." She said it with her eyes half-closed in the manner of all just-woken adolescents. She didn't seem surprised. Jim didn't know what to make of her lack of surprise at seeing him.

"Hey, Darla. Sleep okay?"

"Uh . . . yeah. Did you? I mean, did you sleep over?"

Sleep over. The juvenile term made something in his heart bend backwards. Yeah she was twelve, and twelve was still just a kid, a *little* kid at that. She probably hadn't even meant to say it like that.

He very nearly touched her cheek, but resisted. Darla was not his kid. She was Travis's. His best friend Travis.

That thought brought the morning into stark relief: he and Jenny had a shit job to do today, and part of it was going to have to include telling Darla that her grandmother was gone and her grandfather blinded just like her dad. Oh, and that the cops were worried she might be next.

He reached out and tousled her hair. She let him. "Yeah, I slept over. Your mom and dad wanted me to stay."

The words came frighteningly easy. Was it a lie? Half a lie? No, he decided. Once Travis understood the stakes, he'd be grateful as hell that Jim had stayed overnight. Overnight and awake with a Glock, to be specific. Yeah, he'd appreciate that.

"Because of what happened to Dad?"

"Yeah," Jim said, trying to sound matter of fact. He blinked his eyes blearily. His eyelids felt like fine-grit sandpaper. "You want to go see him this morning?"

"Maybe." Darla slid down the hall, scratching her head with both hands.

Jim couldn't tell if that was a yes, a no, or an actual maybe. Well, the hell with it, that would be between her and her mother. He went on into the bedroom, shut the door, and fell face-first into the mattress. He slept with scent of Jenny's lavender body lotion tickling into his nose.

○

Darla went.

They took the Jeep again. Jim crammed a three-hour nap in before being roused by Jenny. She looked put-together but not over-dressed. Darla, naturally, had chosen a green and white striped rugby shirt that may as well have been a dress in its own right. Jim had brought no extra clothes, and so contented himself with a few splashes of water on his face and treating everyone to Starbucks on the way. His Americano was hot and bitter and perfect, scalding the night's terrors from his entire body as the too-hot water rushed down his throat.

There hadn't been time or opportunity to converse with Jenny about how Darla thought the day was going to go. What did she think she was going to see? To hear? Well, they'd find out soon enough. He wasn't sure he liked the idea of surprising her, but he also wasn't about to bring it up now. Darla, no matter how much he cared about her, was simply and utterly not his. He was not her dad, he was not even a blood relative. However Jenny wanted to handle things that was up to her, and he'd support it. As best he could, anyway.

All was fine until they reached Travis's hospital room door.

Darla planted her feet on the slick tile. Her body locked up like she'd hit an invisible wall.

"No."

She stated it without hysterics or attitude. Just a fact. Nope, she was not walking through that door.

"Hon," Jenny said, "it's your dad, he'll want to know you're okay."

Darla took a step back, eyes locked on the pale wood door. "Then tell him. I'm not going in there."

Jim put a hand on her shoulder. "What is it, D?"

She shook her head. "I don't want to see him like that. I can't. I can't do it."

Jim met Jenny's eyes over Darla's head. *Flashbacks?* he tried to mouth. Jenny only shrugged quickly. He tried to mouth the letters P-T-S-D but gave up, feeling foolish.

"Okay, hon," Jenny said. "It's up to you. If you don't want to go in, that's fine. But I *do* need to go in, and I can't have you out here by yourself."

"I'll stay," Jim said, catching the hint. He was surprised to sense relief in his belly. He didn't want to go in, either, but didn't know it until he no longer needed to. "We'll grab a seat in the hall over there."

Jen nodded. "Okay. Thanks, Jim. Darla, if you change your mind, just come on in, okay?"

Darla nodded and broke for the central nurses' station, situated like a hub from which four hallways extended like spokes. Jenny touched Jim's arm in thanks before letting herself into the hospital room, gently saying Travis's name.

Jim followed Darla to the hub and sat down on a padded bench beside her, leaning his head against the wall. He sipped his coffee. "Want anything?"

"No, thanks."

"How you doing? Really."

Darla sighed theatrically, but Jim sensed sincerity in it.

Understandably. After what she'd seen in her room that night, she had a right to feel put-upon. Hell, she didn't even know about her grandparents yet; how would she stomach *that* information?

"I mean, okay, I guess," Darla said. She pulled her legs up to sit cross-legged on the bench in a maneuver Jim hadn't been to accomplish in twenty years. Fuckin' kids, he thought with affection. Darla ran her forearm under her nose as if it were leaking. "I keep . . . *seeing* it."

Jim pulled away from the wall. "Seeing your dad?"

She nodded.

"Hey, that's totally understandable," he said. "That was a hell of a thing to go through."

"Not as bad as what happened to him."

"No, but . . ." He waffled. How to handle this? Darla was confiding in him, and he didn't want to ruin it. He took a deep breath and dove in. "Look, the thing is, when something bad happens to someone else, that doesn't invalidate how you feel about it. Or how you react. You know? When 9/11 happened, lots of people who were not anywhere near New York developed panic attacks and PTSD symptoms. That was real for them. And they were allowed to feel those things. No point in pretending they didn't feel that way. Does that make sense?"

Darla nodded again, her expression nominally thoughtful. Mostly, Jim thought, she looked guilty. For not having been hurt, and/or for not being in the room right now with her dad. Hell, maybe even for some lingering doubts over the divorce. He knew it fucked kids up in one way or another, or so he'd read. Things between Trav and Jenny had been bad, but never abusive, not that Jim ever heard. It wasn't one of those situations where the kids breathe a sigh of relief now that the trauma is finally over. No, theirs had been one of those "we just don't fit" type breakups, and Jim wondered if those were harder on the kids than the other kind.

The elevator dinged across the room from them, and Detective Beard stepped out. He caught Jim right away, and ambled over. Jim suddenly wondered if the cop ever changed his suit, if he only had on the one, or if he just looked the same no matter what he was wearing.

"Morning," Beard said with an invisible hat tip. "This must be Darla."

Darla looked up at him, squinting. She did not ask the obvious question, so Beard answered it himself.

"I'm Detective Beard," he said to her. "I'm in charge of the case involving your dad."

"Did you find someone?" Darla's voice was frighteningly adult, Jim thought.

"Well, no, not yet, but we are working on some leads."

Jim blinked. Was that true, or was the cop being patronizing? He couldn't tell.

Beard gestured to him. "You mind if I talk to Mr. Luxe for just a minute?"

Darla turned to Jim, her face questioning. Jim pointed down the hall. "Just over there. I'll still be able to see you."

Now Darla's expression turned to youthful contempt. "Why does that matter?"

Shit, Jim thought. He'd played that wrong. She doesn't know she might be in danger. She has no reason to think that, so I just look like an overprotective goon.

He forced a smile. "Right. Sorry. We'll just be a couple

minutes. Think about if you want anything else to eat, okay?"

Darla managed to shrug, nod, and shake her head all at the same time in the way only kids know how to do. Jim rose and followed Beard down one of the hallways, out of Darla' earshot.

"Was that true?" Jim asked right away. "You've got some leads?"

"We have, uh . . . something." Beard cleared his throat. "Is Mrs. Rosemont here with you?"

"She's talking to Trav. Telling him about his parents, I believe. I'm not sure. Darla didn't want to go in, so we were waiting out here."

"And he—Travis Rosemont, he never talked about any brothers? Sisters?"

"No. He's only child."

Beard nodded a bit. "What room's he in?"

"Three twenty-four." Jim pointed. "What exactly's happening?"

"I'm not sure, Mr. Luxe. I need to talk to Mr. Rosemont right now."

"Can I come?"

"Doesn't matter to me, that'd be up to Mr. Rosemont."

Jim glanced quickly at Darla, who sat typing and swiping on her phone. "Let me just check in with her."

Beard indicated his willingness to wait. Jim jogged to Darla and crouched in front of her.

"Listen, I'm going to go with the detective in to see your dad, okay? You'll be okay out here?"

"Where better than a hospital for something bad to happen to me."

Her angsty sarcasm was rather refreshing. He half-

479

grinned and said, "Okay. I'll be right back. Stay here."

Darla gave no indication she heard or that she would obey him. He figured it was the best he'd get. He returned to Beard, and the two men walked to Travis's room.

Jim went in first. Jen sat by the bed, but was not—as Jim discovered he'd been expecting—holding his hand or touching him any way.

Travis lay on his back just as Jim had seen him previously. He thought the bandages around his head were fresh; bright white and lacking stray strings. His mouth was set, jaw clamped tight.

"Trav? It's Jim, man."

Travis gave no indication of having heard. Jenny faced him, and while she was not weeping, her face was strained. She'd definitely told him.

"There's a cop here to see you," Jim went on, approaching the bed. "Is that okay, man? I can tell him to go."

Travis turned his head side to side, minimally.

"He can stay?" Jim asked, to clarify.

"Sure," Travis croaked. He sounded like needed water badly.

The detective introduced himself and approached the opposite side of the bed. "Has your ex-wife told you what's happened?"

"Yes."

Jim thought he saw Travis's jaw trembling, but wasn't sure. He crossed his arms.

"Your mother and your father?"

"Yes. Is my dad still alive?"

"He is. He'll recover, ultimately, it sounds like."

"But not with any eyes."

Travis's voice was a monotone, and reminded Jim somehow of the flatline of a heart monitor.

Beard sniffed as if unsure how to respond. He let the comment pass. "Mr. Rosemont, your father isn't being particularly helpful with his own case. I'm sure you can appreciate that we have some concerns about your daughter's safety."

"Darla!" Travis barked, sitting up in bed. "She's here, she's safe, right?"

"She's right outside," Jim said quickly. "She's fine, man."

Travis stayed up on his hands for a moment, breathing hard, before slowly letting himself back down to the pillows.

"Your father did say one thing that struck us as a little strange," Beard went on once Travis was settled. "Then he clammed up. What can you tell me about your brother, Mr. Montrose?"

Jim reared back, looking at Trav as if Trav could betray something with a look in his eyes. Travis went stolid again, mouth set in a grim line.

Jenny glanced at the cop, at Jim, and then back to her ex. "Travis? What's he talking about?"

"You think it's him?" Travis asked the cop.

"Who him?" Jenny demanded, her voice edging toward shrill.

"I didn't recognize him . . . it's been so long, I thought he was dead, I hadn't thought about him in ages."

"Travis?" Jenny said. "What are you talking about?"

Travis's mouth twitched. "I don't know his name."

He said this so quietly, with such the barest movement

of his lips, that Jim wasn't sure he'd even heard correctly. But Beard leaned a little closer and Jenny leaned a little further away so—yeah. He heard it.

"What?" Jenny whispered. "Travis—"

"We were twins. But something was wrong with him."

Jim felt his stomach twist, and laid a palm across his belly. Wherever this story was going, it wasn't going to end well.

"I don't know what. Physical. Mental. Both. Mom and Dad tried to help him at first, I think. When we were little. But they couldn't do it. Aw, Jesus . . ."

"What happened, Mr. Montrose?" Beard asked. His voice sounded kind, but Jim didn't believe it.

Travis was breathing hard now, chest rising and falling rapidly. It reminded Jim of how he sounded after a basketball game, but there was a different quality to it. It wasn't the healthy gasping of a forty-something guy keeping tabs on his heart by shooting hoops. It was the terrified breathing of an animal, trapped.

"They had to keep him in a room," Travis said through his teeth. "They couldn't control him. Piss and shit everywhere. *He was a fucking demon.*"

Jenny brought her hands to her mouth, stifling a sound. Jim winced.

"Never had a name," Travis said, easier now, like he'd said the worst of it. "Just 'your brother,' that's all they'd call him. Go take this up to your brother, go hose down your brother—"

Travis stopped short, as if catching the terrible admission he'd just made. *Hose* him down? Jim thought, and glanced at Beard to see if he'd heard it.

He had. The cop's eyes glinted in the florescent light

above Travis's head, and then Jim fought to choke down an insane giggle: what did Travis need an overhead light for?

Maybe you should go, he told himself. Maybe you should just sit tight out there with Darla and not listen to all this.

But Darla was the very reason he needed to stay. He'd already jumped to a conclusion, and he was sure Beard was there already too. Had been at that conclusion before he got here. Of course.

"Brother" had come home. But from where?

"Where is your brother now, Mr. Montrose?"

Travis shook his head against the pillows. "I don't know. They took him away eventually. I was nine, maybe ten."

"You were *both* nine or ten," Beard clarified, and Jim thought, *You bastard.*

"Yes. I guess we were."

"They took him away—to where, did you say?"

He *didn't* say, Jim thought, and again lowered his estimation of the cop. He seemed to be enamored of his own authority, cribbing lines from fucking cop shows.

"I *don't know*," Travis emphasized. "I asked once, when I noticed it was quiet in the room, and my dad smacked me across the face. He said, 'We don't ever talk about him, never again.' So I didn't. After a little while . . . he just never existed."

"Jesus," Jenny whispered, now covering her eyes instead. "How could you not tell me that?"

Jim knew the answer. He was surprised Jenny didn't know or guess, but then maybe it spoke to why they were exes instead of married. Frank Montrose was a sonofabitch, that was why. Whether he'd always been that way or because of this second child he'd abandoned—and worse—Jim didn't know, but he knew from how Travis talked about him right now that, yeah . . . Travis was still in some way afraid of his old man.

Travis didn't answer her. "You think it's him? You think it's my brother?"

"Can't say for sure, of course, but it's something I'm going to follow up on."

"Ya think?" Jenny snapped at the cop. "Jesus Christ! Some fucking freakshow is out there hurting and killing the members of his family, which might very well include my daughter! How about you get the fuck out there and detect some shit, huh?"

"I'll, uh, go check on Darla," Jim said before Beard could respond. He let himself out quickly.

Holy fucking *shit*, he thought as he walked briskly down the hall toward the nurses' hub. That is a goddamn horror show is what that is. Good God. It sounded like some real V.C. Andrews type shit.

So what had happened to "Brother?" he wondered. What was wrong with him? What did they do to him? Or *with* him for that matter? Clearly, as far as Jim was concerned, whatever the Montrose couple had chosen to do with the kid, it hadn't worked.

If this was him. That was the most obvious choice, but still . . . what has to happen to a human being to make him search out and mutilate the members of his own—

"Darla?"

Jim stopped dead in front of the nurses' desk. The girl wasn't sitting on the bench.

He turned to the nurse behind the desk. "Excuse me,

did you see where the girl sitting here went?"

The nurse looked up, at the bench, then around the circular room. "Uh . . . elevator."

"She *left?*" He said this while bolting for the elevator doors. "Up or down?"

"I don't know. Down?"

"Ah *fuck!*" He stamped on the down button.

"Sir, I need you to please keep your—"

The elevator dinged and opened. The car was empty.

"Fuck off!" he growled, leaping inside and thumbing the ground floor button.

He raced from the cab as soon as it opened, startling two elderly women who looked like sisters. Jim muttered an apology and turned left for the cafeteria. That made the most sense, he told himself; she'd gotten hungry. Sure.

It took less than a minute for him to pace between the tables and scan the entire room. Not here. He cut in front of the checkout line and gave a cashier her description; no luck.

Swearing again, Jim went into the lobby and stopped in the middle, glaring all around. He tried the gift shop; nothing. He covered as much of the ground floor to which he had access, then took his search outside.

Darla was gone.

five

Jim walked a lap around the hospital grounds, scanning in all directions. He took his phone out and let his thumb hover over Jenny's number; he didn't have Darla's or else he'd have called her himself. Now he'd have to bring Jenny in. He tried not to think of the consequences of such a choice, desperately wanting to find the girl himself first.

But no. Either he'd passed her in his haste somewhere, or Darla was well and truly gone.

By herself or not—that was the real question.

Jim paused as he reached the lobby doors after his route around the building. Okay, he thought. Okay, if some mutant psychopath had shown up and grabbed her, *most likely* the nurse would have mentioned that, right? Right. Okay. So she left of her own accord.

Sure, he thought, going back inside and aiming for the elevator. She's a young girl still, and she's been through a lot, just like you told her yourself. She wanted to take a walk or . . . or go to the mall or whatever it was twelve-year-old girls did when they were freaking out. Maybe she had a friend nearby. Sure. Any number of scenarios were possible. Perfectly reasonable, safe scenarios.

But he had to have Jenny call her.

Jim pulled back from the elevator bank at the last second, figuring he may catch Darla coming back inside or even coming out of one of the elevators; bunching up in the third floor wasn't going to help.

He tapped Jenny's button. She answered after two rings. "Jim?"

"Hey, listen, Darla took off."

"*What?*"

Shit. "Yeah, I went out to the hall and she was gone. The nurse said she got into the elevator. I've been all over the grounds, inside and out, I can't find her. Can you call her?"

"Jesus," Jenny spat, and the line died.

Jim pinched the bridge of his nose. My thoughts exactly, sweetie.

He moped outside again, thinking if Darla was inside the hospital still, she'd end up back where she belonged without his help. If she'd left the building, maybe he could catch her coming in.

Because she has to come back, he thought as he turned right out of the lobby, headed for the downtown area. Lots of shops and restaurants that way, maybe she'd wanted to get something substantial to eat, and the thought of hospital food turned her stomach.

He was right.

Jim stopped short as he turned a corner, spotting the wayward pre-teen on a public bench outside an olive oil store. Darla sat with her arms wrapped around her middle, leaning forward as if about to puke.

Jim approached carefully, like approaching an off-leash

unfamiliar dog. Then he paused and thumbed a quick text to Jenny—*Found her she's fine call you soon*—before slipping his phone into his pocket and continuing his approach. He got to within ten yards before speaking.

"Hey, Darla."

She didn't look up, but he could tell she heard him just fine. She made no move to bolt, so Jim slid onto the bench beside her.

"Yeah, you scared the crap out of me," he said as if picking up the middle of a conversation. He wanted to add, *I fucking told you to stay where the fuck you were goddammit!* but sense won out and he kept his mouth shut.

"I'm sorry," Darla whispered after a moment. "I shouldn't have even come."

Feeling a bit more in control, Jim relaxed against the bench. "What makes you say that?"

"I don't even like them."

"Like who?"

"My parents, dude, who else?"

Jim felt his phone buzz, and ignored it. It would be Jenny. Speaking of which:

"You got your phone?"

"Yeah, I'm not answering it right now."

"Your mom's going to freak out."

"Oh, well, there'd be a change of pace."

Jim snorted. The noise brought a quick glance and quicker smile from the girl, both of which were gone a heartbeat later.

He let the silence grow. The important thing was she was safe. If Darla wanted to confide any more, that would have to be up to her.

"I mean, it's not like I'm glad he's hurt," Darla said.

Jim nodded.

"But also like, maybe he had it coming, you know?"

He thought about Brother, and wondered if she was right. Granted, he'd been not much older than Darla herself when . . . when what? How had the Rosemonts dealt with Brother, anyway? Maybe it was best not to know.

"Divorce is shitty," Jim said. "No way around it."

"Yeah." Darla sniffed. "I guess I should go back, huh?"

"I think so, before your mom sends the brute squad."

She met his eyes, wrinkling hers. "What's that?"

Jim grinned and stood. "Have you not seen *The Princess Bride*?"

She followed him up. "No, what's that?"

"Oh, D. We have a lot to show you. Maybe tonight, even. Come on, let's head back."

She nodded glumly and allowed herself to be led back to the hospital. Jim nearly put an arm around her shoulders, but didn't. Jesus, navigating this whole not-his-own-kid thing was getting to be a hassle.

Now that she was accounted for, Jim noticed the adrenalin rushing through his body He was ready to attack, and only slowly was that feeling dissipating. If Travis's fucking brother showed up, he'd have to get through Jim first.

It won't come to that, Jim told himself as they reached the lobby doors.

It won't.

six

Jim, Jenny, and Darla piled out of Jim's Jeep two hours later with bags of burritos from a local place that was usually one of Darla's favorites. Jim was unconvinced she could be bought off so readily, but didn't argue with Jenny, who was still steaming about her disappearance and Jim's inability to keep tabs on her.

"Dar?" she said now as they slammed the Jeep's doors. "Listen, hon, after we eat, we need to talk, all right?"

"About what." A statement. Darla wasn't having it.

"About a lot of things," Jenny said with a warning note. "Just humor me, Darla."

Darla shrugged carelessly and let herself into the house. She was in her room, the door closed, by the time Jim and Jenny had come in and closed the door behind them.

"Fun stuff," Jim said, setting his burrito on the table.

Jenny slammed herself down in a chair and rubbed her eyes. "Christ, Jim. I need a Xanax or something, those are the stress pills, right?"

"I think so." He took out the rest of the food and spread it out in front of her. "So what'd Beard say, what happens next?"

Jenny sighed and picked up her burrito. It was fully half the size of her head. "We don't have anything to worry about, or at least that's what *he* says. This . . . brother of Travis's is showing a ritualistic pattern, he said. Just going after the people he thinks harmed him. Or, probably did, I should say. He and the FBI think it's, quote, 'very unlikely' he'll try to hurt Darla."

"Or you."

"Yeah, or me."

"You don't look convinced."

Jenny finished a healthy bite. "Jim, my mother-in-law is dead. Travis's brother, her own son, who I didn't even know goddamn existed until this morning is the one that killed her. Travis and his dad are recovering from a—what did Beard call it—a life-altering violent crime. The fucking Feds are involved, Jim! You're goddamn right I'm not convinced."

She tossed the burrito down and sat back, crossing her legs and bouncing her foot.

"Sorry," he muttered. He was still hungry but set his own burrito down too. A show of solidarity, or so he hoped. "What can I do?"

"You can watch my fucking daughter next time!"

Jim lowered his gaze, deciding he had this coming and he may as well take it. Jenny ranted at him for a full five minutes, and Jim was sure Darla heard it all. He only nodded and offered the occasional "You're right" or "I know" to let her know he was listening.

And he *was* listening—he felt like shit, he felt like an asshole . . . he felt like an asshole shitting, for that matter.

He figured she was done when she took another bite

of her burrito. Jim blew out a breath and took one of his own. They chewed in silence.

"I'm so sorry," Jim said at last. "You're absolutely right, and it won't happen again, I swear to you. I love that kid, you know that, right?"

Jenny rolled her eyes first, nodded her head second.

"Do you want me to stay tonight?"

"Yes." While Jenny's face showed frustration, her response came instantly.

"All right. What about telling her about her grand-parents? You want me here for that or not so much?"

Jenny continued eating, eyes drifting thoughtfully around the kitchen before answering. "No. I'll do it. Do you need to grab some clothes and whatnot?"

"Yeah, I probably should." He finished his meal and crunched the paper in between his hands. "I'll do that now, take my time. She's expecting you to talk to her about something anyway."

"Yeah. Jesus, Jim, what a goddamn nightmare."

He stuffed the trash into the kitchen garbage and put a hand on her shoulder. "It is, it really is. But they'll catch him. Everything will be okay."

"Who's going to take care of Travis?"

Jim jerked, and hoped it didn't transmit down his hands and into Jenny's shoulders. "I don't know. I mean, I'll help him, of course. But he won't be an invalid, either, Jen. Being blind isn't the end of the world."

"Easy for you to say."

"True."

Where was this headed? Good God, she wasn't going to take him back after all this, was she? Blind or not, they weren't a good match. Jesus, what if she got it into her head to pity fuck him? Oh shitballs, what a mess *that* would be . . .

"I should go." He lifted his hands and patted his pants for his keys. He hoped she'd say something affirming, something like Hey, don't worry about us, we'll still be together. Only she didn't.

"See you tonight," he said quickly, and let himself out.

○

Jim came back at six bearing Chinese food. Whether he should do so or not was the first text he sent Jenny since leaving. She'd replied with a thumbs-up emoji and nothing more. That was the moment he felt it; felt the door shutting on their little tryst. He told himself he was being hypersensitive; then that he was being *in*sensitive; then that he was being premature. It hadn't been the best week for her family after all, and who knew how Darla was dealing with the information Jenny had to give her that day. No, probably Jenny was just exhausted and a thumbs-up was all she could reasonably manage.

He made that his mantra. The alternative soured his stomach. But he'd felt it before, back in high school and college; the somehow inevitable snap of a relationship ending. Something he saw in their eyes, or the way messages became terse or outright unresponsive. That's what that little brown thumb felt like.

Jim let himself into the house. He found Darla parked in front of the TV, a pillow crunched against her torso, knees draw up. On the screen, rich white twenty-somethings pretending to be teenagers tried to stop an evil supernatural event.

"Hey, D. Hungry?"

She didn't answer. Her expression reminded him of someone completely stoned.

He set the bags on the coffee table. "D? You okay?"

"Pretty much not okay, dude."

Jim sat down on the far end of the couch. "Where's your mom?"

"Bathroom. Shower."

"Did she, uh . . . how'd, how'd the talk go?"

"You mean did she tell me my grandmother was dead and my grandfather had his eyes ripped out just like my dad? Yeah. It was lovely, thanks for asking."

Jim let the sarcasm glide off him as best he could. "Were you close to them?"

"Psh. No. They were assholes."

"Yeah, that's kinda what I heard, too. Are you scared?"

Darla pulled her eyes away from the screen and lit them on him. "What do you think?"

"I don't know, D, that's why I'm asking. I'm trying to be helpful over here, to you and your mom."

"And that includes boinking her?"

Jim made a noise, some cross between a laugh and a groan and a gasp. "Wh-what makes you say that?"

The derision in her gaze said it all. Jim's shoulders slumped. "I have, like, literally nothing to say right now."

Darla turned back to the TV, studying the used car commercial as closely as she had the show. "I don't care. Go for it. Whatever."

He gambled. "I don't think you mean *that*. That you don't care."

"Well what should I say, dude? 'Stop?' You're grown ups, you do what you want no matter what I say, so, have fun. Have a *baby*."

That time he did laugh, because the thought was absurd, but the laugh fell from his mouth with the weight of a bowling ball.

"That's not in the plan, D."

She shrugged.

Jim pulled her seared shrimp out of the white plastic sack and set it on the table in front of her, then added napkins and a fork. The rest of the bag he bunched up into a handle as he stood.

"Can I tell you something? If you really did say stop, I would. I *will*. You're more important."

He walked out, feeling very dramatic and adult. The sensation passed by the time he reached the kitchen ten feet away—by then he just felt like a dick. Literally and metaphorically, just a big dick.

Jenny came walking in, barefoot and naked except for a large bath towel wrapped around her body, and a second hanging from her head like a new crop of hair. "Hey."

"Hey," Jim muttered back, and unpacked the sack. "Darla knows."

"Darla knows what? About her grandparents? Yeah, we talked earlier. She took it okay I think."

"About *us*."

Jenny froze, peering at him as if from under a wizard's hood. Her voice hissed from the darkness of it. "You told her about us?"

Jim kept his voice low. "Christ, no. She figured it out somehow, I don't know how."

Jenny groaned and flung herself into one of the chairs. "Perfect, that's—yes, yes that's exactly what I need right now. Shit."

Jim lifted a white container. "Mu shu, anyone?"

Jenny glared up at him—then smirked. "Fuck off, Jim. Gimme that."

"You want to get dressed first?"

"Oh, I guess. Thanks for picking this up."

He nodded.

Jenny rose and went back to the bedroom, leaving Jim alone in the kitchen with rapidly cooling Chinese chicken that somehow summed up how he felt about this life right then—lukewarm, a little greasy, and while better than nothing, not exactly a feast.

The thought made him smile grimly. He opened the box and dug in with a plastic fork, feeling vaguely fraudulent somehow for not using chopsticks.

Glass broke.

Jim looked up, mouth full of food. He waited for Jenny to shout for help, but no shout came.

"What was that?" Darla called from the living room, where she clearly meant to stay.

Jim stood and walked to the hall, frowning. "Don't know. Jenny?"

Jenny didn't answer.

From the bedroom, Jim thought he heard a thump. What the—

Oh, fuck! he thought, and ran.

He turned into the bedroom and saw the bathroom door was shut, but something thumped again inside. Adrenalin flooded his system as he tried the door. It was unlocked, but he could only open it a quarter-inch. Something heavy blocked its swing, and pushed it shut again.

It's him. It's Brother.

These words were not actual words in his head; they took the form of images and nonsense sounds that swirled around like blood in a drain.

"*Jenny!*"

Impulsively, he kicked the door as hard as he could just below the doorknob. Something grunted and the door opened partially. Jim caught a glance of something brown and rough-woven, some piece of clothing.

In the gap, he heard Jenny choking on a scream, calling for him through a gurgle. Swearing, his vision beginning to tunnel, Jim threw his entire weight against the bathroom door.

Jenny lay naked on the floor. Her towel bunched beneath her hips. She clawed at the tub, trying to pull herself up with one hand while massaging her throat with the other.

Beyond her, also on the ground, was a man.

seven

The stranger wore mostly brown, or else whatever colors the clothes had once been had morphed to brown after years of not washing. He was the very picture of homelessness: a thick, wiry gray beard, skin tanned taut and red by the sun, clothes soiled with unknown fluids, teeth yellow and black. A sharp, rancid smell rose from him, assaulting Jim's senses under the lavender and flowery scents lingering from Jenny's shower.

"What the fuck!" Jim roared, but didn't move. The unreality of the moment clamped him in place. This kind of shit just didn't happen. Right? Right?

Might wanna ask Travis about that, his guts snickered at him.

So this was Brother.

The man grinned and snarled at the same time and launched himself at Jim. Still incapacitated by his brain's inability to respond, Jim stood there and let the attack hit him full force in the body. The man's crushing blow drove them to the bed, the man on top, hands wrapped around Jim's throat.

Jim heard Jenny screaming and the sounds of his own muffled gurgling, but nothing else. The man above him leered down, grinning. Even as his breath choked deep in his throat, Jim could see the man was well beyond sanity; the blue of his eyes shone brightly like an animal's, whose only impulses were feeding and fucking. Which of these he was about to do Jim, he couldn't tell.

Jim's body finally fought back without him, determined to preserve itself despite his fear. He pulled hard at the man's arms. He pried and bent and twisted, but the homeless man's strength was preternatural. Jim could feel that the man's arms were much thinner than his own, but his muscles were fueled by something far stronger. Hate, perhaps, or madness. It was the stringy strength of a man whose body was his primary tool for survival. He didn't have to fear a heart attack from too much sitting in an air conditioned office.

Jim couldn't fight him.

The man was too strong, too determined. Jim's vision corkscrewed as his mind sent frantic warnings: not enough air, shutdown imminent, red alert red alert—

Jim drove his right knee upward.

Whatever else the man might be, he was still a man. Jim felt his testicles smashing flat for a moment under the momentum of his knee.

The man barked and rolled away. Jim scooted back, bunching up the comforter beneath him, holding his throat. He took deep, scathing breaths that seemed cradled in fire.

Seeing the man in agony pleased him. Since his knees were still bent from scooting backward, Jim used the potential energy to fire a kick into his attacker's face.

Either he was too weak from fear or the man was too focused on his balls, but the kick didn't do much. Still—it felt good to try.

Jim checked on Jenny. She was on her feet, but unsteady. Jenny hovered over the tub, half-bent, holding her breasts with her left forearm and steadying herself on the counter with her right hand.

"Cops," Jim coughed. "Call the . . . cops. Get—Darla—"

Jenny, her face strained tight, stumbled toward the bathroom door. She hesitated when she saw she'd have to pass the homeless man to get out of the room and to her cell, which was still in the kitchen.

Jim forced himself up and spun around wildly, looking for some way to tie up their assailant until the cops come.

Way to go, his brain cheered as he rushed to Jenny's bureau and pawed through it. Way to go, Jimbo, you're the hero of this story! You see me there, Jen? You see what I did? Fuck yeah, I got this!

"*Mom!*"

Jim whipped around. Jenny screamed Darla's name.

Darla stood in the threshold between Jenny's bedroom and the hallway. Her arms were straight down at her sides. Darla's eyes were wide and unblinking, her throat pulsing with fast gasps of breath. She sounded as if she were having an asthma attack.

Does Darla have asthma? Jim thought with animal stupidity. That's—

Then he understood.

Jim could only barely process what he was seeing: Clawed hands held Darla's upper arms flat against her sides. A crouched figure hunkered behind her, as if using her as a human shield. As he stared, Jim's hands went cold, then his feet, then the rest of his limbs as someone peeked up and over Darla's shoulder.

Its hair stuck up and waved like a baby's, fine and translucent. Its head seemed pointed at the crown, or else its slick, sloped forehead gave that impression. The eyes were blue, as brilliant as Travis's had been just days ago; as brilliant as Darla's were now.

But as it continued to lift its head higher, Jim realized this thing was only next-door to human, some cousin of humanity, not the real thing.

The skin around its mouth pulled backward tightly, like a face-lift gone terribly wrong. Its mouth was small, firm, and circular. Jim could make out tiny triangular teeth behind its thin lips. The thing moved its jaw up and down, but the mouth didn't seem able to close all the way; doing so would strain its skin to the point of tearing.

It may have been talking, but Jim couldn't tell over Jenny's screams and threats.

"Let her go! Let her go you fucker I'll kill you I swear to God you fucking let her go—!"

The homeless man rose and backhanded her. Jim crouched, ready to attack . . . but he stopped, shooting a glance back at the thing holding Darla.

Jenny stepped back, holding her face. The homeless man pointed at Jim while massaging his groin with his other hand.

"Don't," he said. "Just sit down, boy."

"Mommy?" Darla gasped.

The situation changed then. Jim felt it in the air before anything happened.

Jenny raised her hands toward her daughter. "Okay! Okay. Please. Please. Just don't hurt her. I'll give you anything you want just don't hurt my daughter."

Jim darted his eyes between them all. So too, it seemed, did the monster behind Darla.

No—not just a monster.

Brother.

This was Brother, not the crusty homeless motherfucker who'd attacked them. Maybe he was related too, somehow. Not that it mattered at the moment.

The homeless guy lifted a filthy eyebrow at Jenny, his gaze taking in her naked body. Jenny glared back at him, trembling.

The guy turned to Jim. "On the floor, boy."

Jim licked his lips and again took stock of the scene. Goddammit, he was not trained for this kind of scenario! He could try to rush Brother and Darla, knock them apart, give Darla a chance to run. No one had any weapons— well, except for the two-inch brown curved talons sticking out of Brother's fingers. They may have been fingernails, left to grow and mutate and snap off.

So his assets included himself—a lanky desk jockey—a naked woman, and a twelve-year-old girl being held still by a mutant.

"Okay," Jim said. He lifted his hands to show they were empty as he slowly knelt on the floor. "Okay, I'm going. Don't hurt them."

"Oh, shut the fuck up." The homeless man booted him in the face. Jim grunted and hit the ground.

The man knelt on his back forcing a cough out of Jim's lungs. "Hands behind your back," the man ordered. To Jenny, he snapped, "You, on the bed, face-down, don't move. You hear me?"

Jim twisted his head, nose brushing the carpet, and watched Jenny climbing onto the mattress. She didn't make a sound. From his vantage, he could now only see the soles of her feet.

The guy rummaged around in the drawers Jim had opened. Something slithered past Jim's arm, and then one of Jenny's thin leather belts bound his wrists behind him. Grinding his knees into Jim's back, the man spun and did the same to Jim's ankles.

With a grunt, the man got up. He stood over Jim, hunched. "You really cracked my nuts, boy. God damn. Yeah, you did."

He fired another boot against Jim's cheek. Jim heard the crack of his cheekbone fracturing, his vision going dark. It felt like a brick had smashed his face.

When he was able to open his eyes again, the man was crawling onto the mattress with three more belts and scarves dangling from his hand. Jim knew exactly what was next.

Oh, Christ, no, he thought. Jesus, Jesus, no.

"Please," he heard Jenny saying. She was not screaming, and not even begging. "Please let my daughter go now, I'll do anything you want."

"Yup," the man said. Jim saw him straddling her back. "I know you will, sugar."

"Let her go!" Jim shouted, pointlessly.

"Ah, shut your fuck hole," the man said, casting only the barest of glances behind him. "You fucked up my balls. I need 'em looked after."

"Jesus, man, then let the *kid* go!" Jim roared. He pulled hard against his restraints. The belt around his ankles seemed to slip a bit, but he wasn't sure. "Don't make her stand there!"

"That ain't up to me, that's up to my little buddy there."

Jim snaked his body to the left to better see Darla and

Brother. They hadn't moved from the threshold. Darla glanced down at him, her face tight as she breathed noisily between her teeth. He tried to will her to fight, to struggle, but either Brother was too strong or she was too scared.

The man grunted. Jim turned toward the bed again, his heart turning to ice—but the man was still clothed. The grunt had come from him tightening the belts around Jenny's hands, lashing her to the wrought iron headboard.

"No!" Jenny cried. "Please just don't hurt my daughter!"

The guy astride her laughed. "Hurt her? He ain't gonna hurt *her*. He's here to take care of her, you stupid bitch."

Take care of her? Jim thought madly. Take care . . . ?

He heard Jenny's voice muffle a moment later, and Jim realized the man had stuffed something into her mouth as a gag.

Oh, God, this is really happening. And when it's over this guy is going to kill us all. Or, at least the two of us. Take care of Darla, that's what he said, really? Why—?

Jenny issued a cry through the gag. Jim's body tensed. "Get the fuck off her, you bastard! I'm gonna fucking kill you!"

"No you ain't." The man slid off Jenny, pausing only long enough to slap her ass a couple times with one crusty hand. The gesture enraged Jim.

He nudged Jim onto his back. Jim felt the belt around his ankle slip a little more.

"Now as I was saying," the man said, tugging his pants down to reveal a long, narrow penis, white as an icicle against the rest of his tanned hands and face. "You racked my balls and I need them to feel better, so open up, boy."

Jim blinked, struggling to comprehend. As the man stroked his dick over Jim, his intent crystalized.

Jim's mind sent up flares. Jenny was safe—safe-ish—for the moment, he wasn't going to rape her. Darla had not been physically harmed . . .

There was something he could do, there was something . . . something he'd missed.

Brother.

Brother was here to take care of Darla—to *care for* her. He wasn't going to hurt her. Under any circumstances? Well, that he couldn't know that for sure. But in Brother's mind, he was helping her. He was being protective, not violent.

That meant Darla was not a chip on the table. The homeless guy was still a threat, but probably not to Darla, not directly.

He was somehow *working* for Brother.

Yes, yes, that's it, Jim chanted silently as the man's erection took shape in his leathery hand. Brother had assaulted the people who'd hurt him, who'd ignored him. Jenny was not on that list, just like Beard had said. Neither was Darla. No, Darla was a relative, a child, and Brother was going to protect her from any and every person in the family who could even theoretically hurt *her*.

How this motherfucker with the shit-stained clothes was involved, Jim didn't know and couldn't guess. And as the man began to bend over Jim's face, he figured, well, it probably wasn't important right now.

The belt came loose from his ankles.

Jim struck.

eight

Using muscles he'd long forgotten existed, Jim curled his feet upward off the floor and slammed them into the man from behind. Caught off-guard and with his pants still puddled around his ankles, the man stumbled forward and crashed into the wall.

Jim tossed himself to the right and managed to get to a kneeling position. The man cursed and spun, his erection bobbing ridiculously before him. Jim launched himself, driving a shoulder into the man's midsection. They smashed into the wall together, groaning and growling like animals.

"Run!" Jim screamed, hoping Darla knew it was her he was instructing.

But he couldn't turn to look. The man snarled something foul and brought his fists thumping down across Jim's back, knocking more breath from his lungs again. Christ, this malnourished stringy bastard was fucking *winning*.

From this awkward position, there was one bit of unguarded flesh bouncing in front of Jim's face, just now starting to sag but still stretched upward.

Oh, God, Jim's soul said deep inside, and vomited spiritual disgust inside him.

But years of passive ingestion of movies and television finally served a purpose: he understood right then that this man was, in fact, a killer. Either he'd done it before, or wouldn't mind giving it a try. Whatever his connection to Brother, he must have known what Brother was doing this past week.

If you don't stop him right here, right now, he will absolutely kill you, Jim's brain calmly informed him. You know that.

So make sure he can't.

Jim dipped his head further down and bit.

The tip of the man's penis came off surprisingly easy, though that was likely due to the adrenalin coursing through Jim's body. His teeth clamped down and masticated until meeting together again, a half-inch of engorged flesh in his mouth.

He straightened and spit out the chunk. The man mewed plaintively, kitten-like, as blood rocketed from his member in a flood of crimson that splashed on the carpet. His hands cupped beneath the wound but did not touch it, as if he were afraid of causing more damage. His penis shrank instantly, forcing more of its blood pumping out across his own boots.

Jim whipped around, savage, lips pulled back, searching for Darla.

She was gone.

So was Brother.

The man whimpered behind him and fell to his knees. "My dick! Oh, my dick, you bit m'dick off!"

Breathing hard, Jim struggled against the belt wrapped around his arms. It came off with relative ease, and he shook his hands free. Twisting his right shoulder back, he swung the mightiest fist he could manage at the man's face.

The punch connected solidly. The blow sent the man's head twisting practically over his shoulder. With a soft grunt, he fell forward in the squishy pool of his own blood.

Jim raced to Jenny, wiping blood off his face with his forearm as he went, spitting again. He yanked one of her hands free.

"He's got Darla!" Jim shouted, and left Jenny to undo the rest of her binding. "Tie that fucker up!"

By then he was in the hall, running hard for the living room.

Nothing. The TV blared Darla's show, that was wall.

He dodged into the kitchen. Nothing—but the garage door was open.

"Darla!" He kicked the door wider and threw himself inside.

There.

Brother had nowhere else to go. He'd backed into a corner with Darla still held out in front of him like a shield. Darla didn't look harmed, just terrified.

Jim instantly lifted his hands in a peaceful gesture, then quickly wiped blood from his chin again, trying to look less frightening—if anything indeed could frighten the monster he was looking at.

"Okay, okay," he said, trying to sound gentle but gasping each syllable. "We can work this out. All right? We can work something out."

Brother peered at him over Darla's shoulder. Jim

could not read his expression at all, although his posture suggested he was at the very least a bit worried. Considering all he was capable off, Jim had to believe he was nominally feral, and that he'd act like a trapped animal if pushed any farther.

On the other hand, he'd also managed to break into three locations and mutilate people without being caught, so he was not devoid of intelligence.

Watch your step, Jim thought.

"What's your name?" No one had mentioned one.

Brother blinked and tilted his head.

Jesus, he doesn't have a name . . . or he doesn't even understand the question. What the hell did they do to you?

Jim kept his eyes on the pair in the corner while letting his periphery scan the rest of the garage. They didn't have much room to maneuver; his Jeep and Jenny's car took up most of the available space. Brother and Darla were backed into the furthest possible corner opposite the kitchen door. Landscaping tools hung from friction clamps on the wall behind them, and red plastic bins were stacked in a rack overhead. The garage door opener was mounted on the wall by the door, near Jim, and there were no windows. The only way out was back through the house.

Through me, Jim thought sickly. God, how do we end this well? How?

The gun.

His Glock was in the Jeep still, but locked up and unloaded. Under the best of circumstances, it would take him well over a minute to get into the car, unlock the case, slap a magazine in and rack it. Too long.

"Please do something," Darla whispered. Her voice shook.

Jim nodded and risked a slow step closer. Brother didn't react.

"You're worried about her, aren't you?" Jim asked. "That's why you came here. To take care of her?"

Brother nodded. Okay, good; he understood the fucking language, that was a start . . .

Brother let go of one of Darla's arms, but Jim saw his other hand squeeze harder. He wasn't letting her go. He raised the free hand, his left, to his eye and tapped one claw near his eyeball.

Christ, what does that mean? Jim raged silently. Then he switched gears: No, wait—Jenny will be on the phone with the cops any second now if she isn't already. They'll be here soon. Just got to keep Darla safe and Brother busy. Then they'll take it from there.

Brother wasn't waiting that long.

Darla came flying toward Jim, screeching. Jim pinwheeled backward as she crashed into him. They fell to the concrete in a tangle.

"Fuck!" Jim cried, trying to right himself. He got a handful of Darla's rugby shirt and hauled upward as best he could, aiming to get her toward the door. "Go!"

She managed to land a foot in his midsection as she pushed herself up. Jim grunted and doubled up, still on his ass.

Darla tumbled into the kitchen. "Come on!"

"Close the—!" Jim began, but then the breath coughed out of him as Brother tackled him flat.

He heard the door shut. Good girl.

Then came bright white terror as he realized he was pinned to the ground beneath Brother and his claws. Those claws that had torn out three pairs of eyes.

"Oh, fuck," Jim whined. "Fuck, no, please—"

He struggled against Brother's weight, but the mutation clearly knew what he was doing. Jim was more immobile now than when he'd been tied up with Jenny's belts.

Brother tilted his head again, bird-like. Jim could smell the warm breath bellowing out of his mouth-hole, a green and fetid cloud that made Jim want to vomit as he thought about the smell of eyeballs crushed in Brother's maw.

"I'm begging you," he grunted. "Don't do it, don't."

Brother tipped his head the other way, as if trying to comprehend.

He raised a hand. The claw shone dully under the garage light that had popped on when they entered.

Jim squeezed his eyes shut—then opened them wide instead. No need to blind himself before the moment arrived . . .

Staring down at him, Brother pricked the corner of his own eye. A drop of blood appeared, then grew to a flow as Brother pushed harder.

Jim's mouth fell open in shock. Blood ran down Brother's arm and dripped from his elbow, landing on Jim's face. Jim shut his mouth in response.

Then Brother dug in.

Jim turned away, but it did little good. Brother shrieked in agony as he dug the claw into his own eye socket and worked his finger like key in a lock.

"God, fuck, ugh!" Jim groaned as more blood and thick fluid poured down Brother's arm, coating Jim's face. Drops landed in his ear, partially deafening him.

Jim wrestled himself back and forth, praying for some room to knock this creature off of him. Only distantly did it occur to him that this was, at least, better than his own eyes being ripped out.

He thought her heard a pop as Brother pulled the eye out and dangled it in front of Jim. Brother was panting now, fast agonized breaths, and Jim could hardly believe he'd managed the operation while remaining conscious.

Brother gripped Jim's mouth. His head become frozen in place. Great Christ, his *strength* . . .

It took only a second for Brother to wrench Jim's mouth open. Jim fought uselessly against him.

Brother gazed him with his one eye, pitying somehow . . . then forced his half-mashed eyeball into Jim's mouth.

Jim screamed as best was possible as Brother switched his grip to clamp Jim's mouth shut.

My God what hell is this, what hell is this, Jim's mind chanted at him as hot puke worked its way up his throat. No, no, don't puke, you'll choke, oh fuck, don't puke—

Contracting every muscle in his body, Jim swallowed. The organ was warm and slick, salty somehow, perhaps with tears or blood or both. Pretend it's an oyster, pretend it's anything, oh *God*!

He went deaf.

He went deaf and entered some fourth dimension, some netherworld where everything in sight was inverted. He could breathe easily again, so that was nice. The weight was gone from his body.

Jim rolled over and pulled himself lupine, looking at the kitchen door.

A uniformed cop stood in the doorway, weapon raised. Smoke drifted from the barrel as the cop stared past Jim.

Jim turned to look.

Brother lay on his back, motionless, his head twisted to one side, the side facing Jim. In addition to the cavernous black hole of his empty eye socket, another hole had opened up in his chest, only mildly bloody, but Brother's chest didn't move. Brother was dead.

Jim turned away, stared blankly at the concrete floor, and vomited until he ruptured a blood vessel in his eye.

nine

Jim stood up from the café table when Beard entered. The men shook hands.

"Get you anything?" Jim asked.

"No no, I'm fine. Thanks."

They sat.

"Thank you for meeting me here," Jim said.

"I knew you'd want to know."

"Did you tell Jenny and Travis?"

Beard sat back. "I did. You've not spoken to them?"

"Not really. Jenny and I are over. Which is fine. For the best. I don't think either of us could really have a relationship any time soon after all this. So the homeless guy . . ."

"Burt Standford. Been on the streets for thirty, thirty-five years. Living underground."

"That sounded literal."

"Yes. Literally. There's a lot more underground space in Phoenix than you might think. We don't broadcast it."

Jim blew out a sigh. He didn't want to know, really. "Why was he helping Travis's brother?"

"Still piecing that together. They had a relationship of some kind, from a long time ago. At the moment, it looks like Standford found the boy when the Rosemonts got rid of him. Took him in, raised him up. If you could call it that. I can't imagine just how mentally damaged the kid was after what his parents did, then you add in homelessness on top of it, being coached on survival by a guy like Standford . . ."

Beard shook his head.

"But Standford, he'll be in jail?"

"The rest of his life, whatever's left of it. Might be better off there, really. He didn't contest anything, but he's also not entirely sane, so, we'll see where that goes. But yeah. You don't have to worry about him again."

Beard cleared his throat and leaned forward.

"Listen, not for nothing, but you might want to get some help after all this. You know? Professional help. Even if you don't think you need it."

"Oh, I need it." Jim half-grinned. "Don't worry, I am. Didn't eat anything for a week, but."

Beard offered him a sympathetic dry chuckle.

"Why'd he do that?" Jim asked suddenly. "It's the piece I can't figure out. Why would the brother make me . . . ?"

Beard shook his head. "No way to know, I'm afraid. But my feeling is he was done. He was cornered, and he knew it. I think maybe he was either making amends or . . . or just doing what he thought the entire Rosemont family deserved, which included him. Who knows. Sorry I can't answer that."

Jim nodded. "Well, thanks for coming."

Beard stood. "No problem. We shouldn't need anything else from you. I hope everything works out."

"Thank you."

Beard tipped him a nod and walked out of the café. Jim watched him through the windows and let him drive out of the lot before leaving himself.

He still had to hit the library to pick up some more audiobooks for Travis.

t h e   e n d

bigfoot

originally published by Asylum Ink

"Those are certainly big feet," Jessica said, squatting down beside her partner, Dr. Steven Moody. She cast him a serious glance. "Is this for real?"

Steven frowned as he measured the fresh footprint in the black Oregon soil. "Off hand, yes," he said. "But the forgeries get more and more clever each year. Get the plaster from the truck, would you, Jess?"

Jess nodded and paced quickly through the lush ferns, dodging giant pines until she reached the back of the old Chevy holding their gear. She stopped short and gasped as three men faded into view at the truck's front bumper.

"Oh!" she said. "I'm sorry, I didn't see . . . hello."

"Hiya," the man in the center said, offering a surprised smile of his own. His eyes traveled up and down her slender body, still tan from a summer in California.

Jess tugged at her T-shirt, realizing it was much tighter than she'd remembered. She cleared her throat. "Can I help you?" she asked.

The man shook his head, eyes still fixated on her torso. "I don't suppose so," he said, and hitched his jeans. "I was gonna ask you the same question. Truck break down?"

"No," Jess answered shortly. "I'm here with *Doctor* Steven Moody?"

"Ahhhh," the three men echoed simultaneously in varying degrees of understanding and dismay.

"The Bigfoot Hunter," the center man said, nodding. "We've heard of him."

"We've just found a print," Jess offered, then wondered if she should have.

"Yep, not surprised," the man said.

Jess was mildly pleased to see that none of them had moved any nearer the truck. Or her. The big grey Chevy still blocked them from approaching her directly; if they had nefarious plans, she'd have time to sprint back into the forest and alert Steve. Not that he'd be much help, she thought. Dr. Moody was damn near as thin as his measuring tape; if he turned sideways, he'd disappear. Still. Two on three wasn't bad odds if these characters meant any harm.

Plus, Jess realized as she glanced at each man in turn, all three strangers sported handsome guts over their jeans, and Jess imagined she could smell beer coming from their mouths. They weren't drunk, not in any apparent way; but quite suddenly, she wasn't as put off by their appearance here in the woods as she had been a minute ago.

"You're not surprised he's here?" Jess asked. "You've heard of him?"

Many people hadn't.

"Oh, yeah," the man in the middle said. "Hell, three-quarters of the town's business is based on old Sasquatch. We meet just about every big hunter and scientist who comes through, or hear about them from others."

"We was on Discov'ry," the man on the left said, grinning happily.

Jess forced a smile back; his teeth were practically rotted through, and there was something idiotic in his gaze and voice. She wasn't sure whether to be comforted by or afraid of the fact.

"That's right," their spokesman said calmly. "The Discovery Channel has been through a few times over the years. Great for business. Tourists, you know."

"Oh, sure," Jess said vaguely, remembering then that she still needed to get the plaster gear back to Steve. "Well, it was nice to meet you, Mister . . . ?"

"Klingler," he said, smiling again in a nice, neighborly way. "That's with two L's. Kling-ler. Hard to say sometimes."

"Mister Klingler," Jess said correctly. "Got it. Is there . . . anything else I can do for you?"

Klingler shook his head dismissively. "Nah," he said. "We were just gathering some firewood for our campsite, saw the truck coming up the road, thought we'd say hello. That's all. You say you found a footprint, eh?"

"Yes," Jess said, wondering now if she should've kept quiet about the find. "I was just getting some of our plaster to take a cast. You—wouldn't like to see it, would you?"

She seasoned the question with enough ill ease to make clear she didn't want them to come with her.

"Nah," Klingler repeated. "Seen plenty myself. Now you find me a body, or some droppings, or a real live Sassie, well then you'd have yourself a deal."

"Sassie?"

"Sasquatch is a bit of a mouthful," he said. "Kind of like Klingler." He laughed.

Jess smiled in return. "Fair enough. Well, I'll just be heading back then. Nice meeting you."

Jess turned to go and made it as far as the tree line surrounding the clearing when Klingler's voice stopped her.

"Didn't catch your name," he called.

She paused. "Jessica."

"Nice to meet you, Jessica."

"Likewise. Bye, now."

"Jessica?"

She stopped again. "Yes?"

"You forgot your plaster. For the cast?"

Damn, Jess thought. "Right," she said, and turned back toward the truck.

They'd silently surrounded the vehicle.

Klingler was now next to the driver's side door. The idiot was on the opposite side of the truck, near the tailgate. The third, who'd watched the exchange impassively, stood quite near the tailgate and pile of plaster supplies in the bed.

Damn, *shit*, Jess thought.

Steeling herself, Jess approached the truck, waiting for any sign that the men were going to move to invade her space. Her self-defense training in L.A. had prepared her as much as she thought was possible—but with a spindly Ph.D., her own wits, and not so much as cell phone reception to protect her, her training seemed sorely lacking in the face of three townies.

"Ever seen one?" Jess asked as she moved closer, trying to keep them occupied. "Sasqu . . . I mean, Sassie?"

"Once," Klingler said, leaning casually against the door, hands in his pockets.

He's either harmless, or trying to distract me by looking harmless while these two jump, Jess thought. *Watch them. He can't get to you from there.*

She continued moving toward the tailgate.

"Yeah?" she said. "What happened?"

"Was out camping," Klingler said, looking away from her for the first time and into the forest. "Son of a bitch came barreling right toward me. I was alone. I damn near sh—that is, had a little accident, if you know what I mean, I was so scared. He came and stamped out the fire and took off into the dark. Had a rifle with me, but the whole thing happened too fast, couldn't even get a shot off."

Jess was at the tailgate now, keeping a wary eye on the silent man and the idiot.

"That's sounds terrifying," she said, reaching for the gate handle.

"Jessica."

Despite herself, Jess paused. Knew it was a mistake as soon as she did it.

"You'll want to be careful out here," Klingler said. He hadn't moved. "People get lost. Did you know this whole area has the highest rate of missing persons outside of the big cities?"

"No," Jess said, and forced herself to pick up the big white bucket with the plaster supplies.

If anyone moves, I'll scream, she thought. *Just scream, then go for the cash and prizes: Balls, throat, eyes. Balls, throat, eyes. Balls, throat—*

She pulled the bucket out and took a step back away from the silent man, who hadn't moved, only watched her.

"Yes ma'am," Klingler said, still at the door. "People go missing all the time. Most we never find. Hell, I'm on a search team once, twice a month. Right boys?"

The other two nodded seriously.

Jess backed up two more steps, too far for the man to reach.

"That's crazy," she said.

"We did find . . . have you all heard about the, uh . . . bodies?"

Safe enough now, five or six yards from any of them, Jess stopped. "Bodies?"

"The ones we did find."

"Yes," she said. Which was true. It was one of the reasons this area had appealed to Steven in the first place. Around the small town over the past ten or so years, several bodies had been discovered either by organized search parties or unfortunate campers.

In each case, the victims had been dismembered. Premortem.

"You say you've seen one?" Jess asked Klingler, fighting a sudden urge to puke.

"Once, yeah," Klingler said, and shook his head. "It wasn't pretty. Arms torn off, legs pulled off. Sassie did a number on them."

"If he exists," Jess couldn't resist saying.

For the first time, Klingler shot her a truly upsetting look. "What's that?"

"I said, if he or she exists," Jess said. "Bigfoot."

"You don't think so?"

"I'm not sure," Jess said. "I'm a grad student. I'm still collecting data. I think it's possible, but unlikely."

Klingler grinned at her with a pitying look. "Oh, I see," he said. "You're not one of those true believers out to prove what the rest of us already know. You're a, what—skeptic. Right?"

She shrugged.

"Trying to prove Sassie doesn't exist, huh?"

"Like I said, Mr. Klingler, I don't know yet. We have this footprint, and plenty of evidence to go over from previous expeditions. But you do know the Patterson tape was finally shown to be a forgery, right?"

"Yep," Klingler said, laughing slightly. "Any idiot knew that the day it came out."

Her curiosity piqued. "Why do you say that?"

Klingler returned her shrug. The other two hadn't moved. "That thing on the tape," he said. "It wasn't *big* enough. No way."

"But at first the size seemed consistent with the footprints on file."

"No," Klingler said. "Not nearly. You want to know something? A little inside information? Just because you're a pretty girl?"

The last bit stung and made her blush at the same time. She fidgeted with the bucket, trying to suss out the best way to respond.

"Okay," she said cautiously, narrowing her eyes. Make eye contact, her instructor had said in L.A. So *they* know that *you* know you've got them pegged.

The advice made sense on the mean streets of Los Angeles. In forests of Oregon, it didn't seem to make much difference.

"Truth is," Klingler said, leaning off the truck door now, but keeping his hands buried in the pockets of his jacket, "about ninety, even ninety-five percent of those footprints are faked. Hell, people up here and in California'll fake them just to keep the tourists and monster hunters coming."

"But you wouldn't do that," she risked.

Klingler laughed. "Me? Hell, no No reason. Plenty of other fakers running around. Now, I'll admit, if we lost the business in town, that would be a big problem. But no, nobody I know's ever faked a print. Some kids in town maybe. No, Jessica, I have to tell you . . . folks around here know a lot more than we say."

Her arms were getting tired, holding the bucket. She set it down and shook her arms.

Damn and shit again, she thought. *Now you look weak.*

"We know that Sassie's out there, and she's a mean old cuss," Klingler said. "Big and mean. Best keep that in mind as you, uh—pursue your studies."

"Will do," Jess said, tiring of the conversation. "Nice to meet you."

Klingler nodded. He did not, Jess noticed, move away from the truck.

She gave the other two men a short wave, picked up the bucket, and began walking through the woods back toward Steven.

Stupid, she thought. *They could still be dangerous. They could disable the truck.*

And if they did, what could you do about it? she argued back silently.

She opted to shake the encounter from her mind. If they were up to anything, they would've made a move. If they were going to disable the truck, they would, and she and Steven would hike out of the woods if necessary.

"Steven?" she called as she walked, navigating the dips and branches that threatened to topple her. "Dr. Moody?"

No response. He was still too far away, she reasoned,

or perhaps too engrossed with the footprint. Or better still, maybe he'd found another, or some other revolutionary bit of evidence. When on the hunt, Dr. Moody had a tendency to white out, to not hear a single word spoken to him. *A caricature scientist,* she thought, and smiled.

"Steven?" she called again. "I've got the plaster. Steven?"

No answer.

Jess stopped. *Did I get turned around?* she wondered. *Am I going the right way? Good God, I don't want to ask those thumb suckers back there for directions.*

Movement, perhaps fifty yards ahead, caught her eye. She released a breath she hadn't realized she was holding.

Cheered by the thought of being again in the doctor's proximity, Jess set off through the trees, growing mystified at the scent of burning wood teasing her nose.

"Steve?" she said, as she entered the area where they'd found the footprint.

Steve was nowhere to be seen. Jess walked to the area where they'd spotted the footprint; it was still there, fresh and new in the moist soil.

So was Steve's measuring tape.

Jess scanned the woods. "Dr. Moody?" she called, expecting he'd gone to relieve himself in the bushes during her absence.

No response. But the smell of a campfire was steadily growing.

Or . . . what if it's not a campfire? she thought nervously. *What if it's the start of a forest fire, and we're right here in the middle of it . . . ?*

Dropping the bucket of plaster, Jess ran further into

the forest, following her nose. The fire was nearby, she was certain of it.

"Steve!" she called, shoving aside branches and brambles. "Steven?"

There!

In a small clearing, another fifty yards away, she saw flames dancing. Jess saw at once that it was in fact a campfire, well tended and safely away from any trees or scrub brush.

Two figures stood on either side of the fire, erecting what appeared to be a spit. Hunters, she thought. Like the townies back at the truck.

"Hello?" she called as she drew nearer. "Excuse me?"

The two hunters turned toward her voice. One raised a gloved hand.

"Hi," Jess said, somewhat breathlessly after her jaunt through the trees. "I'm looking for—"

I'll be damned, she thought, and narrowed her eyes at the two men.

In a cluster nearby one of them lay a pair of shoes. But not hiking boots, not tennis shoes, not running sneakers.

The shoes were enormous. The sole seemed just about the length—no, the *exact* length, Jess realized—of the footprint they'd found.

And designed in no uncertain terms to look like a giant bare foot. Both of them.

Fakers.

"You want to explain those?" Jess snapped, pointing to the shoes.

The two men looked at the shoes, then back at her.

"Makin' tracks," one of them said carelessly.

"God dammit!" Jess roared at them. "How could you?"

The man who'd spoken shrugged. "Works every time," he said.

"Works to do what, exactly?" Jess demanded. "To fool the monster hunters? Huh? Damn it, do you realize how much time and energy we just wasted getting ready to make a cast of one of your little jokes?"

She thought immediately of Mr. Klingler's admission that certain townspeople took it as a matter of self interest to keep the myth of the Sasquatch alive. Jess didn't blame them, necessarily. Still. She felt like a fool to have believed in the monster, even for a moment.

"I should take a picture of both of you and confiscate those fake feet right now," she threatened, knowing she could accomplish neither goal if they didn't want her to.

The faker shrugged again. "You could do that," he said. "Billy, gimme a hand with the meat?"

Billy nodded. They reached down, and either man took one end of a long steel pole, the middle of which had been neatly hidden by the height and breadth of the fire.

They lifted the pole up and set each end down in the brackets of the spit.

Jess swooned.

Dr. Steven Moody had been run clear through. His arms and legs hung limp. The spit had gone in somewhere in his backside while the other end protruded from his mouth, forcing his jaws open, as if his lifeless body was trying to take a bite of the steel rod. His clothes had been removed.

Both men turned to her.

"You could do that," the first repeated. "But it won't get you very far. Ain't that right, Harley?"

"That's true," Jess heard Mr. Klingler say behind her.

She whirled, seeing that Klingler and the other two men had already surrounded her.

How quietly they moved, she thought helplessly. *How quiet.*

"There's no Sassie," Klingler told her, almost gently. "Not that we ever seen. But a couple of prints here and there keep the meat coming. Sorry to keep you so busy at the truck talking all that nonsense, but we needed some time. Hope you don't mind."

At last her tongue loosed and Jessica screamed, inhaling the acrid odor of woodsmoke and Steve Moody's slowly roasting flesh.

They fell upon her.

killercon

The agenda for the convention looked promising. Mike was anxious for it to start, and he squirmed impatiently while in line for his name tag.

8 am – Coffee and continental breakfast hosted by Starbucks.

9 am – Walking vs. Running: How to catch sprinting co-eds while moving at a brisk walk through thick foliage.

12 pm – Lunch. Cannibal-friendly.

1 pm – Machete or Axe? How Weapon Choice Affects Performance

4 pm – Dinner

6 pm – We Don't Need No Stinkin' Chainsaws: How Moving Parts Can Ruin a Good Massacre

8 pm – Film Festival. Hollywood's laugh-out-loud take on the profession, and how they get it all wrong. Complimentary popcorn and soft drinks! Cash bar available.

Grinning to himself, Mike turned over the flyer to see the following day's activities. Like any convention, attendance would be low Sunday morning, but the Con was thorough, cramming as much information into the weekend as possible. Mike figured he'd at least pick up the presentations that began after lunch.

11 am – To Mask or Not To Mask? How concealing your identity works for and against your victims.

12 pm – Luncheon and networking. Poolside! Visit our exhibition booths for free blade sharpening, with skin-crafts for the kids!

2 pm – Racism and Sexism in the Profession: Why always pick on the minority in the group? Plus, why sexually active teens must perish in fountains of their own arterial blood.

4 pm – Awards Ceremony

Mike's black, merciless heart gave a little jump. The awards ceremony! He dared to imagine his bloodstained fingers grasping the KillerCon Best Member Award this year. That damned sociopath Jay had cheated him out of it three years running, and it was time the organizers of the event realized Mike's talent. Didn't mutilations count for anything anymore? What about unique use of weaponry? Jay was a hack-and-slash man all the way, had been since birth, but Mike had never limited himself to a solitary weapon--weapons of opportunity were his stock in trade, from butcher knives to hacksaws.

Plus, Jay always wore that stupid clown mask all the time, even during the convention. It was permitted, but frowned upon. How come, Mike wondered, when every other serial killer and mass murderer was willing to show his face, Jay was rewarded for covering his own?

Mike dropped the convention program and flyers back into the bloody canvas tote the Con had provided for all the attendees. He glanced down into the bag, still waiting in line to receive his nametag. This year's swag wasn't as outstanding as last year's, he noted with some disdain. A sharpening stone (so trite), a knife-shaped letter opener (cliché), and brand-new work gloves for the more down-and-dirty work their trade required.

Mike rolled his eyes. If he didn't win Best Member this year, he determined, then this was his last Con for awhile. So what if they cancelled his membership? It wasn't a union; his work would go on unimpeded. And, he further determined as his mind wandered on the gory subject, he'd make this year his most fatal yet. Twenty co-eds? Heck with that, he was going for a whole dorm full of them! Let's see Jay keep up with that kind of body count at a stupid summer camp!

Mike grunted as someone bumped into him from behind. He turned slowly, letting his bloodshot eyes narrow into crimson slits.

It was Jay. Mike recognized the dopey clown mask instantly.

"Hello, Jay," Mike said, sneering.

The clown mask bobbled. "Mike," Jay replied.

Mike continued to peer through the mask's eyeholes, burning his hatred into the other killer. "You gonna apologize or what?"

"For what?"

"You bumped into me!"

"Mike, you're being overly sensitive."

"Overly what!? Why you third-rate, maim-only, sequel-bombing! . . ."

Jay's machete cut cleanly through Mike's neck, sending

the other man's head toppling end over end past the line of convention attendees. There was a shocked gasp through the crowd--not at the grisly sight of Mike's lips fish-mouthing foamy cries of agony, but rather at the breach of etiquette. Killers didn't kill each other at the Con, that was the rule.

Jay stared at the rest of the attendees in line, who turned away and waited for their nametags. No one wanted to cross a three-time Best Member award winner. Jay wiped his machete off on Mike's grease and blood-stained coveralls, noting with detached delight that one foot was still twitching. The rest of the convention passed uneventfully, and everyone went back to work Monday with a greater appreciation for their chosen career.

It was going to be a red-letter year.

alone

I am lonely.

It's a tangible thing, more tangible than me. They see right through me, now as ever, only now, it's for real.

I've never been so alone in my entire life.

Wait.

That's not exactly true. I've never been so alone in general.

I've also never been so cold.

I wander the halls of my school, growing more and more angry that this is where I ended up. Of all places.

Sometimes I try to sleep, but the most I can manage is sort of a floating doze.

This sucks.

Monday is hard. School is packed full. I guess I don't get a holiday named after me. I drift from group to group, listening carefully. But I don't even hear my name mentioned.

Guess I shouldn't be surprised. I didn't exist then. I don't exist now.

When Jordon Kersey and her clan of pretentious troglodytes talk about my best friend Hallie, though, that's even worse. I swing at Jordan, because really, what's anyone going to do about it?

I don't connect. Of course. I am a ghost.

Her clan starts heading for the staircase leading down to the first floor, and I follow along, swinging, swinging, nothing happening, and it makes me even more mad.

Then, just as she's taking the first step, I scream as loud as I can and use both hands to push. The scream, of course, is composed of pure silence, an empty orchestra.

But my ghostly hands connect.

Jordon gasps and flies down the stairs. She lands once somewhere in the middle, bounces, and flies again before sliding to a stop on the linoleum floor.

Some people laugh. A few shout in surprise. Some applaud, like Jordon's committed the worst high school blunder ever.

She doesn't get up.

That's when the girls' coach crashes through the crowd that's gathered and checks for a pulse.

That's how I learn that I can kill. Not all at once, but by degrees. One by one.

I stalk through the halls each day, watching them go busybusy helterskelter to this class and that, did you hear what Ricky said to Sheila last night omigod! My ears burn and bleed at the sound they make, except my ears can no longer hear for they are not there.

Nights are easier. Quiet. There's an occasional hum that I learned came from the air conditioning units. I can thrust my incorporeal head into the workings and I've learned a lot about these machines. I would have been a fine air conditioning repairwoman.

Dude did you see the game last night, dude of course I did dude!

My parents are so totally lame I sweardagod did I tell you what they did yesterday?

Ohmigod I failed algebra my mom will kill me!

Not if I kill you first, I think. At least, I think I think. What do you think, I ask as if aloud, but it's silent and quiet, because my body has long since gone.

I want to leave the school but I don't. I am a superhero, I am X-Man Kitty Pryde. Walls are no longer barriers to me, but still I avoid the gym. They killed me there. With their mocking, their hate, their vitriol, ha ha ugly girl, can't get a date, can't go to parties, can't be cool like us.

I think (if I can think) there was something wrong from the beginning, from before I was born perhaps, some defect or misalignment of my heart that made it give up the ghost, ha ha, at the age of fifteen. Panic struck me daily, taxing the organ, boiling my blood and twisting my guts like snakes in burlap, until that day during gym class when it became too much and my heart said "See ya!" and lay down and slept. I watched, invisible and go-through-able, as they kept on with their jokes, made fun of my body until someone finally realized this was no game, no show, no fake, that I was dead and gone, then hushed ripples of disbelief echoed around the gym. I watched it all, floating above them.

I wonder (if I can wonder) what my father did with my body. I think I can leave the school, I think I could go and see, but I don't. I stay and watch because I do not sleep now, and I test the limits of my disembodied strength, and finally learn that I can kill.

I tried Jeff a week after Jordan, exerting my will on

him and throttling his veins until an embolism shocked his brain to death.

I hear them talking these days about the school being haunted. That some thing is watching and choosing and waiting and striking.

They are right.

But I am still alone.

I have not seen Jordan or Jeff. They are not bound here like me, it seems. I wonder why. Or maybe they are here, but even I cannot see them. That's not what the movies would have me believe. I haven't seen a movie in a long time.

I watch my best friend Hallie closely. I pretend I am her guardian angel, and perhaps I am. They have always attacked her as they did me, but her heart is strong, she will not perish like I did, panic and fear choking the drumbeat in her chest to stillness. She is sad that I am gone, so I am sad for her. I never meant to leave her. But I follow her every day, watch her in class, try to whisper answers in her ear that I don't think she can hear.

So when she choked on a piece of meat at lunch yesterday, my heart (if I had one) was torn apart. I watched my best friend die. It was long and painful, not the brief spasm I had felt. I screamed and no one heard. I wept and no one could dry the imaginary tears.

But I heard laughter. Laughter that wasn't from a living thing. I heard laughter and taunting, the sound of victory, the sound of a girl and a boy celebrating. I am a ghost, yet felt a chill.

I am not alone.

panic

Originally published in the anthology
Z Resurrected as a companion novella to *Sick*

Tuesday, November 12
Phoenix Metro High School
Phoenix, Arizona

5:04 p.m.

Um—

My name is Laura Fitzgerald, I'm seventeen . . . and I really, really want to be eighteen someday.

I don't know what's going on, exactly. It feels like the world is ending out there. I'm scared, and there's no one else in here but me. This is Cody's phone, not mine. I guess you know that. Whoever you are. Whoever finds this, I mean.

If Cody's mom or dad hears this, I'm sorry about Cody, I did everything I could. I swear.

God . . .

I don't know . . . I don't know how long I can stay in here. I don't have any food or water. But they're still out there, I can hear them. Sometimes I hear someone scream out there.

Um . . .

Honestly? I'm kind of surprised I can even talk right now, usually I'd be curled up in a little ball somewhere. That's what I really want to do. But I can't. They'll get me if I do.

Oh, God. God.

No. Okay. Stop. Breathe. I can do this. I can do it.

Uh—

I just, I thought I should explain everything, because maybe it will help? I don't know. I don't know if anyone will ever find this . . . but, um . . .

Okay.

This is what happened.

Tuesday, November 12
1:50 pm

"This is my worst nightmare," I told Mackenzie Murphy as I forced one step after another toward the gymnasium. Around us, hundreds of other students pushed and shoved and yelled and cussed. It felt like being in human soup, drenched in clammy sweat and the breath of thousands of other high school students.

I don't do well in crowds. Phoenix Metro High School grew exponentially a few years ago when another school closed down. There are way, way too many of us. Definitely way too many for me.

Kenzie smiled and tugged my pony tail. I yelped, and Kenzie laughed. "Don't worry, you've got a bratty-little-sister-type friend going with you to keep you all distracted."

Despite how my arms and legs shook under my hoodie and jeans, I managed to smile back at her. Kenzie's brother Brian had broken up with me a few weeks ago, but Kenzie didn't act all weird about it, thank God. She kind of *was* like a little sister to me, even though she wasn't that much younger.

I forced myself to take as deep a breath as I could. It

wasn't easy. I wanted a pill. All I had to do was reach into my bag and grab my bottle of clonazepam and in twenty minutes or so, I'd be able to handle all the noise and shoving and shouting, mostly because I'd be a half-asleep zombie.

But I didn't do it. I didn't take one. I didn't want to *have* to anymore. It was something I'd been working on for a while.

"I can't believe Brian didn't come with us," I said to Kenzie as people jostled into us. Each anonymous touch made my stomach clench.

Kenzie grabbed my arm and pulled us out of the worst of the foot traffic. I appreciated it. It made it easier to breathe. Our classroom buildings are all open, not enclosed; not indoors. That meant we had to deal with whatever the weather happened to be. Today, it was nice outside, sunshiny and a little cool but not cold. It wouldn't get cold until December, or even January. We never got snow, and it only rained maybe a dozen times per school year. The roofs and awnings over the sidewalks were mostly for providing shade.

I think the open hallways helped me deal with my panic disorder and agoraphobia. I could usually handle being in classrooms, but gatherings any larger than that made me feel like I'd been put into a coffin and pushed out to sea like Danae in the Greek myth—enclosed and muffled in darkness, lolling out into an endless rollercoaster ocean, sick to my stomach and utterly trapped.

It wasn't the greatest way to spend each day.

"Fuck Brian," Kenzie said, sincerely but without any real hatred. She loved her brother a lot. "He's being an ass-bag."

"But gosh, how do you *really* feel, Kenzie?"

"He is!" Kenzie kept me moving toward the gym, but an angle, out of the bulk of the foot traffic. "You are awesome and so totally good for him, and one day, he'll figure that out."

"Yeah, we'll see."

I drew in another breath. It came back out like a stutter.

"Hey," Kenzie said, as we reached the doors to the gym. "You got this. And if you don't, we'll mosey. I'll go with you to Nurse Garrett or whatever. Okay?"

"Thanks. But, no. I can do it. I can do this."

Kenzie lowered her voice. "Have you taken anything?"

She and our friends knew I carried a couple bottles with me in my bag at all times. Klonopin and Paxil. The Pax I took twice a day, but the Klonopin I took as needed. I usually needed one a day. Sometimes two. That had been normal up until a few weeks ago. I'd started a lower dosage of Paxil, and been avoiding the Klonopin as best I could. But no one besides my doctor and my parents knew that yet, not even Kenzie or Brian. Maybe it was stupid, but it was a fight I wanted to take on myself.

I stopped walking and pulled away from the gym doors. Kenzie came along without protest. Someone behind us said, "Look out, bitch!"

The outburst certainly did not help calm my nerves. Phoenix Metro High School isn't the friendliest place on Earth.

"Listen, I need to tell you something," I said as the bell signaling the start of seventh hour went off.

"Totally," Kenzie said, her eyes serious.

"It's just that . . . I haven't been taking all my pills all the time."

Kenzie's eyebrows rose. "Yeah?"

"I've been backing off them. Slowly. Lower dosages and stuff. So this whole pep rally thing, it's kind of an experiment, you know? Like, if I can sit through this, then maybe... I don't know."

"Okay. What can I do?"

"Nothing, just.... I just wanted you to know, so in case something really bad happens to me—"

"Do whatever you have to. I'll be there. Does Brian know?"

"Not yet. That's what I wanted to talk to him about tonight."

Brian and I had crossed paths earlier that morning, before he and his friends Chad and Jack ditched fourth hour. When I'd told Brian I wanted to talk to him, I think, or maybe *want* to think, that he looked happy about it. Or at least intrigued. We'd stayed friends since we broke up, because we hung out with a lot of the same people, like Cammy and her boyfriend Hollis. Them, Kenzie, Chad, Jack—we hung out a lot at lunch and things like that. They were my best friends. When Brian said he thought we needed a break, I'd had a pretty epic meltdown afterward, worried that all my friends would stop talking to me. It turned out to be the opposite. Honestly, while I know we were all still friends, I think they were angry with him about the breakup.

I'd be lying if I said that didn't make me a *little* pleased.

Kenzie's surprised expression changed to suspicion. "Okay, Laura? It's really cool that you're willing to try going to this dumb pep rally thing, and I'm happy for you. That's awesome you've been able to back off the meds. But you're not doing it for Brian, are you? Because, seriously? Don't."

"No, not *for* him. It's more like—I don't know. He kind of had a point. I should be able to go to a movie, you know? I should be able to go out to eat with him, or with anyone, not just stay home all night. That's all. But no, I'm not doing it for him."

"Okay," Kenzie said. "That's good."

A security guard shouted at us to either get into the gym for the pep rally or get to class. Kenzie and I hurried into the gym. The doors closed behind us.

I sucked in a breath the instant we passed through the lobby and my Vans touched the hardwood floor. The gym, decked out in our red and white school colors, overflowed with students. The band had already started playing on the visitor's side of the bleachers, while the cheerleaders did routines on the floor. The football team lounged around at the opposite end of the gym, waiting for a cue to run out and be introduced to the crowd as if we didn't go to class with the athletes every single day.

"What do you want to do?" Kenzie said over the noise as I froze in place. The noise assaulted me, and I could feel the walls closing in. I felt like a rat in a maze.

Our friend Cammy became head cheerleader this year, and she executed perfect backflips across the basketball court. At the end of her flips, she saw me cowering against the wall. She couldn't wave, because it would be like breaking character, but she smiled big and sent me a wink.

That helped. Cammy is the opposite of everything I am. I wished sometimes I could be more like her.

"I'm okay," I said, half truthfully. "I'm okay."

I stepped toward the stairs leading up the collapsible aluminum bleachers. Kenzie and I found seats at the very top, near all the depressed smokers who always seemed to congregate together. They were harmless, though, compared to some of the other students.

"All right," Kenzie said, making sure I had the aisle seat in case I needed to run. "See? Not so bad. You got this."

I nodded, but couldn't respond. I had to focus hard on my breathing. Panic attacks usually feel like heart attacks, except panic won't actually kill you—it just feels like it. Already my chest felt constricted, but I'd been practicing some breathing and meditation techniques. I focused on them now: *Breathe in one two three four, breathe out five six seven eight . . .*

I was jealous of every single person in the gym. Many were bored, a few seemed genuinely excited, not counting the cheerleaders and dancers. They were so lucky, and they didn't even realize it. To them, it was just *ho-hum, another day of school, at least I get to get out of math this period.* For me, it was anything but. It was *everything.*

Kenzie put a hand on my knee, her crimson nail polish glaring beneath the high florescent lights. Into my ear, she whispered, "You're shaking."

I rubbed my arms, pretending like I was cold, even though I didn't have to do that with Kenzie.

"Chilly," I lied. And my friend Kenzie nodded. It's hard to describe how much I appreciated that.

Then the gym exploded. So did my heart.

1:56 p.m.

It started with someone screaming a cuss word from among the group of football players. Everyone looked.

From the direction of the locker rooms, a guy came barreling toward the football team on his hands and knees, like an ape. Even over the band and the general chaos, I could hear him *growling*.

The team turned toward him just as the guy leaped. It seemed inhuman, like no person should have been able to jump that high from that hunched of a position. The guy tackled one of the football players, taking him to the ground.

People started screaming. I stood up, legs quaking, wanting to head straight down the stairs and out of this gym and out of this school and *home*, please, God, just let me go *home*. . . .

The hunched-over guy grabbed the player's arm in his hands, and bit him. The football player on the ground shouted and started punching the guy in the head, but it had no effect. Even from as far away as I stood, I could see blood flying across the basketball court, staining the wood.

I could see the football player's face go from surprised to angry to being in serious pain.

The team went to work. They dogpiled the two of them as security and teachers rushed to the scene. Everyone in the gym was on their feet now, some cheering, a few wincing, but all watching. We'd been transported to the Roman Empire, become spectators in the arena.

On the court, the fight slowly got contained. Someone got on the gymnasium PA system and said, "All right, everyone sit down, it's over, sit down please . . . it's under control, please sit down, everyone."

Most of us did. I didn't. I couldn't. My feet had melted and become stuck to the aluminum bleachers, my arms cramped straight down and motionless.

Our school resource officer, Doug Shepherd, had the attacker face-down on the court and in handcuffs. Officer Doug bled from his hands, and the guy flailed like a fish out of water. The football team congregated at the end of the gym again, several of them holding wounds on their arms or faces.

The crazy guy had done a whole lot of damage in not very much time at all.

Kenzie summed it up best: "Holy *shit!*"

"Yeah," said a kid sitting next to her. It was one of the smokers dressed head-to-foot in black—jeans, jacket, shoes, cap. He looked as spooked as I felt. Either he was naturally pale, or else the fight had drained the blood from his face. He seemed young, maybe a freshman.

Kenzie took my hand. "Laura? You okay?"

I closed my mouth as a janitor came out and began pouring bleach on the floor where blood had spilled and pooled. Officer Doug wrestled the crazy guy out of the gym somehow while we all watched. Then someone started applauding, and pretty soon the whole gym was cheering and clapping. I wanted to think it was for Officer Doug, but wondered if it was for the fight. For the blood.

Somehow, I managed to sit down. "Yeah," I told Kenzie. "I'm... no, I'm not okay. But I'll make it."

I forced myself back to my deep breathing practice while teachers got the gym under control. Several football players left the gym with a couple of coaches, headed back into the locker rooms, I assumed to get bandaged up.

I took my phone out and tapped Brian's name. I sent him a text: *Big-time fight at rally. Not feeling real good but I am here!!!*

On the one hand, maybe I shouldn't have even bothered touching base. On the other, I needed him to know I could sit at a pep rally without going catatonic. Technically, that remained to be seen, but still. It felt right to point out something scary had happened and I'd survived.

Kenzie leaned over as I typed, and smiled. "Yeah, that's it. Shove it in his face."

Something resembling a laugh coughed out of me, and I set the phone down beside me. I might need to dial 911 before the pep rally was over, the way things were going.

"I never seen anything like that," the kid next to Kenzie said, and wiped his face. I could smell the cigarette smoke on his clothes. "Man, fuck this place."

Kenzie gave him an understanding grin. I found myself nodding. I wasn't a big fan of this place, either.

"I'm sorry my brother's such a tool," Kenzie said as things settled back down and Cammy got the cheerleaders arranged on the sidelines. She seemed to be giving them a little pep rally of her own, getting them to focus.

"It's not your fault," I said. "I get it. I wouldn't want to hang out with me, either."

"Oh, he wants to hang out with you," Kenzie said, grinning a grin far too sly for her age. "He wants to do a lot more than hang out with you."

I poked her leg, which made her cackle.

The band started playing again, and Cammy guided her cheerleaders back onto the floor, well away from the area the janitor marked off with orange cones and yellow Wet Floor triangles. I thought I could smell the bleach he used on the blood.

Cammy got on the PA microphone. "Whew, okay! How's everybody doing?"

The students roared back. I guess they were doing great. I guess seeing people bleed was exciting for them.

"That was really crazy," Cammy went on. "But you know what? We're cool now! Yeah! Let's hear it for Officer Doug!"

Cheers. I shrank in on myself, rolling my shoulders forward. Kenzie put a hand on my back.

"Now let's focus on the positive, all right? Let's talk about how our team's gonna smash the Sabercats!"

Oddly, I think Cammy managed to change the overall feeling in the gym right then. I don't know how, but it felt to me like the excitement turned to actual school spirit. Or maybe the difference between smashing Sabercats and the team smashing the crazy guy just wasn't all the big. As long as someone was getting smashed, our student body was all for it.

Cammy began announcing the team by name. The guys would come forward one at a time, jogging to the center of the court, slapping hands with the guys who'd already been called. They looked even more cocky than normal, probably still pumped from beating up one guy.

"Spirit Week," Kenzie grumbled, shaking her head. "It's Tuesday for God's sake. Why are we even doing this?"

"We're not in class," I said. "So that's something. I think they're trying to make us happier to be here."

Kenzie snorted, looking more like a worldly college student than a sixteen-year-old sophomore. The truth is, this fight we'd just seen wasn't unusual in and of itself. I didn't think people normally got bitten in school fights, and I didn't think a single person could usually draw so much blood from so many other people. But an on-campus brawl wasn't unheard of by any means. We had one once a month, I'd guess. Once, there'd been a riot. Windows broken and everything.

Needless to say, I hadn't handled *that* day very well, and I hadn't even seen it in person. I'd been shaking under the American flag in my history class, the lights off, as Principal Winsor announced a lockdown.

A tall white fence surrounded the entire campus, supposedly to keep us safe. What it did instead was make the school feel like a prison. Brian and his friends knew how to jump the fence, which freaked me out because the ends were tapered to points, and I worried they'd impale themselves one of these days. We used to have an open campus for lunch, but they closed it a few years ago. So, combine all that with adding twice as many students than the school was built for, many of whom had to get up extra early in the morning to bus in from an entirely other side of town, and it was no wonder tempers flared.

Not exactly the kind of place for a girl with my particular mental baggage.

Still—here I was, and while I definitely didn't feel at ease, I hadn't bolted for the doors, either. Thanks to Cammy's cheering, a sort of positive energy began building in the gym. As I let my gaze drift across the bleachers opposite ours, I spotted our friend Jack standing near the bottom bench, doing some kind of hip-pumping dance and making a selfie-style duck-face with his lips. Typical Jack. Not everyone saw the humor in it, but I kind of did. He caught me watching him, gave me a surprised wave, and proceeded to pantomime about a dozen sexual positions, only half of which I've ever even heard of. I tapped Kenzie and pointed Jack out. She saw him and cracked up.

So when my phone vibrated the bench under me and I saw Brian had texted me back, I think I even managed a smile. With the fight over, and practicing my deep breathing, Jack's antics, and now Brian returning my message . . . I almost felt *good*.

"Hey," I said to Kenzie, loudly over the drums and horns and shouting. "Look."

I showed her my screen. Kenzie grinned. "See? He's not a complete idiot. Still an idiot, but, you know. Not *completely*."

I laughed. I couldn't remember the last time I actually laughed while at school.

Turns out it didn't matter, because then I screamed.

I wasn't the only one.

2:51 p.m.

At first, I assumed it was a joke. Maybe some kind of belated Halloween thing, but Halloween was two weeks ago. Then I thought maybe it was some kind of school spirit skit. That didn't work either. My last hope was a senior prank.

It wasn't. It wasn't any of those things.

Less than an hour ago, one crazy student tried taking on members of the football team. Those athletes had been led away toward the locker room. Now they'd come back.

And they all acted just like the crazy guy had.

One moment, Cammy's leading the cheerleaders in a spirited chant that's starting to catch on in the stands. Then the doors to the locker rooms flew open and the football players who'd been hurt in the fight sprinted toward their teammates, the cheerleaders, kids sitting on the lowest benches . . . anyone they could reach.

The cheerleader closest to the lead player didn't even see him coming. He ran full speed, hunched over, and smashed her to the ground. He buried his face against her throat before anyone else could even move. Suddenly the athlete pulled his head back for a second—and in that second, we all saw everything our nightmares were made of.

Bright blood washed his face. A patch of skin from the cheerleader's neck hung from his teeth. Even over the noise of the band still playing and other cheerleaders still chanting, I heard a nauseating gurgle coming from the cheerleader's mouth as blood sprayed out of her. She grasped for the wound, as if trying to scoop the fluid back into place, her sneakered feet thumping helplessly against the court floor. The athlete lunged back in again and . . .

. . . and I am almost certain that he began to chew on her throat.

"What the—" Kenzie said, and stood.

In the amount of time it took her to say it, the other enraged players raced onto the court, attacking anyone within reach. One of them grabbed some boy in the first row of bleachers across from us, and yanked him off his feet. The football player gripped the boy's arm in both hands and bit down. He tore skin and muscle away from the bone as if the boy's limb was a raw drumstick.

My stomach lurched so hard it brought me to my feet.

"*Jee-zus!*" the smoker kid beside Kenzie squealed. He stood up, too.

All of us were on our feet by then, screams piercing through the voices of the cheerleaders who didn't yet realize something had gone hellishly wrong.

Pills, I thought. *Need my pills, need to have a pill or two or ten, oh God please just let this stop now—*

Cammy caught on faster than some of the others. She started shoving her cheer team toward the exit, shouting, "Get out of here! Go, go! Run!"

Her directive acted like a light switch, empowering everyone in the gym to bolt for the exits. Everyone not being attacked, I mean. By then, there were a dozen or more people bleeding from wounds. All the wounds were the same, it seemed—arms and necks. One cheerleader sat on the floor, trying to pull herself backward on her hands while one of the possessed athletes gnawed on her shin.

And for me, things got quiet.

Muffled. I knew where I was, and saw but didn't understand what was happening around me. All my muscles loosened and went slack. My heart went from stuttering at a hundred miles an hour to an impossibly slow thunk behind my ribs, barely enough to pump my blood.

Blood—

So much of it now on the floor. Spraying through the air. Like a war.

Over the chaos, I thought I heard someone talking over the school PA system. Principal Winsor maybe. I only made out a few words: "Faculty—students are—remain—for the—period—lockdown—"

I felt Kenzie grabbing me, shoving, trying to get me to move. I couldn't. My fight-or-flight responses failed completely and chose instead to make me just stand there, motionless, maybe hoping the monsters in the gym wouldn't notice me at all.

My hand began to shake. No—vibrate. I raised it to my eyes and saw that I'd accidentally tapped Brian's contact button while his message was still on my screen.

When a recording kicked in reciting his number back to me—sending the call to voicemail—something inside me twitched and my panic came back in full force.

"We gotta *go!*" Kenzie screamed.

The smoker kid beside her shouted "Fuck this!" and ploughed past both of us, trying to scramble down into the exodus below. Everyone in the gym had flooded toward the exit leading out to the breezeway, the main sidewalk that split the campus in half from north to south. But the stampede resulted in a human traffic jam. It also allowed the bloodstained football players to pick off anyone being kept from the doors. One by one, they'd leap and drag to the ground anyone pressed up against the tide of humanity trying to squash through the double doors. It looked like trying to use a funnel the wrong way around.

"Here, take . . ." I said, and pushed my phone toward Kenzie as my brain spun on a merry-go-round, trying to find a safe way to get out of here.

I barely heard her talking behind me as we both took quiet steps down the bleachers, keeping our backs to the wall. I still wore my backpack over both shoulders, so I pulled it off and carried it in one hand while trying to unzip the front pocket with the other. If I could just get to my pills—

One of them saw us.

I stopped in place and Kenzie banged into me as the football player, mouth ringed with crimson matching the red school color of his jersey, came scrambling over the bleachers toward us. His eyes gleamed yellow and his mouth and arms seemed swollen as he slobbered and growled his way up the bleachers.

He did not stalk us, did not try to pin us in place by how he moved his body. I only know that in retrospect— in the moment, all I knew was this big guy was coming at us and wouldn't stop for anything. And I know *that* much because I said it: "Stop."

Just said it. Didn't scream, didn't throw up my hands to ward him off. Just, "Stop."

It didn't work.

The athlete dribbled thick strands of saliva and blood from his mouth. It swung back and forth as he leaped at us.

My body took over. I used the only weapon I had.

I'd taken my pink backpack off and held it by the loop while I'd tried to find my pill bottles. As the athlete came at us, I swung the bag as hard as I could at his face. The bag connected, my heavy English textbook thunking him solidly enough to disorient him for a one heartbeat's worth of time.

"*Go!*" Kenzie screamed at me.

And I went. We both did, sliding more than running down the bleacher steps to the floor. By then, much of the traffic jam had cleared as kids ran the opposite direction, toward the locker rooms or else climbing and dodging up and down the bleachers, pursued by guys who trained to do things like run up and down steps for an hour at football practice.

Kenzie and I pushed toward the doors. A few people were still jammed up between the doorframes. I looked back into the gym, trying frantically to comprehend the carnage.

In that moment, I didn't think I'd ever sleep again.

The gymnasium floor was half covered with bodies. Some of them didn't move, lying in thick puddles of their own blood that poured out of ragged throat wounds. Many rolled around, coating their clothes in the fluid of others, screaming or moaning, holding arms or legs. One kid howled, "*Mommy! Mommy!*" as his forearms spilled red. The crazed athletes continued their hunt, knocking people over and attacking their throats or arms.

Something else I didn't realize until later: They weren't working as a team. Each guy initiated his own attack. Every so often, one would stop and sniff at a dead or dying student, growl, and move on. They didn't stalk, didn't select victims. It wasn't as if they targeted smaller kids, younger kids, black kids, white kids, brown kids, boys, girls... just whoever was closest. They used no athletic moves, like juking or faking, the way I saw football players do when my Dad watched NFL games. They just charged, like animals, unstoppable, no pausing to stop or consider or listen to pleas.

What *was* this?

I don't know how long I stood there before Kenzie pulled me by the sleeve. I stumbled after her, thinking, *My pills, my bottles, in my bag, my bag, need my bag...*

Outside was no better than inside. People ran screaming down the open-air hallway, headed toward the performing arts department that anchored the south end of campus just like the gym anchored it north. In between those two points, the two-story A, B, C, and D buildings were emptying, students and teachers alike scurrying like insects into and out of doors as they tried to make sense of the chaos. Those buildings sat like gargantuan rectangular cinder blocks on either side of the breezeway, with a staircase tethering each one in the center. The staircases overflowed now with escaping students, like fans at a concert trying to rush the stage.

"Laura!" Kenzie gasped as we came to a stop in the middle of the breezeway. "We gotta get outta here, the— the parking lot, maybe—"

Then she was gone. Fleeing students bashed into us, knocking Kenzie one direction and me another. I hit the concrete on my elbows with a shriek, realizing only vaguely that the soft material of my hoodie probably saved my bones from splintering at the impact.

I shouted for Kenzie as she was half-carried down the sidewalk by students trying to escape. I lost sight of her maroon shirt a moment later, buried amongst hundreds of other people.

"*Help!*" someone cried. "Help me, please!"

I turned my head. Lying on the ground no more than a car length away, a girl younger than Kenzie gripped her ankle. She wasn't bleeding though. I guessed she'd been hurt in the mad stampede from the gym, trampled by the running, panicked boots and sandals and sneakers of a hundred high school students.

Our eyes met. Hers were brown. They were also wide with terror.

"Please," she said—maybe whispered, though how I could've heard a whisper over the insanity going on around us, I don't know.

"Help me," she went on. "I can't walk. *Please.*"

I pulled myself to my feet and stood still, staring at her. I mean—I'd *heard* her. I'd heard her perfectly clear. I even saw that her expression shifted as I stood up, as if thinking I'd risen specifically to come over and help her.

Except I didn't.

All the shouts and screams climbed into my ears like

fire ants, stinging and poisoning me. I lifted my hands to my ears and squeezed my arms as tightly to myself as I could. Yet even as I did this, I gave the campus a lighthouse scan, right to left, and saw nothing but blood and dust and the dead or dying.

I had no concept of how long it had been since the football players came tearing out of the locker room. Maybe a minute, maybe an hour, maybe a year. But however long it had been, they'd decimated what looked like a quarter of our school's population.

I turned back to the girl. She had a hand raised toward me, expecting me to help her up. I stood there and stared at it.

For me, there are many kinds of panic. There are the attacks that raise my heart rate to terrifying speeds; I start babbling and shaking, and feel like I'm going to puke non-stop for the next week and a half. Then there are the attacks that go way past scared, and deep into paralysis.

When that happens, it's almost a relief. My heart almost stops. My skin tingles, then numbs. I can't hear anything. It's what I imagine a stroke must feel like, staring at some blank point in space, unable to move, to talk, to think. It's acceptance, in a way. A fundamental shut-down of all my systems as my body and mind prepare to give in to whatever fate I'm doomed for. It's the worst kind of attack, and also kind of the best, because there is no fear exactly—just a mantra, a chant, telling me *You're going to die now. You're going to die now. You're going to die now.*

The girl's expression shifted again. I'm almost eighteen, and in the past seventeen years, I'd never seen a human being give me or anyone else a look of such utter shock and disgust. She looked at me like I'd just admitted to murdering her family, friends, and pets.

I lowered my hands.

No, I told myself. *No, don't let this beat you, dammit, don't let it. Help her, help her now—*

I swear to God I thought those things. I did.

But then she was gone and it was too late. A blur of red slid into her with a teeth-rattling crash, followed by an almost cartoonish puff of dust as she smashed out of my line of sight and out of my periphery. It was like I was a movie camera and she'd been knocked out of frame.

When I turned to look for her, I wished I hadn't. What I saw there—what I saw the guy who'd smashed into her *do* to her—

His mouth opened wide, wider than should have been possible, I think. His hands seemed covered in some kind of yellowish scales, and with one of them, he yanked her chin backward, exposing her throat. He rammed his teeth into her neck, shook his head like a dog with a toy, then pulled away, taking flesh with him.

I could have fit a fist in the hole he left behind. The girl issued a burbling, choking sound as blood spewed out of her. The guy spit pieces of her flesh out of his mouth, then dug into the hole with his fingers, yanking pieces from inside her throat, bringing them to his nose, sniffing, then discarding the bits he didn't like . . .

Or feeding himself the bits that he did.

She died quickly. Her head fell to one side, brown eyes fixed on mine. I think I was the last thing she ever saw: the girl who stood and let her die.

Something inside me shuddered, and I felt the paralysis

start to creep in again. I might have stood there until one of the athletes came for me, except right then, my brain finally did something useful for once: It pointed out that I was still alive, but wouldn't be for much longer unless I found somewhere to hide, fast.

I'll never know or understand why none of the players tackled me in those moments while I stood uselessly on the covered sidewalk. Probably it was dumb luck. There were plenty of other people around, plenty of targets to choose from. I honestly believe it was all a matter of chance.

"Run," I said out loud, and finally, my feet became unglued and I took off for the C buildings, which were closest to me. There was too much anarchy happening further down the breezeway, past the B and A buildings, and admin and cafeteria beyond.

Past that was the performing arts department, where Brian and his best friend Chad were supposed to be this period. I wondered where they were. If they were—

Impulsively or instinctively, I don't know which, I raced for the nearest set of stairs to go up to the second floor of the west C building. The stairs were empty now. I didn't want to be on the first floor, not on the ground with these insane killers. On my way, I saw the smoker kid dressed in black who'd been sitting next to Kenzie. He stood pushing on a door to one of the first-floor classrooms, screaming to be let in.

It wasn't happening. I reached for his arm as I ran past.

"This way!" I said, and pulled him along behind me— maybe to make up for what I'd just done, or not done, for the girl with the broken ankle, the girl I'd watched get torn apart.

I must have sounded like I had a plan, because the kid came willingly. We bolted up the stairs and around a single switchback, toward the nearest classroom door as one of the mutated athletes roared and gave chase behind us.

Me and the kid both screamed as the athlete propelled himself up the stairs on his hands and feet, bellowing with each step as if in agony, his face contorting. And his face—the skin seemed to be melting somehow, falling down from his skull... *my God.*

We reached the door, which opened readily; the classroom was empty, the lights on. We leaped inside and shut the door. I flipped off the lights while the kid backed away from me, holding his left arm to his chest. I felt around the doorknob to throw the lock, realizing only then that the classroom doors had to be locked from the inside or outside with a key; there was no way to lock the door without one. Funny, the little details you don't notice even after three and half years.

"Shit," I whispered.

"What do we—?" the kid started, but I waved at him to shut up, pressing my ear to the door.

I could hear the athlete bellowing wordlessly, but not right outside the door. I thought he was most likely still on the stairs, possibly on the broad landing where the staircase switched back on itself. I could also still hear screaming outside, but further away.

After another minute, the groans of the athlete faded, and I heard nothing immediately beyond the door. I realized then that I was also listening for sirens, but not hearing any.

I slid my way up the door, keeping my body pressed against it, and searched for my phone. Nowhere. Dammit, Kenzie had it last.

"I think we're okay," I whispered to the kid.

He nodded and licked his lips, then winced.

"What's wrong?" I said.

"My arm." He walked over to me, pulling up his long black sleeve. "One of those fuckers bit me. Look."

I did. The kid had a chunk of his skin missing, and the wound still dripped blood. But it wasn't deep, and it was on the top of his arm, not near a vein.

"Keep pressure on it," I said, sounding for all the world like I knew what the hell I was talking about, which I didn't.

He nodded and wrapped his right hand around the wound again.

"What's your name?" I said.

"Cody. You?"

"Laura."

"What the hell is going on out there?"

I shook my head. Tried to form words. Couldn't. Shook my head again.

Then I looked at the clock.

2:54 p.m.

"We should put something in front of the door," I said.

Cody nodded. I tried shoving the teacher's desk, but it wouldn't budge. Together, lifting and dragging, the two of us managed to move it in front of the door. I glanced up at the windows. In these buildings, the only windows were narrow and set high in the wall by the ceiling—plenty to allow natural light in, but not allowing anyone to look out of. God forbid we get distracted or daydream.

I hopped onto the desk and stood on tiptoe, using my fingers to pull myself up one more inch. This wasn't the best vantage point in the world; I could only see a sliver of the ground past the second-floor railing, and maybe ten yards up and down the sidewalk outside this classroom. The only really helpful thing was I could see the stairs plainly, and at that moment, they were empty.

"It's clear," I said, feeling like a weak parody of an action movie hero. I climbed down and sat on the desk, elbows locked beside me, taking deep breaths.

"Man," Cody said, and that was all for a little while. Then he said, "We need to call the cops."

I got up and went to a tan phone embedded in the wall. It had probably been installed when the school was built. I picked up and immediately tried 911, but didn't get so much as a dial tone or busy signal. I tried the zero button. Same result.

By the time I'd hung up, Cody had a cell phone out and up to his ear. I watched nervously, waiting.

Cody shook his head. "Nothing."

"Who did you try?"

"My mom. I'll try my dad."

"No, 911 first."

"Oh, yeah, huh? Good call. What're you, a senior?"

I guess he was making a joke. Sadly, I couldn't laugh. But then Cody didn't look like he expected me to.

He dialed the number and turned on his speaker. The line seemed to ring for way too long a time. Then a click sounded, and I involuntarily took a step closer.

We are currently experiencing a high volume of emergency calls. Please hang up and try your call again.

"Whoa," Cody said. "That's not good."

I didn't bother to reply. He was right.

"Damn," Cody muttered, setting his phone down on a desk and gripping his arm again.

"How is it?"

"Hurts. God *damn*. What kinda pussy bites someone? Er—sorry. I don't mean that, I mean, like . . . chickenshit. He was a chickenshit."

"It's okay." I didn't think either term fit for the type of person who could do what I'd seen done in the past ten minutes.

"What's the matter with them?" Cody said.

"I don't know. But they were hurt. Something's wrong with their faces. And skin."

"Maybe they're sick," Cody said.

"Yeah, maybe." My gaze dropped to his phone. "Hey, is your internet working?"

Cody started pacing, holding his arm tight to his chest. "Try it."

I picked up his phone and sat down in a student desk. He had the same phone I did. I opened the browser, then hesitated, not sure where to even start. I tried a local news site first.

We'd made the news. Not Phoenix Metro High School, but the entire *city*.

Several hospitals in town had been quarantined. Every available law enforcement officer had been called into duty, and were already stretched thin. Two fires raged in downtown high-rises, though they couldn't be connected directly—yet—to what was going on in the rest of the city.

And what was going on amounted to panic. The news sites told people to stay home, or to go indoors right away, lock doors and windows, and not let anyone in because 911 was overwhelmed and police couldn't necessarily respond quickly. This announcement had apparently then led to isolated looting, but the looters hadn't gotten very far because they were "allegedly" being attacked by "concerned citizens" on the street.

I didn't think they were concerned citizens at all. Concerned citizens didn't usually bite people.

I swiped the browser closed. "Can I check your socials?"

Cody nodded, his face masked in pain.

His networking sites were more helpful, and much worse. People were already uploading videos and photos of attacks. They looked pretty much like what I'd seen in the gym. The most recent posts began sharing one common thread. It almost became a meme all on its own.

Don't get bit!

I gave Cody a clandestine look as the individual pieces of today's events started clicking into place. The news sites seemed reticent to leap to conclusions, and that was fine, that wasn't their job. Social media and citizen journalism, on the other hand, notoriously leaped to conclusions. But this time, the conclusions seemed pretty consistent: I was sitting in a barricaded classroom with a kid who would eventually become one of the raving maniacs who'd bitten him in the first place.

My trusty old fear came flooding back into my system. I tried to order it back.

No, I thought. *Stop. Think. You're alive, you're not hurt. If you want to stay that way, you have to STOP and THINK.*

"How's your arm?"

"I told you, it hurts," Cody snapped. "Jesus."

"We should clean it out. Sterilize it."

"How you plan on doing that?"

"I'm not sure. Just saying."

Cody rolled his eyes. "What'd you find out online?"

"Um—not much, still looking. Give me another minute."

I'm not a good liar, but Cody didn't come try to look at his screen. I kept searching, trying to find something to help me. Most of what I found were instructions on how to clean out and bandage bite wounds.

575

Tapping onto a website, the page wouldn't load. I tried again. Nothing. So I tried another. Then another. And realized as I waited and tapped and waited and tapped that things were definitely going from bad to worse.

We'd lost the web.

Heart beating more quickly now, I tried my mom's number. No connection. Hers was the only one I had memorized, but I had a feeling it didn't matter what number I tried.

Cody stopped pacing suddenly, and twisted his shoulders back and forth as if trying to crack his spine. "God, now my back hurts. Suck."

I stood. "I think we need to try and get you to the nurse's office."

"Screw that, I'm not going out there!"

"But that . . . bite. We've got to clean it out."

"Look, we go out there, we're both getting a lot worse than bitten."

He had a point there. But I couldn't stay in here with him, either. I had to decide whether or not tell him what I'd read.

"Cody? Listen."

Like a professional little brother, he huffed out a sigh and cocked out one hip as he looked at me.

"The web is down. Phones aren't working. 911 isn't even working anymore. Something really big and really bad is happening right now."

His little brother act dissolved. "You mean besides school?"

"Yeah. It might be the whole city. There's no telling when someone might be able to help us. Do you understand?"

"Uh, no?"

"Okay, well, it sounds like maybe people who get—"

My breath caught and I couldn't finish. Cody stared at me, waiting to finish. Then he finished it on his own. I watched his expression change from irritated to understanding to dread.

"Bit," he said. "That's what you were going to say, right? Bit? What? What happens? Aw, Christ, were you gonna say that I'm gonna... naw, no, no way."

I held up my hands. "That's why we have to get to the nurse's office. We've got to try and clean it out, it might help."

"Is that what it said?" Cody demanded. Even as he spoke, he rushed toward me. I stepped out of the way, but it wasn't me he was after. He went to his phone and began trying to get a site to respond. "Goddammit! Is that what it *said?* I'm gonna turn into one those things?"

"Not if we can kill the germs."

I hadn't actually read that online, but I'd read enough to know that human bites could be very dangerous no matter what. I figured—hoped, maybe—that if we could treat his wound fast, it might prevent or delay what people were saying on the social networks, because what they were saying was exactly what Cody guessed. Sooner or later, he'd become like those guys in the gym.

Cody cussed again and kicked at a desk, which slid a few feet and toppled. We both stood still a moment, both of us breathing hard.

"Okay," he said after a minute. "Okay. How? We can't just waltz down the sidewalk. If they see us, they'll come after us."

"It's not that far," I said. "Just admin. I mean, it's a one minute walk on a normal day. We could either run for it, or sneak from place to place, or start with sneaking and then run if we need to. I don't know."

"What do we do when we get there?"

"Peroxide. Bandages. Wrap it up good. Ice pack, if you want."

Cody chewed on his lips, nodding. "Man. I knew I shoulda ditched the assembly."

I thought of Brian. Of Chad. Jack, Hollis, Cammy— everyone. I wondered where they were. Most of the guys had ditched class until after lunch. Jack had been with them, so they were probably on campus. Everyone except Hollis, who Cammy said stayed home sick. Now I couldn't help wondering just what *kind* of sick.

"Listen," I said. "I'm really scared. Okay? I am. But I'm a lot more scared of what'll happen if we don't get you some help."

Cody glared at me. "You think I'll come after you."

"I didn't say that."

"Didn't have to. Jesus."

"Are you going or not?"

Cody flinched a little at the tone in my voice. I could barely believe I'd said it myself. Where had *that* girl been my whole life?

"Yeah, okay," Cody said. "Just, lemme smoke first."

He pulled a pack of cigarettes out of his hip pocket, lit one, and shut his eyes. He looked even younger as he did it; not just too young to be smoking, but too young for us to be having a life or death conversation. He looked so thin, and so pale against his all-black clothes.

I checked the window again, and didn't see anything. Maybe the cops were already here, containing the situation. During a lockdown, like in case there was a shooting, we were supposed to stay in our classrooms with the lights off and the door locked. This was nothing at all like a shooting, though. Maybe if Cody hadn't been bitten we could stay put, which was exactly what my body wanted to do.

But I couldn't risk it. Cody would get sick too, he was getting sicker even as we sat here.

Cody stomped his foot on the end of his cigarette. "Okay. Let's go."

We got next to the teacher's desk and were just about to lift it together when the PA system popped to life, scaring me almost into a coma.

"Uh . . . This is . . . this is Vice Principal Brandis. We have, uh . . . a slight . . . *situation* . . ."

Cody and I traded looks. Mr. Brandis, a slender man with an easy smile, always came off to me as very calm. Even when something crazy happened, like the riot, Mr. Brandis had looked upset but not worried. Or scared.

He sounded scared now.

"Students are re-re-requested to go to their classrooms and remain there until . . . until we, uh—"

Suddenly a crash sounded on his end of the line, like a microphone being dropped, and it made me jump. Over the speaker, I heard something like a snarl, as if from a mountain lion. Then a growl, as if from a grizzly bear.

Then silence.

Cody and I looked at each other again.

"Maybe we should stay here," he whispered.

I nodded. "Thirty minutes?"

"Maybe like an hour. Or two. Maybe tomorrow."

I didn't answer. From what I'd read, two hours might be more time than he had. Still. After that announcement, I started thinking maybe waiting would be a lot safer.

For the moment, anyway.

I sat under the white board with my back against the wall and my knees hugged to my chest. Cody paced nervously at the other end of the room, smoking cigarette after cigarette. I watched him go back and forth like a ping pong ball, flicking his cigarette every three seconds or so. He spit, too. Into the carpet. Normally it would have grossed me out. Normally the smell of smoke would have irritated me. Not today.

Maybe my mind was elsewhere.

It wasn't like the movies. Not at all. Sitting there, I'd somehow imagined us talking to fill the silence. Sharing stuff with each other and all that. In the movies, that's what would happen. We'd sit and talk, tell each other our deepest secrets. Probably cry about some mean thing one of us had said to our mom that morning, the morning that we hadn't realized would be our last.

None of that happened. Other than Cody asking once if the smoke bothered me and me shaking my head, that was all the communication we had. We didn't talk at all.

So I watched the clock. And I watched Cody.

I didn't know what exactly to look for, but thirty minutes into our wait, I thought I could see changes. They were small, but there. I don't think Cody noticed them.

At first it was just how fast he walked back and forth while he smoked. When I'd noticed he'd slowed down, I chalked it up to just running out of steam, or maybe his lungs getting clogged up with smoke. But it wasn't either of those things.

Had I not been watching, I might've missed it. But as the clock ticked off the minutes on the wall above him, Cody began to lean his torso forward, his shoulders rolling in. He also began absently rubbing the base of his spine.

"Cody?" I said as the clock marked off one full hour.

He lifted a fresh cigarette to his mouth and cupped his hands around a silver lighter. But he hesitated, too.

"It's been an hour," I said. "What do you think?"

Cody didn't move. He seemed to be staring at something. He finished lighting the cigarette, and dropped his left hand. His right hand he kept up near his face, the lighter glittering in his palm.

"Um," he said, his voice muffled by the cigarette between his lips. "Maybe we should go."

I stood up, my knees popping. "Why?"

He didn't answer, and didn't come over. So I walked to him.

And sucked in a breath when I saw his hand. The knuckles had crusted over with yellow, translucent scabs.

"Does it hurt?" I said.

Cody made a fist, wincing and grunting. "Yep. Fuck. Yeah." He took a quick puff of his cigarette and then stomped it out. "God damn, it feels like I'm being *stabbed*. Shoulda listened to you about the nurse."

"Do you want to—?"

"Fuck it. Let's go."

4:23 p.m.

We moved the teacher's heavy desk again together, one of us on each short side. Immediately, I felt naked and exposed with the door unblocked. I wanted my pills so badly.

But I forced myself to the door, and put a hand around the knob. "Me first?"

Cody nodded, looking even paler than he had an hour ago. The smell of cigarette smoke hung heavy around him.

I listened at the door, and heard nothing. I twisted the handle, expecting it to get ripped out of my hands by one of those creature-students from the gym. Instead the knob turned easily and the latch unclicked.

I pulled the door open slowly, trying to split my attention between listening and keeping my heart in my chest instead of letting it thump out of my mouth entirely, which it sure seemed like it was trying to do. Apart from that, I didn't hear anything.

"Okay," I whispered. "We'll go slow. If we have to run, try to run back here."

"Why."

"Because at least we know we're safe in here."

Cody snorted, but didn't say anything. Maybe it wasn't the best plan, but taking some kind of action felt good. Our friend Chad had this thing he liked to say: The best plans in the world go out the window when the first shot is fired. He was going straight into the Marines after he graduated this year, so maybe he knew something I didn't.

Still. For as terrified as I was, I wasn't just sitting around, either. Maybe people who've never been truly frightened day in and day out wouldn't understand that. People like Chad, for instance, who wasn't afraid of anyone or anything. For me, on the other hand, anything other than crouching in a corner was an improvement.

"What're you waiting for?" Cody rasped.

I blinked. Maybe I wasn't being as brave as I'd thought.

I opened the door and stepped onto the sidewalk. The campus seemed dead, for lack of a better term. I didn't hear anything at all. Maybe everyone had been evacuated.

Cody and I slid across the covered concrete sidewalk to the top of the stairs. I peeked over the railing of the sidewalk down to the first floor, and saw a body. From up here on the second floor, I could see the motionless form of the girl with the broken ankle. The girl I'd left behind. The top half of her body lay in a gelatinous puddle of blood, her arms splayed wide, her knees cocked over to one side as if doing some kind of permanent yoga pose.

I wondered what her name was.

Whatever sad semblance of bravery I'd imagined having drained out of me. I could practically feel it rushing out my feet and through the soles of my purple Vans and spilling down the steps as surely as that girl's blood had spilled from her neck. My breath shallowed, and I couldn't lift my hands off the stair railing.

"What?" Cody said.

"Can't," I whispered, my eyes refusing to blink or leave the shape of the dead girl's body. "Can't do it. I can't."

Because here it came, roaring into me like a train—the panic, the terror, the sensation of suffocating in the open air. I had to get back inside the classroom, had to go *now*, had to go—

"Fine," Cody barked, and took a tentative step down on the stairs, wincing. "I'll fuckin' go myself."

He took another step, and another, moving awkward and slow as if his knees wouldn't bend.

Clenching my eyes shut, I said, "Wait."

I could not let this happen again. Not after the girl. I had to help Cody, had to try. I opened my eyes and forced myself down the stairs past Cody.

"Sorry," I said. "I'll go first. I'm okay."

Total lie. But it felt good to say.

Together now, we took cautious steps down the staircase until we reached the bottom floor. I felt as if we'd moved onto a tightrope stretched across the Grand Canyon, where one wrong move would kill us both. I guess that wasn't so far from the truth.

Now that we were on the ground, I could see more bodies. At the far end of the east C buildings, I saw a few people lying on the concrete. Smears of blood stained the sidewalks all around us. But I didn't see any of the crazy athletes.

We shifted over to the nearest classroom door on the first floor, pressing ourselves flat against it.

"Should we check the classrooms?" Cody said.

It wasn't a bad idea. Having more than two of us making a break for the nurse's office might improve our odds. I definitely wouldn't be opposed to the help.

But another thought crossed my mind at the same time. "Problem is they might not want to let you to go one we got inside," I said. "Or they . . . might not want us in with them at all."

Something like hopelessness passed over Cody's pale features.

"Either way, I think we might be better on our own right now," I said.

Cody nodded, slightly, like there was no point in anything. Maybe there wasn't. Maybe he already knew that.

We followed the wall to the corner and peeked around, first to the north. In that direction stood the D buildings and gym. The doors to the gymnasium were closed, and other than several bodies, we saw nothing.

Turning to look the other way, south down the main sidewalk, we saw them.

"Ah, *shit*," Cody whispered.

I counted six students for sure, but they kept moving, sliding dumbly across the concrete of the breezeway, making it hard to keep track. They weren't all football players, for one thing. For another—they were monsters.

All of them moved on their hands and feet, reminding me again of giant jungle gorillas. A few wore short sleeves, and I could see clustered crystalline formations on their forearms and hands. Their faces had that hideous melted look I'd seen earlier, the red of their lower eyelids visible even from a distance, their mouths deformed and lips jutting down to expose their lower teeth. All of them had bloodstains on their skin or clothes.

They wandered aimlessly near the B buildings, only four or five car lengths away. Beyond them sat the A buildings, then the cafeteria and administration, which lay across the breezeway from one another. The nurse's office was inside admin, so that meant getting past those monstrous kids.

"Go around?" Cody whispered.

I nodded. We scurried—slowly and quietly—back the way we had come. Each of the lettered buildings stood alone, surrounded by a concrete sidewalk; only the central sidewalk was covered by a blue awning. We headed west to the opposite end of our C building and checked around the corner.

More of them. A lot more of them. Ten, at least. Guys, girls, athletes—it seemed like one example from every clique and style was represented. Whatever was going on, it was spreading. Fast.

I didn't see my friends among the group of them, though. Not Brian or Kenzie, not Chad. Not Cammy or Jack or Hollis. Maybe they were alive. Maybe I could find them.

"*Shit!*" Cody said again. "Now what?"

I bit my lips, mind spinning. How could we get past them? Run? No. I didn't like those odds.

Distract them?

Yes. Maybe. Yes.

How?

"You have your phone?" I whispered.

Cody pulled it out and tapped on the screen. "You

587

said the phones weren't working. And I don't think I got time for someone to come get me anyway, know what I'm sayin'?"

I took the phone from him. "We'll set the alarm, slide it toward them here. Maybe when it goes off, it'll distract the ones in the breezeway. Then we can run to the nurse."

"That's a pretty big fuckin' maybe."

"It's all I got. You have any ideas?"

Cody grunted softly as he switched positions. Already I could see the scabs on his hands had spread.

"Okay, no. Do it. Jesus this hurts."

I felt the urge to touch his shoulder, to reassure him. But I didn't. Because I also didn't want to come into contact him.

I set his alarm for two minutes, then waited, peering around the corner, hoping like hell none of them would wander this way. They didn't, and when their collective backs were to me, I tapped the start button and slid the phone on its back toward them.

I spun to Cody. "Go!"

We rushed to the other end of the building, and kept an eye on the monsters in the breezeway. Then Cody's alarm went off.

The speed with which those kids in the breezeway sprinted toward the noise took my breath away. They'd appeared to be in so much pain, the way they moved slowly, but it was like they disregarded that pain as soon as they thought someone might be nearby.

So *fast*.

But now the breezeway was clear, all the way to administration.

"Come on!" I said, and together, Cody and I ran for the building.

Or, rather, that was the plan.

All the plans in the world go out the window when the first shot is fired. Our first shot was not realizing how bad off Cody already was.

He took one big step with me as we started our run. I must've gotten five or six yards away from him, focused exclusively on getting into the safety of admin, when he screamed as though being stabbed.

I skid to a halt and looked back. Cody's eyes widened in agony as he held both hands to his back.

"Go, go!" he said through clenched teeth. He took a shambling step forward, and another, biting back wails with each movement.

They'd hear him. I knew it. They'd hear him and come after us. We had to move.

I raced back and grabbed his arm, bringing another cry from him that he couldn't contain. His skin felt hot and brittle.

"Run or die," I said.

He twisted his head to look west, down the length of the C building. And one of the monsters spun around the corner, roared, and galloped toward us.

Without a word, Cody leaned forward and began to run. I held on to him and followed suit, my breath scorching and my heart shooting warning flares in my chest.

It's coming, my mind chanted as we tried to run. *That kid is coming, more will be coming, they'll take us down and that will be it—*

We passed the intersection between B and C, and saw

several of the monsters just coming around the corners, spotting us, and giving chase.

Keep going, keep going, c'mon Cody, keep going . . .

We passed the B buildings, then A. Behind us, dozens of whatever those kids had become fell into a wave of snarling, feral hunger, intent on taking us both to the ground. They were maybe twenty yards away.

We reached the admin building, and only dimly did an alarm go off inside me when I saw the windows facing the breezeway had been broken out. Some kind of fight had happened here.

No time to assess. As Cody cried out from the agony in his body, I flipped open the admin doors and yanked him inside after me.

Of course, locking the doors behind us was another story. School administration doors didn't come with giant oak beams to drop across them to keep student monsters from chasing you.

So we rushed for the nurse's office without even trying to block the doors in any way. We did get a short break when the doors latched; opening them required a thumb button to be pressed, and it took the monsters a second to figure that out, it seemed, which bought Cody and me just enough time to make it into the hall that led to Nurse Garrett's office.

Nurse Garrett herself showed up in the doorway of another room between us and her office. She wore her dark blue scrubs as usual.

And streaks of blood. On one of her forearms, through a bloody tear in her sleeve, I saw a mouth-sized gash had recently congealed.

I almost said her name. I almost felt relief. A teacher, a nurse, someone who would know what to do.

But Nurse Garrett wasn't Nurse Garrett anymore.

With an inhuman screech, teeth bared, she leaped at us.

Nurse Garrett's arms had already sprouted the disgusting yellowish crystals, and her eyes had become jaundiced. With another feral yell, she came at us, fingers outstretched, seeking our flesh.

Cody had ended up in front of me in the narrow hallway. The nurse jumped, grabbed his shoulders—

And threw him aside.

Cody stumbled past her, collapsing into her office with a shout. Nurse Garrett lunged for me, and took me to the hard tile floor in one jarring crunch.

We hit the floor, with her on top of me, pinning my shoulders down and snapping for my throat.

4:31 p.m.

It's a strange thing to die. For one thing, I wouldn't have expected to have the clarity of mind to think something like, *It's a strange thing to die.*

Time slowed down as she killed me. I thought of the songs I'd never hear again. *I Got You, Babe,* by Sonny and Cher, which my parents sang to each other in the kitchen sometimes and laughed. Boy-band love songs I pretended I didn't listen to after age twelve but still secretly danced to when no one was around. Kenzie's beloved Green Day songs.

I thought about the food I'd never eat again. Mom made this Italian meatloaf that I always asked for as my birthday dinner. Or Dad's cookies baked from scratch. Peanut butter only. It was the only thing he knew how to cook, or so he claimed, and they were really, really good.

I'd never know what sex was like. Brian and I hadn't done it. Partly, I felt bad that we hadn't, but I also felt kind of proud. Either way, it would have been nice to at least know. And it would have been nice if it had been Brian.

It didn't matter anymore, because any second here,

any moment now, this woman was going to tear my throat out with her teeth the way the girl with the broken ankle had had her throat torn out while I watched. I suppose I deserved it. I'd feel Nurse Garrett's teeth puncture my skin and cartilage, pulling, tearing, the way a tooth feels when your dad has to use string to yank it out, only so much worse.

So much more blood, so much more pain, and no more music and no more Dad's cookies and—

"*No!*"

The scream came out of me with such force that for a second, I thought Nurse Garrett really had torn my throat apart. From somewhere inside me, a burst of crazed adrenalin exploded, and I managed to shove the monster off my shoulders.

She was still on top of me, but I used the short break to scrunch my body to one side, which put my shoulders against the wall. It gave me the leverage I needed to push again, and put a little space between me and her.

As Nurse Garrett shifted to spring at me again, I kicked as hard as I could at one crystalline arm. The scabs broke and the nurse pierced the walls with her scream. I shuffled to my feet and sprang for her office, slamming the door shut and falling with my back against it.

That's when, at last, I cried.

With fear, with relief, with gratitude to be alive just one more minute. How much was a minute worth now, what could I buy with just sixty more seconds of breath? I hoped to find out someday.

I don't know how long I sat there. I only know that no one—nothing—came banging at the door after us. I didn't want to think about why.

When I stopped crying, it slowly dawned on me that Cody was crouched in the far corner of Nurse Garrett's office. It was a small room, with white-painted cinderblock walls, a low vinyl-upholstered couch with a roll of paper spread across the top, a small desk, phone, and some cabinets. The paper on the couch was rumpled and smeared red. Cody huddled beside the desk, arms wrapped around his legs, his forehead on his raised knees.

Still breathing hard, I stared at him.

"She didn't come after you," I said, the words ragged.

Cody lifted his head. The whites of his eyes had become almost completely yellow, a hideous, cancerous jaundice that gave him a canine appearance.

"I think you better go," he said.

I slid to my feet, shaking. I went to one of the cabinets and opened it up. "We'll get some peroxide or something, clean out the bite, she's got to have—"

"Laura."

I froze, but did not turn to look at him. His voice was demonic, as if a lifetime of his smoking habit had caught up with his vocal cords all at once.

"You have to go."

I slammed the cabinet door. "Yeah? How? Huh? Where am I supposed to go? They're out there, just waiting for us."

Cody stood, very slowly, like an old man climbing out of bed. He reached for one of two crutches leaning against the wall near Nurse Garrett's desk.

"No," he said. "They're waiting for you. They don't want me anymore."

I couldn't answer.

"We'll try the doors to the parking lot," he went on

through clenched teeth. There was a small guest parking lot right outside admin, and the school fence didn't go around it. If those doors were open, I could get off campus. Not sure what good that would necessarily do, though. Off campus and into what kind of nightmare waiting beyond?

"The lock down," I said. "They're probably locked."

"Still gotta try," Cody said. "If they are locked, we'll clear a path down the breezeway if we have to. Best we can. Get back to the classroom, like you said. At least it's open and you'll be safe there."

"I can't move the desk by myself."

"I think . . . we'd better . . . hurry."

There was no time to come up with a better plan. So I nodded, and Cody limped toward me. I got out of his way, then stood behind him as he put a hand on the door knob.

He hesitated. "Hey. Thanks for trying."

"Sure."

"Maybe there's a cure, huh? It's not like I'm gonna die, right? Those guys out there, they're not dyin', right?"

"Right," I said. And thought, *No, not dying. Just killing.*

"Okay. Cool. Here we go."

He opened the door.

4:35 p.m.

The hall outside Nurse Garrett's office was empty. Cody shuffled along the tile floor, holding the crutch in both hands like a lance. We both froze as a rustling sound crept around the corner toward us.

Cody motioned for me to stay put. So I did. He went forward with the crutch, peeked around the corner, then stepped out of the hall into the lobby. He was looking toward the admin doors leading to the parking lot, which is exactly where I wanted to go. Forget staying on campus, never mind the supposed safety of the classroom, and I didn't care what might be waiting outside. I wanted out of this place. Now.

The thought made my heart race harder, and I realized then how thirsty I was. I'd had nothing to drink since lunch time.

"Come closer," Cody whispered, sort of out of one corner of his mouth as he kept his eyes fixed on the doors. "But don't run till I tell you."

I slid along the wall, leaving clammy handprints on the white paint.

"What is it?" I whispered, still in the hall and unable to see whatever he was looking at.

"Four of them," Cody said in a low voice. "Even if the doors are unlocked, you won't make it to the parking lot. Try for the classroom."

I carefully moved to the opposite wall so I could see more clearly out the broken admin windows. It was a narrow view, and I saw nothing from this vantage. That didn't mean much—there could be a school full of monsters on either side of the admin windows and I'd never know it until I went out there. Then . . . well, then that would be that.

A flat run toward the C buildings would require pure and simple luck. That was it.

"What about you?" I whispered.

"I'll follow best I can. Keep your back clear. You ready? When I say go, you gotta go."

"Okay."

I crouched a little and braced a foot against the wall like I was on the school track. I didn't consider myself out of shape, exactly, but I also didn't go to the gym or anything. On the one hand, years of just staying home scared hadn't exactly built up my muscles or endurance. On the other hand, if I didn't run fast enough, well . . . I'd just have to. It wasn't a question of—

"*Go!*"

I sprinted toward the admin doors, not looking back. They couldn't have been more than twenty feet away, and the creatures behind me roared just as my hands landed on the crash-bar door handle.

I smashed through the doors and took off madly down the breezeway as I heard Cody shouting in the lobby. I risked a glance backward, and saw him swinging the crutch at the four monsters, buying me time.

But further behind me in the breezeway, down toward the performing arts building at the south end of campus, a group of the creatures saw me running and gave chase.

I had a good head start, though. So long as I didn't fall and didn't run into any more of them between here and the C buildings, then maybe—*maybe*...

From near the gym, more monsters wandered onto the breezeway. I stopped—stupidly—as I hoped somehow they wouldn't see me.

No luck. One immediately howled and took off down the sidewalk at me.

"Shit!" I wheezed, and turned left between the B and C buildings, remembering there hadn't been as many of the creatures on that side, and hoping maybe there weren't now. Again I'd have luck and nothing more to get me through this.

Then I slid on dust and hit the ground as I rounded the corner between the B and C buildings. My hip cracked against the concrete, sending pain riffling down my leg. I bit back a scream and pulled myself to my feet. My spill had let the monsters close the distance.

Barely able to breathe now, I skidded around the far west side of the C building. No monsters. I swung myself against the wall to catch my breath, chest aching horribly, and peeked around the corner the way I had come.

The monsters—six, I think, maybe more—tumbled into the intersection where I'd slipped and began looking around, trying to figure out where I'd gone.

Good. They didn't have super-senses or anything like

that. They'd have to find me the old fashioned way, by looking and listening.

I clutched at my throat, trying to force my breathing to slow, but terror kept my muscles tight. The staircase up to my classroom refuge was only around the corner and halfway again down the building, but who knew how many of the monsters might be there by now? All it would take is one of them to be hanging around the base of the staircase, and that would be it. I'd have nowhere to go. I'd have to run, and just keep running, and I could not do that, not forever. They wouldn't tire, they wouldn't stop. They'd come at me like cheetahs bearing down on prey in the savannah.

I'd run from C to admin, then basically got in a fight with a some diseased creature-nurse, then run again from admin back to here . . . my legs felt like plastic sacks of jelly and my heart seemed to have swollen up and pushed my lungs to the side.

The staircase wasn't more than forty yards or so from my position at the side of the building, and I *could not make it.*

My heart skipped one beat. Then another.

It's a disconcerting feeling, like the muscle is doing somersaults and predicting a heart attack. Now, in addition to being out of breath and weak from the exertion, panic started racing up my spinal nerves and electrifying my limbs.

Outta luck, Laura, outta luck, you got away with it this long but now time's up and they've got you.

"Please," I whispered. "*Please.*"

The powerlessness of my legs suddenly didn't matter

anymore, because fear rooted me in place. This goddamn panic, this useless *fucking* panic—

The monsters in the breezeway shuffled away, banging accidentally into each other like mute fish in a tank. Others joined them from the area of the gym. Some I recognized as athletes from the initial attack.

They'd lost me, and were wandering now. No longer a group. I knew if just one of them saw me and bellowed, the others would come charging, but until then, they'd given up on me.

Okay. Okay. Breathe, Laura. Breathe. You've got a minute, here. You got a minute. Slow down. Take it easy. You might even be able to walk to the stairs if there aren't any of those things on that side of C, so take easy. Calm down. Calm—

An alarm went off.

The creatures on the breezeway looked up at the same time, then down the length of the sidewalk to where I stood still peeking around at them.

I gasped and pulled myself back from the corner, hoping but not believing that they hadn't seen me. I looked down and to my right, trying through my fear to figure out what sound had tipped them off . . . and saw Cody's cell phone.

One of the monsters must have picked it up or somehow unintentionally tapped the snooze key on the phone's screen after the alarm went off before, when we'd used it to distract them. Now it blared to life again, beckoning every creature within earshot, and thus every other creature who saw their new brothers and sisters shouting and running for fresh meat.

A helpless squeal squeaked out of me, and I tried

to run for the opposite corner toward the staircase and classroom. I only managed a weak shuffle. I checked around the corner to examine the stairs, and saw creatures racing down the breezeway, but not headed this direction. Not yet. The coast was as clear as it was going to get.

I swept Cody's phone into my hands and smashed a numb finger against the screen, silencing the phone before turning the corner. Again I tried running, but still couldn't do it. The panic in my veins wouldn't let me. It wanted me to give up, to lay down, to die.

No!

I pushed hard against the cement, fighting the pain and fear with each step toward the stairs. *Just make it that far*, I thought, *just make it that far*.

And then, at the east end of the building, he came around the corner.

My limbs locked in place just feet from the bottom step of the staircase as Cody turned the corner and glared at me. Even from that distance, I could see the yellow in his eyes, or maybe I just imagined I could. His skin had already begun to fall and slide from his skull, and he was almost bent in half at the waist.

He made no sound as he broke into a ravenous run.

I rushed for the stairs. I had a huge head start, all I had to do was get up them, into the classroom—

And then what? I couldn't move the desk myself. I couldn't block the door.

My body paid no attention to these random thoughts. All I could do, all *it* could do, was move and take each second as it came.

With each one of those seconds, Cody got nearer. I

couldn't believe how fast he moved now, as if whatever pain he was in was so severe the only way to alleviate it was to run. He wasn't on his hands and knees yet like some of the others, but his fingers hung only a few inches from the concrete as he charged, his diseased arms swinging numbly from side to side.

I reached the steps and grabbed the hand railing. The certainty that Cody would reach me stiffened each of my joints, making them hard to move.

I pulled myself along. One step up, then the next, and the next. I couldn't tell the last time I'd taken a breath.

Then his hands were on the hem of my hoodie. I felt the jacket being pulled away from me. The sensation tripped something inside me; I screamed and my joints unfroze. I kicked backward, connected with some part of him, and he let go of my hoodie.

I rushed up the stairs, not using the rails anymore. Cody growled and followed. I imagined feeling his breath on my legs as I climbed.

Reaching the second floor sidewalk, I lunged for the classroom door and got one hand on the knob before he crashed into me, sending me flat against the door and the knob drilling into the same hip I'd landed on earlier. Any breath I had left inside coughed out.

His teeth buried into my right shoulder.

I pushed against the door, sending us both toppling backward across the sidewalk. He rammed into the railing and barked out a howl, releasing me. Screaming, I spun to face him, then charged forward with both hands out. I caught Cody in the chest, and for one sickening moment I felt the thick, sharp crystal formations on his chest through his black T-shirt.

Then he flipped backward over the railing.

Cody didn't have time to make a sound. I just heard the awful thunk of his body landing below.

I peered over the railing. Cody lay on the ground, one foot twisted in a terrible direction, not moving. I'd killed him.

No—

He got up.

He got up and shook his head, now hunched completely over like the others, his hands on the ground, knees bent a little, back hunched. He twisted one shoulder upward to look up at me. I watched as he clambered toward the steps . . . paused . . .

And then he wandered off, making obscene chuffing sounds like an angry dog. He limped a little, but otherwise seemed either unhurt or uncaring that he was hurt. Just a skinny, pale kid dressed in black looking for a victim.

I went into the classroom.

Once I'd closed the door, I tried to push the teacher's desk against it, but like I'd expected, I couldn't move it on my own. So instead I made a pile of desks, a tangle of blue plastic chairs and wooden armrests in front of the door. I didn't think it would necessarily keep anything from getting in, but it would slow them down.

When I'd finished, I checked my shoulder. There were damp marks on the fleece where Cody had bit me, but all he'd gotten was a mouthful of my hoodie. He hadn't even bruised my skin. A lucky break.

Lucky. Could anything in this day really be called that?

What I wanted next was to sleep, but I didn't know that I could. Plus I needed one more thing. I searched but couldn't find quite what I was looking for until I spotted the American flag in one corner.

I grabbed it and yanked the flag off. Weren't you supposed to not let it touch the ground or something? I tossed it onto the teacher's desk. Like the pile of desks, it wasn't much, but the pole felt stout and heavy in my hands. It was the best weapon I could find.

Finally I sat down cross-legged at the far side of the room, holding the flagpole under my arm like a lance— like Cody had done with the crutch. As I sat, I felt Cody's phone in my pocket, and pulled it out.

I tried every number I could remember, and got no responses. The internet didn't work, either, but all the apps native to the phone worked fine.

Fighting thirst, I decided I'd leave a record in case it would be helpful later. A record, or maybe an elegy.

Wishing for just one drink of water, I tapped the phone's audio recording button and began to speak.

7:57 p.m.

And that's it. That's everything that happened. I've been in here ever since, waiting, too nervous to sleep. I'm hungry. I'm so thirsty. I don't know when—

Wait.

. . . I heard something. Outside.

Oh, God.

Something's coming. They found me.

Okay. Okay. Shit. Okay.

Mom? Dad? If anyone finds this, I love you, I love you so much.

This. . . oh, my God, this might really be my last moment on earth.

. . . Fine.

Fine. I'm not going to die on my knees. So help me God, I will fight whatever comes through that door. Mom, Dad, I love you. If you ever get this, I love you and I want you to know I beat it. I beat this. No matter what.

And Brian and Kenzie, I hope you're okay. Cammy, Hollis, Chad, all you guys, I hope you're all right. I hope I see you again. You were such good fr—

. . . It's here.
It's coming toward the door.
I have to go. I love you.
I love you.
I'm sorry.
But I'm not afraid.
. . . Bye.

the end

i love you, marie

The undead had ruled for eighteen months when I met Marie. She was quiet, pale, and thin. As one of only a hundred survivors, competition for her affections was high. I never learned why she chose me.

Marie stayed close from the moment we met during automatic weapons training that took place in the field behind our new home: a school we survivors fortified to protective ourselves against the zombies. I was determined to protect Marie, to not let her become infected by a zombie's bite. Marie had asthma; she would take a slow, deep breath before speaking. She could only speak as long as her breath allowed, then would take another breath to finish her thought. She needed someone to protect her. Marie was innocent and beautiful. She had something to offer whatever world was left if the living won the war against the undead.

We were alone in what had once been an English classroom. People had spread out and found privacy among the school's many classrooms. The cafeteria had become our hospital, and the auditorium was used for daily tactical updates. That day's update had been grim: The zombie attacks were growing in frequency. Another attack was expected this night. I was due to relieve another guard posted at the compound's west wall. Marie was exempt from guard duty, working instead in the hospital. I didn't envy her; one of the jobs our "nurses" had was to burn recent corpses to ashes in the school's furnace—otherwise the dead victim would rise and attack us, whether bitten or not. I'd asked Marie how she could handle working in the hospital; she'd replied in her shallow voice that it was easier than shooting zombies.

"I gotta go," I told her as we cuddled behind a teacher's desk.

Marie inhaled. "I know," she breathed, and licked her dry lips. Water was our biggest concern after the undead. Pure water was in short supply, and it bothered me to see Marie so in need of it.

"You gonna be okay?" I asked.

"Yes," Marie said. "I know I'm safe with you."

I smiled. In our dire circumstances, it was good to be affirmed, needed. I hugged her, trying to warm her skin against mine.

A little smile appeared on her lips. That small gesture twisted something in my chest, and I swallowed hard. I fought the urge to kiss her, something I'd wanted to do since we'd met.

"Marie," I said, "I know it's only been a few months, but I wanted to say . . . I wanted to tell you . . ."

Marie moved away from me and knelt on the floor. Her eyebrows knitted. "No," she said after a breath. "Please don't say it."

"Marie . . ."

Marie lowered her head. "Can they think?" she asked quietly. "The undead."

"Think?" I echoed. They don't think. They're dead."

"Isn't it possible there. s some small part. f them that still. eels?"

I felt a sneer curl my lips. The thought that the undead had any vestige of humanity in them disgusted me. They were flesh-eaters. And we'd killed hundreds. One good shot to the skull put them down. But if they were in any way human, that made us . . . what?

"They're not human," I snapped, and stood up. "We're all soldiers now. It's re-kill or be killed, Marie."

She lowered her head. I regretted my tone, but I was angry. I took her cold chin in my hand. "I have to go. Please wait for me. I need to tell you . . ."

Marie wheezed in a breath. "Just go."

At a loss, I went. As feared, a horde attacked that night. My heart raced as the zombies tried to scale the walls. I could barely hear our automatic rifle fire over the crescendo of the undead's insensate groans. Congealed blood and bits of grey matter decorated our walls, our hands, our faces.

We slaughtered them and cheered wearily afterward, knowing it was a brief respite. More would come. Exhausted, reeking of flesh and sweat, I went back to the classroom. Marie was there, nestled against the desk, her eyes wide and staring at me as I came in. I wished I'd washed first, but the water shortage prevented it.

"Hey," I said.

Marie smiled and held a hand toward me. She was never bothered by gore. I took her hand and sat beside her. Marie looked at me, her eyes dull in the morning light.

"I love you," she breathed.

Despite my aches and nausea, my heart beat happily under my ribs. "I love you too, Marie."

She pulled me close. I rested my head below her collarbone. "I know," she said, and kissed my hand. I smiled and closed my eyes, savoring this moment more than anything since before the undead had arisen.

Marie continued to kiss my hand.

Then to lick it.

I opened my eyes. My hands were covered with blood and the flesh of the dead and undead. Marie was feasting on the remnants. Though her face was dry, it looked like she was crying.

"Marie!" I said, then stopped. Listened. Pressed my ear against her chest. She didn't have asthma as I'd assumed; Marie needed to force air past her larynx to speak.

She had no heart beat.

"Thank you," Marie said, a moment before I shot her.

I carried her re-killed body to the furnace and cremated her, tears of rage cleansing my face. I checked my hands, my body; no bites. She hadn't infected me. I wondered why. I went back to the classroom and lay back on the linoleum.

"Can the undead think?" She'd already known the answer.

Could the undead love? The living could. The living did. I did.

"I love you, Marie," I whispered aloud, and let unconsciousness take me away to a land of nightmares and grief.

cooped up

First appeared in *SoWest: Love Kills*

Brian built the cage in a day. The chickens needed a bigger coop, and he was thrilled to be able to build one for his father.

His dad, Bill, sat on the back porch of his out-of-the-way single-bedroom home outside Sierra Vista. Brian had only known about the place for a week, ever since his dad reached out after three decades of separation.

"There's some things I need to say," Bill had told him over the phone. He sounded frail. "Will you come, son?"

And of course Brian said yes, because obeying one's father was just what one did.

He didn't want to disappoint.

He took a day off work and drove down from Phoenix in the relentless July heat. That morning, at dawn, the temperature clocked in at 90. That meant 115 or more by afternoon.

So be it. His curiosity was too piqued to be put off by heat. He'd spent a lot of time under that Sonora sun as a kid. It wouldn't bother him.

The little house wasn't a shack, but it wasn't much

more, either. A dusty Chevy pickup sat parked on the gravel driveway—same model, different year as Brian's own. The echo unnerved him; he'd somehow bought the same damn car as his dad. *Christ.*

The property had no fence; it sat at the bottom of a steep dirt hill on its own small, flat plot. Creosote, mesquite, and saguaro surrounded the house at irregular intervals. There was no garage, no carport, not even a pavement slab, just tan gravel spread around the house to a distance of about ten feet. Brian saw a long, low chicken coop on the west side of the little house, and the sight of it made his heart twist. Dad had raised chickens as far back as he could remember. At a glance, Brian figured about five Cochins and three Gold Sex Link hens, scratching in the dirt. The coop was simple: two-by-fours and hexagonal wire mesh, four feet tall by ten or so feet long.

"Still at it," Brian muttered, and parked the truck next to his dad's.

When the front door opened, Brian wasn't sure he'd concealed his shock at Dad's appearance. The man was *old*—shockingly old. His feet were enormous and swathed in Ace bandages. His forearms and biceps had withered, and he required a walker.

Dad blinked at him and seemed to search for a smile to put on a face that hadn't smiled for as long as Brian had been alive.

"You came."

"You called."

"Well." Dad turned and shuffled into the house, so Brian followed, closing the door.

He took note of things as Dad went into the living

room. Bedroom off the entry hall, dark and crowded with bookshelves and boxes. What might be in those boxes, Brian could only imagine. The entry spilled into a living space and open-floorplan kitchen, with Spartan appointments. A big TV was set up in one corner in front of a blue recliner and side table, on which sat a plate of crumbs. A wheelchair was folded up and resting against the wall nearest the recliner. A sliding glass door showed a covered tile patio and small patch of dead grass beyond.

Past the tiny yard, desert landscape extended to the horizon, broken only by distant bruise-colored mountains. No other houses, no buildings, no electrical poles. Thinking back, Brian guessed it had been five minutes or more between the last house he'd seen and arriving here.

Dad was totally isolated.

There was a stout round table shoved gracelessly into the corner near the glass door, and Dad sat on one of its two chairs. Brian wondered, but didn't care, who in the hell would ever sit in the other one. He stayed on his feet, hands in the pockets of his cargo shorts.

"I, uh . . . just wanted you to know that I . . . I maybe coulda done things differently, is all." Dad coughed a little bit and sounded like he swallowed whatever came up.

Brian fought a disgusted sneer. "That's all, huh?"

"That's all."

"Is that an apology?"

"Well, it's what I got, son."

"Why? Because you're old and dying?"

"Well . . . that might have something to do with it."

Simultaneously uncomfortable with the closest thing to affection he'd ever experienced and swelling anger at the past coming back to haunt him, Brian paced to the sliding glass door, looking past the patio and yard to the distant mountains.

"You must not get a lot a visitors down this way," he said, folding his arms.

"No, not many."

"You look like you could use some help, to be honest."

"I get by."

Brian's gaze drifted to the chicken coop. The hens poked around in the dirt and sipped from a tin waterer.

"How do you feed the chickens?"

"Toss the feed in through the wire. It's easy. Getting out there and back is a chore these days, but."

"But you don't get to go inside the coop. You know, like the old days."

Dad sighed. "No. That's true."

Brian faced him. "I don't have to be home any time soon. Let me put up a new coop for you. So you could go inside."

"Oh, for heaven's sake, Brian, you can't—"

"Sure I can. Hell, you'd be amazed at what I can do." He jingled his keys. "There's not much more to really say, is there, Dad? It's early, and I passed a Home Depot on the way in, about, what, twenty minutes from here? I know how much you love those old girls. Look, I'll be right back."

"Son—"

"Back in an hour."

He was out the door before Dad could say anything else.

Not a handy person but not unfamiliar with tools, Brian ran mental calculations as he drove to the big box hardware store. Just in case Dad didn't have tools at the house, he'd have to invest a little there, but no big deal. Lumber, a screw gun, some fasteners, tacks, chicken wire, hinges . . . no problem. It didn't have to be perfect. Just big enough for Dad to get inside and be with the chickens.

The heat punished him as he loaded his haul from a big orange cart into the bed of the Chevy. God damn, it was not going to be a good time out in Dad's back yard as the sun rose higher. But what the hell. It was the least he could do.

Brian backed the truck alongside the west side of the house. He unloaded the materials to the center of the patch of dead grass, carelessly piling everything up. The bed of the Chevy was half empty when Dad wheeled himself onto the patio and watched.

"You don't have to," he called.

"Too late, already done," Brian called back, and dumped the last load.

He got to work on the image in his head, laying out wood as the new DeWalt charged up. He expected Dad to call out instructions or corrections, but the old man was still, not even sipping water in the heat. For his own part, Brian let himself into and out of the house for frequent water breaks, not wanting to end up passed out from heat exhaustion. Who knew if the old man would bother calling for help. He certainly didn't have the strength to pull Brian into the shade or get him more water; he'd barely managed to maneuver himself out to the patio in the wheelchair.

The coop took shape more readily than Brian had expected. But then, by mid-day, he was motivated to wrap up and get home. He kept himself cooled off with a hose coiled near the extant chicken coop, and by lunchtime stepped back to take in his creation.

"I think that'll work," he announced.

Dad may have nodded a little, Brian couldn't tell. The chickens by then had retreated to the relatively cool darkness of their covered nesting boxes.

The new coop stood eight feet tall and sixteen feet long. The fresh chicken screen sparkled, shiny and strong. Brian tested the simple door he'd constructed on thick metal hinges. It swung easily and silently. The hasp-and-staple style latch clanged.

"So," Brian said. "Let's give it a try."

He remembered how to do the next part from Dad.

The nesting boxes had a rear door that could be lowered to gather eggs. There weren't but a few eggs when Brian opened it. The girls had gone into hiding from the terrible sun, so it was an easy if dusty experience moving each hen to their new home.

"There's no nesting box in yours," Dad called.

Brian got the last chicken in and shut the gate, slapping the latch closed. He dusted his hands together. "Yeah, I just realized that. That's okay."

"It's not okay. They'll burn up. Be like some KFC out here in the yard in this heat."

"Huh. You think so?"

Dad nodded.

Brian gazed at the structure for a long time, debating. Then he shrugged and went to go get behind Dad's wheelchair.

"Let's try it out," he said, and wheeled Dad off the patio. "Make sure you can get in okay."

The chair rocked and bobbled over the rutted landscape.

"There's no ramp," Dad said, hands dangling limp off the sides of the wheelchair.

"Oh, that's okay. I'll just help you over the threshold."

"How am I supposed to do it myself?"

They reached the coop. Brian stepped on the little footrests at the rear of the chair and leaned his dad back. "Not sure. I hadn't thought that far ahead."

"Son . . ."

Brian opened the gate, shoved the wheels up and over the two-by-four at its base, and got his dad into the coop. The girls clucked and fluttered but none tried to get out. They knew Bill well.

Brian sighed satisfactorily.

He remembered how to do the next part from Dad, too.

Brian stepped out of the coop and closed the gate. He brandished a new padlock from one pocket and snapped it closed over the latch.

Dad still faced away from the gate in his chair. "What was that? What did you do?"

Brian stepped into his view and half-hunkered, his hands on his knees, staring into his father's eyes. "Let me know if this starts ringing any bells, Dad."

It did. Brian could see it did. Terror rose up in the old man's eyes like a spider climbing a thread. "You . . . you can't leave me out here."

"Yes I can."

"The heat. I got no water. I got no shade . . ."

"Nope."

"Dammit, boy, get me out of here!"

Brian shook his head. "You shouldn't have called me. You shouldn't have moved to a place where no one can hear you and where no one cares. *You shouldn't have locked me up in a fucking chicken coop.*"

The old man's voice trembled. "Only when you were bad . . . just once or twice . . ."

"For *years*. Till I got strong enough and had the balls enough to kick my way out of it. You remember that day? You left me and mom a week later. Three, four, five times a week, for hours at a time you put me in there. What, you thought I'd forget, is that it? Because I didn't, Dad. I didn't. Not even after thirty-whatever years. You should have just moved out here and died. Oh, well."

"You were bad," Dad pleaded, as if this would make everything all right. "You had to learn . . ."

Brian stood straight.

"Looks like I did. I'm leaving now. Although, wait. I do have to wonder . . . without any feed, what do you think the girls will eat?"

His father cast a comically worried glance at the chickens clucking around him.

"You can't do this!"

"You were bad. So you'll stay in there as long as I say you stay in there."

"*Brian!*"

Brian ignored him. He walked quickly to the Chevy, slapped the tailgate shut, and climbed in.

He watched in the rearview mirror as Dad pushed against the wire with both hands, his fingers like chicken's claws. Brian watched, and waited.

The screen held. He'd tripled up on the U-shaped tacks

and Dad was far too scrawny in his upper body to push it loose.

Brian glanced at the digital thermometer readout on his dashboard.

One hundred sixteen.

"Thanks for the call, Dad," he said, and drove the truck over the gravel and on to the dirt road.

dead street

I wrote this in 8th grade, so age 13 or so. I have made no revisions, only minor copyedits for spelling and the like. Enjoy!

The sign on the way into the small town read:

Welcome to Windsorville!
Pop 287
Founded 1959

People talked about Windsorville the same way some folks talked about 'Salems Lot. In some aspects, I guess it was the same. Now I'm not sayin' that Windsorville is haunted by vampires . . . but it definitely got somthin' to hide .

It's been a few years since the incident, but in all that time, Windsorville ain't gained one new townsman. I guess the property value's low . . . makes you wonder why no big-assed corporations move in (which just goes to show ya that even the developers are scared of the place). There ain't no oil or gold or nuthin', or if there was or is, no one never said anything.

And I guess that the things that happened between the year that the town was founded and today still seem to scare people, even those big "tough" guys from the city. Why one city-slicker went in there once, and well . . . I won't get into that.

I was born in 1930—I'm affectionately called an "Old Fart" by my children behind my back. In 1959, I was working for a trucking business. I'll never forget that day that the new fella . . . a kid actually . . . was assigned to drive with me. Damn fool. Said if we went through Windsorville, we'd save ourselves a heap of time getting to Citycorporation.

Forget it, I tells him, no one cares if we go around . . . they all understand.

"Understand what?"

"That the place is . . . well . . . different." We drove along that old dirt road on the way to Citycorporation. And even though they were big-winded businessmen, they let us go around Windsorville.

"See," I tells this kid, "there's something about Windsorville that no one understands. No person has ever gone into that town, and not one has ever come out. And yet, there's never any news about what's happening there. No deaths, no births. It's like the place is just one big dead spot."

The kid's hands opened and closed irritably on the wheel. Suddenly, he shouted, "Fuck, man, I'm goin'," and before I could stop him, he drove straight past that sign, and into Windsorville. He was whistling a Buddy Holly song through his teeth.

We stopped in front of this little coffee place. I asked

the kid why he wanted to stop. He claimed he was thirsty. But I saw that look in his eyes. He was still living in a world that despised wimps, and a world where you couldn't back out of a "Triple Dog Dare" so that his ego said, "Screw you guys, I'll show you fuckups that there ain't nothin' to be afraid of." What he didn't know was that even the stupidest kids around our town didn't step foot into Windsorville— not even on a "Triple Dog Dare." He continued to whistle Buddy Holly.

And I, not knowing what to do, followed him in. My black hair swept about my forehead as a gust of wind blew some tumbleweeds past the place.

"Jeezus," I whispers, and walked in.

A few people sat in this place, at the barcounter. The kid sat down in a stool at the end of the bar, and I took the seat next to him. The music which had been droning in the musty air wound down slowly. Everyone sitting at the bar put down their coffee—one man spilled his he slammed it down so hard.

I noticed with a small revulsion in my stomach that it wasn't brown—it was red. Thick, red coffee. The kid didn't notice. He was smiling a broad smile, thinking that this was just one merry adventure. The waitress came up to us, a glare in her eyes. She didn't say anything, but the kid started to.

"I'll have a," he started, but the waitress just tossed a cup of coffee on the bar. I put my hand up before she could hand me one.

The kid nodded at the others at the bar, who were eyeing us with distaste. He smiled, picked up his cup and drank.

"Oh God," I muttered sickly as the cup came down. The kid licked his lips free of the red stuff.

"Good coffee," he said. He hadn't even realized what it was. Still he whistled. (Damn, that got on my nerves.)

"Okay, you quenched your thirst," I said, "let's get out of here." I stood up, ready to leave, when I bumped into a burly man dressed in overalls. He had been standing behind my chair.

He smiled then, a smile that would make hippos thankful.

One tooth was pure black, others were brownish-yellow. Most were crooked, others were missing all together. But all had one thing in common. They were rimmed with red. "Blood," he rasped at me, and his hand pulled out a scythe.

I would have been wasted right away, if the kid hadn't saved me.

I heard a click, and the next thing I knew, the kid's switchblade was against this guy's neck.

"Drop it, pal," he whispered. The kid was still smiling. Dear Lord, was he enjoying this?

I thought for sure the man would do just that, but instead he laughed with that raspy voice, and pressed the knife against his throat.

"Christ!" the kid screamed.

Blood poured from the wound, and then I began to scream too as I saw the man not die, but to feed himself. His hand cupped under his neck, collected the blood, and he drank it.

But it ran back out the slit, so he drank again, and there he was, caught in a never-ending blood feast.

I now knew the horrible secret of Windsorville.

Zombies. Cannibals. Perhaps both. But I knew one thing. Unless we hauled ass, we would become permanent additions to this ghastly place. I grabbed the kid's arm and ran out of the coffee shop.

We ground to a halt as we saw a man bending over the front of the truck, the hood raised over his head. The man came back up, and in his hands were all of our wires needed to run the vehicle.

"Holy shit," the kid said.

Still hanging on to him, I took off down the street.

It was only after about three blocks that I noticed I was heading in the wrong direction.

We stopped in the middle of the main street, the deserted street.

"Gotta quit smoking, gotta gotta gotta," the kid stuttered.

"Gotta get the hell outta here," I choked.

"Eat-my-fuck-and-spit-it-out look!" he cried.

I did and wished I hadn't. All the people in the shop were following us, running, waving blades and clubs.

"C-mon," I wheezed. I ran over to a fence, and jumped into a back yard.

Coming around a corner, I froze in my tracks. A man stood by a grill, flipping raw bloody steaks over and over.

But there wasn't any fire going. Nearby, seated at an old picnic table, a lady and two kids chewed the bloody morsels with relish. Twisting my head away, I saw what remained of the family dog.

"Oh my God. . ." the kid whined.

I said nothing, only ran back over the fence.

But now the people were closer, so we continued to go down the main street. The dead street.

Suddenly as hell, the kid tripped in the street and fell down. He tried to get up, but his ankle was busted up.

"Run!" he yelled at me.

I did. I looked back once, and saw him trying desperately to fend of the bloodsuckers with his switchblade. Then he screamed and died, as the others continued to swallow his blood.

But this didn't stop the people. They kept after me until I finally got to the town limits. I chanced a look back and saw with horror that the kid was running with them now, face pale, teeth red, switchblade waving for me. He wanted me, wanted my blood.

I thought that I'd drop dead right there. "He's one of them," I thought sickly, "he's one of them!"

I stomped over the city limits, and promptly fell down. There, I waited. Waiting to die. There was nothing I could do; too tired to run away. Maybe they'd get it over with quickly .

They came. But then they stopped. I couldn't figure it out. Then I noticed that they weren't crossing their border. Not so much as a hair crossed over. Finally, seeing that I wasn't about to come back in, they walked off.

And that's the story, friend. Take it or leave it.

I'd much rather leave it, if ya knows what I mean. I never went back to that place, and I never intend to. Windsorville just lies there, dead.

But one or two things gotta be mentioned.

First, my family was worried as hell when I returned. Remember my black hair? It had gone dead white, and stayed that way for damn nears a week.

Then there was the whistling. People comin' in at night after having passed Windsorville swear that they'd heard a whistling, a whistling that resembled Buddy Holly.

But finally, there was the sign. Remember what it said? "Pop. 287"? Well, honest to God, when I passed it on the way out, it read "Pop. 288." Take that for what it's worth.

So if you're ever around in these parts, go everywhere and see everything, everything except Windsorville. Some people that come this way say they don't go because it's a tourist trap.

I just smile back and say, "It's a trap all right."

dinosaurs
downstairs

When Bill went downstairs to the street to start his car that morning, he was dismayed to see it had been crushed flat.

His baby, his darling 1966 Camaro, cherry red, was now reduced to a foot-high mass of rectangular metal. The other cars lined up on the street were untouched. Bill knew immediately is was his downstairs neighbor, the dinosaur.

They shouldn't let dinosaurs sub-let here, Bill thought angrily. There were plenty of apartments in the city, why on earth did the management feel it was imperative to allow an extinct species to live here next to so many humans?

Plus they were dangerous. Sure, the Tyrannosaurus Rex downstairs had sworn up and down that he was reformed, that he'd converted to a heart-healthy vegan diet, but Bill wasn't convinced. The ripping and tearing sounds he'd heard coming from beneath his apartment suggested a feast of meat, not dainty baby corn and bean sprouts. Bill had complained to the manager, who'd only shrugged and said the Rex paid his rent on the dot every month, so it wasn't any of his concern what went on in the privacy of the dinosaur's apartment.

The manager had, no doubt, informed the Rex of Bill's complaints. And that's why his Camaro was now the height of a fire hydrant.

"Fricking dinosaurs!" Bill turned on his heel to go back into the building. Will insurance even cover this? he wondered as he banged into the building.

We won, they lost! he thought as he stomped up the stairs to the second floor. "Dinosaurs had their shot, and nature selected them for extinction," was a line from some dinosaur movie he'd seen once, and those words delighted him endlessly. It was a mammal's world now, Bill told himself, and dinosaurs had no business taking homes and jobs away from decent, hard-working, tax-paying citizens like himself. They flooded the health care system, took resources away from the schools—nothing good ever came from a dinosaur! Well . . . maybe oil, but that was eons ago.

Bill worked himself up into a rage by the time he reached the Rex's apartment on the second floor. He pounded on the door.

"I know you're in there! I can hear you stomping around! Come out here! I want to know what you did to my car!"

Bill was surprised when a brachiosaur opened the apartment door. He almost couldn't see the tiny head perched atop her long neck.

"Oh! I—I'm sorry, I—I'm looking for the tyrannosaur."

"He's not here," the brach said stiffly.

"Oh . . . Well, you tell him from me that I know he's the one who crushed my Camaro out there, and he's going to have to pay for it. Every last cent! You got that?"

The brachiosaur nodded. "I'll let him know."

Bill was suddenly certain the brach had no intention of reporting his complaint. His anger blossomed fully, and he aimed to take it out on the plant-eater.

"Fricking herbivores! Now you look here! I don't care how few of you there are left in the world, but you can't just barge into my town and start crashing around like you own the place! We're the dominant species, see? This is our world now, and you don't belong here. Why don't you just go back to where you came from? Fricking dinos! If it was up to me, I'd send every last rotten one of you back to your—"

The brachiosaur stepped on Bill. His skeletal system collapsed instantly, and he was reduced to a crimson stain about the thickness of a manhole cover. Ironically, he could likely fit into the Camaro now.

"Honey?" the Rex called from the bathroom. "What's going on? Did you feel the floor shake just now?"

The brachiosaur wiped her foot on the welcome mat, and shut the door easily with one faint brush of her tail. The Rex poked his head out of the bathroom, trying to floss several pounds of cabbage and onions out from between his razor teeth with a length of nylon rope. His weak forelegs weren't up to the task, and vegetation clung stubbornly to his gums.

The brachiosaur turned to him, smiling sweetly. "Nothing to worry about. It was just a mammal."

acknowledgements

An enormous thank you to all of the backers who helped bring this project to life! It is literally true to say I could not have done this without you:

Amelia Bennett
Lorre Gillespie
Backer #3
Lauren, the best librarian ever!
Ames
Justin Care
Bernie
Erica Oesterle
Samuel Todd Gdula
Patrick Kellner
Krista Hammock
Craig Hackl
John Groseclose
Thomas D.
Trevor O. Clevenger

Marsha Tufft

Phyllis Gibson

Dani Hoots

Khepre Bailey

Backer #23

Michael Polo

The Carpenter Family

Benjamin Garren

Jacob H Joseph

Daniel Hanson-Brown

Lauren Verlaque Hall

Russell Nohelty

Rachel Noble-Galusha

Tina Edwards

Robin Ginther-Venneri

William O'Broin

Jim Brownrigg

Chris Rose

CJ McCubbin

Brittney Bluhm

Tianna Tagami

Margaux, Fanny, Léna LENAIN

Backer #44

Steven J. Scally

Danalynn Donovan

Lisa Mc

Jeffrey C

Charles D. Moisant (silverphoenix.net)

D. Kleymeyer

Threnody Cassidy

Melanie B.

Made in the USA
Middletown, DE
07 January 2023

21619326R00378